"My lipstick i

"What?"

"Kissing will make my lips red. Don't you know that?"

"I..."

Lacey caught the front of Gabe's sweatshirt and pulled him forward, planting a kiss smack on his lips. For a moment he was caught off guard, but found himself responding.

Pulling back, she licked her lips. "Cool and chocolaty. Nice." She puckered up. "Are they pink?"

He cracked a smile. He couldn't help himself. She was infectious and tempting and drawing him into her delightful personality.

"You are crazy."

"See?" She touched his lips with one finger, and he wanted to grab it with his teeth and nibble and... "I made you smile. It helps to be a little crazy and not take life so seriously."

TEXAS
★ COUNTRY LEGACY ★

LONE STAR WISHES

Linda Warren

Cathy Gillen Thacker

Previously published as *A Texas Holiday Miracle* and *The Texas Christmas Gift*

ISBN-13: 978-1-335-20957-3

Texas Country Legacy:
Lone Star Wishes
Copyright © 2020 by Harlequin Books S.A.

A Texas Holiday Miracle
First published in 2014. This edition published in 2020.
Copyright © 2014 by Linda Warren

The Texas Christmas Gift
First published in 2013. This edition published in 2020.
Copyright © 2013 by Cathy Gillen Thacker

Recycling programs
for this product may
not exist in your area.

For questions and comments about the quality of this book, please contact us at CustomerService@Harlequin.com.

Harlequin Enterprises ULC
22 Adelaide St. West, 40th Floor
Toronto, Ontario M5H 4E3, Canada
www.Harlequin.com

Printed in U.S.A.

CONTENTS

A Texas Holiday Miracle   7
by Linda Warren

The Texas Christmas Gift   233
by Cathy Gillen Thacker

Two-time RITA® Award–nominated author **Linda Warren** has written over forty books for Harlequin. A native Texan, she's a member of Romance Writers of America and the RWA West Houston chapter. Drawing upon her years of growing up on a ranch, she writes about some of her favorite things: Western-style romance, cowboys and country life. She married her high school sweetheart and they live on a lake in central Texas. He fishes and she writes. Works perfect.

Books by Linda Warren

Harlequin Heartwarming

Texas Rebels

A Child's Gift

Harlequin Western Romance

Texas Rebels

Texas Rebels: Egan
Texas Rebels: Falcon
Texas Rebels: Quincy
Texas Rebels: Jude
Texas Rebels: Phoenix
Texas Rebels: Paxton
Texas Rebels: Elias

Visit the Author Profile page at Harlequin.com for more titles.

A TEXAS HOLIDAY MIRACLE

Linda Warren

A special thanks to my go-to ladies,
Cindi, Joan, Charissa and Tammy,
who know everything from kids to Christmas
to plotting. Thank you!

Dedication

I dedicate this book to the readers, who
write to me, buy my books, come to book
signings, encourage me and support me.
Your friendship means the world to me. Wishing
you love, joy and happiness this holiday season.
And a miracle or two. Love, Linda

Chapter 1

Christmas was the happiest time of the year for many people, but for Lacey Carroll it would be the saddest. Too much had happened to...

The front door slammed with the strength of a gale-force wind. She paused in spooning macaroni and cheese onto a plate. Not another bad day. This would make four in a row. She placed the pot on the stove, wiped her hands on a Frosty the Snowman dish towel and made her way into the living room.

Her six-year-old half sister, Emma, sat in the middle of the sofa with her arms clutched across her chest, her face scrunched into a dipped-in-vinegar frown. One of her pigtails had come undone and stuck out in a snarl on the left side of her head. Grass and bits of leaves were tangled in her blond hair. Smears of dirt marred her face, her red T-shirt and her jeans. Her sneakers were filthy, the shoelaces undone. She'd been fighting. Again!

Before their father, Jack, had passed away five months ago, he'd asked Lacey to care for Emma, so Lacey was now Emma's legal guardian. She couldn't refuse her father's dying wish, even though she had a good job in Austin and her own life. At twenty-eight, she'd made a life-changing decision because she loved her sister. Days like this, though, tried her patience and reminded her how ill equipped she was to raise a child.

She'd bought child-rearing books and kept a mental one filled with common sense in her head. On most days she needed both.

"What happened?" Lacey asked in her best authoritative voice.

"Don't talk to me. I'm mad," Emma shot back.

"Lose the attitude. What happened?"

Emma glared at her through narrowed eyes. "I told you don't talk to me."

"And I told you to lose the attitude. Now!"

Emma turned her face away in anger.

Lacey sat beside her. "What happened?" she asked again, this time in a more soothing tone.

Emma whipped her head around. "I wanted to hit him in his big fat nose."

Oh, good heavens. Lacey took a deep breath. "Who did you want to hit in the nose? You know hitting is against our rules. Daddy's rules."

"Brad Wilson. Daddy would've hit him, too."

"I don't think so. Daddy didn't believe in violence."

Emma's face crumpled. "He said…said…there's no Santa Claus, and Jimmy and I…were big babies for believing in him."

Oh, no! Lacey flipped through pages of the mental book in her head. She knew what Emma's next question was going to be and she had to have an answer. A good one.

"Is it true, Lacey? Is there no Santa? Did Daddy put my gifts under the tree?" Big green eyes, just like Lacey's, begged for an answer.

As Lacey saw it, she had three options. Lie like she'd never lied before. Tell Emma Brad was teasing her. Or offer the truth. How could she tell a six-year-old there was no Santa Claus?

Her father had told Lacey he wanted her always to be honest with Emma just as he'd been honest with Lacey. Still…

She searched for the right thing to say. Lie, lie, lie, her inner voice kept chanting. If she did, Emma would find out soon enough. But she'd still have time to believe like a little girl should.

Lacey scooted closer and wrapped an arm around Emma. "You know there's more to Christmas than Santa Claus and receiving gifts."

"No, there isn't. Christmas is about getting gifts from Santa Claus."

Lacey prayed for patience…and wisdom. "Christmas is about the birth of Jesus Christ, and we celebrate his life by giving gifts. Sometimes giving is better than receiving."

"No, it isn't. Without Santa Claus there is no Christmas." Emma's eyes widened in realization. "There is no Santa Claus. No!" She fell sideways on the sofa and howled as if the world had come to an end.

Lacey gave her a minute and frantically breezed through the book in her head, but the pages were blank.

Maybe mothers who had given birth had all the parenting answers. Lacey didn't have a clue how to soothe a little girl's broken heart, except to love her. She gathered a wailing Emma into her arms. Hitting Brad in the nose didn't seem like a bad idea at the moment.

"Shh." Lacey stroked Emma's hair, picking out bits of grass and leaves. "We'll still have Christmas. When you wake up Christmas morning, all your gifts will be under the tree and we'll have hot chocolate and cookies like always. Nothing has changed."

"It has, too." Emma sniffled into Lacey's chest. "I don't want any gifts if they don't come from Santa Claus."

"Not even that red bicycle you've been wanting?"

Emma thought for a second. "No. I don't want nothin'."

Lacey cradled her sister close. "Sweetie, Christmas is a feeling that you have in here." She placed her hand on Emma's chest. "It makes you feel good to believe in an imaginary figure who will grant your every wish. It's every child's dream. But in reality it's those people around us who love us and give us that feeling and make us feel joy and love." She poked Emma in the chest again. "All you have to do is believe in Santa, and he's right there, just like Jesus Christ. You learned that in church. As long as you believe, no one can take that feeling from you. It's warm and comforting and brings unimaginable joy. You'll feel it's Christmas because I love you and I will make Christmas as special as I can."

"But you're not Santa."

"I am Santa." She tickled Emma's rib cage. "Don't you feel all warm and fuzzy inside?"

Emma giggled. "You're weird, Lacey."

"But you love me."

Emma snuggled closer. "Uh-huh."

Lacey sagged with relief. Maybe they could get through this.

The doorbell rang and Emma rose. "I'll get it."

"No. You go brush the trash out of your hair and I'll get the door."

"Aw, Lacey."

Lacey pointed toward the hall. "Go." Emma dragged her feet toward her bedroom and Lacey went to answer the door. Sharon Wilson and her two sons stood there.

Emma came racing back, her fist raised in the air. "I'm gonna hit him in his big fat nose."

Lacey caught her before she could accomplish her goal. "Stop it."

Sharon and her boys took a step backward. "She is a little aggressive, Lacey."

Lacey bristled. "Your son just ruined her Christmas, so I'd be careful what you say."

"I'm sorry, Lacey. My husband will handle this when he comes home."

"I'm not sure what your husband can do. The damage is already done, and I'm not happy about it. Your son was very cruel to ruin their Christmas."

"They're stupid kids, and…"

Sharon popped Brad on the back of the head with her hand. "Shut up. Your father will deal with you when he gets home. Go to the house and wait for me." Brad ran away, but Jimmy waved shyly at Emma before following.

"Could we talk for a minute?" Sharon asked.

Lacey nudged Emma toward the hall. "Go brush your hair." Surprisingly, she went.

Sharon twisted her hands. "I know Emma's been

through a rough time and I understand that, but I feel it's best if our kids don't play together anymore."

You hussy almost erupted from Lacey's mouth. The woman had nerve. Lacey quickly calmed her rising temper. Jimmy was Emma's only playmate, and her sister needed a friend. Since their father's death, Emma had alienated everyone around her. Lacey was working to change that, but days like this didn't help.

Lacey swallowed her pride. "Emma and Jimmy play well together. It's your older son who's causing all the problems."

"I know. Since he turned ten, I can't handle him anymore. I leave that up to my husband. I'm really sorry, Lacey. Jimmy likes Emma."

"Can Jimmy come here to play with Emma, because I really don't want Emma around Brad?"

"Well, I guess that would be okay." Sharon looked toward her house down the street. "I better go before the boys get into another fight. Again, I'm sorry."

Lacey closed the door and made her way to the kitchen. Emma bounded in with her hair all around her face and climbed onto a bar stool.

"Did you wash your hands?"

"Yes."

"We'll have to wash your hair tonight."

Emma brushed it from her face. "Why?"

"Because it's dirty."

"Lacey, you always make me do things I don't want to."

"That's life, snuggle bunny." Lacey placed a plate in front of Emma and sat beside her on the other bar stool.

Emma stared at the food. "What's this?"

"Supper. Your favorite mac and cheese out of a box. Green beans, turkey and cranberry sauce left over from Thanksgiving."

"But you burned it."

"I cut the burned part off and the turkey is still good. Eat it."

"You're gonna kill us, Lacey. You're not supposed to eat burned food."

"Eat and stop complaining."

Emma ate the mac and cheese, most of the turkey and picked at the green beans. Lacey had to admit she was a lousy cook. Her mother was, too. Her dad had been in charge in the kitchen. It shouldn't be that hard, but she seemed to burn everything she made. In Austin, she ate out mostly because she was so busy. But a child needed a healthy diet.

"These beans are yucky. You're supposed to put butter on them or something. Daddy did."

Butter. Why hadn't she thought of that? She had to buy a cookbook or something. Eating at the local diner was getting old. She'd attempted Thanksgiving dinner because she wanted it to be special for Emma, but she wasn't fooling anyone. It had been a disaster. And kind of lonely with just the two of them.

She carried her plate to the sink. "If you're finished, go take your bath and I'll do the dishes. I'll be in to help with your hair."

Emma climbed off the stool and dashed down the hall. After putting the dishes in the dishwasher, Lacey wiped the counter. A banging sounded from next door. Their neighbor, Gabe Garrison, was working on something. He always was.

Lacey had never actually had a conversation with the man. Her father had introduced them months earlier and Gabe had said hello and walked away. Her dad had explained that the man's son had been killed in an

ATV accident—an ATV that Gabe had bought the child for his birthday.

According to her father, Gabe had been a lawyer in Austin. After the accident, he'd tried to continue working, but hadn't been able to. He and his wife had divorced and he'd moved back to Horseshoe, where he'd been raised, to grieve alone. He wanted privacy and Lacey understood that, but that was hard to explain to a six-year-old.

Gabe's son's dog, Pepper, was in the backyard and a big temptation for Emma. Lacey lost track of the number of times she'd told Emma not to go into Gabe's yard. Emma never listened. If she heard the dog, she went over, and then Lacey would get a short lecture from Gabe on respecting a man's privacy.

Leaning against the counter, Lacey wondered what her friends in Austin were doing. Probably getting ready to go out for the night to a club to party. That had been Lacey's old life, and she missed it in ways that were hard to explain. Maybe because that life had been carefree with very little responsibility. Now responsibility weighed on her like an anvil around her neck. Some days it was hard to stand upright for the weight. She didn't regret her decision to raise Emma. She just regretted she wasn't more experienced at being responsible.

Her parents had divorced after nineteen years of marriage, and Lacey's young life had been thrown into turmoil. Her college dream had been forgotten because there was no money to send her, so she worked at Macy's in the makeup department. Her mother worked there, too. It hadn't been ideal, but it had been a job.

A short three months later, her mother had remarried and Lacey had moved out of the house and been on her own. She'd gotten a job with a party-planning company. She'd loved it, and she'd been away from the influence of her mother and her mother's new husband.

Her dad had moved back to Horseshoe, where he had grown up. A year later he'd married Mona and they'd had Emma. Her father had been happier than Lacey had ever seen him. She'd continued to visit, much to her mother's displeasure, and had enjoyed spending time with them. Never in a million years had she imagined her dad's and Mona's lives would be cut so short.

She tucked the memories away and hurried to help her sister. Bathed and in her jammies, Emma carried her soft blanket, her Pooh bear and a pillow to watch TV.

"I'll see if I can find a Christmas show." Lacey flipped through the channels.

"I don't want to watch a Christmas show. There is no Christmas."

Lacey let that pass, hoping Emma's attitude would change. At six, it changed often. Sometimes faster than Lacey could keep up. "*Shrek the Halls* is on. You like Shrek."

Emma curled up with the blanket on the sofa and watched without complaining. Score one for Lacey. "I have to get clothes out of the dryer, but I'll be right back to watch it with you."

"'Kay."

Lacey folded the laundry and put it away. She thought of taking a shower, but decided to wait until Emma had gone to bed. Her sister needed all of Lacey's attention. She stopped short in the living room doorway. The blanket, Pooh Bear and pillow were on the sofa, but Emma was not.

"No! No! No!" Lacey ran for the back door. The only place Emma would go was to see Pepper, and Lacey did not want another confrontation with Gabe the Grouch.

Her father had installed a privacy fence around their backyard. A gate opened into Gabe's yard. Lacey rushed through it and stopped suddenly. Gabe stood there with a scowl as big as Texas on his face.

The man was tall, six foot or more. He wore jeans and a dark flannel shirt. He looked foreboding. A chill slid through her that had nothing to do with the temperature. His hair was long and his face unshaven, as if he didn't care, which Lacey knew he didn't. His jeans and shirt seemed to hang on his thin body. He probably ate very little, but he still was a very handsome man in roguish sort of way.

"Would you please keep your sister out of my yard?" The words were cold and sharp, just as he'd intended, she was sure.

She stepped around his dark presence and went to Emma, who was kneeling by Pepper. The black lab was lying in a dog bed and Emma was stroking her.

She reached for Emma's arm. "Let's go. You're not supposed to be here."

Emma looked at her with beseeching eyes. "But Pepper wants me here."

The dog whimpered as if it were in pain. Was the dog sick? It was none of her business, she had to remind herself. She tugged on Emma's arm and half dragged her back toward the gate.

It was a chilly winter night and Emma just had on her PJs. "Run to the house. I'll be right there."

Emma glanced at Gabe and then raced for the back door.

Lacey faced the dark knight, not sure what to say, but she knew she had to say something.

Gabe didn't give her time to voice her feelings. "If

she comes into my yard one more time, I'm nailing the gate shut."

Lacey looked into his eyes. If she had never known or felt pain, she would know what it was by that one glance. The crevices around his eyes were permanently etched in place as if forged by fire. His eyes were hollow, dark pits, and the only emotion he showed was the anger that flared from their depths. Normally, when she saw all the angst on his face, her retorts died on her lips. The man had been hurt enough. But today she didn't back down.

"That gate is half mine, and if you nail it shut, I will un-nail it." She was ready for battle, but then he did his usual thing. He turned and walked away.

Chapter 2

Gabe tuned out the woman. He had no desire to talk to her or anyone. He didn't understand why she couldn't respect his privacy. When Jack was alive, Gabe had had no problems. Now the kid was out of control and the woman had no idea how to handle her. Both of them had tried his patience for the last time. He would nail the gate shut without a second thought.

He opened the back door and then picked up Pepper, bed and all, and carried her inside. She was getting too weak to walk. As he placed her by the sofa he noticed she was trembling in pain. Gritting his teeth, he knew he had to give her another shot. He went into the kitchen and got the medication the vet had given him. After giving her an injection, he stroked her until she drifted into sleep.

Sinking back onto the sofa, he drew a long breath.

The vet had said it was time to put Pepper down. She was in too much pain from cancer, but she had been Zack's dog and he couldn't bring himself to do it. He looked at all the pictures of Zack he had hung on the walls. His son was in this room. He was everywhere. And Gabe had to take care of the dog his son had loved.

He rested his head on the back of the sofa and closed his eyes. The moment he did he saw his laughing, happy son and pain pierced his heart. Pain was all he felt these days. Life meant nothing to him. He couldn't understand how fate could be so cruel as to take a child from his parents. Gabe didn't know right from wrong anymore, and it didn't matter. All that mattered was that he remembered his son every moment of every day.

That was the only thing that kept him going.

The next morning Lacey let Emma sleep in. Last night, they hadn't talked because Lacey was too upset. She had scolded Emma and put her to bed early.

Lacey was making breakfast when Emma trudged in and climbed onto the bar stool. Smoke spiraled from the toaster and the alarm went off, shrilling loud enough to wake the neighborhood.

"Not again." Emma buried her face in her hands.

Lacey pulled off her sneaker and threw it at the smoke alarm. The device flew off and landed in the kitchen sink, causing the deafening sound to stop. The blackened toast popped up at the same time.

Emma looked through her fingers. "You're gonna kill us, Lacey."

She opened the window to let the smoke out. "I have everything under control," she said, hoping she sounded convincing. Inside, she was shaking and wondering how a twenty-eight-year-old woman could be so hope-less in the kitchen.

She threw the burned slices of bread in the garbage and put four more in the toaster. Stupid smoke alarm wasn't stopping her.

"You have to know when to push up the lever," Emma told her. "Daddy knew."

Next trip to town Lacey was buying a new toaster. She was tired of fooling with this relic. While she watched the bread, she slipped her sneaker back on. Just as the slices were starting to burn, she pushed up the lever, and then buttered the toast, added grape jelly and placed it on the plate with the scrambled eggs.

"Breakfast," she said, sliding it in front of Emma with a smile.

Emma rolled her eyes. "Now we don't have a smoke alarm."

"I'll get the ladder and put it back after breakfast. Nothing I can't handle."

Emma ate her breakfast and Lacey munched on a piece of toast. Nothing like starting the day with a little excitement. She hoped Gabe hadn't heard the alarm. She had a feeling he didn't hear much of anything besides the demons in his head.

Brushing hair from her face, Emma asked, "Are you mad at me?"

Lacey knew Emma was talking about last night. "You disobeyed me."

Emma swallowed a mouthful of egg. "Mr. Gabe doesn't mean it when he says for me not to come into his yard."

"Emma, sweetie, yes, he does."

"But I hear Pepper and I have to go."

Lacey sighed. "Pepper is not our dog, and we have to respect Mr. Gabe's privacy. Do you understand that?"

Emma shook her head.

Lacey was all out of options. She'd just have to watch Emma more closely. She clapped her hands to brighten the moment. "Today we get the Christmas tree. Daddy always got it the Saturday after Thanksgiving."

"There's no Santa Claus, Lacey!" Emma shouted. "We don't need a Christmas tree!"

"Well, I still believe in Christmas, and I'm putting up a tree right in front of the windows in the living room."

"I'm not looking at it." Emma jumped off the bar stool.

"You don't have to." It broke Lacey's heart that Emma was being so adamant about this. Maybe if she kept pushing, Emma would start to believe again. There was no Christmas without the magic of belief. Somehow, Lacey had to find a way to put a little more of that good stuff in their lives. "Go get dressed while I put our dishes in the dishwasher."

Lacey managed to reattach the smoke alarm. The green light came on, so she felt sure it was working and ready for the next round.

The Christmas tree lot was off the square in Horseshoe. People were out and about searching for the perfect tree.

"I'm not looking," Emma told her.

Lacey didn't say anything. She got out of the car and walked around, inspecting the trees. Soon Emma was right beside her. It was taking a while, but Lacey was learning parenting tricks.

She picked out a seven-foot Douglas fir and had the

man put a stand on it. Then he tied it on to the top of her SUV.

While they were waiting, a little girl came over and said something to Emma. To Lacey's shock, Emma frowned and kicked at her with her sneaker. The little girl ran back to her father, who was measuring a tree.

This wasn't the place to discipline Emma. She'd wait until they got home. Lacey didn't know if she had the strength or the capabilities to continue to deal with this kind of behavior. But she would keep trying.

As they pulled into their driveway, Lacey saw Gabe in his front yard digging up a shrub that had died. The black knit cap he wore on his head gave him a dangerous, fierce look. He didn't even raise his head as they got out. He just kept digging.

Before Lacey could stop her, Emma darted over to Gabe. Lacey wanted to pull out her hair. This was turning out to be the worst day ever. She ran behind Emma and caught her just before she reached the man.

"Whatcha doing?" Emma asked.

Lacey took her hand and led her back toward their house without saying a word to the man who was glaring at them.

"You disobeyed me again. Go into the house and sit on the sofa until I get there. And do not turn on the TV. Do you understand me?"

Emma nodded and stomped toward the front door. Lacey unlocked it and Emma went inside. First, Lacey had to get the tree off the SUV, and then she would deal with her sister.

She grabbed a pair of scissors and the kitchen stool. She cut the strings off the tree and tried to lift it from the SUV, but soon found she couldn't. The stool gave her some height, but not enough for her to hoist the heavy tree. The branches scratched her face and she said a cuss word under her breath. How was she going to get the tree off the car?

Gabe kept digging, trying to ignore the crazy lady on the rickety kitchen stool. She was going to fall and break her neck, but it was none of his concern. She stood on tiptoes and tried to heave it off, but to no avail. The woman was a menace. Her smoke alarm went off regularly. He'd heard it that morning. Evidently, she couldn't cook. The stool wobbled and she grabbed the car to keep from falling.

Do not help. Do not help.

The warning in his head was clear, and he always obeyed it because he didn't want to interact with anyone. But even he had a breaking point. He propped the shovel against the house and walked over.

With one gloved hand he gripped the tree trunk and lifted it from the SUV.

"Oh…oh…" she stammered, almost falling off the stool again.

"Where do you want this?" he snapped.

"Uh…" She climbed off the stool and headed for the front door. "In here."

Inside the house she pointed to the living room windows. He placed the tree in the spot.

"Hi, Mr. Gabe," the little girl said from the sofa.

He didn't want to engage in conversation, so he left. On his way back to his house, he cursed himself. He didn't want to get involved, and helping the crazy lady was a sure way for that to happen. He was trying desperately to keep his privacy, and he'd probably just made a big mistake.

That suffocating feeling came over him, and he went into the house to check on Pepper. She was better this morning and had even trotted outside to do her business. The shots always helped for a while. How he wished they could last longer. Soon he'd have to make a decision, and it was tearing him up inside. He just couldn't let go.

He wasn't sure what he was afraid of. The vet had said it was the best thing for the dog, but how could killing something be good? If he did what the vet had suggested, it would be like letting go of Zack all over again.

Some things were just too painful to endure twice.

Lacey was stunned. The Grouch had helped. She was still trying to digest that. Maybe things would change. Maybe he would be friendlier. And maybe she would sprout wings and fly. Oh, yeah. Gabe Garrison had not changed. She had no idea why he had helped, and he probably had none, either.

She had other important matters to take care of. For the first time, she'd become aware of how Emma brightened when Gabe was around. She'd formed a connection with him and Pepper.

Their father had raised Emma. Mona had died six months after Emma's birth. While Mona had been pregnant, the doctors had discovered cancer. Mona had refused any treatment until after the baby was born, but by then the aggressive cancer had spread. She hadn't lasted long.

Emma was more comfortable around men, and she'd somehow transferred that need for a father figure to

Gabe. That was why Emma kept saying Gabe didn't mean what he said. *Another problem.* Lacey had too many to deal with. She'd tackle the most pressing first.

"Mr. Gabe brought our tree in," Emma said, her eyes bright. It didn't escape Lacey that Emma had said *our.* Maybe Lacey was winning her over.

She knelt in front of Emma, who sat on the sofa. "Why did you disobey me again? You're not supposed to go into Gabe's yard."

Emma twisted her hands. "I forgot and I wanted to see what he was doing."

"Emma…"

"Really. I forgot."

Lacey had a feeling she was fighting a losing battle about Gabe and his privacy, so she decided to tackle another problem. "What did the little girl at the tree lot say to you?"

Emma looked down at her hands. "She said hi."

"Then why did you kick at her?"

"'Cause I don't like her."

"Why? She seemed real nice and she was there with her daddy…." Lacey's voice trailed off as something occurred to her. "You don't like her because she has a daddy and you don't."

From the shattered look in Emma's eyes, Lacey knew she was right. She wanted to stand up and do a jig. She'd gotten it right. Maybe parenting didn't come through the birth canal. Maybe it was trial and error.

She sat next to Emma. "You have a father, and he loved you more than life itself. You do know that, don't you?"

"But he's not here." The little voice wavered. "Why did my daddy have to go?"

Lacey gathered her into her arms. "I don't know, sweetie. I wish I had an answer that would make you feel better, but I don't. Sometimes bad things happen in life, and we have to adjust and go on. That's what Daddy wanted for you, and you promised him you wouldn't be sad."

"I miss Daddy," Emma cried.

"I do, too." Lacey held her sister and hoped by talking she could ease some of her pain. "Close your eyes."

"Why?"

"Just do it."

Emma scrunched her eyes together.

"Now, can you see Daddy? Try to see him."

"I can. I can see Daddy."

Lacey held her tighter. "Is he smiling?"

"Yes. He's smiling at me." Emma's voice grew excited.

"When you're feeling lonely and when you think other children have a daddy and you don't, just close your eyes and your daddy is right there. Always. And I'm right here. Always."

Emma leaned away. "Are you mad at me?" It was Emma's stock question when she'd done something wrong.

Lacey kissed her forehead. "No, sweetie. I'm not mad at you. But the next time that little girl says hi to you, I want you to say hi back. I do not want you kicking at anyone. Understand?"

Emma nodded.

"I'll call Sharon and see if Jimmy can come over and play for a while."

Emma jumped up. "Oh, boy! I'll get my Legos out."

And just like that the morning turned around. For the time being.

Jimmy came over. Lacey made them peanut-butter-and-jelly sandwiches for lunch, and then they returned to building stuff in the living room. As Lacey wiped the counter, she heard banging. And it was close. He wouldn't!

She ran outside and pushed on the gate, but it wouldn't budge. She used her body and shoved with all her might, and still the gate wouldn't move. Damn him! She wasn't going to let Gabe get away with this.

Back in the house, she hollered to the kids, "I'm going outside."

"'Kay," Emma shouted back.

Lacey went into the garage and found a hammer. Then she grabbed the kitchen stool that was still by the car and marched around to the fence between Gabe's and their house. She stepped up on the ladder and then vaulted over. Misjudging the height, she landed on her butt. She was winded for a moment, but she still had the hammer in her hand.

Getting to her feet, she took a long breath and marched to the gate. A large board was nailed across it. She tried to pry it away with the hammer, but she wasn't strong enough. Damn! She kicked at the gate. Frustrated, she sank to the ground with her back against it.

"What are you doing?"

She looked up into the brooding eyes of the dark knight. Every time she looked at his sad face, she wanted to apologize or try to make him feel better, like she did Emma. But sometimes there was no way to make things better.

She staggered to her feet. "I was trying to pry the

board away, but you nailed it securely. I hope you're happy."

Gabe just stared at her, his dark eyes orbs of never-ending sadness.

"She's a little girl and she doesn't understand. And I don't understand how you can be so cruel. How would you feel if someone had done this to your son?"

He turned as white as the fluffy clouds over his head, and Lacey thought he was going to pass out. Still, she wasn't in a relenting mood.

"If it makes you happy to keep the gate closed and us out, then by all means leave it nailed up. One day you're going to have to face the outside world and maybe even have to explain how you could hurt a six-year-old child. Your son would be so disappointed in you. Emma's made a connection to you and Pepper, but I will do my damnedest to keep her away. So be happy, Mr. Gabe Garrison. You just secured your privacy."

After saying that, she marched back to the fence and realized there was no way to get over it without the stool, which was on the other side.

Not willing to lose face, she stormed around his house and to the double gates on the other side. Stomping across his front yard, she realized she still had the hammer in her hand. What had she done? She'd traumatized a man who was barely hanging on emotionally.

Placing the hammer back in her father's toolbox, she knew she had to apologize. Later, though, when she wasn't fuming.

Gabe was so locked within himself he probably hadn't even heard what she'd said. She'd take time to cool off and then she would try to make amends. If that was possible.

She was so tired of dealing with grief and pain that she wanted to scream. There had to be a glimmer of happiness somewhere, and she intended to find it for Emma. And for herself.

But for Gabe, happiness was in his rearview mirror. And the road ahead was strewn with heartache and pain. Hope was something he didn't even want or desire. Inside, he was already as dead as his son.

Chapter 3

Gabe walked into his house and sat at the kitchen table, Pepper curled at his feet. The woman had some nerve. She didn't even know Zack or him. He looked up to stare at a photo of his son.

How would you feel if someone had done this to your child?

Don't think.

But his feelings bubbled to the surface. He would be as mad as hell. He ran his hands over his face and a tortured sigh escaped. He would have protected his son with his dying breath, except that when his son had needed him the most, Gabe hadn't been there. He'd failed his son. He'd failed to teach him how important it was to follow rules. He'd failed to discipline him. That was all on Gabe's shoulders. Gabe was the reason Zack was dead.

Another tortured sigh erupted from his throat.

Pepper whined and Gabe reached down to pat her. As he did, he saw his reflection in the glass on the stove. He didn't recognize himself. He touched his bearded face. When was the last time he'd shaved? Or showered? Or had gotten a haircut? He couldn't remember.

Your son would be so disappointed in you.

The woman was right. He recognized that somewhere in the frozen region of his mind. Zack wouldn't approve of him giving up and living his days in regret. But what else could he do? He had no reason to live anymore, but he didn't have the nerve to take his own life. He would never do that. It went against everything he believed in. So he continued to live in a hell of his own making.

One crazy woman was putting doubts in his head. *Ignore her,* he told himself. But he looked at the photo of his smiling son and knew he couldn't continue to live like this. Zack was gone and he couldn't hurt another child. But he could make things right.

It took Lacey about thirty minutes to calm down. Emma and Jimmy continued to play with the Legos and she made them a snack. Afterward, Emma wanted to know if they could go outside and play. Lacey hesitated, but Emma would find out soon enough about the gate. Lacey just had to be ready to explain.

She watched from the window while the kids chased each other and then played with a soccer ball, kicking it. Not once did Emma go to the gate, and Lacey was grateful for a little more time. Sharon called and Jimmy went home.

Not wanting to go to the diner again, Lacey made

hot dogs and they had store-packaged pudding for dessert. She had to do better than this.

Emma took her bath and then curled up on the sofa to watch *How the Grinch Stole Christmas*.

Lacey couldn't get Gabe off her mind.

"Sweetie, I'm going outside just for a minute. I'll be right back."

"'Kay." Emma was already engrossed in the movie.

Lacey went through the garage and walked to Gabe's front door. She rang the bell and waited. After a moment, he opened it.

She could only stare. He'd shaved, and his long hair was slicked back as if he'd just gotten out of the shower. He wore jeans and a black T-shirt and his feet were bare. Raw masculinity seemed to reach out and touch her. She swallowed hard.

"Did you want something?" he asked, his voice wrapping around her in a soothing sensation.

"Um…"

He lifted a dark eyebrow, and his eyes were heated with an emotion she couldn't describe. It wasn't anger this time. Could it be regret?

"Did you want something?" he repeated.

She cleared her throat. "Yes. I want to apologize for what I said earlier. I was completely out of line mentioning your son."

He inclined his head, as if that was a response.

Taking a couple steps backward, she turned and walked to her house. She'd never met anyone like Gabe before. He used a bare minimum of words, and she found that odd for a man who was a lawyer—or who had been one.

Once in her garage, she took a couple of deep breaths

before joining Emma to watch the rest of the movie. But the movie went right by her as thoughts of Gabe filled her head. He cleaned up better than anyone she'd ever known. He was handsome with a rugged, masculine appeal that made her pulse skitter with awareness.

She'd had a boyfriend in Austin, and they had been serious until her father had become ill and Lacey had started spending so much time in Horseshoe. Darin hadn't been happy that she'd taken on the responsibility of Emma, and they'd drifted apart. She hadn't heard from him in months.

Her mother also hadn't been pleased with Lacey's decision. But then she and her mother had never been really close. Her father had been the steadying force in her life as a child and as a teenager. Her mother had worked at Macy's for as far back as Lacey could remember—long hours and all holidays, leaving little time for her family.

Her parents were mismatched, and Lacey had never understood how they'd gotten together. Her mother was a social person who liked to go out after work. Her father had been a homebody who had enjoyed tinkering around the house.

Jack Carroll had been a postman, and her mother always had been on his case about drive and ambition. She'd wanted him to have a desk job. She'd wanted him to have prestige. It had all come to a head after her father had declined a desk job at the post office. Her mother had told him to get out and never come back. And he had. Then she'd blamed him for leaving. Her mother was the victim, and Lacey had grown tired of hearing that story.

But she was Lacey's mother, and Lacey loved her

even though it was hard sometimes to deal with her. She had no idea how she was going to fit Christmas in with her mother, because her mother refused to be around Emma. Somehow she blamed the child for the reason Jack never came back.

Emma was sound asleep, holding her bear. Lacey wondered how anyone could blame an innocent child. And she wondered if her life would be filled with anything other than heartache. Getting up, she yawned, reached for the remote control and clicked off the TV. She lifted Emma into her arms and carried her to bed.

Tomorrow had to be a better day.

And the man next door had to be in a better mood. They'd made a start. Now Lacey waited for the next encounter.

The next morning Lacey was in a hurry to make the ten o'clock mass. Emma was being stubborn, not wanting to wear a dress or put a bow in her hair. But Lacey won that round. They walked through the doors of the little Catholic Church in Horseshoe just as the bell chimed.

Emma fidgeted during the service, and Lacey had to give her a couple of sharp stares to keep her still. Afterward, they came out of church to a cold winter day. In the parking lot, Lacey said hello to Angie and Hardy Hollister. She had met Angie when she'd first moved here. Angie was very nice and had wanted to help as much as she could after Jack's death. Angie's friend Peyton was the same. Hardy was the D.A., and Peyton's husband, Wyatt Carson, was the sheriff.

Emma brightened when she saw Angie and Hardy's

daughter. Erin was almost twelve, but Emma considered her a friend.

Erin took Emma's hand and they ran to say hello to Erin's grandma and the Wiznowski family. They were a big family and owned the busiest place in town, the bakery. Lacey was still learning all of their names.

"Why does Emma look so sad?" Angie asked, her hand on her stomach. She was due at the end of March and she positively glowed.

"Brad Wilson told her there's no Santa Claus and now she doesn't want to have Christmas."

"How awful."

Hardy had his arm around his wife, and he rubbed her shoulder in a loving gesture. "Kids can be cruel."

Erin and Emma came running back and they said goodbye. Angie bent down to Emma. "Merry Christmas."

Emma twisted in her Mary Jane shoes and didn't respond.

Lacey took Emma's hand and they walked to the car. They went to the diner for lunch before heading home. Emma was very quiet. She probably was feeling lonely, just like Lacey was.

Emma plopped onto the sofa. "Can Jimmy come over to play?"

"No. He's gone to his grandmother's today. Change your clothes and we'll play games or something."

"No." The word was spoken in an angry tone.

Lacey gave her a minute. Then she placed her hands on her hips. "Go change your clothes. Now!"

Emma jumped up and ran to her room. Lacey groaned. Another one of those days. They were due for a good one. Soon.

After slipping into jeans and a pullover top, she went to check on Emma. The little girl was lying on her bed, reading a book. She took after her mother. Mona had been a librarian.

Lacey glanced around the lavender, white and purple room she'd helped their father decorate. Emma was not a girlie girl and had not wanted a pink room. Her father had bought all kinds of Barbies and a Barbie doll house and numerous other Barbie toys, but Emma barely touched them. She liked the outdoors and would rather play with a ball instead of a doll. But she did love stuffed animals, and they littered the comforter on her white four-poster bed.

Lacey sat beside her sister. "What are you reading?"

Emma closed *A Light in the Attic* and scooted up. "Why don't I have a grandma?"

Oh, that was the reason for the sulkiness. "You did have a grandma. Two, actually. Dad's mom's name was Martha and your mom's was Ruth. Grandma Martha died when I was fifteen. She would've loved you."

"She would?"

"You bet. She gave big hugs and made everyone feel loved. I always looked forward to staying with her during the summer."

"What about my other grandma?"

Lacey took a breath, hating to talk about so many deaths. But she had to be honest. "She died, too, sweetie. I never met her. She was a librarian like your mother."

Emma stared down at her sneakers. "Why does everybody have to die?"

Lacey frantically opened the book in her head and searched for answers. As always, none was suitable. She had to go with her gut feeling. "That's life, sweetie, and as you get older you'll understand more." That sounded lame even to her own ears. She was terrible at this. Hugging Emma, she said, "You know what? You can call me Lacey or you can call me Grandma. I can be both."

Emma giggled. With a hand over her mouth, she said, "You're weird, Lacey."

"How about if we walk to the park and play on the big slide and swing set?"

"'Kay." Emma jumped off the bed. "They have a really big slide. It makes my stomach feel funny and it's fun."

"Let's get our coats and go, then."

Emma grabbed her coat from a chair. As Lacey went to her room to get hers, the buzz of her cell phone stopped her.

"Just a minute, Emma. I have to answer my phone."

It was her mother. Lacey sank onto the bed, ready for another round of complaints. "Hi, Mom."

Her mother wasted no time getting started. "Since you couldn't spend Thanksgiving with me, I was hoping we could spend Christmas together."

Lacey closed her eyes and counted to three. "Mom, you know I can't leave Emma at Christmas."

"What about me? Your own mother? You have no time for me anymore. I don't know what Jack was thinking when he asked you to take care of that child. You're a young woman and should have your own life."

They had been through this so many times, and Lacey had grown weary of the subject. "It was my choice. Mona's sister offered to take Emma, but she has four children of her own. If Emma was taken from the home she'd shared with Dad, I knew it would be detrimental for her. I love my sister and I couldn't put her through that. I'm here and I intend to stay here. I will work something out for Christmas."

"Like what?"

"If you would just accept Emma, you could come to Horseshoe."

"I'm not stepping foot in the house your father shared with that woman."

Lacey wanted to beat her head against something. "He shared this house with his wife."

"I'll never forgive you for accepting her."

"Mom, have you been drinking or something? You're not making any sense. You're the one who told dad to leave. You're the one who remarried three months later. I don't know why you feel like the victim."

"Jack would have come back if it hadn't been for her."

"You'd married someone else. Are you forgetting that?"

"I only did it to get back at him. That's why the marriage didn't last."

"Mom, I'm not going through all this again. Mona and Emma made Dad very happy."

After a long pause, Joyce said, "Maybe I am being a little irrational, but I loved your father and I never meant for him to stay away. It just turned out that way."

Finally, her mother was admitting the truth. "I know you loved him, but you were miserable the last years of your marriage."

"Lacey," a little voice call from the hallway. "Are we going to the park?"

"In a minute, sweetie. I'll be right there," she called back. "Mom, I really have to go."

"Am I going to see you at all this Christmas?"

"What about Mervin?" That was her mom's new boyfriend.

"He'll want to spend time with his kids, and I don't get along with them."

No surprise there. Her mother enjoyed being the center of attention. "Call me when you have a day off and I'll come for a visit."

"I work a lot during the holidays."

Same old line. Same old verse. "Please think about coming here for Christmas. Once you meet Emma, you'll love her. She had nothing to do with your marriage or your divorce. She's just an innocent little girl."

"I'll talk to you later," her mother said, and clicked off.

Lacey sat for a moment and wished her mother would come to grips with the past and her part in it. But maybe some things just were not doable. Or realistic, considering the way her mother felt.

Now Lacey had a little girl who was eager to go to the park. She reached for her jacket and hurried to the kitchen. But Emma wasn't there and she wasn't in the living room. Or anywhere in the house.

No! No! No!

Lacey ran out the back door and stopped short. The gate was open. Gabe had removed the board? She walked slowly to the opening and could see Emma sitting on a lawn chair, huddled in her red-and-black coat. Gabe sat next to her in a black hoodie and jeans. They were staring at Pepper in her bed. Neither was speaking. There was complete silence.

What were they doing?

Gabe didn't seem upset that Emma was there. Lacey's first instinct was to go over and make Emma come back to their house. But something stopped her.

A plane flew overhead. A car honked and the wind rustled through the leaves of the tall oaks. Other than that, the two of them sat there in perfect harmony. Perfect silence. Lacey couldn't bring herself to interrupt.

Suddenly, Emma said, "Pepper is sick. When I was sick, my daddy took me to the doctor. You have to take Pepper to the doctor."

Gabe didn't answer or look at Emma. His eyes were on the dog.

"My daddy died, so he can't take me anymore. Lacey does. Daddy's in heaven and Lacey says he can see me. But I can't see him. I miss my daddy." Emma wiped at her eyes and Lacey wanted to run over, but again she didn't. "Do you miss your son?"

Lacey's heart sank at the question. She should get Emma before she caused Gabe any more pain. But for some reason she couldn't explain, she stood there, holding her breath, waiting for Gabe to answer.

Chapter 4

Gabe's throat locked tight. He couldn't push a sound through. Nor could he breathe. His body stiffened in protest, needing oxygen. Just when he thought the pain would get him, Pepper saved him. She whimpered, and the child jumped from her chair and went to the dog.

The little girl stroked Pepper and Gabe wanted to scream, *Don't touch her. She's Zack's dog. Get away from her.* But the words wouldn't come. In that moment he realized just how insane his thoughts were, and the lock on his throat lessened. He breathed in deeply, his lungs expanding from the much needed relief.

"Pepper is sick, Mr. Gabe," the kid said.

He knew that. He wanted to tell her it was none of her business and that she should go home. But once again the words wouldn't come. Maybe because Pepper had lifted her head and licked the child's hand. Pepper liked the kid. He'd never noticed that before. He hadn't noticed many things beyond the pain in his chest.

"She's shaking. I think she's cold." The kid noticed the blanket by the basket and gently tucked it around Pepper.

It was getting colder. He should take Pepper inside, but whenever he did, she whined to go out. He was just giving her a little more time.

The kid stood up. "I gotta go. Lacey's probably looking for me. She doesn't like it when I come over here. But you don't mind, do you?"

Yes, I mind. Please, just leave me alone.

"Lacey and me have the same father. We're sisters. Her mama lives in Austin and I've never met her. Do you have a sister?"

Yes. He should call Kate and let her know he was… what? Still living with the pain. She wouldn't want to hear that, so it was best to wait a little longer.

"I gotta go. Don't forget to take Pepper to the doctor. He'll make her all better. 'Bye."

Not this time.

The child ran to the gate. Gabe got up and squatted next to Pepper.

"You like the kid, don't you?"

Pepper nuzzled his hand in approval.

But she's not Zack. She's not Zack.

Lacey hurried into the house and was standing just inside the back door as Emma came through it.

"Oh," Emma said, startled.

Lacey folded her arms across her chest. "You've been over at Gabe's."

She would have to discipline Emma, even though

it would hurt Lacey more than it did her sister. She'd let her disobey too many times, though. Gabe hadn't seemed to mind Emma being there, but Emma had done all of the talking. Gabe hadn't responded once. And Emma needed to know that she had to mind and respect other people's wishes.

"Uh…" Emma twisted her hands. "You were on the phone and I heard Pepper."

"You can't hear the dog from inside the house."

"Yes, I…"

"No." Lacey pointed a finger at Emma. "You've disobeyed me twice today, and now I have to punish you."

"No, Lacey, no. Don't punish me." Emma barreled into Lacey, wrapping her arms around Lacey's waist, and burying her face in Lacey's stomach. "I'm sorry. I won't do it again."

Lacey swallowed, trying to be strong. "You say that all the time and you still disobey me. Go to your room and sit in the time-out chair."

"No. I don't want to."

Lacey pointed toward the hall. "Go."

"No. I'll be good!" Emma wailed.

Lacey took Emma's hand and led her down the hall to her bedroom. Emma sobbed loudly the whole time and Lacey's strength waned. She pulled out Emma's desk chair and placed it in a corner.

"Take off your coat and sit and think about what you did."

"No, Lacey," Emma cried as she removed her coat and sat in the chair.

"I'll come back in about thirty minutes and we'll talk." It took all of Lacey's strength to walk out the door. Emma's wails followed her.

"Lacey!" Emma screamed.

She sat at the kitchen table and buried her face in her hands. How did parents do this? It was pure torture, but she had to start setting boundaries for Emma. She just never dreamed how hard it would be.

"Lacey," Emma kept calling.

The sobs and calling suddenly stopped, and Lacey glanced up, waiting for Emma to walk into the kitchen. But she didn't. Lacey didn't know what she would do if Emma disobeyed her now. Her luck held, and the house grew quiet. After fifteen minutes, Lacey could stand it no longer. She slowly made her way to Emma's room.

Her sister was still in the chair, her head bent as if she was studying her sneakers. She looked up when Lacey entered.

"Can I get up now?"

Lacey sat on the bed and patted the spot next to her. "Let's talk."

Emma climbed up beside her, her eyes still watery, and Lacey felt a catch in her throat. She hated this part.

"Do you know what you did wrong?"

Emma nodded. "But Mr. Gabe doesn't mind me coming over. We talked."

Lacey didn't want to remind her sister that she had done all the talking. "That's not the point. I asked you not to go over to Gabe's."

"But..."

"Emma, sweetie, Dad put me in charge of you and your welfare, and your well-being is my top priority. When you continue to disobey me, I feel as if I have failed in my promise."

"No, Lacey." Emma leaned into her, her face against Lacey's arm. "I love you."

Lacey wrapped her arms around her sister. "I know you do. And I love you. That's the reason I'm here."

"I didn't mean to disobey. You were on the phone and I went outside and heard Pepper and Mr. Gabe. I wanted to see what they were doing. I forgot, Lacey. I forgot what you said. I didn't do it on purpose. I'm sorry."

Lacey hugged Emma tightly. "We're going to make new rules. From now on, when you hear Pepper I want you to come to me and tell me, and then we'll decide if you can go over and visit the dog. That's the way it's going to be, Emma. Do you understand?"

Emma nodded and looked up at Lacey. "Pepper is sick and Mr. Gabe's gonna take her to the doctor. Can we go see Pepper tomorrow?"

"I'll go over and ask Gabe, but we have to respect his wishes."

"'Kay."

"Get your crayons and pencils and drawing stuff out, and I'll go over and talk to Gabe."

Emma jumped off the bed. "I'll draw a picture of Pepper. Are we going to the park later?"

"No. That's part of your punishment. I'm not rewarding you with fun time."

"Oh." Lacey expected more tears, but Emma acquiesced easily, which Lacey was more than grateful for. She was holding on by a thread with her parenting skills.

"I'll be back in a few minutes."

Emma was busy pulling things out of a drawer as Lacey walked out. Lacey had to apologize to Gabe one more time and see exactly how he felt about Emma invading his privacy. And she had to thank him for removing the board.

* * *

Gabe planned to give Pepper a few more minutes and then he would take her inside. He wasn't sure when he realized someone was standing there, but he felt a strong presence and turned his head. It was the crazy lady. Now what?

She stepped onto his deck. "I'm sorry Emma came over here and disturbed you."

He frowned. "Who's Emma?"

She blinked, as if she was caught in the headlights of something disturbing. "She's…my sister. The little girl who is always coming into your yard. Against your wishes."

"Oh." He was losing his mind, and he hated that she was reminding him how out of touch he was.

She motioned toward the gate. "Thanks for removing the board."

"Yeah. I shouldn't have done that."

What did she want? Couldn't she see he was having trouble making conversation?

Pepper whimpered, and she went to the dog and squatted next to her. "Is Pepper sick?"

Go away, he screamed inside his head. But then he heard words coming out of his mouth. "She has cancer."

"Oh. I'm sorry." She patted the dog and seemed generally concerned. But his perception was way off. "Is there any help for her?"

He rubbed his hands together, not wanting to talk, but once again words erupted from his throat. "No. The vet said it's time to put her to sleep. But she was my son's dog and I can't do that."

She continued to pat the dog. "She's trembling in

pain. You have to do something. You can't just leave her like this."

"She's the last thing I have of my son. If she goes, I…"

She got up and knelt in front of him. He looked into green eyes as bright and shining as anything he'd ever seen. Was that a tear he glimpsed?

"She's not the last thing you have of your son." She placed a hand over her heart. "In here you have many memories that no one and nothing can take from you, not Pepper's death or anything on this earth. That love, that feeling, will always be with you."

His gaze narrowed on her face and he saw her for the first time, really saw her. Her hair was blond, a beautiful natural color, and it was short, kind of kicked up at the back and curled around her face. It gave her a young Meg Ryan appeal…. He had no idea where that thought came from.

"I'm sorry, I don't know your name. I'm a little out of touch."

"It's Lacey."

A pretty name for a pretty woman. He shook his head. "You don't understand."

"I do. I lost my father. The one and only safety net I had in my life, and suddenly all that security was gone. It's been hard holding it together for Emma. I know your situation is different, but you can't continue to let this dog suffer. Do the humane thing like the vet suggested."

"I've been trying to do that, but something always stops me."

"I will go with you if that will help."

He looked at her again. He was a man and strong enough to handle anything. He'd dealt with his son's death. Why was he so frightened of what would happen to him once Pepper was gone? Suddenly he saw a life-line in her eyes. That was the way he saw it, and he took it, because it was the only thing he had at the moment.

"Thank you. I... I would appreciate that."

She went back to Pepper. "Do you have anything to give her for pain?"

"The vet gave me some injections. I only have one left."

Lacey sat next to the dog and stroked her. "She really needs something."

He stood and walked into the house, knowing once he gave Pepper the injection, he would have to take her to the vet. It was time.

The woman was still there when he came back. She watched as he gave Pepper the injection. The dog drifted into sleep.

"When do you want to take her in?"

"The medication lasts a little over twenty-four hours. Probably tomorrow or when the vet has an opening." He made the decision and he wasn't panicking, because this woman, this crazy woman as he'd called her, had reached out a hand when he'd desperately needed it.

"Do you mind if Emma says goodbye to Pepper? She's very fond of her, and I don't know how she's going to take this."

He ran a hand through his hair. "Do whatever you feel is best."

"Thanks. You're doing the right thing. I'll... I'll talk to you tomorrow."

Was he doing the right thing? Then why did he feel as if he was in a deep dark hole without any chance for survival?

As she left, he wondered what had just happened. He'd talked so much in the past few minutes that his throat burned. And he realized how much he missed talking. How he missed a lot of things. Maybe there was a light at the end of his long dark tunnel. A green light.

Lacey stood on her patio and took a deep breath. She needed it to calm her emotions before she went into the house. Gabe's pain touched her heart. She feared this might be the last straw for him. But she would do everything she could to help him. She was just glad he was in a receptive mood, because he didn't need to go through this alone.

She knew about loneliness, death, suffering and the unimaginable pain that went along with them. Maybe they could find solace together. She was still reeling from him talking to her. He had a deep, strong voice, and she could picture him in a courtroom. There wasn't much on this earth he couldn't handle, she imagined, except the death of his son.

Shivering, she wrapped her arms around her waist. Soon there had to be some relief for Gabe. He couldn't continue to live the way he had been, and the fact that he'd actually confided in her gave her hope. She wiped away an errant tear.

Now she had another problem. How was she going to tell Emma about Pepper? Once again, death was going to derail them for a short time. It was too much, though. Too much for a six-year-old girl to handle. Too much for a twenty-eight-year-old woman to handle. And definitely too much for the man next door to handle.

She opened the door and went inside. Emma sat at the table, drawing.

Emma lifted her head. "Look. I drew a picture of Pepper."

Lacey removed her jacket and stared at the black dog on the paper with the blue sky, green grass and tall trees. A happy scene.

How was she going to tell Emma?

"Very nice."

"Did you talk to Mr. Gabe?"

"Yes, and—"

The doorbell rang, interrupting her. She hurried to answer it, glad for the reprieve. Bradley Wilson and his son Brad stood on the doorstep.

"Hi, Lacey," Bradley said. "My son has something to say to Emma."

Emma ran into the room. Lacey caught her before she could do anything stupid. "Brad has come to see you."

"I don't want to see him," Emma replied. "I want to hit him."

Bradley poked his son.

"Emma, I'm sorry I ruined your Christmas," Brad said, as if he'd memorized the words or as if someone had quoted them to him.

Emma glared at him and Lacey bent and whispered in her ear, "Say thank-you for the apology."

Now Emma glared at her. Lacey lifted an eyebrow and Emma repeated the words. At the end she tacked on, "I still want to hit you."

"Don't worry, Emma," Bradley said. "Brad has asked Santa for an Xbox, and since he believes there is no Santa and has told this to other children, he won't be getting an Xbox."

"Dad!" Brad wailed.

Bradley looked at Lacey. "I'm really sorry about this."

"Thank you, and thanks for the apology."

They walked off, and Lacey and Emma went into the living room. "That was nice of Brad."

"He's a big baby."

"Emma…"

"It's true, Lacey. He's crying like a baby 'cause he's not gonna get an Xbox."

Lacey sat on the sofa, flipping through the imaginary book in her head. "Let's talk about belief."

Emma hopped up beside her. "Why?"

"Because belief can be a powerful thing. If you believe strong enough, long enough, wonderful things can happen."

"Like maybe there really is a Santa."

Lacey tucked a stray curl behind Emma's ear. "Could be. All you have to do is believe."

"You're getting really weird, Lacey."

Lacey kissed the tip of Emma's nose. "Just believe, that's all you have to do."

"I'll try. But I know the truth and I can't forget it."

Lacey pulled Emma onto her lap, knowing they had to talk about something much more important. She had to tell Emma about Pepper.

Chapter 5

"Sweetie—"

"Are you mad at me, Lacey?" Emma interrupted, resting the side of her face against Lacey's chest.

"No, I'm not mad at you."

"But you punished me."

That obviously stung a little. "Why did I do that?"

Emma played with the watch on Lacey's wrist. "'Cause...'cause I disobeyed."

"Yes, you did. But we talked about it and you're not going to do that again, right?"

"Mmm-hmm."

It was just too difficult to punish Emma, especially at this grieving time in their lives. Maybe she would get better as the years rolled on. Even though Lacey knew she had to be the adult and set rules and boundaries, she would rather that she and Emma be friends instead of Lacey being the stern disciplinarian.

"Lacey, Pepper is really sick," Emma said, and it brought Lacey back to the present problem.

"Yes, she is."

"But Mr. Gabe is going to take her to the doctor and the doctor will make her all better."

Lacey tightened her arms around Emma. "I talked to Gabe, and Pepper is not going to get better."

Emma looked up at her. "Why not?"

Lacey swallowed and glanced toward the ceiling. *I could use a little help here.*

"Why, Lacey?"

"Because like you said, Pepper is really sick. She… she has cancer."

Emma's eyes rounded. "Like Daddy had?"

Their father had died of prostate cancer, which he had let go on too long. Taking care of Mona and Emma, he'd neglected his own health. The doctors had operated, but it had been too late. The cancer had spread.

"There are all kinds of cancer. I'm not sure what kind Pepper has, but it's bad."

"Is she going to die?"

The book in Lacey's head was closed, and there wasn't any reason to flip through it, because there was no answer. She'd read so many books about death and grief, and she still didn't have the answer or the words to make the pain better. The person just had to deal with it. That was the really hard part, especially for a child.

She looked into Emma's troubled green eyes. "Yes, Pepper is going to die."

"No." Emma buried her face in Lacey's chest and cried. All Lacey could do was hold her and pray for the right words. Loud sobs racked Emma's little body, and Lacey's eyes filled with tears as she waited for the cries to subside.

She rubbed Emma's back. "Pepper is in a lot of pain."

Emma raised her head, wiping away tears. "I know. She shakes."

Lacey drew in a deep breath. "Gabe is going to take her to a doctor, but he won't be bringing her back."

Emma's eyes rounded even more. "Is the doctor going to put her to sleep?"

Lacey was startled at the question. She'd had no idea Emma knew about such things. "How did you know that?"

"Last year, Jimmy's cousin's dog had to be put to sleep. He was real sick, too. Jimmy said the doctor took away his pain and now he's in heaven."

Thank you. She glanced briefly toward the ceiling.

"That's what the vet is going to do for Pepper."

"Then he'll go to heaven and be with Zack?"

Lacey squeezed her sister, amazed at her insight. "Yes, sweetie. Pepper will go and be with Zack now."

"I have to say goodbye." Emma began to scramble from her lap, but Lacey caught her.

"Not today. Gabe is taking this really bad, so we have to let him have his privacy. Please understand that, Emma."

Emma twisted her hands. "But…"

"You have school tomorrow, and when you get home you can spend time with Pepper and say goodbye. Gabe said you could."

"'Kay." Emma leaned against her and Lacey just held her as they both came to grips with the situation.

They ate dinner in silence, and then Lacey got Emma's clothes and backpack ready for school the following day. Then they settled in to watch some TV, but Lacey's thoughts were with the man next door. He really didn't need to be alone. If she went over there, she felt sure her visit would be met with a big scowl. She would take baby steps with Gabe. In the days ahead she would make sure he wasn't alone.

The next morning on the way to school Emma said, "Don't be late today."

"I'm never late," Lacey replied as she pulled into the parking lot of the Horseshoe school. Since the town was small, grades one through twelve were housed in one big building shaped like a horseshoe. There were portable buildings to the side for pre-K and kindergarten. A gym and cafeteria were situated at the end of the horseshoe. The metal buildings with the half-brick front had been there for years. Green shrubs enhanced the front. In the spring, colorful flowers would be blooming in the flowerbeds, planted by the agriculture teacher, Mr. Schuldt.

Kids ran to the front door so they could make it to their classrooms before the bell rang. Emma climbed out and so did Lacey.

"Be good today and be nice to your playmates." She kissed her sister.

Emma fidgeted.

"Everything will be fine. I'll be here early if that will make you feel better."

"'Kay. Love you." Emma followed the children into the school, her black-and-purple backpack flopping on her back.

Lacey got in the car and drove home, hoping Emma wouldn't dwell on Pepper too much today. She seemed to be okay with what was happening, and Lacey wanted it to stay that way.

As she pulled into her driveway, she noticed everything was quiet at Gabe's. No banging or sounds anywhere, which was unusual. He was usually outside by now working on something.

She made her way into her house, put her purse on the table and walked over to his deck. He wasn't there. She knocked and got no answer. Everything was quiet inside. Where was he?

She went back to her house and across the yard to his front door. Again, she got no answer. She knew she was trespassing, but she didn't care. Her only thought was of Gabe and his mental state. Without thinking it to death, she opened the double gates by the garage. That was when she heard the sound. A saw or a drill. She didn't know which, but Gabe was working in his garage.

When she tried the garage's side door, it opened easily and the sound was much louder. She stepped inside and saw Gabe working on a large box. Was that a coffin? Yes, there was no mistaking it. He'd made a coffin for Pepper. Her chest ached at the sadness of it all.

He turned off the sander and set it on the floor. As he did, he noticed her. She expected him to be startled or surprised, but he was neither. He just went back to working on the box.

Walking closer, she said, "I knocked, but you didn't answer."

He rubbed the plywood with a rag. "Did you want something?"

She curled her hands into fists. He was acting as if they hadn't talked yesterday, as if they hadn't shared something special, as if he wanted her out of his garage. That wasn't happening. He was putting up every defense he could to keep her away so he could keep feeling the pain. That wasn't happening, either.

"You've made a coffin for Pepper."

"Yes. I'm not just going to throw her in the ground."

The whole attitude thing had resurfaced, but she was good at kicking attitude.

"Did you call the vet?"

"Uh…"

She held up a hand. "Please, let's not go back to the old animosity. Did you call the vet?"

He stopped rubbing the wood. "I was feeling down last night, but today I have everything under control."

"Yeah, I can see that." She glanced at his appearance. He had on the same clothes as yesterday and he hadn't shaved. "Have you been to bed at all?"

He went back to fiddling with the wood. "I don't sleep much."

"Because that's when you dream."

He stared at her. "You don't know anything about me."

"I don't have to. I know you're barely hanging on emotionally, and you don't sleep because that's when you dream about your son. I've been there and I'm still there, and I'm still trying to cope. And I have to because I have a little girl who needs me."

"Well, I don't have anyone, so would you please leave me alone?"

She stepped closer to him. "No, sorry. I can't do that. I promised you I would be here to help you with Pepper."

Their eyes locked. His eyes were cold and dark, emitting a message that she received all too well, but it still didn't deter her.

"I relieve you of that promise."

She shook her head. "I'm not going anywhere."

"This is my house, and I'm asking you to leave." Anger flashed in his eyes. Her first instinct was to turn and walk away and let him live in all the pain he had created. But something beyond her control made her lay her hand on the box.

"This is really nice. Zack would be very proud of his father."

Gabe froze, just as she had expected. She'd said Zack's name on purpose, because it was the only thing that caught his attention.

"Are you dense? Get out of my garage."

A tremor ran through her, and she knew she couldn't continue to be stronger than she was. It was taking everything she had to stand her ground. She didn't know what would have happened next if Pepper hadn't come into the garage.

"Oh, Pepper is better." She went to the dog and stroked her.

Gabe glared at Lacey and she continued to pet the dog.

"The medication helps," he said so low that she barely caught it.

"Did you call the vet?" she asked one more time.

"Yes. And he said he will come to the house in the morning at ten and do the procedure here."

"That would be much better and less stressful on Pepper. And you."

"I'm not worried about me," he snapped.

"I'm well aware of that."

Pepper whimpered.

Lacey hugged her. "Are you in pain, girl?"

"She wants to go outside." He wiped his hands on a rag. "Come on, Pep. We'll go outside." Gabe walked past Lacey through a door into a utility room. Pepper trailed behind, but she wobbled. It was clear she was very weak.

Lacey had the choice either to walk out the garage door and retreat to her house or to follow them. She did the latter. In the kitchen, Pepper's strength gave way and she sank to the floor. Gabe picked her up as if she weighed no more than a feather and carried her out the back door.

Lacey was dumbstruck by the scene before her. The kitchen had a table and one chair. The counters were bare; nothing was on them. It looked as if no one lived there, except for the dog dishes on the floor. She gasped as she saw the wall.

Photos of a brown-haired little boy covered it, from the day he was born until the day he'd died. Zack in a crib, crawling, walking and holding on to Gabe's fingers, on a tricycle, then a bicycle, a skateboard and doing numerous other activities. Zack's life was on this wall.

She peeked through the doorway into the living room. There was a sofa, chair and a TV on a box, but she didn't think it was plugged in. And another wall dedicated to Zack. Gabe had made his house a shrine to his son. It was the most depressing thing Lacey had ever seen. She shook off the morbid feeling and went outside.

Pepper was curled up in her bed and Gabe sat in a lawn chair, watching her. Lacey took the other chair and they sat in silence, much like Gabe and Emma had yesterday.

Pepper laid her face off the side of the bed and kept a close eye on the backyard. "She likes it out here," Lacey said.

"Yes, but sometimes it's too cold." His voice was similar to yesterday, so she kept talking.

"I didn't know a vet would come to the house."

"I didn't either, but I like the idea much better than Pepper being in a strange place."

Since he seemed to be in a better mood, she suggested, "I can sit with Pepper if you'd like to take a nap or...a shower."

He rested his elbows on his knees and rubbed his hands together. She waited for sharp words to hit her.

"I... I think I will take a shower." He went into the house without another word.

Lacey exhaled deeply. How did the man keep going without sleep? And then it dawned on her that that was the reason he was so grouchy. She might be in over her head with Gabe, but she couldn't make herself turn away from someone in need.

Pepper moaned and stretched out. Lacey eased to the deck and sat by her, stroking her. The poor thing was in so much pain, She was glad Gabe had made the right decision for the dog. She just hoped it was the right one for Gabe.

Gabe showered quickly and decided to shave. The crazy lady was annoying the crap out of him, but in a way she was holding him accountable for his actions. He didn't need her telling him what to do. He didn't need her at all. He...was lying to himself. He'd reached out to her last night because he was losing control of his faculties. There was only one thing to do concerning Pepper, and he had needed someone to give him that push. It just happened to be the lady next door. Now he had to get rid of her, because he could handle this all by himself.

After changing into clean clothes, he went back outside. He paused in the doorway. She was sitting on the deck talking to Pepper.

"I bet you'd like to chase squirrels. My friend had a dog, and when we took her to the park she would spend all her time chasing squirrels. It made her happy." Pepper raised her head as if she understood, and the woman kept talking. "Oh, you like squirrels." Her voice dropped to a tone of sadness. "I'm sorry you're in so much pain, but it will get better soon. And there are a lot of squirrels in heaven, I'm sure."

"Do you really think she understands you?" He couldn't keep the derision out of his voice.

She looked at him. "I choose to believe she does, Mr. Garrison. It's all about belief."

He returned to his chair. "Please don't talk to me about religion."

"Oh, please, like I would dare." She pushed to her feet, and he couldn't drag his eyes away from her slim body. That surprised him, because he didn't really want to see her. He tried to remember her name and couldn't.

"I'm talking about believing that there is a better place for us when we die. I have to believe that because I know my father is in a better place than the hell he was in here on earth." Her voice wavered, and he felt a catch in his throat, an emotion he hadn't felt in ages.

"I'm sorry about your father," he found himself saying. "I didn't know him all that well, but he was a good neighbor."

She sat in the chair. "Yes, my father was an exceptional man. I miss him every day, and I'm so afraid of doing all the wrong things with Emma."

"She seems well-adjusted and happy."

"I'm sorry she bothers you so much, but she loves Pepper. I've been thinking about getting her a dog."

He was supposed to say something here, but he wasn't sure what it was. The kid did bother him and he really did want to be alone. But he didn't voice his real feelings, because for the first time in two years he felt someone else's pain, and it blindsided him. Maybe into reality. Maybe into accepting that he had to go on. That was his only choice, and it came from a woman who knew about grief.

All of a sudden he didn't want to get rid of her. He wanted to keep talking. But what would that accomplish? He had to make her see that he didn't need her. Or anyone.

Chapter 6

Gabe got to his feet. "Pepper doesn't need a babysitter. She'll lay out here and enjoy the fresh air. I have to finish the box, but I'll check on her every now and then." He looked directly at Lacey. "And I'm sure you have things to do at your own house."

"Actually, I have laundry waiting for me." Lacey stood and faced him, even though it was like facing a towering inferno of attitude that was leveled right at her. "I'll go on one condition."

"I don't do conditions."

She ignored the warning in his voice. "I'll go if you come and eat a sandwich with me at lunch."

"I don't eat at a set time. I eat when I get hungry and I never watch the clock."

She placed her hands on her hips. "Today at twelve."

His eyes darkened. "Listen…hell. I don't even remember your name."

"It's Lacey," she replied with as much patience as she could find.

"Lacey," he said with a husky growl that seemed to come from somewhere deep within him. "I am not coming to your house for lunch at twelve or ever."

She sat back down.

"What are you doing?"

"If you're not coming, then I'll just stay here. I have the whole day free. Isn't that nice?"

By the narrowing of his eyes it was clear he considered it anything but nice. He threw up his hands. "Okay, okay. I'll come over at noon. Now will you please leave?"

Once again she stood, her eyes catching his. "Since you asked so politely, I'll go. See you at noon." She turned and walked toward the gate, forcing herself not to look back at the scowl on his face. But there was a moment of victory in her heart. She'd won this round.

She went inside and sat at the kitchen table. All those creepy-crawly doubts niggled her. What was she doing? She was trying to help someone else when some days she was barely holding it together herself. But there was no one else to help Gabe. She remembered those days after her dad had passed, the horrible sadness, the debilitating pain and trying to hold it all together for Emma. They'd come a long way in five months, but occasionally they needed a helping hand, and the people of Horseshoe had been very kind to them. And she had to be kind to Gabe. It was that simple for her.

She stripped the beds and put the sheets in the washing machine. All the while she was thinking she should fix something appetizing for lunch. Since her culinary skills were limited, she called Angie.

She came straight to the point. "I need help with a cooking problem."

"Okay. I need details."

"I have ham and cheese. How do I make that into something special in a sandwich?"

"Grill it in a frying pan like a grilled cheese. Use butter." Angie went through the process step by step, and Lacey wrote it down. "Serve with a pickle, chips and beverage of your choice, and you have an appetizing lunch."

"Thank you. This sounds simple—so simple I think I can accomplish it."

Angie laughed. "Call if you run into a problem."

Lacey hung up and went to work. By noon she had the sandwiches on a plate without a burn mark on them. She added cherry tomatoes, a pickle and chips, then waited for Gabe. At five minutes after twelve she had a sneaking suspicion he wasn't coming. With her back to the stove, she tapped her foot, counting off the minutes on the coffee mug–shaped wall clock. When the big hand hit the quarter hour, she marched to the door.

She yanked it open and jumped back. Gabe stood with his hand in the air, getting ready to knock.

His perpetual scowl was firmly in place. "I told you I don't watch a clock. I was washing my hands in the kitchen when I noticed the time, so I came without changing clothes because I knew you would be storming over if I didn't."

Sawdust coated his jeans and a brown stain marred his T-shirt. She wanted to laugh. She'd made an impression. Even though he might not admit it, he didn't want to upset her. He was thinking about other people, and that was good.

She stepped aside and opened the door wider, letting his remarks fade away. "Are you still working on the box?" she asked just to make conversation.

Before coming in, he brushed the sawdust from his jeans. "I finished sanding it and stained it. It's ready."

She motioned toward a chair. "Have a seat and I'll bring our lunch. Would you rather have coffee or tea?"

"Coffee, black, but I'm really not hungry."

He was eating if she had to force it down him. She had to suppress another laugh at the thought. Carrying the plates to the table, she noticed he'd taken a seat. At least they wouldn't have to argue about that. She hurried back with the coffee and tea and sat down.

"It's grilled ham and cheese," she said as she picked up her sandwich.

"It looks tasty, but…"

"It is, and for the record, my cooking skills are limited, so it's best to take what you're given here."

He took a sip of his coffee, his big hand engulfing the white cup. "How many fire alarms have you gone through?"

She held up one finger. "I just put them back up and they keep working."

He shook his head and the scowl on his face lessened. "I hear it regularly."

"I'm working on changing that." She nibbled on a pickle. "I had a busy life in Austin and rarely had time to develop any culinary skills." She resisted the urge to wink.

"What did you do in Austin?"

He was asking questions. That was good. She didn't know if he was doing so out of curiosity or boredom, but she'd take either. "I worked for a big party-planning company. The holidays are the busiest time of the year."

He picked up his sandwich and took a bite. "You planned parties?"

"Yes, big extravagant parties. For banks, large companies, law firms, weddings and people who wanted to make an impression. We did a lot of private parties in lavish homes."

"Isn't there food involved?"

"We hired caterers for different parties. Janine is the woman who runs the company, and I was her personal assistant. It was a fun job and I met a lot of people—nice people. I miss that part of my life."

While she'd been talking, he'd eaten the whole sandwich, probably without even realizing it. His cup was empty, so she got up to refill it.

"People just call you and tell you what they want and you do the rest?"

"That's about it."

"I worked..." His voice trailed off.

She resumed her seat. "Where did you work?"

"Doesn't matter." He clammed up, apparently realizing he was getting into personal territory.

"Dad said you were a lawyer."

Gabe studied the coffee in the cup. "A lifetime ago." He glanced toward the living room. From his chair he could see the undecorated Christmas tree. "You haven't done anything with the tree?"

"No. That's another problem. Emma doesn't want to decorate the tree."

"Why not? Kids love that kind of stuff."

Lacey pushed the chips around on her plate. "One of the Wilson kids down the street told her there isn't a Santa Claus, and now she doesn't believe and doesn't want to have Christmas."

"A kid her age should believe, and no one should take that from her."

"I agree. Kids grow up much faster these days, but I'm not giving up. I'm working on changing her mind. Did Zack like Christmas?"

Gabe stood up suddenly. "I've got to go."

She'd crossed a line, but she couldn't take the words back. She followed him.

At the door, he said, "You don't have to fuss over me. I'm fine."

"Well, you'll excuse me if I believe otherwise."

"You don't know me and I don't know you. I wish we had kept it that way."

"But we're neighbors and see each other every day. We can at least be civil."

He ran a hand through his hair. "I just want my peace. That's all."

"For today and tomorrow you'll have to put up with Emma and me. I promised her she could see Pepper this afternoon, and you're not going back on your word."

His eyes narrowed on her face, and her bravado faltered for a second. "You're very pushy, do you know that?"

"No. I'm usually a very agreeable person and easy to get along with."

He rubbed his hands together and looked at them, as if he was gauging his next words. But then he turned toward the door. "I have to go."

"Gabe, it really would help to talk about your son. I know you don't believe that, but it would. Earlier, when you spoke about my dad, it gave me a warm feeling, and if you talked about Zack it would help you."

His eyes caught hers. Once again she saw all that anguish etched across the strong lines of his face. Her breath stalled.

"I can't. Please understand that."

She wanted to reach out and touch him, hug him, comfort him in some way, but she knew that was the last thing he wanted from her.

"Gabe..."

He walked out the door.

Lacey let out a long breath and then closed the door. Gabe had taken a step forward, but now he'd taken several backward, and he still had tomorrow to get through. He wouldn't be alone, though.

Pepper was asleep and seemed peaceful, so Gabe went to the garage to see if the varnish on the box had dried. It hadn't. He sat on a stool and tried to collect his thoughts, tried to find reason and sanity in all the misery that clouded his mind.

It really would help to talk about your son.

How could she say that? She didn't know. He jammed both hands through his hair. Talking about Zack would tear out his heart. But then, his heart had already been destroyed. Maybe she was right. Maybe. But he still held on to every memory of his son and he held them close to his heart where no one else could ever touch them. Tomorrow, though, he would let go because it was the right thing to do. And, God help him, he couldn't do it alone.

He wasn't quite sure why it was hard to admit that, but Lacey knew. She saw right through him and she still kept pushing him even when he resisted her efforts. She was a very strong lady, and he really should be grateful she was willing to help him.

He got up. What did he care? After tomorrow, he would sink into that oblivion of complete pain, and there was no way to stop it. Not unless he reached out a hand for someone to save him. In that moment he saw her green eyes, and he shoved the image away. He didn't want to be saved. But a part of him was fighting back. A part of him was remembering what life was about. A part of him was waiting for the light to completely engulf him. If that were possible... For the first time he realized he was still living, and it was up to him to keep fighting for that light. That right.

Lacey picked up Emma and they headed home. "Do you want to stop for hot chocolate and a kolach?" Emma loved the pastry brimming with different fruit mixtures in the center.

"No, Lacey. We have to go home."

Lacey knew better than to ask. Emma had her mind set on one thing—Pepper. As soon as Lacey parked in the driveway, Emma jumped out of the car and ran for the front door.

Before she opened it, Lacey said, "Remember, we talked. We're going over to Gabe's and you can stay for a little while, but then you have to come home because Gabe wants his privacy. Understand?"

Emma bobbed her head. She shot through the house like a bullet, throwing her backpack at the sofa. Lacey followed slowly.

When she reached Gabe's deck, Emma was sitting by Pepper, lovingly cuddling her. Gabe sat in his chair, watching. He'd changed clothes—that was the first thing Lacey noticed. The box must have been finished. She could only imagine how much pain it had caused him to make it. But then again, it might have been cathartic. She never knew with Gabe.

"Pepper's real sick, Mr. Gabe," Emma said.

"Yes, she is," he replied, surprising Lacey. She had expected him to remain silent.

Emma kissed the dog and then walked to Gabe. "The doctor's gonna make Pepper's pain go away?"

Gabe visibly swallowed. "Yes."

Emma crawled into the other chair and no one spoke, just like the other day. Lacey went back to her house and let Emma have this time with Pepper and Gabe. Emma was attuned to Gabe's pain, as was Lacey. She just wished he would let them in.

Later, Emma came back.

"Did you have a good visit?"

"Yes, but it's getting colder, and Mr. Gabe said I should probably go home."

"And you have homework to do."

"Yeah." Emma sat at the kitchen table.

Lacey was making dinner, but she caught her sister's somber tone and wondered if Gabe had said something to her. Lacey wiped her hands on a dish towel and walked to the table.

"Did you and Gabe talk?"

Emma shook her head. "I just helped him be sad."

"What?" Lacey was thrown by the answer.

"Gabe is sad and doesn't want to talk, so I don't talk, either. I just help him be sad."

Lacey reached over and hugged Emma. "You're getting so grown up. I'm proud of you."

Emma wiggled away as if the compliment had embarrassed her. "What's for supper? Are we going to the diner?"

"I'm making hot dogs. It's all we have. I have to go to the grocery store soon."

"It's okay. I'm not too hungry."

A sense of sadness lingered in the room. They ate supper in silence. Then Lacey had an idea. "I'm going to make Gabe a hot dog and take it to him. Get your books and start on your homework."

She left Emma at the table working on math. It was dusk, and a yellow glow had settled over the neighborhood. The air was brisk. By morning the temperature probably would be freezing. Traffic sounds softly echoed, and a dog barked in the distance.

Gabe sat on the deck as usual, and Pepper was in her bed. Going up the steps, Lacey said, "I brought you supper."

"I'm not hungry," he said. "And it's not your job to feed me."

She let his sharp words flow over her and took a seat in the other chair with the food in her lap. "We had hot dogs, so I brought you two with a thermos of coffee. And Oreos. Everybody loves Oreos."

"I'm not everybody."

"Okay, we've established that." She handed him a hot dog wrapped in aluminum foil. He stared at it for a full thirty seconds before he took it. Unwrapping it, he took a big bite and then another.

She held out the thermos. "You might need something to wash it down."

He took it without a sharp quip. While he ate, she nibbled on an Oreo, and then offered them to him. He took the bag without a word and they ate cookies in silence.

Pepper didn't move. She was stretched out with her head on the corner of the bed. The poor thing had suffered enough, and Lacey's heart broke at what would happen tomorrow. But it was time.

"I'll be here after I drop Emma off at school in the morning."

He didn't respond.

Darkness now bathed the neighborhood, and the air had grown colder. The outdoor noises had gone quiet like the hush before a storm. Lacey didn't know whether to go or stay. Gabe was clearly struggling.

He gave her the thermos. "I… I've made up my mind, so I'll be fine. But thanks for being here and thanks for lunch today and supper. I forgot to thank you earlier."

Her throat closed up. He was so sincere, and she knew the battle inside him was ongoing. The thermos wasn't empty, so she handed it back to him. "You'll need something to finish off the cookies."

He looked up at her, and from the deck light she could feel the heat of his eyes. She wanted to reach out and hug him like she had at lunch, but she knew he wouldn't welcome that intimacy.

"Thanks," he said simply.

"You're welcome." Darkness fell like a wall, shutting out the outside world. It was just the two of them. And Pepper. Lacey wrapped her arms around her waist to ward off the chill of the night. "Even though it hurts, you're doing the right thing."

"Yeah." He twisted the thermos in his hands.

Unable to stop herself, she touched his arm. "Try to get some rest. Good night."

The muscles under her fingers tightened, and she felt his strength like a band of steel. And that epitomized Gabe. Strong. Hardened. But vulnerable. Tomorrow his nerves of steel would be tested. She left with an ache in her heart.

Chapter 7

The next morning started with an argument. Lacey wanted Emma to wear her candy-cane tights with ankle boots, and Emma wanted to wear jeans and sneakers. In the end, Lacey gave up because she had other things on her mind.

After breakfast, Emma insisted on going to see Pepper. Lacey didn't object because she wanted to check on Gabe, too. It was cold outside—not quite freezing, with the temperature in the high 30s. She bundled up Emma and they walked next door. Gabe wasn't outside, so she knocked. He opened it almost immediately. She expected him to be unshaven and wearing the same clothes, but his long hair was slicked back and still slightly damp from a shower. And he wore clean jeans and a T-shirt. An almost forgotten longing pierced her lower abdomen.

"Uh…can Emma see Pepper one more time, please?"

He opened the door wider and Emma ran to where Pepper lay in her bed near the cabinet.

"How's Pepper?" Lacey asked Gabe, and she noticed the bags under his incredibly sad eyes. She wondered when he'd last slept.

"The shot has worn off and she's whimpering a lot."

Emma sat on the floor next to Pepper. The dog didn't even raise her head.

Emma kissed Pepper. "It'll be okay. You'll feel better soon."

"We have to go, Emma, or you'll be late for school." Lacey hated to leave Gabe, but she would be back in just a few minutes.

Emma got up and walked to her, still huddled in her coat. Blond hair peeked out from the hood. All Lacey could see were her big green eyes.

"I don't want to go. I want to stay with Pepper."

Lacey hadn't been expecting this. She had to be firm. "You have to go to school."

"Why can't I stay? Pepper wants me to."

Another unsolvable problem. Lacey did not want Emma to witness Pepper's passing. At her age, she'd dealt with enough. Lacey guided her to the one chair in the room and Emma sat.

"Sweetie, this is not something for a little girl to witness. The vet will take care of everything and Pepper will be at peace. Just know that."

Emma frowned. "I have to be here."

"Emma…" Lacey didn't know what else to say. She understood Emma loved the dog, but watching the procedure was out of the question.

"Why do you have to be here?" Gabe asked Emma, startling Lacey. She had expected him to ignore them.

"Because Lacey wouldn't let me be there when Daddy went to heaven, and I want to be here when Pepper goes to heaven."

Lacey was stunned. She'd had no idea Emma felt this way. She knelt in front of her. "Sweetie, I was in the hall with you when Daddy passed. The doctor asked us to leave the room. If I had had any idea it was his time, we would never have left. I just…just didn't know." A sob clogged her throat and she had to stop. She had failed Emma. And she'd failed herself.

"We should have been there, Lacey," Emma said.

Yes blocked her brain with so many regrettable memories. She'd done the best she could at the time, and there was no going back to change that. When the doctor had come out of the room and told them their father had passed away, she'd felt as if someone had pulled the floor out from under her and she was tumbling, tumbling down into the deepest hole of despair. But she'd had to get up. She'd had to get up for Emma.

Lacey gathered Emma into her arms and sat with her in the chair. She had to make a decision and she had no idea if it was right or wrong. But then, every decision she'd made since their father's death had been that way. She'd been going on faith, and she had to lean on it now.

Emma rested her head on Lacey's shoulder. "Please let me stay. I'll be good. I won't cry. I promise."

Lacey looked at Gabe. The lines around his eyes weren't as intense because his attention was on something other than Pepper. It was on Emma. "I'll call the vet and see what he says."

"Thank you." His offer was like a morsel of food to

a starving person. She desperately needed someone to advise her, and the fact that it came from Gabe gave her a warm feeling.

Gabe went into the other room to make the call. Lacey untied Emma's hood and pushed it from her head. "If the vet says no, you have to accept that. Understand?"

Emma remained silent, and Lacey knew what that meant. *Trouble.*

"Emma…"

Emma sat up. "You don't understand."

"What don't I understand?"

Emma studied the tips of her sneakers. "I… I have to be with Pepper when she goes to heaven because I want her to take a message to Daddy."

Lacey swallowed hard and she couldn't say another word. Tears stung the backs of her eyes and threatened to erupt. The only thing Lacey knew to do was to go with the moment and let Emma have this time she thought she needed. Lacey couldn't take that away from her, even if she knew life didn't work that way. Dogs didn't take messages to heaven. But what did she know? Maybe they did. After all, it was the holiday season and a time for miracles.

Gabe came back into the room. "Dr. Morris said children are often present. It's a simple procedure and as long as the child understands what's going to happen, it usually works out well."

"Do you mind if she stays?" Lacey had to ask because Pepper was Gabe's dog and he might want to do this alone.

He shook his head.

She could tell by the softening of his eyes that he was okay with the situation, so that made things a lot easier.

"But we will have rules," Lacey said.

"You always make rules," Emma grumbled.

"Rules," Lacey stated firmly.

"'Kay."

"I'm going outside to get everything ready." Gabe laid his cell phone on the table and headed for the garage. "I want it done on the deck were Pepper loves to stay."

"I'll help." Emma tried to jump from Lacey's lap, but Lacey held tight.

Gabe paused in the doorway. "You can watch Pepper while I'm busy."

"'Kay."

Lacey unbuttoned Emma's coat. Emma sat on the floor, talking to Pepper. Lacey wondered what message her sister wanted Pepper to take to heaven. It was clear Emma didn't have closure about their dad's death. Lacey wasn't sure she did, either. They were both going through the motions of living. Just like Gabe. Hopefully, today would be a turning point for all of them. And not a step backward.

Since Gabe's phone was right there, she decided to use it to call the school about Emma. She didn't think he'd mind. Gabe was so out of touch that she was surprised he had a cell. She didn't mean to invade his privacy and it was none of her business, but when she opened the phone she noticed there were twenty-two missed calls from Kate Rebel. Lacey quickly made her call and clicked off.

Glancing out the back door, she saw him setting up a card table. The coffin was next to it on the deck. He worked thoroughly engrossed, as she'd always seen him do. Who was this woman who was desperately trying to reach him? Again, none of her business.

"Lacey, why is there only one chair?" Emma asked, getting bored as six-year-olds were known to do.

"I don't know."

Emma looked at the wall of photos. "Why are there so many pictures?"

"Gabe likes looking at his son" was the only answer she had.

"Oh." Emma turned her attention back to Pepper. "She's whimpering."

"Just stroke her. It helps her relax."

The doorbell rang. Lacey opened the back door and said to Gabe, "I think the vet's here."

Gabe came into the house. He wore just a black hoodie, but he didn't seem to be cold. "I'll let him in."

A young man in his thirties with blond hair and blue eyes followed Gabe into the kitchen. "This is Dr. Morris, and Dr. Morris, this is Lacey and Emma Carroll, my neighbors."

They shook hands and Dr. Morris looked at Emma. "So you want to be here today for Pepper?"

Emma stood up and brushed blond hair from her face. "Pepper is my friend and I want to be here when she goes to heaven."

"That's very brave," the vet told her, leaning down to Emma's level. "Do you know what an IV is?"

"Yes. My daddy had one when he was in the hospital."

"Good. I'm going to put an IV in Pepper's foreleg so I can give her medication that will gently put her to sleep."

Emma rubbed her head. "Will it hurt?"

"No."

"Then she'll go to heaven?"

"Yes. It doesn't take long. I'm going to go outside with Gabe and get everything ready, and when it's time your mother can bring you out."

"Lacey's not my mother. She's my sister," Emma quickly corrected him.

"Oh, sorry." The vet seemed confused. "You look so much alike."

"'Cause we're sisters," Emma stated.

Dr. Morris nodded. "Yes. I know now."

Without another word the two men went out onto the deck. Lacey could see them talking, and then Gabe came back into the house. He knelt down by Emma and Pepper.

"I'm going to take her outside."

Emma kissed the dog. "Goodbye, Pepper."

Lacey couldn't believe Emma was taking this so well. Tears burned her eyes, and she feared this might not have the outcome Emma wanted. But she would be here to help her. And Gabe.

Gabe picked up the dog bed with Pepper in it as if it weighed no more than his phone. She held the door open, and he carried Pepper outside to the table. Their eyes met briefly. All she could see was resignation mixed with pain.

Emma ran to her and wrapped her arms around Lacey's waist. "The doctor won't forget, will he, Lacey?"

"No, sweetie. Put your coat back on so you'll be ready."

Emma did as Lacey asked, and they waited. Gabe stood by the table, his hand on Pepper while the vet worked. Tall, strong, yet vulnerable like the big oak that was not twelve feet from him. She wanted to go to him, but she had Emma to think about. She was torn about who needed her most.

It was a relief when Gabe motioned for them to come outside. Emma shot out the door and stood next to Gabe, touching Pepper gently. Lacey stood on Gabe's other side.

The vet had his hand over the IV in Pepper's foreleg. "Say goodbye," he said, and then she noticed that with his other hand he injected the medication into the IV.

"Bye, Pepper. I love you," Emma whispered. "When you see my daddy, tell him I love him."

The words were low, but Lacey heard them. Her chest tightened in pain. Emma hadn't had the chance to say that to their father before he'd passed, and obviously it had bothered her. Lacey didn't have time to dwell on it, as she felt the man beside her tremble. She rubbed his back in reassurance, just as she would have done to Emma. He leaned into her hand as if he needed her support.

The vet removed the IV very quickly so Emma couldn't see. Pepper took a short breath, and then she was still. Gabe stroked her head, "Goodbye, girl. You're at peace now. I'm sorry it took me so long to do…this." His voice wavered on the last word, and Lacey clutched him around the waist for reassurance.

The sun popped out like a cork from a bottle, spreading its goodness everywhere and lighting up the cold, dreary day.

"Is Pepper gone?" Emma asked.

The vet nodded. "Yes."

Emma glanced toward the bright sunshine. "She turned on the light for us."

It was a moment of relief for all of them. The vet put everything back into his bag and helped Gabe lift Pepper into the coffin, bed and all. Gabe covered her with a big quilt and positioned the lid on top.

"Would you like me to help?" the vet asked.

"No, thanks. I have it from here." The two men shook hands and Dr. Morris left.

Until that moment, Lacey hadn't noticed the big hole Gabe had dug against the wood fence. He must've stayed up all night digging.

Gabe picked up a nail gun from the deck and nailed the coffin shut. Emma watched all of this without saying a word. She seemed fine, but Lacey was skeptical.

When Gabe finished, Lacey stood at one end of the box. "I'll help you carry it."

Gabe didn't respond. He just picked up his end and they carried it to the hole. Emma followed without saying a word. Gabe jumped into the hole, and then picked up the coffin and slid it in. He had to step on the box to get out. Then he marched toward the house.

"Where you going?" Emma called.

"To get a shovel to close the hole."

Emma made a dash for their house. Lacey had no idea where she was going until she came back with a small shovel their dad had bought for her to help in the yard. Lacey wasn't going to be left out, so she went to the garage and found their father's spade.

The three of them shoveled dirt over the coffin. Lacey's arms grew tired, but Gabe and Emma kept dirt flying. Gabe stopped long enough to remove his hoodie. She could see the muscles in his arms bulging as he worked in just a black T-shirt. Lacey stopped for a moment just to watch, and then she caught herself. This was definitely not the time.

Gabe used a rake to smooth out the dirt. Pepper had been put to rest. Emma glanced toward the bright sunshine.

"Pepper's happy now."

"Yes," Lacey agreed, and thought it chased away the sadness of today. "Time to go to school."

"'Kay." Unexpectedly, Emma hugged Gabe around the waist and he tensed. "Bye, Mr. Gabe." She ran for the house.

"I'll be back as soon as I can," Lacey said to Gabe.

"There's no need. I'm fine."

She eyed that strange look on his face. He was shutting her out again. Shutting out the world because he felt safer that way.

"You did the right thing. It was a big step forward. Keep taking those steps."

"I don't need your armchair psychology. I think it's best if we went back to being—"

"What?" She lifted an eyebrow. "Neighbors? Enemies? Friends? Or maybe nothing at all would suit you best." She shook her head. "But that's not going to happen. I'll be back whether you like it or not."

She left him standing in the backyard with a befuddled look on his face. She'd never met anyone so conflicted. She supposed he had reason, but two years was long enough. Gabe had to start living again. Why that was so important to her, she had no idea. Maybe the pain in her reacted to the pain in him. Whatever it was, she was determined they would at least be friends.

* * *

The house was very quiet without Pepper. Even the deck was lonely, and that loneliness went all the way to Gabe's soul. He cleaned out the garage from building the coffin and put everything away. Keeping busy kept him from thinking. After everything was back in its place, he went for a jog. He did that often to keep the memories at bay. Up and down Horseshoe streets he jogged, around the business district and to the school. He didn't stop until he was so tired he was forced to.

Breathing deeply, he sat on a curb. He purposely stayed away from his house because he didn't want Lacey to baby him, to think he needed her. He was doing fine on his own.

The people in Horseshoe avoided him and didn't speak when they saw him. They knew he wouldn't accept their hand in friendship. And that was the way he wanted it. But as he sat on the curb and listened to the thud of his heart against his ribs, his loneliness was more than painful, it was debilitating. This wasn't the normal way to live, and avoiding Lacey wasn't going to help. He stood up, feeling weary and lost. Slowly, he made his way back to his house. Back to the memories. Back to the pain.

At first, Lacey was surprised when she found Gabe gone, but then she got angry. He didn't need her, and he was making that more than clear. When she thought about it, he'd never asked for her help. She was the one who offered, so she had to take a step back and leave him alone like he wanted.

She went to the grocery store, stocked up and then

came home and put everything away. Not once did she think of going to Gabe's. She couldn't believe she had been so pushy. Now she had to concentrate on Emma and her well-being.

Emma's teacher was standing outside with a group of kids when Lacey arrived at the school. That wasn't a good sign. Mrs. Fillmore obviously had more complaints about Emma's behavior, which seemed to happen about once a week.

Getting out of her car, Lacey took a deep breath and said hello to the teacher. The woman wasn't frowning like she usually was.

"Good afternoon, Lacey," Mrs. Fillmore said cheerily.

Lacey wondered what had happened to make the teacher so happy.

"Good afternoon."

Mrs. Fillmore was somewhere in her forties with brown highlighted hair and a shaken–soda can personality, bubbly and lively. The kids loved her. "I wasn't sure what to expect when Emma returned to class today. The death of a beloved pet is traumatic for a child."

"What happened?" Lacey asked.

"She came into the classroom and took her seat. I was just going to resume the class when she raised her hand. She wanted to know if she could tell the class about Pepper. I was hesitant at first, but agreed. I can't tell you how well it went. It was marvelous. She opened up to the kids and they responded. It was wonderful to see. I hope the old Emma is back. I'm almost positive she is."

Lacey could hardly believe her ears. "Emma stood up in front of the class and spoke?"

Mrs. Fillmore nodded. "She did. I'm so happy to give you good news for a change."

"And I'm happy to hear it."

Childish giggles echoed, and Lacey glanced to where Emma was standing with Jimmy and two other kids. She was actually talking with them and not frowning or hitting. When Emma saw Lacey, she came running over with the little girl Lacey recognized from the Christmas-tree lot.

"Just wanted to give you the good news," Mrs. Fillmore said, and walked back into the school.

"Thanks," Lacey called after her.

"Lacey, this is Bailey. Look what she gave me." Emma twisted her wrist and Lacey saw a stretchy band with sparkles that a lot of little girls were wearing. "Isn't it pretty?"

"Yes. That was very nice of Bailey."

"Can she come play with me sometime?"

Yes, yes, yes! Lacey wanted to shout. It was the best news she'd heard in a while. Emma was making friends again, fitting in.

"If her mother says it's okay."

"Bye, Bailey." Emma waved as the little girl ran off. "Don't forget to ask your mommy."

Lacey had hoped for a miracle and she'd gotten one. For Emma. But Gabe's miracle was yet to come.

Chapter 8

Gabe sat looking at his backyard. The large oak to the right had died during the drought of 2011. Tomorrow he would cut it down. It would be his goal for the week. His eyes slid over to the fresh mound of dirt on the left.

Rest in peace, girl.

He'd prolonged her life more than he should have, because he'd known that once he let go of Pepper he would have to face reality. A reality that was too dark and disturbing to even think about, so he had kept putting it off to another day.

If Lacey hadn't pushed him, Pepper would still be in pain. He needed to thank her for that, but she probably wasn't going to speak to him anytime soon. Maybe that wasn't a bad thing. He couldn't make himself believe that, though. He ran both hands through his hair with a long sigh.

Voices caught his attention, and he glanced up to see Emma and Lacey coming through the gate. Emma bounded up the steps with a handful of yellow flowers. They looked like daisies. She walked right up to him.

"Do you mind if we put flowers on Pepper's grave?"

He swallowed. "No."

Lacey stood in the yard, and he noticed that hurt look in her eyes. Damn! He hadn't meant to hurt her, but then what had he expected?

Jumping down the steps, Emma went to Lacey and they walked to the grave. Emma knelt down and carefully placed the flowers. She said something to Lacey, but Gabe couldn't catch it. It was getting colder again, and Lacey pulled her brown jacket tighter around her. Taking the child's hand, she led her back to the gate.

He had a new ache in his gut, an unfamiliar one he didn't like. She had been nothing but kind to him and he had hurt her in return. Drawing in a deep breath, he called, "Lacey."

She stopped with a puzzled look in her green eyes.

"Could we talk for a minute?"

"I suppose." She looked down at Emma. "Go start your homework and I'll be there in a minute."

The child darted off and he made his way to Lacey. "I'm sorry I bailed on you today."

She brushed blond hair from her forehead. "Why did you?"

He studied the wood grain on the weather-worn fence. "I was feeling claustrophobic and had to get away and be by myself. I know you don't understand that, but it was something I had to do. I walked around Horseshoe until I couldn't breathe, then I sat on a curb and tried to remember exactly what I was doing. Nothing makes much sense to me. I think you already know that."

"Yes." She shoved her hands into the pockets of her jacket. "I was just worried about you, that's all. And I shouldn't be because I barely know you. But you're hurting and I can identify with that. If I'm overstepping my bounds, I'm sorry."

Staring into her eyes, he wondered how she could know him so well. No one understood him. Not his exwife. Or his sister. Or his friends. But she seemed to reach a part of him that he kept hidden. Maybe that was why he'd had to get away. He hadn't wanted to expose that part of himself.

"I… I…"

She touched his arm and he stiffened. She'd done that once before and it had thrown him off guard. Human contact was alien to him now, but it seemed natural when she did it.

"It's okay. I understand. Take all the time you need. I'm right next door if you need anything." She turned and walked to her house.

He sucked in the cool air, and it chilled all the aches and pains inside him. Would there ever be an end to his agony? Maybe not, but he would not hurt Lacey again.

When supper was finished, Lacey sent Emma to take a bath, and afterward Lacey brushed Emma's long hair.

"You had fun in school today?"

Lacey sat on Emma's bed, and Emma stood between her legs. "Yes. I like Bailey."

"I'm glad you found a friend."

"She gave me something. I need to give her something back. You make my bows. Can you make her a bow?"

"I certainly will, but not tonight."

"Ouch. You're pulling my hair."

"Sorry, snuggle bunny." Lacey patted the bed beside her. "Let's talk for a minute."

Emma groaned as she climbed onto the bed. "What did I do?"

Lacey put her arm around her sister. "You didn't do anything wrong. I just want to tell you how proud I am of the way you handled today."

Emma rested against her. "Oh."

"Sweetie, you do understand why we weren't in the room when Daddy passed?"

"Yeah. But it's okay now."

"'Cause Daddy knows you love him?"

Emma drew back, her eyes big. "How do you know that?"

Lacey squeezed her. "Haven't you figured out by now that I know everything?"

"You're weird, Lacey."

"If you have questions, I'll try to answer them."

Emma burrowed farther into her. "Daddy's never coming back, is he?"

Lacey's voice was clogged with tears, and she didn't bother to look for an answer in her imaginary book. She had to go with the feeling in her heart. "No...no, sweetie. He's never coming back." She laid her hand on Emma's chest. "But he's right there." Then she laid her hand on her chest. "And he's right here. He's with us all the time in spirit."

"Is Pepper there, too?"

"You bet." She kissed her sister's forehead. "It's homework time."

"Aw, jeez."

"You have math problems to do."

Emma made a face. "I hate math."

"Get your books and you can work at the kitchen table."

Emma trailed behind her, grumbling as they made their way to the kitchen. Lacey set up everything and Emma went to work.

"Sweetie, I'm going next door for a minute."

"'Kay."

She couldn't get Gabe out of her mind. He'd said he was sorry and that meant a lot to her. Caught off guard, she'd failed to thank him for letting Emma stay today, and she needed to do that. Maybe it was just another reason to see him. Or maybe she was pushy.

It was already dark and she didn't like leaving Emma, but she'd only be gone a few minutes. She found her way to the deck, but the light wasn't on. Had he gone to bed? She tapped on the door, but he didn't answer. She tried the screen door and it opened, as did the door.

"Gabe," she called into the dark house. Still no response. A light was coming from the living room—a very dim light. Acting braver than she was feeling, she walked into the kitchen and then into the living room. A lamp was on next to the TV. Gabe sat on the sofa in jeans and a black T-shirt. His head was tilted back, and his bare feet were outstretched.

"Gabe," she said tentatively. He immediately raised himself up.

"Lacey. What are you doing here?"

"I called, but you didn't hear me, and I got worried."

He swiped a hand through his hair. "I must've been half-asleep."

She wanted to ask if he was okay, but she knew better. He was tired of that question. "I won't stay. I just wanted to thank you for letting Emma stay today. It has made a world of difference in her attitude. I never realized she needed to tell our father she loved him before he passed."

"Yeah. It seemed important to her. I'm glad it helped."

Going where brave angels feared to tread, she sat beside him without an invitation. "Did it help you?"

He lifted an eyebrow. "Doing your psychology thing again?"

She stood up. "I was only trying to help. I'll leave you alone." It was the last thing she wanted to do, because she could hear the panic in his voice. But she wasn't sure how to help him other than to annoy him, which was how it usually turned out. She took a step toward the kitchen.

"I don't know what to do with myself." The words came out low and husky, but Lacey heard them. "I go outside and then I come back in. I feel lost, without any direction, like a car without a steering wheel. I don't know where to go or where to turn. I've lost the most important part of myself. I've lost my son. Zack is dead." The last word came out on a choked sob, and more sobs followed.

At the gut-wrenching sound, Lacey's heart plummeted to the pit of her stomach, and she sat by him again, wanting to give him some sort of comfort. "Gabe…"

"Zack is dead."

She wrapped her arms around him, and he sobbed into her chest, saying the words over and over. Her heart rate was dangerously close to overload at the pain in his voice, and she didn't know what else to do. Clearly, he had never said the words out loud. Her guess was that he'd never openly cried over the death of his son. He had never allowed himself that weakness.

His arms gripped her, and he held on as if she were his anchor. His sobs did a number on her control and she was glad when he silently laid his head on her shoulder. Suddenly, he leaned away, wiping away the telltale tears. "Sorry. I lost it for a minute."

"Is this the first time you've cried?"

He rested his head against the sofa. "Yes. My ex-wife couldn't understand why I didn't cry. She called me hard and unfeeling. She called me a lot of things, but I knew if I allowed myself that weakness, Zack's death would be real, and I didn't want it to be real."

She stroked his arm, and he didn't pull away.

"Zack was a mischievous, happy kid, always laughing, always teasing. I don't understand how someone with so much life in him can suddenly be gone."

"We'll never have an answer for that."

"No, we won't. I kept holding on to Pepper, determined not to accept the reality. But…my son is dead and he's never coming back." He said the words with a finality that was as real as it could get. Lacey thought it strange that she'd had this same conversation with Emma just a few minutes ago.

"No." She laid her hand on his chest, as she had Emma. "But he lives in here."

"Yeah." He caught her hand and entwined his fingers with hers. Her heart skipped a beat. "Thanks for listening. Saying those words was long overdue."

He closed his eyes and she waited for him to speak again, but there was only silence. Then his chest rose and fell quietly. He had drifted into sleep—a much-needed sleep. Removing her hand, she reached for the blanket at the end of the sofa and spread it over him. She didn't want to wake him because he desperately needed to sleep. The urge to kiss him was strong, and she didn't know why. She couldn't be attracted to him. There was no future with Gabe Garrison. He lived in the past, and she had a six-year-old to raise. But there was a connection she couldn't deny.

She let herself out of the house and locked the door as she left, feeling good that Gabe had finally admitted something he'd been denying for two solid years. His son was gone and he had to go on living. Maybe there was hope for him.

Gabe woke up to a surreal feeling. For a moment he didn't know where he was, but then he saw the photos on the wall and all that pain blindsided him. It wasn't like before, though. Something was different.

Sitting up, he realized there was a blanket over him. And then it all came back. Lacey. The tears. Oh, God. He'd made a fool of himself. Strangely, he didn't feel like a fool. He felt revitalized. He got to his feet and an old urge hit him. He wanted coffee. For years, that had been the first thing he'd done every morning. Lately, he hadn't cared whether he had coffee or not.

In the kitchen it became very clear he didn't have any coffee or a coffeemaker. Glancing at the clock on the stove, he saw it was after nine. Had he slept all night? He never slept for more than two hours. Finding his boots, he pulled them on. He knew where to find coffee.

Going out the back door, he glanced toward the mound of fresh dirt and the pain wasn't there like before. Just an incredible gratitude that he had gotten through yesterday. And grateful that Pepper was now at peace.

Lacey should be home from taking Emma to school. Lights were on in the kitchen. He gently knocked.

"Just a minute," she called. A second later she opened the door.

At the sight of her, his mouth fell open and he quickly closed it. She was dressed in dark skinny pants and knee-high leather boots with a lime-green turtleneck sweater. Her short blond hair framed her face. For the first time he realized how beautiful and sexy she looked. How had he not seen that before?

Parts of the previous night came back to him: the fragrant scent of her hair, the softness of her skin and the gentleness of her touch. It had been a long time since he'd held a woman, and all those old urges were still alive in him. He wasn't sure how, because most of the time he had felt dead. But not today.

"Good morning," she said with a smile in her voice. "Come in."

He motioned toward her. "Obviously, you're getting ready to go out, so I won't bother you."

"I'm going to Temple to Christmas shop. That can wait for a few minutes. Would you like a cup of coffee?"

He stepped into the warm house. "That's why I came over—to bum coffee."

"You're in luck because I'm out of my Keurig cups and had to make a regular pot this morning."

He slid onto a bar stool and watched as she reached for a cup and filled it. The boots gave her height, and his eyes strayed to the roundness of her bottom and fullness of her breasts. A new energy surged through him.

She placed the steaming mug in front of him. "Did you sleep well?"

"Yes. All night, actually, and I feel rested." He lifted the cup and took a sip.

"I'm glad."

His eyes met hers over the rim of the cup. "Sorry I unloaded on you last night. You're very good at dealing with grief."

"I know deep in my heart that one day Emma and I will get past it. And you will, too. They say that time heals all wounds, and I'm counting on it."

"You're a very strong lady."

She tossed her head. "Oh, please. Don't tell my irresponsible nature that. In Austin, I lived an easy, carefree lifestyle. Work and play—that was it. My biggest responsibility was to make sure my paycheck went into my account before I paid bills." Her green eyes grew thoughtful. "But it's strange when responsibility is thrust upon us—we either fold like a cheap tent or rise like a phoenix. I'm somewhere in between—a work in progress."

"I don't believe that for minute. In my experience,

there aren't many young women who would take on the responsibility of raising a six-year-old, especially when their whole life is ahead of them."

"Didn't I tell you I'm a martyr?"

He got lost in the sparkle of her eyes, and it was the best way to start his day. This was his first step forward. He slid off the bar stool.

"I'll leave so you can do your shopping."

"Wait." She reached for a cabinet door and opened it, pulling out a thermos. "You can take the rest of the coffee."

"I have a thermos of yours I need to return."

She handed him the filled thermos. "Now you have two."

With the thermos in his hand, he knew he should say something, but looking at her his words were all jumbled with the new feelings inside him. He wasn't ready for any kind of relationship, and he had a feeling she wasn't, either. He wasn't even sure if that was what he wanted. The only thing he knew was that he liked her and she was easy to talk to, easy to be with. And right now that was the most valuable thing in his life.

He raised the thermos. "Have fun shopping."

She followed him to the door. "I ordered Emma a red bicycle with a white basket in front, and they called that it was in so I have to pick it up. I'm not sure how I'm going to hide it from her. I think I can get it into the attic."

"You can hide it in my house."

She seemed taken aback for a moment. "Oh. I wasn't hinting at…"

"I know. But I have lots of room, and it's the very least I can do for a neighbor."

"Gabe, it's… Thank you."

He tipped his head and walked out, feeling alive and taking baby steps back into a world that didn't seem so bad after all.

Chapter 9

All the way to Temple, Lacey resisted the urge to go back. Gabe had seemed to want to talk this morning, which was so unusual for him. But last night had been a breakthrough, and she wanted to be there for him if he needed her.

The moment she thought that, she realized she was getting involved too quickly. Gabe had made it clear on more than one occasion that he'd rather be alone, and she had to respect that, just as she kept telling Emma. But she couldn't get the vulnerable man she'd held in her arms last night out of her head.

She had an appointment at the bank and she made it just in time. Her father had had a excellent life insurance policy and Lacey wouldn't have to worry about work for some time. But cleaning house and doing laundry were going to get old quickly. Once Emma didn't need her so much, Lacey would have to find something to do. In Horseshoe that would probably be difficult. For now, though, her goal was to make the best Christmas possible for Emma.

The appointment went well. She'd put a large sum of money in a trust fund for Emma's education and she had to sign papers to finalize everything. From there, she went to the mall and shopped. She bought Emma two outfits, another pair of boots, a couple of games and an iPod. The Christmas music piped into the stores put her in the mood for the holiday season. She only hoped that as Christmas drew nearer, Emma would feel the same way.

After leaving the mall, she stopped at a craft store and bought stretchy string to make bracelets for Emma's friends. Then she bought beads and ribbons, and supplies to make a wreath for the front door. She bought more than she'd planned, but it was Christmas.

Her last stop was the sporting-goods store to pick up the bicycle. She waited at customer service and was shocked when the guy brought out a box.

She looked at the ticket in her hand. "You have the wrong order. I bought a bicycle. It's red and white."

The teenage boy with a pimple on his forehead, which she tried not to look at, replied, "This is it. You have to put it together."

"What?" She had no idea how to put together a bicycle.

"No. I picked one out that was put together. It had a white basket on it."

The kid shook his head. "That's the display."

"Well, that's the one I want."

"It's not for sale," the kid said in a slow voice as if

he was talking to a child. Lacey realized she might be overreacting. Evidently this was normal.

She took a deep breath and tried again. "Can someone in the store put it together? I'd be willing to pay."

The boy pulled on the earring in his ear as if he was trying to conjure up someone else to talk to her. "There's a guy here that does that, but he's pretty booked up. I'm not sure you can get it by Christmas."

This was getting her nowhere. She had to do a lot of things with tools while decorating for parties, so surely she could put together a bicycle. If not, she'd have to ask someone for help. Maybe even Gabe. But that might be too painful for him.

"Could you please put it in my car?"

The boy sighed with obvious relief. "Yes, ma'am."

In a matter of minutes she was on her way to Horseshoe with the bicycle in the box. She had almost reached town when she noticed pine trees and the ground beneath them littered with pinecones. Two young girls about twelve were selling bags of them. Pulling over to the side of the road, she waited for the traffic to pass and then she turned around and went back. She bought three bags.

When Lacey arrived home, she carried the craft items and pinecones inside and put them in her bedroom. Then she was off to find Gabe. Her heart hummed a little faster at the thought. A loud sound echoed across her backyard, and she knew Gabe was working on something again.

She peeked out her kitchen window and couldn't believe her eyes. Gabe was at the top of the dead oak tree in his yard sawing limbs off with a chain saw. Oh, good heavens! The man was going to hurt himself. She hurried outside.

Gabe's yard was littered with dead branches. The sound of the saw was deafening. There was no way to get his attention. But just then the sound stopped. Gabe placed the saw in the crook of a branch and made his way down the tree.

His dark hair was tousled, and sweat soaked his T-shirt. She thought he'd never looked so handsome because that blank look in his eyes was gone. There was actually a light there now. A burning light that bode well for the future.

He removed his gloves. "You're back."

"And you're cutting down a tree all by yourself."

He looked at the mess in the yard. "Yep. Should keep me busy for a few days."

"Is that your goal? To always stay busy?"

He inclined his head. "Just about. How was the shopping?"

"Did you know that a bicycle comes in a box? And you have to put it together like a puzzle?"

A slight grin touched his mouth. It was the most beautiful sight she'd ever seen. It released the sad grieving man and made him irresistible.

"Yes. That's how they come."

"Well, I wish someone had told me that."

He stuffed his gloves into his back pocket. "Would it have stopped you from buying the bicycle?"

"Probably not."

"I'll help you. It's not hard if you follow the directions." He eyed her briefly and blood rushed to her face. "I have a feeling you don't follow directions too often."

She frowned. "Why do you say that?"

"The burned food, for one thing."

"Okay, you have a point." She glanced toward her house. "Can I please put the bicycle in your house? I have to pick up Emma in a few minutes, and she gets all paranoid if I'm not there exactly on time."

Lacey wound up putting all of the gifts in his spare bedroom, which was empty. The whole house was just about empty.

Gabe stared at the pile of gifts. "That's a lot for one child."

"Did you not buy a lot for Zack at Christmas?"

She thought he would shut down immediately, but he didn't. "Dana, my ex, would go overboard every year, even though we would say each time we would cut back. We never did and now I'm glad we didn't. Zack had the best Christmases." He looked away as he said the last word.

She wanted to hug him. She didn't know why she always had that feeling when she was around him. Maybe because a man who was hurting as much as he was needed lots of hugs.

He quickly recovered. "You'd better go or you'll be late."

"Oh, yes, and thanks." She ran for her car, once again feeling as though she didn't want to leave him. But Gabe was doing fine and didn't need her fussing over him.

Gabe grabbed a bottle of water out of his refrigerator and headed for his deck. He actually had bottled water because he'd gone shopping that morning after Lacey had left. He'd bought food, too, and a coffeemaker.

He stared at the mess in his yard. It would take him about a week to get it all cleaned up, and then he'd have a lot of firewood. He thought of stopping to put the bike together, but he'd rather do that with Lacey because he felt she would want to be a part of it. And she might get upset with him if he did it on his own.

Lacey was like a breath of fresh air in a world that had become dark and stale to him. For months he hadn't even known she was there. Hadn't wanted to know. He'd even cringed whenever he'd seen her and the kid outside. She'd invaded his privacy more than once, and her audacity had angered him. That same audacity had sparked a flame inside him that lit the fuse of his emotions—emotions he'd thought had died with Zack.

All day he'd been waiting for her to come home. He didn't know why. He just liked being with her. She made the loneliness bearable. And that was saying a lot.

He heard a sound and realized it was his cell phone. Where was it? He followed the sound into the kitchen and saw it on the counter. It was his sister. Most of the time he just ignored it, but today he clicked on.

"Hi, sis."

"You answered."

"Sorry about the other times." He sat at the kitchen table. "I just wasn't in the mood to talk."

"I worry about you."

"I know, but I told you I needed my space."

"So what's different now?"

He told her about Pepper and Lacey and Emma.

"That's Jack Carroll's family?"

"Yes. Emma was very fond of Pepper."

"I'm glad they were there for you, but if you had called I would've been there."

"Kate, don't mother me. You have seven sons for that."

"Like any of them listen to me."

"Oh, they listen."

Kate chuckled. "So tell me about this Lacey. Is she raising the little girl?"

"Yes." The question was an awakening moment. He knew nothing about Lacey's personal life other than she was raising her sister.

"How old is she?"

"Kate, stop with the inquisition. I know very little about her because I value my privacy."

"Oh, please don't start that again."

"And that's the reason I don't answer my phone most of the time. You treat me like one of your sons."

"Okay, I get it. But please come out to the ranch for supper one night. We'd all love to see you."

"I'm not making any promises, but I'll think about it."

"I just want you to be happy again."

Gabe didn't know if that was possible. "Bye, sis."

He walked out to his deck, his head filled with thoughts of Lacey. Taking a seat, he knew he was having a surreal moment, which wasn't unusual. He had those daily. This was different, though. He'd leaned on someone for the first time in his life, and he knew little about her except that she was kind, compassionate, understanding and selfless. She wasn't like anyone he'd ever known. And he was thinking too much about her. He drank the last of his water and went back to work, but thoughts of Lacey lingered.

When Lacey arrived at school Emma wasn't there waiting. Lacey got out and looked around. A moment of panic ran through her until she saw a group of kids. She started over and Emma broke away and ran toward her.

The first thing Lacey noticed was the fear on Emma's face. Second, the headband and bow Lacey had made were gone from Emma's hair.

Lacey hugged her and asked, "Did school let out early?"

Emma shrugged. "We had a program and when it was over, they said we could go home. And you weren't here." Her bottom lip trembled.

"I didn't know you were getting out early."

Emma had been very afraid Lacey was going to leave her. Lacey had done everything to reassure her that she wasn't, but Emma's fears were very real.

"I will always be here, sweetie. Please remember that."

Emma hiccupped. "'Kay."

"What happened to your bow?" Lacey asked as they got into the car.

"I gave it to Bailey."

"Why?"

"She gave me something, so I gave her something. You can make me another and she liked my bow."

"Sweetie, I don't want you giving away your stuff."

"But…" Lacey looked in the rearview mirror and saw Emma's bottom lip tremble again.

Oh, good heavens. Lacey had wanted Emma to make friends and now Lacey was spoiling it. She couldn't have it both ways.

"It's okay, sweetie. I'll make you another. Now let's go to the bakery and get a snack."

The scent in the bakery was decadent. Lacey could gain five pounds just from the smell.

"Hey, cutie," Angie's sister, AnaMarie, said from behind the counter. "I missed you yesterday."

It was an opening line for Emma to talk about Pepper. AnaMarie listened avidly as she prepared Emma's cherry kolach and hot chocolate.

"Sweetie, I'm going to speak to Angie for second. I'll be right back." Lacey went down the hall to Angie's office. Angie was an accountant. She did just about everyone's taxes in Horseshoe, and she did the bakery's books.

Lacey tapped on the door frame. "Are you busy?

Angie glanced up. "Well, look at you. All dressed up. What's the occasion?"

Lacey took the chair across from Angie. "I had to go into Temple today, so I made an effort with my appearance. I'll be back in jeans tomorrow."

Angie leaned back in her chair. "Cooking lessons and dressing up. I get the feeling it's for someone special."

"I wish." Lacey couldn't believe she squirmed in her chair like a teenager. "I have to admit, though, the sandwiches were for my next-door neighbor."

"You mean Gabe Garrison?"

"Yes. I just wanted to lift his spirits a little. I'm hopeless in the kitchen, so I don't know what I was thinking."

"It's so sad about his little boy."

"Mmm. And he had to put his son's dog to sleep."

"Oh, no. We've all tried to reach out to him, but he's made it very clear he values his privacy. Hardy knows him and so does Wyatt. He attended Horseshoe schools. He's a couple years younger, I think. I vaguely remember him. Very handsome with a brilliant future ahead of him."

"My dad had mentioned he was from here."

"Is Gabe doing okay?"

"It's hard to tell, but I think he's getting better. At least he's friendlier. And that brings me to my next question."

Angie smiled. "I can almost guess."

"I want to cook a really good meal. Believe me, the man could use it. So can you tell me how to do a roast the simple way?"

Angie pulled a pad and pencil forward. "I'll write it down step by step."

The front door opened and Peyton Carson, her two-year-old son, J.W., her daughter, Jody, and Erin came in. Jody and Erin were inseparable and best friends.

"One daughter delivered safe and sound," Peyton said. Peyton was a beautiful blonde who caught everyone's eye.

"Hi, Mama." Erin kissed her mother.

J.W. ran through to the kitchen. "Jody, get him," Peyton said to her daughter. Looking over Angie's shoulder, she asked, "What are you doing?"

"Writing out a recipe for Lacey."

Peyton held up two fingers. "I have two words for you. Crock-Pot. Or is that one word?" She shook her head. "Doesn't matter. You just throw everything in there and let it cook. Simple. Wyatt actually thinks I'm a good cook and I'm never telling him differently."

"That's the lazy way of cooking," Angie told her.

"Don't listen to her." Peyton laughed. "She cooks everything the hard way. Really. I mean who does that? No one but Angie."

The two were best friends, and Lacey knew they were teasing each other.

Angie handed Lacey the recipe. "Text or call me if you have a problem."

"Thanks." Lacey rose to her feet. "I better get Emma and go home. It's been a long day and I'm ready to get out of these boots."

"Crock-Pot," Peyton called as Lacey walked out of the bakery.

Lacey smiled. It was nice to be around women near her age. She missed that connection she had in Austin. Every day life seemed to get a little better. She still had Christmas and Emma to worry about, but she was going to cook Gabe a delicious meal whether he wanted it or not. She might burn the house down doing it. The smoke alarm would save her, though. God bless that annoying little piece of technology. But who would save her from Gabe and her growing feelings for him?

Chapter 10

The next morning after dropping Emma at school, Lacey went to the supermarket. She'd seen Angie at the school and Angie had given her more cooking advice. Angie had said the man at the meat counter could help Lacey select a roast. He did, and she took what he suggested. Emma liked mashed potatoes, so Lacey bought potatoes and a peeler. She was set for a day of cooking.

As she unpacked groceries, she could hear Gabe's saw. It had been buzzing until late the previous night. He was determined to finish the tree.

Lacey laid out Angie's instructions on the counter and went to work. With the roast browned on one side, she flipped it over to brown the other. Her cell buzzed and she fished it out of her purse. It was Janine, her former boss.

"Hey, Janine." Lacey went into the living room and sat on the sofa.

"How are things going?"

"Pretty good. I have a roast in the oven."

Janine laughed. "You're getting domesticated."

"We have to eat, so I'm trying to learn."

"Why not come back to work and pay someone to cook?"

"I wish I could, but there's no way I can leave Emma. I have to be here when she gets out of school. Besides, the drive every day would kill me."

"Have you thought of moving back to Austin? We have a lot of good schools here, and you and Emma could start over."

The thought was so tempting, but she pushed it aside because it wasn't really what she wanted. "This is Emma's home, and I don't know how she would react to leaving all the memories of our dad. She's still grieving." *And so am I.*

Janine sighed. "I gave it a shot. We're so busy with the holiday season, and I could really use your help."

"Sorry. I'm dealing with a little girl who doesn't believe in Santa Claus, and that takes all my energy." Lacey told her what had happened.

"I'm sorry, Lacey. I know you have your hands full, but remember to have some fun for yourself."

The smoke alarm shrilled and Lacey jumped to her feet. "I gotta go. I'll call you later."

She threw the phone on the sofa and ran. The kitchen was filling up with smoke coming from the oven. Damn! The shrilling sound jabbed like sharp needles at her brain. She quickly turned off the oven and then removed her sneaker and threw it at the pesky thing.

The alarm flew off and landed in the dining room. She picked it up and threw it out the back door. Opening the oven door, she coughed as smoke billowed out into the kitchen and dining room. Damn! Her dinner was ruined. What was she thinking? She couldn't cook. She sank to her knees, slapped away an errant tear and had her own private pity party.

Gabe was going into his house for water when he heard the alarm. Not again. What was she doing? Unable to resist, he strolled over. As he neared her back door, the smoke alarm landed at his feet. He retrieved it from the dry winter grass and then opened the door. Smoke engulfed him.

He covered his mouth. "Lacey, are you okay?" He saw her sitting on the floor and went to her. "Lacey?"

"I burned my beautiful roast," she mumbled. "It's black. What's wrong with me that I can't cook?"

"Is it just the roast? Nothing else is on fire?"

She nodded and he took her arm and helped her to her feet. "Let's get out of here until the smoke clears."

As she limped toward the back door, he realized she had on one sneaker. Searching the kitchen, he found the other one on the counter. He opened the kitchen window and followed her out the door.

After taking a seat at her patio table, he handed her the sneaker and she slipped it on. She ran her fingers through her short hair and fluffed it. Even with tear trails on her face, she looked beautiful.

"I'm hopeless."

"Have you never cooked?"

Her eyes narrowed, and he was expecting a whole lot of attitude, but she replied, "Not really."

"Why?"

The eyes narrowed even more. "Don't push your luck. I'm not in a good mood."

"I'm just asking a question."

"I liked it better when you were quiet."

He leaned forward. "I know very little about you. Is your mother still living?"

She laughed, a bubbly sound that lifted his spirits.

"What's so funny?"

She pointed a finger at him. "You wanting to talk."

Their eyes met, and he felt a chink in that solid armor he'd built around his heart. To avoid further analysis, he asked, "Any brothers or sisters?"

She shook her head. "I was an only child until Emma."

"A spoiled, pampered child?"

She closed her eyes as if giving it some thought. "Yes, mainly by my father. My mother worked a lot and still does."

"It must have changed your world when Emma came along."

She tucked her feet beneath her. "Not really. I wasn't as spoiled as you might think. The thought of having a sister was exciting, and I loved her the moment I saw her. I couldn't wait to leave work and come see her. And Mona was very good about letting me visit any time I wanted."

"That was your stepmom?"

"Yes."

She rubbed her jeans absently. "She only lived for six months after Emma was born, and I think she leaned on me a lot to care for Emma. Dad did, too. He had his hands full taking care of Mona. It was so sad. My dad deserved happiness, not what he got." She brushed away a tear and Gabe's stomach clenched. He wanted to take away her pain just as she had tried to take away his.

Before he could say anything, she continued, "My parents had a lousy marriage. They argued all the time. After nineteen years, my mom told my dad to leave and he did. It shocked her, I think. Anyway—" she waved a hand "—it was a bitter divorce and I was caught in the middle. My mother wanted me to hate my dad and I couldn't. Now she wants me to hate Emma, and I can't do that, either. Suffice to say, Mom and I are always at odds. I love her, but it's hard dealing with her."

"Where does your mother live?" He was caught off guard by the words coming out of his mouth, but he found he was curious about her.

"In Austin. She got our family home in the divorce. She wants me to come home for Christmas, but she doesn't want me to bring Emma. That's causing a lot of friction, because I can't leave Emma."

He'd never met anyone quite like Lacey. She had sacrificed her chance at a life so a little girl could have a home. The more he talked to her, the more he admired her.

"I'm sure it will work out."

"You don't know my mother."

If she was that hard-hearted, Gabe didn't want to know the woman. But then, he wasn't in the mood to associate with many people. Lacey was an exception.

"So your mom didn't cook?"

Lacey smiled a smile that rivaled the sun, and for moment he was lost in her charm. "Getting back to the cooking, huh? No, she doesn't cook. My dad did all the cooking. Sometimes I would help, but he did all the major stuff. I just played. He was an awesome dad. I don't know why he thought I would make a good mother for Emma. I'm terrible at it. Every day I feel like a failure."

"Every parent feels that way. You never know if you're doing the right thing. You just have to trust your instincts and your heart. When Za…" Gabe caught himself in time. He couldn't talk about his son.

She looked up. "What about Zack?" He should've known she wouldn't leave it alone.

"Nothing," he replied sharply, hoping she got the message.

She stared at him, her green eyes soft and understanding, as if she knew what he was thinking, and she was urging him toward something he didn't want but desperately needed.

Before he knew it, words tumbled from his throat. "When Zack would misbehave, my wife, Dana, always expected me to be the disciplinarian. And it killed me. I hated that part of being a parent. I guess if I had been sterner and not so lenient, Zack wouldn't have…" He drew a deep breath and knew he had to say the words. He couldn't just think them. "Za… Zack wouldn't have disobeyed." A wad of guilt burned his throat.

"What did Zack do?" she asked softly.

Gabe focused on a terra-cotta pot on the patio table. "When we got the four-wheeler, we sat down and made rules. Zack could only ride it on weekends when I was home. During the week he had homework and school activities. He agreed and I trusted him. I put the key in my nightstand." Gabe drew another breath. "Dana always picked him up from school. She was doing some legal work for one of our neighbors. She left Zack to

do homework and drove to their house to leave papers.
When she returned, she couldn't find Zack. She immediately called me and I came home. He'd found the key
and had taken the four-wheeler for a spin. He'd turned
it over, and I found him with the vehicle on top of him.
His chest was crushed and… I pulled it off and carried
him to the house. An ambulance was on the way…but
it was too late. My son…was dead."

Lacey slipped onto his lap and wrapped her arms
around his neck. "I'm so sorry."

He sucked air into his tight lungs. "I think we've
done this before."

"You're talking about it, and that's good. It doesn't
help to keep it all bottled up inside."

Her hand stroked his neck, and he lost his train of
thought. The pain inside him ebbed and new, vibrant
feelings emerged. She smelled of smoke mixed with a
flowery scent that was all woman—a delicate fragrance
that filled his nostrils and awakened needs deep inside
him. His hand rested on the curve of her hip, and the
urge was strong to move upward to her breasts, to feel
their fullness.

"The smoke has cleared," he said, getting to his feet.
He needed to put distance between them. "Let's check
out the damage."

She followed him inside. "This is my last attempt
at cooking. From now on, we're eating sandwiches."

He opened the oven door. "You don't seem like a
person who gives up that easily."

"How many times have you heard the smoke alarm?"

"Point taken." He found a hot pad on the counter and
lifted the pan out of the oven. Inside was a charred lump
of meat. "How long have you been cooking this thing?"

"Not long."

He placed the pan on another hot pad. "This is really burned. Maybe there's something wrong with your oven."

She smacked her forehead with the palm of her hand and he wanted to laugh, which felt good. "The oven. Why didn't I think of that? Please let it be the oven."

He closed the door and set the dial to two hundred degrees. They both stared through the little glass window. It was an electric stove, and the coils became red instantly. "Whoa. It's heating up fast. That's not normal. The thermostat must be broken."

"Really?" Her voice rose with excitement. "Could that be the problem?"

"These houses were built about twenty years ago, and this is probably the original oven. A repair guy will cost a lot of money. It might be best to just replace the built-in oven."

"This was Mona's house, and when she married my dad, he replaced the floors, painted and did some updating. I don't think he replaced the appliances. Maybe I'll just buy a new one, but I'll have to get someone to install it."

"I'll do it," he offered. "If you're free in the morning we can go to Temple and pick out a new one. I'll measure it so we can get the right size to fit."

"Thank you." She reached up and hugged him, and he tensed. He couldn't help that reaction. His feelings were all over the place and he had to take a step back. He didn't want to cause either of them any more problems.

"Where's your ladder? I'll put the smoke alarm back up."

"In the garage."

It didn't take him long to reinstall the alarm. He carried the ladder back to the garage and made his getaway.

He felt like a coward, running away, but that was all he could do at the moment. Lacey was too nice for him to hurt and he'd realized recently that soon he'd have to return to his old life. When that would happen, he wasn't quite sure. Right now, he was enjoying the crazy lady next door.

Lacey hurried to pick up Emma. As soon as Emma walked into the house, she said, "Not again, Lacey. What did you burn?"

"It wasn't my fault. We need a new oven."

"You're blaming the oven?"

"Yes, smarty-pants, Gabe said the thermostat is broken."

Emma threw her backpack on the sofa. "I'm gonna go see Gabe." Lately, Emma had dropped the *Mr.* from Gabe's name, and Lacey saw no need to correct her. Emma and Gabe were now friends.

"Wait a minute. Gabe is busy working on the tree and you might be in the way."

"I want to see if my flowers are still on Pepper's grave."

"Just stay a minute because you have homework to do."

"'Kay."

Emma shot out the door, and Lacey resisted the impulse to go with her. She wanted to see Gabe, too. But she'd sensed his withdrawal from her. She should give him his space. They were drawing closer and it was making him nervous. It made her a little nervous, too, but she found it exciting at the same time.

The evening went as usual. Emma complained about homework and about washing her hair, but eventually Lacey got her into bed. The morning came quickly. She dropped Emma at school and hurried home.

As soon as she pulled into the driveway, Gabe came over with a measuring tape. He got the serial number and make off the door, and then they were on their way to Temple. He insisted on going in his truck. She got the impression he didn't trust her driving.

The truck was nice, with heated leather seats. In his other life, she realized he must've had money. As he was a lawyer, she could understand that.

"You can do a lot of things," she remarked.

"I was raised with seven nephews, and my brother-in-law made sure we knew how to survive in this world."

"What happened to your parents?"

She expected him to clam up, but he didn't. "My dad left soon after I was born. He was a truck driver and traveled all over the States. He met my mom when he was passing through Horseshoe. Settling down wasn't his thing. I met him for the first time about five years ago. I tracked him down. He had remarried three times after my mom. I was his only child, though. He lives on the Gulf Coast, fishing, these days. Even after all this time, he still wasn't interested in being a father. We parted amicably."

How sad, Lacey thought. "And your mom?"

He shifted uneasily in his seat. "She died when I was fourteen. I have a half sister who is eighteen years older than me, and instead of seeing me put into foster care, she insisted I live with her and her family. She and her husband, John, already had seven sons, and they accepted me as one of them."

"Seven sons?" Lacey tried to keep the awe out of her voice, but failed.

"Yeah, seven rambunctious boys in about eight years. Two were born in the same year. Jude was born in January and Phoenix in December."

"Where do they live?"

"On a ranch not far out of Horseshoe."

"And they never visit you?" That question might have been out of line, but she couldn't take it back.

His hands gripped the wheel, his eyes glued to the highway. "I told them not to. I needed my space and they respected my wishes." He zoomed around a car that he obviously thought was going too slow. "At least my nephews have. My sister, Kate, hasn't been quite as accommodating. She tends to treat me like one of her boys."

Kate. "Kate Rebel?"

He glanced at her. "You know my sister?"

"Um…" She should have kept her mouth shut. Now she had to tell him what she'd done. "No, not really. The day the vet came to put Pepper to sleep, I used your phone to call the school about Emma. I was going to ask you, but you were busy with the vet. I didn't think you'd mind one phone call. I just happened to see all the missed calls from Kate Rebel."

He spared her another sharp glance. "You used my phone without permission. Do you even know what the word *privacy* means?"

His reprimanding tone needled her. "Okay. I did it. I'm sorry. Spank me."

The corners of his mouth twitched. "Do you know you're a little crazy?"

"Yep. And lovable."

"And infuriating."

"But you like me."

His eyes met hers. "Yes. I like you."

That was more than she'd ever thought she would hear from him. And it was enough.

Chapter 11

Shopping with Lacey was like nothing Gabe had ever experienced. She looked at all the ovens, even the ones that wouldn't fit her space. Grabbing her attention to focus on what she needed was like catching dust motes in his hand. Impossible. Then, after looking for more than an hour, she decided she didn't like any of them. At the third store, he'd had enough.

"This is it," he told her. "You're picking out an oven that will fit your kitchen and we're not looking at ones that will not."

"Maybe," she said, sliding out of the truck.

He groaned, but followed her inside. He found one that was almost the exact measurements and showed it to her.

"This will do. The measurements are an eighth of an inch off, but I can make it work."

She pointed to one farther down the aisle. "I like that one."

He counted to three. "It's a double oven. You have a single oven."

"Okay. Don't get testy."

He bit his lip. "See. This one has a timer and push buttons. Easy to use."

"I like that."

"Good." He motioned to the salesman. "We'll take it." He waited for her to object, but she didn't. They bought the oven and were soon on their way back to Horseshoe.

"Let's get an ice cream."

"No," he replied. "I can have the oven in by this afternoon."

She turned in her seat to face him. "There's no rush. You can do it tomorrow or the next day. I'm not exactly Rachael Ray tied to the stove. You need to lighten up and have some fun."

"I don't know what having fun is like anymore."

"I'll show you." She pointed to a Dairy Queen up ahead. "Pull in."

"No. We can be home in no time."

"Pull in."

He pulled in. Rolling into the drive-through, he pushed a button to lower his window. She leaned across him and said to the young girl, "Two medium ice cream cones, dipped."

"I don't want one."

"He does," Lacey stated, but the girl hesitated. "He does," she repeated, and the young girl turned to make them.

He was fighting a losing battle, so he gave in. He

took the cones and handed them to Lacey while he paid the girl. "I can't drive eating ice cream."

"Oh, my, the man who can do everything can't eat ice cream and drive."

"It's not safe."

"Then find a spot and we'll eat them here."

He found a parking space and turned off the engine. She handed him a cone and he ate it like a good little boy. There was blissful silence for a change.

After wiping her mouth, she placed the napkin on the console and turned his rearview mirror toward her. He gritted his teeth.

"There's a mirror on your sun visor."

"Oh. You should have said something."

"You never give me a chance."

She made a face at him, and then turned to look in the mirror. "My lipstick is all gone. Kiss me."

"What?"

"Kissing will make my lips red. Don't you know that?"

"I…"

She caught the front of his sweatshirt and pulled him forward, planting a kiss smack on his lips. For a moment he was caught off guard, but found his lips responding in the most sensual way.

Pulling back, she licked her lips. "Cool and chocolaty. Nice." She puckered her lips. "Are they pink?"

His lips cracked into a smile. He couldn't help himself. She was infectious and tempting and drawing him in with her delightful personality.

"You are crazy."

"See?" She touched his lips with one finger, and he wanted to grab it with his teeth and nibble and… "I made you smile. It helps to be a little crazy and not to take life so seriously." She glanced at her watch. "Oh, we have to hurry. I can't be late for picking up Emma."

It amazed him how she could go from fun loving to responsible. He started the truck, and once again they were on their way home. Gabe felt something different, unusual and welcoming. A sliver of light opened in his heart. He could feel it—warm and comfortable, like sunshine, filling his system with much-needed nourishment. And at that moment he realized he needed a little crazy in his life.

Lacey was there when Emma got out of school, and they went to the bakery for a snack. She thought she'd give Gabe some time to do what he had to in the kitchen. With her and Emma underfoot, he'd be scowling the whole time. Much like he had been today.

She'd been silly on purpose to draw him out of his serious mood, which he always seemed to be in. And it had worked. He'd smiled for the first time. It was breathtaking to see the change on his face. He'd allowed himself to feel something other than pain. If she had to be silly to accomplish that, then so be it.

At the bakery, Angie laughed about the burned roast, but was glad to hear it was the oven's fault. Lacey bought kolaches to take home for dessert. Emma was all excited when Lacey told her Gabe was putting in a new oven. She could hardly wait to charge into the house.

Lacey was surprised to see Gabe was almost finished. With some kind of tool, he was tightening the screws to the cabinet.

He wiped a rag over the front of the new appliance. "All done."

"We have a new oven. Now Lacey won't burn our food," Emma said.

Gabe put his tools back into a toolbox. "There's some sawdust on the floor. I had to shave off some wood to make it fit, but the lip on the oven covers it."

"I'll sweep it up." Lacey went to get the broom out of the utility room.

"The old one is on the patio," Gabe told her. "I'll haul it to the dump in the morning."

She tilted her head. "Thank you, kind sir. And for your reward we're having fish sticks, macaroni and cheese and kolaches for supper. You're invited to stay."

"Thanks, but I'm not really hungry."

"You'll come anyway." Her eyes held his, and for a moment she thought he was going to refuse again.

"Okay, but I want to work on the tree for a while."

"Deal."

He paused at the door with the toolbox in his hand. "You know, it's getting very hard to say no to you."

"Let's keep it that way."

A smile touched his face, and it was so beautiful. It softened those hard lines that were etched by pain and suffering and made him attractive and appealing. Maybe a little too much for her peace of mind. She liked Gabe, but they really had no future. He would soon get his life together. He was already taking steps in that direction, and she would stay here in Horseshoe and raise Emma. There was nothing wrong with them being friends, though. Yet her heart wanted so much more.

"Lacey, did you make my bow?"

Emma's question brought her back to reality. "No. I haven't had time."

"Bailey and I are dressing alike tomorrow and I have to have it."

"Really?" She stared down at Emma, who obviously thought she could pull rabbits out of hats. Or would that be bows? "You could have told me that earlier."

"I did. I told you I needed another bow."

"Okay. I'll do it tonight. Start on your homework and I'll get supper started."

"I want to help Gabe."

"Not tonight. Gabe is busy."

"You're no fun, Lacey." Emma stomped to the table and crawled onto a chair.

"I'll have you know I'm lots of fun." With the broom as a prop she started twerking, twisting her arms and legs in a spastic sort of way. Turning around, she saw Gabe standing in the doorway with a stunned expression on his face.

"Oh."

"Lacey's being silly." Emma came to the rescue.

"I thought she was having a seizure."

Emma laughed and Lacey frowned.

"I just wanted to tell you that I'm taking the old oven and putting it in the back of my truck. I had no idea I was in for a show."

"Lacey's weird." Emma pulled books out of her backpack.

Lacey lifted an eyebrow, daring him to say one word.

"Hmm." He walked out, and she sank back against the counter. After a moment, she recovered and started supper.

Gabe came over and ate with them, as promised, but he didn't stay long.

That night Lacey made the bow, and the next day

Emma and Bailey marched into the school dressed alike in their candy cane outfits. They looked adorable.

Lacey didn't dawdle, though. Since Gabe had helped her yesterday, she planned to return the favor. He had the tree completely cut down—only a stump remained, but branches were strewn all over his yard. He was cutting the branches into firewood.

"Good morning," he said, turning off the chain saw. "Where do you want the wood stacked? I'll help."

"You don't have to do that."

"And you didn't have to install my oven, so let's don't argue. Where do you want me to stack the logs?"

He pointed to a place near the house where he had already started a pile. They worked in silence, except for the chain saw. She paused every now and then to watch him. Since the sun was out, he'd removed his hoodie. His black T-shirt emphasized the muscles in his arms. He'd put on a little weight and he looked damn good.

His cowboy boots were worn and dirty and his long hair dripped with sweat. Masculinity with a capital *M*. She had never been more aware of it than she was today.

Lacey was exhausted by the time she had to pick up Emma, but Gabe's yard looked a little better. There were still branches and debris everywhere, but most of the big branches had been cut up and stacked.

She had a few minutes before she had to leave, so they sat on his deck, drinking water. The weather was beautiful—sunny and in the sixties. A slight breeze ruffled her hair, and she felt relaxed just sitting there with him. She wondered if he felt the same way.

"What are you gonna do with all this wood?"

"Burn it in the fireplace when it gets colder. You and Emma can come over and I'll make s'mores."

"You're inviting us over?"

"Why not?"

"Exactly." She placed her bottle on the floor. "I'm going to try to get Emma to decorate the tree this weekend."

"Just take it slow and don't force her."

"That's what all the books say, and I've read just about every one, but it's so frustrating. I want her to believe and to feel the excitement of Christmas like I did as a child. I want her to have good memories. I want her to be a little girl with stardust in her eyes."

"What does Emma want?"

"What?"

"You keep saying what you want. Ask Emma how she wants to celebrate Christmas. Give her a chance to express her feelings and gradually pull her in. I know you can do that because you're constantly pulling me in to things I don't want to do."

She placed her hands on her hips. "Like what?"

He took a big swig from the water bottle. "Like… making me smile and making me realize that I'm still alive."

"Poor you."

"Yeah, poor me."

She wasn't offended by his words because there was a slight smile on his lips. And she loved it—loved that he was finally letting go of all the pain. Little by little he was getting better. But when he reached the pinnacle of full recovery, would he still hang around Horseshoe, Texas?

Gabe never knew what to expect from Lacey. That was part of her charm. She was now in full Christmas mode and totally involved with cooking. Whenever he'd go over to her house, she was either watching cooking shows on TV or reading recipes on the internet. Every night she made something different and he ate with them. She was getting good, and it wasn't hard to get caught up in her excitement.

If she wasn't trying a recipe, she was decorating or making pinecone wreaths for the door and the fireplace. He'd helped hold the cones so she could tie them in place on a rounded wire. And he'd helped hold the red plaid ribbon she then wove through the pinecones. She'd added red berries for an extra touch.

She was very good at crafts. There were now a lot of decorations for Emma to put on the tree, but it wasn't working. The tree still stood, looking lonely and bare, in the living room.

As he returned from his morning jog, he noticed Lacey on the ladder in the front yard nailing Christmas lights to the house. He watched her for a moment, enjoying the view. She wore tight-fitting jeans and a knit top that showed off her figure to perfection. And he was happy to recognize that he found her curves enticing.

He walked up to her. "What are you doing?"

She looked down at him. "Uh…it's not hard to figure out. I'm going to light this house up like Cowboy Stadium. Emma has to get in the Christmas mood soon."

"I could say you're crazy, but I think I've covered that."

"Yes. Crazy like a fox. I have no idea what that means, but I've heard it all my life."

He didn't feel the need to enlighten her. Lacey was just Lacey—charming.

"The wind is picking up. You need to get down from there before you break your neck."

"Oh, please. This is what I did in my job. Hang decorations for ladies who wanted everything just right. Believe me, when you have to hang decorations in a ballroom, it takes a tall ladder and a steady hand."

"I thought you were an assistant."

"Yes. The person who does things when an employee doesn't show up for work. The party must go on, you know."

"I had no idea. All I know is you're too high in the air for my peace of mind."

"I'm not getting down until I finish."

"I'll go get my ladder and help you."

"Ah, a man after my heart."

For the next hour they used a staple gun to secure lights all over the front of the house. It really was going to light up the night. But then, Lacey could do that with just her smile. She scurried down the ladder to turn them on and they gazed at their handiwork.

Lacey clapped her hands. "Oh, Emma has to be excited about this."

"Yeah. Planes are going to mistake your roof for the Austin airport."

She poked him in the ribs playfully. "How about some coffee?"

"You read my mind."

He was very comfortable in Lacey's house. The more time he spent there the more he wanted to come back. Lacey's cheerful personality was inviting, and he needed that in his life right now.

He sat at her table and she placed a steaming mug

of coffee and a plate of something chocolaty in front of him.

"It's fudge. I made it last night. Taste it."

"Am I a guinea pig?"

She took a seat with a gleam in her eyes. "Maybe."

"Mmm," he mumbled, munching on the sweet treat. "You're getting this cooking thing down."

Her eyes twinkled even more. "Thank you very much. Now, if I could just get Emma to believe in Santa again…"

"You have about three weeks before the kids at school will get excited and she will, too. You just have to give her time and don't push, but I don't think you hear me when I say that."

Lacey fiddled with her cup. "I try, but I don't know. Emma's very adamant. She's lost her father and now Santa has been taken from her. I can sense her stubbornness and anger, and I worry about that."

"Anger is not a good thing to live with. After Zack died, I was filled with rage. I took a hammer and beat that four-wheeler into a million pieces. Even that didn't stop the fury building in me. I snapped at everyone, and when I almost hit one of my colleagues for laughing in my presence, I knew I had to get away. I threw some things in a bag and started driving. The next thing I knew I was in Horseshoe."

He took a breath, hardly believing he was sharing that awful time.

"Did you tell your wife?"

He ran his finger over the handle of the cup. "Two weeks after the accident she moved in with her brother and his wife. She blamed me and I blamed her, but our marriage had fallen apart long before the accident. She was busy building her career and so was I. Zack was our only common interest."

"I'm sorry."

"See." He slapped his hand on the table, jarring the coffee in his cup. "You have me talking even when I don't want to."

"You do want to talk. That's why you're doing it. And it's long overdue."

"I suppose," he admitted, and wondered why it was so easy to talk to her.

"Did you come to Horseshoe to visit your sister?"

"I guess that was my destination, but I wasn't thinking about it consciously. Turns out I wasn't ready for all her smothering and sympathy. I love her, but I just couldn't handle it at that time. I slept in my truck until I saw a house for sale. I made the deal and the next day I moved in. The sofa and table were already here, and that was all furniture I needed. The sofa was my bed for a long time until I finally broke down and bought a mattress for the old iron bed in the bedroom."

She reached out and clasped his hand on the table. Her hand was so fragile compared to his, or at least it looked that way. Fragility disguising an enormous strength.

"I'm so happy you're doing better."

"Yeah." He entwined his fingers with hers, her softness soothing against his calluses. "You're there for me and Emma. Who's there for you?"

Her green eyes clouded for a moment. "The people of Horseshoe have been very nice to us."

"How about your mother?"

"She was angry that I had accepted the responsibility of Emma and tried to persuade me to send her to Mona's sister in Midland. I couldn't do that, so I handled it alone. When dad died, Emma and I came home and we sat in his recliner and fell asleep. We stayed there the whole night. She cried. I cried. She clung to me like a leech and was afraid for me to get out of her sight. The following weeks were really hard trying to hold it together. But time moved on and people came by and brought food, visited and offered their condolences. We made it. But we're not quite there yet."

"You're amazing. Do you know that?" A smile curved her lips, and he watched it transform her into a beautiful, irresistible woman.

"And a little crazy?"

"I'm beginning to really like crazy."

Silence stretched, but it wasn't uncomfortable. It was that of two people dealing with their emotions and enjoying the moment of having someone who understood. Someone who cared.

Chapter 12

Lacey could hardly wait for Emma to see the house. She'd turned on the lights before she left so Emma would see them as they drove up.

For the school Christmas program, the first graders were going to sing carols. Today was their first practice, and she'd thought Emma would be all excited because she loved to sing. But when she got into the car, she was somber and quiet. Lacey asked her a few questions but then stopped. Emma was clearly annoyed about something. The house would cheer her up, Lacey was sure.

Emma crawled out of the car and then stopped as she saw the lights. Her face scrunched into her trademark frown.

"What'd you do that for?"

Lacey unlocked the front door. "Because it's Christmas and Santa has to be able to see our house."

"There is no Santa, Lacey. Sometimes you make me mad."

Lacey bent down to her level. "Sometimes you make me mad, too. So there."

"Daddy puts the lights on the house. And you're not Daddy." Emma shot toward her bedroom, the backpack in her hand.

Lacey's heart took a jolt. She'd screwed up. She sank onto the sofa and buried her face in her hands. Gabe had told her to take it slow and not to force Emma. She should have listened. After a moment, she walked down the hall to Emma's room. Emma lay curled into a fetal position, the backpack still looped around her arm. She faced the wall, away from Lacey.

Needing time, Lacey went to her room, pulled out a couple of parenting books and tried to figure out how to make this right again. The message was clear: never force a child, be patient, be understanding, be supportive, ask their opinion, let them share their feelings, love them and let them know you love them.

She laid the book on the bed. Gabe was right. Lacey was doing what she wanted, not what Emma wanted. Damn! How could she have screwed this up so badly? She took a deep breath and went to Emma. As she removed the backpack from Emma's arm, Emma turned over. Her face was blotchy and her eyes were red from crying. Lacey could hardly stand it. She willed herself not to cry. But hurting Emma took a toll on her.

"I know I'm not Daddy, but I'm doing the best I can."

Emma flew into her, wrapping her arms around Lacey's waist and crying into her chest. "I'm…sorry I was mean to you. I'm sorry…"

"Shh." Lacey stroked Emma's hair and then lifted

her sister into her arms. She sat on the bed with Emma in her lap. "It's okay. Stop crying."

Finally, Emma's wails ebbed.

As Lacey held her sister, it occurred to her that Emma's reaction was over the top. When Lacey had gotten the tree and put up the wreaths and other decorations in the house, Emma had complained, but not paid much attention to what Lacey was doing. Today was different. She thought about Emma's reluctance to talk earlier.

"Sweetie." Lacey brushed hair away from Emma's face and removed the bow that was hanging loose. "Did something happen in school today?"

Emma rubbed her face against Lacey shirt. "No. Why?"

"You're very upset."

Emma played with Lacey's watch. "I told Bailey about Pepper and Daddy, and that I sent Daddy a message with Pepper when she went to heaven, and Bailey said—" Emma hiccupped "—she said...that dogs can't talk and Pepper couldn't give Daddy my message. Now Daddy doesn't know I love him." Emma buried her face in Lacey's chest and sobbed.

So that was it. Unknowingly, Bailey had taken away Emma's happiness. Lacey reached for Emma's chin and pulled up her face.

"Daddy, Pepper and Zack are in heaven, and heaven is a beautiful place where everything is perfect. There's only one voice, whether it's a person or an animal, and it's understood by everyone. Pepper's probably licked Daddy's face, his hands and his feet in excitement to give him your message. Daddy knows, sweetie. He knows. Don't let anyone ever tell you different. You tell them to talk to your big sister, and I will set them straight."

Emma sat up, her eyes like big shiny marbles. "They're in heaven."

"Yes."

"Oh." Emma threw her arms around Lacey's neck. "I love you."

Lacey's heart melted into a drippy mess. "Love you, too, sweetie. Please talk to me when you have a problem, or when someone tells you something you don't understand or when you're just sad."

"'Kay."

"Now I'm going to fix supper. Wash your face and then you can go tell Gabe supper will be ready in a few minutes."

Emma jumped off her lap and ran to the bathroom. Lacey made her way to the kitchen, feeling a little better. Actually, she felt a lot better. Finally, she was getting this parenting thing down—at least until the next crisis.

Gabe pulled off his gloves. A couple more days and he'd have the backyard clean again. Emma came through the gate and jumped up the steps on the deck, and then slid into a chair.

"Hi, Gabe."

"Hi, kiddo." He sat in the other chair and waited for her to speak, because obviously she had something on her mind.

She scooted to the back of the chair, her feet dangling over. "Do you believe in Santa?"

"I did when I was a kid. It was the most exciting time of the year. I couldn't wait for Christmas morning to see if I'd gotten everything I'd asked Santa for."

"I'm not supposed to tell anyone, but you're an adult, right?"

He suppressed a smile. "Yeah."

She leaned toward him and whispered, "Santa's not real. Our parents put presents under the tree."

"How do you know that?" He knew the answer, but he wanted her to talk about it. It might help Lacey in her quest to get Emma to believe in Santa again.

"Brad Wilson told me and Jimmy, and it's true 'cause I asked Lacey and she doesn't lie."

"Is that why you're sad?"

Emma kicked with her feet. "My friend Bailey told me that Pepper couldn't tell Daddy my message, because dogs can't talk. That made me sad, and then I told Lacey she wasn't Daddy and she shouldn't have put up the lights."

Lacey had worked so hard on the lights. He wondered if she was over there crying. That bothered him. He didn't want her to be sad. He had to restrain himself from running to her. First, he had to talk to Emma.

"Did you apologize?"

"Yeah. Lacey said that Daddy, Pepper and Zack are in heaven, and in heaven everybody understands each other 'cause it's heaven." She raised her hands palms up to emphasize this miracle. "Lacey knows everything."

He agreed with that wholeheartedly. Lacey was wonderful.

"So why are you sad?"

"Lacey wants me to believe in Santa again, but I can't."

He scooted his chair closer. "Why not?"

"'Cause he's not real."

"You believe in heaven and you don't know that it's real."

Her eyes narrowed. "It is real. My daddy is there."

"Belief is a powerful thing. It can lift our spirits, get us through bad times and work miracles. You just have to believe sometimes. You have to trust. You believe that heaven is there because you have to know that your daddy is in a better place. I believe, too, because I have to know the same thing about Zack. I'm going solely on belief."

She looked at him, her green eyes wide. "So Santa could be real?"

He shrugged. "If your belief is strong enough, anything is possible."

Suddenly, her bottom lip trembled and he tensed. "I'm too little to know this stuff. I just want my daddy to come back."

Gabe reached out and lifted her into his arms, trying not to let his emotions overtake him. "I want Zack to come back, too," he said, his heart tightening in pain, but he had to go on for Emma. "But there's a difference between reality and belief. And yes, you're too little to understand that. So we're not going to be sad because Lacey would be very upset with us."

Emma rested her face against his chest, and he held her as if she was the most precious thing in the world. He was beginning to believe she was. He'd thought no one could ever touch that part of him that belonged to Zack. But like her sister, Emma was working her magic on his heart.

"Oh." Emma sat up. "I forgot. Lacey said supper's ready."

"Then we'd better go. Maybe she'll dance for us."

Emma giggled. Still holding her, he stood and carried her back to her house, enjoying the feel of a child in his arms again.

Lacey was making a salad. She was cutting a tomato with more force than necessary. It was obvious she was upset.

"Go wash your hands, Emma. Supper is almost ready," she said.

Emma darted off and Gabe went into the kitchen, grabbing Lacey's arms from behind, stopping her chopping motion.

"What's wrong?"

She laid the knife on the cutting board and turned in the circle of his arms. "I'm getting everything wrong. I can't seem to do anything right concerning Emma. I keep causing her more pain."

"She told me what happened."

Her teary eyes opened wide. "She talked to you?"

"She told me what her friend Bailey said about Pepper, and that she'd hurt your feelings and she was sorry."

"You were right. I should stop all this Christmas stuff and just let her celebrate the way she wants. But I…"

He pulled her into his arms. She rested against him, and a warm glow settled around his heart. "Just take it slow. That's all you have to do. She asked me about Santa, and I think she's opening up to the idea. Just give her time. But prepare yourself for the fact that she may never believe in Santa again."

"I think I'll take down the lights tomorrow."

"Not unless she asks you to. I think I might have to explain what *slow* means."

She raised her face with a smile, and everything was

right in his world in that moment. "I don't think it's in my vocabulary."

"I don't think it is, either." He turned her toward the hall. "Go take a hot bath and relax while I put supper on the table."

"I can't. I'm in the middle of making a salad."

"Go. I can finish." He gave her a gentle push and she went.

A moment later, Emma came running back. "Why is Lacey taking a bath? Did she get dirty?"

"We're giving her some time alone, so that means you have to help me."

"I can! I can!"

She was eager to help, and they had the table set and all of the food on it by the time Lacey made her appearance. That tired, sad look was gone from her face. The resilient, vibrant Lacey was back.

"Look, Lacey, we did supper, 'cause we love you."

Love. Time stood still for Gabe. Love was something he hadn't thought of because he had been unable to give it anymore. And he hadn't wanted to lead Lacey on. Or Emma. He was getting too involved, and the last thing he wanted was to hurt them.

After supper, he quickly made his exit. That might have been the coward's way out, but he needed time to think about what was happening with his feelings.

Since it was Friday and there was no school the next day, Lacey pulled out the bag of crafts she'd bought, and she and Emma made stretchy bracelets for Emma's friends. Some had beads and some were just plain, but the important thing was that Emma was happy again.

As Lacey crawled into bed, she wondered why Gabe

had left so quickly. He had been in a good mood earlier and as sweet as he could be. She smiled at that description. The grouch had turned into a sweetie. She curled up in bed and it hit her.

'Cause we love you.

She sat up. That was it. Gabe was afraid she was taking his attention for more than it was. The silly man. They were both holding on by their fingernails, and neither was ready for a serious relationship. Couldn't he see that? Silly, silly man. Tomorrow she would set him straight.

The morning didn't start well. Lacey burned the toast again and the smoke alarm went off. Emma covered her ears until Lacey knocked it off the wall. Gabe rushed through the back door.

"Lacey did it again, Gabe," Emma said.

"It's the toaster," she told him.

He shook his head. "You do know they sell those."

She stuck out her tongue. He ignored her and opened the kitchen window. "Seriously."

"Sit down and I'll fix breakfast."

"I just wanted to make sure everything was okay. I have work to do."

"You have time to eat eggs and toast."

He glanced at the trashcan. "It's burned."

"Oh, please. Like that's never happened before." She inserted more slices of bread.

"You have to watch it, Lacey," Emma said.

"If someone would stop distracting me, I could."

"I couldn't find my shoes."

In minutes she had toast and eggs ready for them. Gabe ate. Emma went to put on her shoes and Lacey slid onto Emma's stool.

"You know, I expect a marriage proposal for this."

His head jerked up.

"Do you really think I'm ready for a relationship? Or that you are? That's what you thought last night when Emma said y'all loved me, didn't you? You thought I wanted more from you than you're willing to give."

"More than I can give."

"I know that, Gabe. So please don't think I'm searching for a wedding dress on the internet."

He smiled and her heart lifted. "You're always surprising me."

"Sometimes I surprise myself."

Emma charged in. "I'm dressed," she announced.

Gabe slid from the stool. "I'm stacking wood to make a fire outside, and this afternoon we can do hot dogs and s'mores. My treat, since you're always cooking for me."

"Can I help you, Gabe? Please," Emma begged.

"If it's okay with your sister."

"Go, but please mind Gabe."

"I will."

Lacey expected him to go out the back door, but instead he went into the garage, got the ladder and put the smoke alarm back up.

"If you're not careful, I will be looking for that wedding dress," she whispered for his ears only.

He winked and ushered Emma out the door.

Lacey sighed and leaned against the cabinet, vowing this day would be a good day and sadness would take a break.

Emma followed Gabe around like a shadow. He made a pile of twigs, short limbs and logs. Emma worked alongside him. He imagined she had helped Jack in the yard. He vaguely remembered a few of those times.

As he worked, he thought of Lacey's comment about him getting scared of commitment. She was right. He wasn't ready for that. It was a little uncanny that she could read him so easily. But then, they had a connection that was all tied up with grief and death. They understood pain and were struggling to find sunshine in their lives. They were becoming good friends, but part of him yearned for much more. He wasn't sure what that was at this point. All he knew was he liked being around Lacey and Emma.

Lacey came over at noon and they stopped for lunch. She had sandwiches made for them. Afterward, he said, "I'm going to the grocery store to get the things we'll need for later."

He felt energized doing something for them.

It was nice to relax and let Gabe do all the work. He had the fire blazing when she walked over and plastic-covered cushions for them to sit on. Emma was hopping around like a grasshopper, helping him. Lacey sat on a cushion, feeling like a queen.

They made hot dogs first, which tasted great after being grilled on the fire. The night air was chilly, but the fire kept them warm. Gabe had all the food on a tray and kept getting up to make sure they had everything they needed. Emma sat in front of the fire between Gabe's legs. He helped her roast a marshmallow and put it on a graham cracker with a piece of chocolate. Emma giggled and basked in Gabe's attention.

Gabe made Lacey one and fed it to her. She felt a little naughty as she ate from his fingers. The glow of the fire warmed them, but she was feeling a different kind of glow.

To still the beating of her heart, she suggested, "Let's sing songs."

"Which one?" Emma asked.

"Christmas songs, of course."

She broke into "Frosty the Snowman" followed by "Jingle Bells" and "Rudolph the Red-Nosed Reindeer." Emma joined in, and when they sang "Deck the Halls," Gabe's deep tones echoed through the night with vivid clarity and spine-tingling emotions.

Overhead, stars were showcased in a spectacular winter sky. Lacey pulled her jacket tighter around her as the temperature continued to drop. Emma's head rested on Gabe's chest. Chocolate was smeared on her face, but Lacey didn't worry about that. Emma had found a remarkable man to fill the empty place left by their father. But it was only temporary.

A chill ran through Lacey. She raised the fur collar of her jacket and scooted closer to Gabe. He looped an arm around her, and they sat listening to the snap and crackle of the fire. It was peaceful and relaxing, and Lacey allowed herself to drift into a fairy tale. She could see herself in a beautiful white gown walking down the aisle to a man with dark eyes. But she was old enough to know fairy tales didn't exist. And she'd told Gabe she wasn't interested in a relationship.

She'd lied.

Chapter 13

The days passed too quickly for Lacey. Christmas was two weeks away and Emma hadn't changed her mind about Santa. The Christmas tree stood by the windows looking like a lonely soldier needing a hug. She had considered taking it down, but she would follow Gabe's advice and go slow.

He ate with them every day without complaining or making a quick exit. Having a man around was nice, especially since he was handsome and made her happy just to see him. It was too late to chide herself for letting her heart get involved. Gabe was a part of her life, but she didn't know for how much longer. She was grateful for every day and grateful he'd survived the biggest tragedy of his life. Whatever happened next would be up to them.

She still had to make arrangements to visit her mom

before Christmas. Time seemed to be running out and she had a lot to do before the big day arrived. The number one goal today was to put the bicycle together. After dropping Emma at school, she hurried over to Gabe's. He sat on the floor in an empty bedroom with parts of the bike laid out.

She stared at all the bolts, screws and pieces. "When they say you have to put it together, they're not kidding."

Gabe looked up from a page of instructions. "It's really not that hard."

"I'll take your word for it." She held up the bag in her hand. "I brought paper, ribbon and tape to wrap Emma's other gifts."

She sat down and went to work. But she kept looking up to watch him, and the way his hands and arms worked with confidence and ease. His hair was really getting long. Today he had it combed back, and it hung past the collar of his T-shirt.

"Have you always worn your hair long?"

He didn't even look up as he attached the front wheel. "No. I got a haircut about two months after I moved here from the only barber shop in town. It's run by two old cowboys and they asked a lot of questions. They were just being friendly, but I wasn't in a friendly mood, so I never went back."

"It gives you a roguish-outlaw look."

He sat back on his heels, his eyes gleaming. "You like roguish outlaws?"

"If they have dark eyes."

He pointed a wrench at her. "You're distracting me."

"Me? I'm just wrapping presents."

"Mmm." He went back to the bicycle with total concentration, or at least it appeared that way.

She finished the gifts and stacked them in a corner. When she turned around, Gabe stood there with the bicycle completed.

"Oh, it's beautiful. I have to go to the house to get ribbon to put around the basket. It has to have a red bow. I'll be right back."

In a matter of minutes she had returned. She threaded a ribbon around the white basket and finished it with a big bow.

"Do you put a bow on everything?"

She straightened with a piece of ribbon in her hand. "Yes." And before he could stop her, she caught his hair and looped the ribbon around and tied it.

"Take it out," he said in a warning voice, moving closer to her.

"No. I like it." She took a step backward.

"Take it out."

"No." She stood her ground for a split second before he grabbed her. He held her hands up to his face. Their eyes met and everything faded away except the feelings between them. His head dipped and his lips captured hers in a time-standing-still type of kiss. The laughter and playfulness turned into serious emotional need. She wrapped her arms around his neck and pressed her body into his, loving the feel of his hard angles against her softer ones.

The kiss went on and on until they finally sank to the floor. His hand slipped under her blouse and touched her breast. An ache shot through her—a familiar ache she welcomed. She ran her fingers through his hair, loving the thick texture and the scent of manly shampoo.

Just when she thought the world would spin away, her

cell phone rang. It took a moment for her to realize what the sound was. Gabe pulled away, back in total control.

She crawled on her hands and knees to her purse and found her phone. She couldn't let it keep buzzing. It could be about Emma. It wasn't. When Lacey saw it was her mother, she wasn't going to answer, but one look at Gabe's face and she knew the moment had passed.

"Hi, Mom."

"You haven't called about Christmas."

Christmas was the last thing she wanted to talk about right now. "I was thinking next week one day. When can you be free?"

"Christmas Day."

Lacey wanted to pound the phone on the floor, but instead she replied, "You know that's out of the question unless you plan to come to Horseshoe."

"I guess I'm pushed aside for any old day."

Gabe put tools back into his toolbox, and Lacey was very aware of the frown on his face. Her mother's words went right over her head. "How about next Wednesday?"

"You know it's hard for me to get off during the holidays. We're so busy."

"Whatever, Mom. I've told you what I can do. I don't know what else to say except that I love you and I'd love to spend some time with you."

A heavy pause followed. "Wednesday will be fine. You can pick me up at work and we'll go to a nice restaurant."

"That sounds good. I'll see you then."

Lacey clicked off, stunned that had been so easy. Three little words had worked magic. She glanced up to see Gabe staring at her. She wondered if they would work on him. But she would never put him in that position.

"Your mom, huh?" He closed the toolbox with a snap.

"Yeah, she's finally agreed on a day for us to visit."

"I'm glad you're trying to work things out."

She disliked the stilted conversation. "Gabe, could we talk?"

"I thought we were talking." He wrapped his arms around his knees and stared at her.

"I mean about what just happened between us."

"Lacey…"

"I'm attracted to you. I think you know that, and I don't want to lie about it or pretend I'm not."

The silence stretched before he finally said, "I'm attracted to you, too. I like touching you, holding you and kissing you. And I shouldn't. I still have a long way to go for full recovery, and I don't want to hurt you."

She crawled on the hardwood floor to him and sat beside him. "You really do need furniture. Do you know that?"

A smile touched his lips. "You have a knack for lightening a mood."

"Because there shouldn't be a mood. We're both adults. What happens between us is our business, and I think we're mature enough to handle it."

He stretched out his legs and leaned back on his hands. "I can't get serious about anyone right now. I have a past I'll have to face someday. I don't want you caught in the middle."

She tickled his nose with a piece of ribbon. "You worry too much. Now, I have to go. It's my day to help out at school and I have to change. Do you mind if I leave the bicycle and gifts here until Christmas Eve?"

"No problem. But I'd better put them in the closet in case the kiddo comes in here."

After everything was stored in the closet, Lacey said, "I'll see you later."

She didn't try to kiss him or touch him because she knew he was struggling with his feelings. She was, too, but somehow she knew what she wanted. Only time would tell if it was real or just the result of being thrown together as next-door neighbors at a time when they'd each needed someone.

The next few days were hectic. The kids in Emma's class were rehearsing for the Christmas program. The girls were told to wear red and the boys were to wear black pants and white shirts. Emma wanted a new dress for the occasion, so they decided to go to the mall on Saturday.

Lacey only saw Gabe at mealtime. He was building a storage shed in his backyard. He seemed to have a need to stay busy. Lacey understood that, but she felt he was putting distance between them. That made her sad, but she was learning the hard way to go slow.

On Wednesday, when she drove to the school to drop off Emma, Mrs. Fillmore was waiting outside. Lacey had wanted to get away quickly so she could leave for Austin to see her mother. Emma had been exceptionally good the past week, so Lacey couldn't imagine what the teacher wanted.

Lacey kissed Emma, who ran off to meet Jimmy.

"Hello, Lacey."

"Good morning, Mrs. Fillmore."

"I know you do a lot for Emma's class, but I'd like to ask one more favor. Most of the mothers work, and I'm not getting any assistance for the Christmas program. I need someone to help me get the children on the stage where they need to be. It just takes a little patience."

"I'll be happy to help. It's next Friday, right?"

"Yes, and thank you. I'm so happy Emma is adjusting after her father's death."

"Me, too," Lacey admitted.

Mrs. Fillmore turned toward the school. "I'll let you know details next week. Have a nice day."

Lacey drove home and dressed for the day in a print skirt, silk blouse and leather boots. Her mother would expect more than jeans. She hadn't told Emma where she was going because Emma would have wanted to go, too, and explaining her mother's feelings would be difficult. She had Gabe's number on her phone, so if she was running late or had problems, she could call him to pick up Emma.

As she brushed her hair, she thought she'd better let Gabe know her plans. She slipped on the cashmere jacket her mother had given her last year for Christmas and went next door.

Gabe was busy laying forms so the concrete company could pour the foundation for the shed. He looked up and saw a woman standing near his deck. Who was she? And what did she want? He got to his feet and walked toward her. The closer he got he realized it was Lacey, all dressed up and looking as beautiful as he'd ever seen her.

He wiped his hands on his jeans. "I didn't recognize you at first."

She lifted an eyebrow. "Is that good or bad?"

"I'm not sure." He was honest. "I feel as if I don't

know you." He looked her up and down. "You're very different from the woman in jeans who makes me smile."

She leaned over and whispered, "I can still make you smile." A whiff of a delicate fragrance reached him, and he wanted to reach out and take her in his arms. He had the urge to get to know this Lacey. And he shouldn't. He was so tired of resisting when everything he wanted was right in front of him.

She nodded toward the forms. "Are you going to be home all day?"

"Where else would I be?"

"As you can see—" she waved a hand down her body "—I'm dressed to go visit my mother, and I wanted to make sure if I have a problem with getting back—like traffic or car problems—that someone will be there to pick up Emma. My go-to person is you. Can you help me out?"

"Just let me know and I'll be there."

She hugged him, and he wrapped his arms around her and held her for a moment. They stood there in the chilly day, and he was never more aware of how much this crazy lady had taken over his heart.

"Gotta go. I'll see you tonight. Bye."

She sashayed toward the gate, and he couldn't stop watching. Resisting wasn't an option anymore. She was pulling him in hook, line and sinker. And he wasn't panicking.

The traffic on I-35 was bad, but Lacey was still early for her lunch with her mother. They'd decided to meet at the restaurant. Lacey parked and went inside. Her mother had made a reservation, so Lacey was shown to a table immediately. The restaurant was very upscale with soft music playing in the background. It wasn't long before her mother arrived.

Lacey stood to hug her. Her mother was a blonde with green eyes, just like Lacey. At fifty-two, she looked more like thirty-five. Her mother had always taken care of her appearance. Today she wore a designer dress with silver earrings, a necklace and high heels.

"It's good to see you," her mother said as she took a seat. "I'm not crazy about the short hair, but it's your hair. And at your age you need to start using more makeup."

Lacey counted to three and then asked, "How's Mervin?"

"Fine. He wants me to move in with him, but I'm just not ready for that."

Her mother never shared these types of things, so Lacey was startled for a moment. Mervin was the type of man her mother should have married. He was in insurance and she assumed he was reasonably well-off.

Lacey placed a napkin in her lap. "Do you mean he wants to get married?"

Her mother glanced up, her perfectly made-up face revealing a wrinkle or two. "Of course, I would never move in with a man without marriage. I jumped into marriage too fast the second time, and I am not doing it again."

"Do you love him?"

The waiter came with menus and they ordered drinks.

"Love is for young folks," her mother said as soon as the waiter was out of earshot. "I just don't want to be alone for the rest of my life."

Guilt slashed across Lacey's conscience. Her mother had always lived her life her way, but Lacey still felt guilty for not spending more time with her.

Joyce opened her menu. "The scallops are really delicious here, and I know how you love them."

Her mother changed the subject quickly, and Lacey let it drop because she didn't know what else to say. They had a pleasant meal and chatted like strangers, not like a mother and daughter who had their ups and downs.

Lacey decided to talk about the holidays. "I wish you would come for Christmas. I want you to. Does that mean anything?"

Joyce laid her napkin on the table very carefully. "I just can't be around that child."

Lacey bit her tongue and prayed for patience. Going on her gut instinct that her mother wasn't as coldhearted as she seemed, she reached into her purse and pulled out a small photo album she kept of Emma. She opened it and laid it on the table near her mother's napkin.

"Look at Emma. She has blond hair and green eyes and looks like me." Joyce picked up her napkin and wiped her mouth, ignoring the photo. "Look, Mom. She's just a little girl. She doesn't know about divorce or resentment or regrets. She's only knows she's lost her daddy and it's still hard for her to accept. That's why she clings to me. I'm the only person there for her. Look at her, Mom."

Her mother finally glanced at the photo album. Lacey flipped it to the next picture and the next.

"She has blond hair and green eyes just like us," Joyce commented. "How is that possible?"

"Mona's eyes were green, but Emma's are lighter

like mine and yours. I don't know how it's possible. I just know that it is."

"Her hair and everything about her reminds me of you when you were that age."

"Everyone who meets us comments on how alike we look."

"You were always your father's daughter."

Lacey wasn't sure how to respond to that, so she didn't, hoping it wasn't going to lead to another argument.

"Sometimes I felt left out. Your father took you to ball games and fairs and carnivals and fishing. Not once did he ask me to go."

Lacey was dumbstruck. "Because you didn't want to," Lacey reminded her.

Joyce waved a hand. "That's beside the point. It would have been nice to have been included sometimes."

"I'm sorry if we shut you out."

"And I'm sorry about a lot of things. It's hard to explain my feelings about Emma. I know they're wrong," Joyce said, leaning back in her chair. "Your father always wanted another child and I kept putting it off. I started having female problems and had to have a hysterectomy. It was too late then."

"I never knew you wanted another child."

Her mother glanced in the direction of a waiter who was clearing a table. "Jack and I argued about it all the time. I regret not listening to him more. I regret so many things, and when I see his child with another woman, I'm filled with such anger, and it's all directed at me. I screwed up our lives and I have only myself to blame."

Lacey's breath caught at her mother's obvious pain. So

many years and she was learning things about her mother that she'd never known. "But Emma's not to blame. She has no grandmothers, only an aunt who doesn't know her. I'm all she has, Mom. She could use you in her life."

"Please don't ask that of me."

Lacey reached across the table and took her mother's hand. Joyce gripped it tightly. "Emma and I need you. Think about that."

They walked to their vehicles in silence. Lacey gave her mother a gift and she accepted one from her. "I'm not going to open this. I'll keep it until Christmas, hoping you'll change your mind."

They hugged and Lacey said, "I love you, Mom." She got in her car and drove away. In her rearview mirror she could see her mother still standing in the parking lot, looking lonely and alone.

Why did life have to be so hard?

Lunch had run long, and Lacey was in a hurry to get back to Horseshoe. She didn't want to be late to pick up Emma, but there was a wreck on I-35 and the traffic was backed up for miles.

She hit the steering wheel with the palm of her hand. "Damn it!"

Thirty minutes later the traffic still hadn't moved, and she knew she wasn't going to make it. She had Mrs. Fillmore's private number, so she called and told her the situation. Thank God the teacher had a heart of gold. She let Emma talk to Lacey on the phone.

"Sweetie, I'm caught in traffic and Gabe will pick you up. Okay?"

"Where are you?"

"On a highway and I can't get to school on time because someone had a wreck in front of me."

"Are you gonna come get me?"

Lacey's heart sank and she repeated, "Sweetie, Gabe will be there. I'll come as soon as the traffic clears."

"'Kay."

Clicking off, she immediately called Gabe. She tapped her fingers on the steering wheel, hoping Emma wasn't going to be upset. After another thirty minutes, the traffic began to move, and she zoomed toward Horseshoe.

It was 3:30 p.m. when she pulled into her driveway. She expected Emma to be in the front yard bawling her eyes out. She wasn't, but that didn't mean she was okay. Lacey jumped out of the car, yanked open the front door, ran through the house, out the back door and through the gate.

She stopped suddenly. Gabe and Emma were working on the concrete forms. Emma knelt in the dirt with a hammer and was beating on something. Gabe was beside her, talking and giving instructions. Emma chatted away, comfortable with Gabe and unafraid. She was okay. Lacey was, too. She took a long breath and relaxed.

Everything was perfect. Just perfect.

Chapter 14

Gabe looked up, saw Lacey and whispered to Emma. Her sister jumped up and ran toward her, screeching, "Lacey! Lacey! Lacey! You're home."

Lacey caught her and lifted her into her arms, kissing her cold cheeks. "Are you okay?"

"Yeah. Gabe picked me up and we're busy working."

"I see." No tears. No fears in her beautiful green eyes. She was adjusting, and that was the best Christmas gift Lacey could receive.

Emma wiggled to get down. "I have to help Gabe."

Gabe had ambled over by then and she smiled into his dark, warm eyes. "Thank you."

"No problem."

"We got ice cream, Lacey."

"You did? That was a treat."

"Yeah. Now we have to get back to work."

Lacey hated to burst her bubble. "Sweetie, it's homework time, and I have to get supper started. You can help Gabe tomorrow."

Emma scrunched up her face. "Aw, Lacey."

Gabe squatted in front of Emma. "Tell you what, kiddo. I'm going to get cleaned up. While you're doing homework, I'll go to the diner and get supper for us. Lacey's had a rough day."

He glanced at her and as he said the last words, she thought if this wasn't love, she didn't know what was. The revelation shook her. She'd considered herself in love with Darin, but the feelings she had for Gabe were different. It was as if he held her heart in his hand and he had to squeeze it for her to breathe. Without him... She stopped herself. These feelings were too new, too soon, and she had to stop weaving dreams that weren't meant to be. She could breathe perfectly well on her own, thank you very much.

She vowed not to overthink their relationship. For now, she would enjoy his company and be thankful that he was growing stronger and stronger emotionally.

The days that followed were easygoing. Gabe continued to work on the storage shed, and she was busy helping Mrs. Fillmore with the school program. Since she wasn't home much during the day, they had very little time alone with Emma there. But it gave Lacey a chance to figure out exactly what she was feeling. She wasn't sure love was supposed to happen that quickly. But then she was a sucker for love at first...grouch.

On Saturday, Lacey and Emma went to the mall in Temple to buy a dress for the program. It was a big mistake. The mall was crowded and it was hard to shop, but they finally found a dress that Emma liked and so did Lacey. It was red with a black-and-red polka-dot ribbon around the waist.

Emma wanted to get something for her teacher, so they searched for that, all the while fighting the crowds. The chatter and noise was loud and festive, and the piped-in Christmas music filled their ears. As they walked toward the entrance, they passed Santa's Wonderland, where a long line stretched into the crowd.

Lacey didn't say anything to Emma and they kept walking. It took everything in Lacey not to point out Santa. But she would not force Emma. That was more important.

Suddenly, Emma stopped and looked back. "I want to talk to Santa."

This was more than Lacey had hoped for. "Um… okay." She had no idea what Emma wanted to say, but Lacey was going to give her the opportunity. Maybe, just maybe, a miracle might happen.

They stood in line for fifteen minutes before they reached Santa.

"Hi, little girl." Santa patted his knee. "Hop right up and tell Santa what you want for Christmas."

Emma crawled onto his knee and stared him straight in the eye. "You're not real."

Lacey gasped and hoped the kid behind her didn't hear. She'd had no idea her sister was going to be this blunt.

Santa was taken aback, but only for a moment. "You don't say. You're awfully young to think that way."

"But it's true."

"Now, I know I'm not the real Santa. He's at the North Pole, awfully busy getting ready to deliver a lot of gifts to children all over the world. I'm just one of his helpers, taking children's wishes back to him."

The expression of stubbornness on Emma's face changed to one of confusion. She wasn't quite sure anymore. Lacey knew her that well. Yes! She wanted to raise her fist in the air, but she waited to hear Emma's next words.

"'Kay. I'll tell you what I want for Christmas, and if it comes true, I'll know Santa is real." Then she did something that made Lacey want to scream. She whispered into the man's ear. Lacey couldn't hear a word. She stepped closer, but the noise of the crowd prevented her from hearing.

"Santa can do some things, but others he can't. Just never stop believing," the man said, and Emma slipped off his lap.

Lacey took Emma's hand and they walked out of the mall. One way or another she was going to get Emma to tell her what she had asked Santa for.

As Lacey buckled her seat belt, she glanced at Emma. "Santa was nice."

"He's just a helper."

Lacey started the car and backed out of the parking spot, trying to be patient. "But you believe what he said to you?"

"I told him what I wanted for Christmas, and if I get it, then I'll know."

One. Two. Three. Be patient.

"What did you ask for, sweetie?"

"I can't tell you, because then I won't know if Santa is real."

Evidently a six-year-old was smarter than Lacey. Emma refused to say what she wanted for Christmas no matter how many times Lacey tried to turn the conversation in that direction. It wouldn't come true if she told Lacey, she kept saying. Lacey would give her time, but she had to find out. Above all else, she wanted Emma to believe.

Gabe spent the morning in Horseshoe. He stopped at a resale shop and bought a patio table and chairs for the deck. He'd seen the set as he'd passed by and had decided that he needed it. At the hardware store he purchased a barbecue pit. He was making hamburgers for Lacey and Emma that night. From there, he went to the grocery store.

He had just finished setting things up when Lacey walked over. From her dazed expression, he knew her mind was somewhere else. She sank into one of the cushioned wrought iron chairs as if it had always been there.

He leaned against the table. "What's wrong?"

"Emma talked to Santa at the mall."

"Well, that's good. It's what you want, isn't it?" He wasn't sure because her expression didn't change.

"She told him what she wanted by whispering it to him, and now I don't know what it is. I'm trying to figure out a way to get it out of her. Nothing's working. She's adamant that if she gets what she asked for, then she'll know that Santa is real." Lacey's eyes narrowed in thought. "Think I'll go back to the mall and try to talk to the Santa and see if he'll tell me. I'll make him tell me."

"S-l-o-w." Gabe spelled out the word patiently and her head jerked up. "You're getting obsessed with this, and you need to take a deep breath, stop and think.

Emma has taken a step forward, so you have to continue to let this happen naturally."

She ran both hands through her hair and fluffed it like he'd seen her do so many times when she was worried. "But if she doesn't get what she asked for, then she'll never believe and I'll..."

"You'll love her and you'll be there for her like you always are. So, please, calm down and just take it slow."

"Why are you always—" She touched the cushion beneath her. "What am I sitting on?"

"A chair cushion."

She jumped up and looked at the patio set. "You bought some furniture." Her eyes went to the barbecue pit. "And a barbecue pit. You're settling in and nesting."

Unable to resist, he pulled her into his arms. "Men don't nest."

"Mmm." She splayed her hands across his chest, and he felt their warmth all the way to his heart. She had that effect on him. "Men hunt. Isn't that a quote from Jerry Seinfeld? So what did you hunt us up for supper?"

"Hamburger meat. And it was hell beating little old ladies to it in the grocery store."

She laughed, a bubbly sound that relaxed every muscle in his body, and at the same time tightened them in a well remembered way.

"Where's Emma?"

"Inside. Jimmy was waiting in our driveway, and they're playing with Legos. I better go check on them. I just had to vent to someone, and you're my go-to guy."

"Happy to be the go-to guy. Come over later and we'll do the hamburgers."

She went down the deck steps and he called, "And stop obsessing."

She stuck out her tongue and made her way to the gate. It seemed like forever since he'd nailed the gate shut. He'd been in that deep, dark hole. Unreachable. Safe. And dying a little each day. She'd had the nerve to bring him back, and a part of him would always be grateful for that. Even though his other life waited, he couldn't see beyond this time here in Horseshoe with Lacey and Emma. If he was living in a fool's paradise, it was the best place on earth.

Lacey spent the entire weekend trying to coax Emma into telling her what she wanted for Christmas. After a couple of dark looks from Gabe, she gave up. He was right, as always. It would work out the way it was meant to be, and she had to accept that.

After she left Emma at school on Monday, she put on her sweats and grabbed her iPod. Gabe had started running every morning and she planned to join him. She really needed the exercise.

Gabe walked out of his house and she met him in the front yard. He gave her a quick glance in the sweats. "What are you doing?"

She jogged in place. "I'm running with you this morning."

"I go fast and I don't stop for anything."

"I go slow and stop for everything. My attention span is not that great."

He lifted an eyebrow. "Mmm."

"I'll hang with you until I drop."

He took off down the driveway and into the street. She followed and tried to keep up with him, but she soon found his long strides too much. Somewhere around the two-mile mark she collapsed on a curb, breathing heavily.

"You okay?" he shouted back.

She waved a hand. "I'm fine."

Her heart ping-ponged inside her chest with painful thuds, reminding her she was in dismal shape. She really needed to work out every day. And she would, just as soon as she could feel her legs again.

Two cars stopped, their drivers asking Lacey if she was okay. She muttered something and they drove on. Mrs. Hornsby, on whose curb Lacey was sitting, came out and asked if she'd like a cup of coffee. The last thing she needed was coffee, but she thanked her, and the elderly lady left Lacey to her misery.

It was about 8:30 a.m. and it was nice sitting there in the cool morning. Or it would be when she could breathe normally. The winter grass was brown and brittle, and the trees had lost their leaves and stood out like stick figures against the cold. A squirrel darted across the street and up one of the trees. Several green cedars stood out in prominence as if waiting to be decorated. That reminded her of the poor Douglas fir in her living room. It probably would never be adorned with the bright colors of Christmas. She wouldn't force Emma, but it was taking a toll on Lacey's Christmas spirit.

She was about to get up when she saw Gabe jogging toward her. He wasn't even breathing hard. He squatted in front of her with his back to her.

"Hop on."

"Gabe…"

"Come on. I need coffee."

She did as he'd asked, feeling a little foolish and very

young. He fitted his arms under her knees and took off toward their houses.

She wrapped her arms around his neck. "I really can walk, you know."

"You're too slow."

"You've wanted me to go slow."

"Different situation. And stop talking. It uses up too much oxygen."

She rested her face in the crook his neck and drew in the manly scent of soap and sweat. It revived her senses.

"I have Oreos and coffee waiting."

He didn't answer, just jogged up her sidewalk through the front door and dropped onto her sofa. He fell one way and she went the other. He was exhausted and she was laughing. She couldn't help herself. Then they both were laughing like teenagers.

"Well, we've given the neighbors something to talk about."

"Yeah." He rested his head back against the sofa. "Things were getting too boring."

She rose on her knees beside him. "I'll have you know I'm never boring."

He turned to look at her with a half grin. "Now, that's the gospel truth."

She poked him in the ribs, and he pulled her onto his lap, his lips finding hers with heat-seeking accuracy. She curled her arms around his neck. Her fingers tangled in his hair, and she reveled in the fire building between them. His lips were cold and hot at the same time and she felt that heat in the regions of her body that really needed it. He groaned and she opened her mouth. The kiss deepened to the point they both needed—somewhere between fantasy and reality. His lips trailed to her cheek and then to her neck. Her skin ached from his touch, and it ignited her senses into full-blown arousal. When she straddled him, not even thinking of consequences, and pressed her body against his, he pulled his mouth away.

"S-l-o-w." Each letter came out ragged, but she knew he meant it. They were going too fast. "You said something about Oreos and coffee."

She kissed the tip of his nose. "I had something else in mind."

"I know. I did, too, but…"

She slid from his lap. "I really hate that word—*but*." She walked into the kitchen and poured coffee for both of them and then found the cookies. He took the cups to the table and she followed, feeling as if she'd already had too much caffeine. Her nerves were jiggy and she was hyped up. It was all about sex, which she hadn't really thought about in a long time. And that was good.

After sitting at the table, she opened the cookies and handed him two. She was about to add cream and sugar to her cup when she noticed the dark liquid. It reminded her of his incredible eyes. She didn't need the coffee. All she had to do was look into his gaze and she'd receive the same thrill, the same lift and the same warm feeling.

Even so, she took a sip and looked at him over the rim. "Are you freaked out yet?"

"A little," he admitted to her surprise. "I've never felt about anyone the way I feel about you. I know we're both adults, but I come with a lot of baggage, and I don't want to drag you down."

She reached out and touched his arm. "Let me worry about that. I'm a big girl. I've been on a date before and in a serious relationship, so I know about pain and dis-illusionment."

He dipped an Oreo into his coffee. "But…"

She groaned. "No buts."

"The concrete people are coming today, so I better get moving." He drained his cup and stood.

"Are you running scared?"

"You betcha. You scare the hell out of me and make me feel things I haven't felt in years. So yeah, it makes me want to run."

"But not too far."

He winked and walked out the door. She finished her coffee and three Oreos. Then she got up and went to take a cold shower.

Gabe hurried inside his house, took a shower and changed clothes. A rumble of thunder echoed, and he walked to the window to look outside. The clouds had darkened, and rain softly splattered the ground. His cell phone buzzed, and he reached for it on the bed. It was the concrete company to notify him they wouldn't be coming because of the rain.

He stayed at the window and continued to watch. The rain would screw up his forms. He'd have to redo them tomorrow or whenever it stopped raining. The dirt around Pepper's grave was sinking in, and he'd have to order more dirt to fill it in.

Drawing a long sigh, he went into the kitchen and made a pot of coffee. He would just as soon have it with Lacey, but being around her was getting harder and harder. Most of the time he was frustrated, because the feelings between them were getting hotter and hotter. Soon he'd have to make up his mind about what he wanted to do: love her or admit they had no future.

He turned and saw the photos of Zack on the wall. Most of the time he would stop and look at them and remember the day each photo was taken and remember all the love and happiness that had filled his heart. But he couldn't live in the past. He already knew that.

He marched to his bedroom and pulled his briefcase out of the closet. It was empty because he'd left all of his work on his desk the day he'd left his law firm. He took it into the kitchen and laid it on the table. One by one he took down the photos. He didn't study them or remember. It was just as Lacey had said. All those memories were in his heart and they always would be. When the briefcase was full, he carried it back to his room and stored it in the closet. Tomorrow he'd work on the ones in the living room. First, he'd have to find something to put them in.

Ironically, as the rain continued to tap against the windows he didn't feel sad. He felt a release, a freedom—a freedom to move forward with his life without guilt. Without regrets. Without pain.

But he would take it slow, just as he'd told Lacey to do so many times. In the days ahead he would know what his future held.

Chapter 15

On Wednesday, Lacey dashed over to Gabe's for a minute. The night before, he'd worked late on the shed after they had poured the concrete to make sure no stray dogs or cats or birds could mess up his work. Emma had gone over and written her name in the wet cement with a stick. But Lacey had had no time alone with him.

Gabe wasn't outside, which was a surprise. She knocked on the door and he opened it immediately with a cup of coffee in his hand.

"Morning," he said. "Would you like a cup?" She didn't need coffee. All she had to do was look at him and the warm fuzzies started.

"No, thanks. I'm on my way back to the school with cupcakes and stuff for the classroom party." She walked in and he closed the door. "It's the last week of school before the holidays and Mrs. Fillmore has roped me into doing all kinds of things. I just wanted to tell you that we won't be home this evening. We have the last rehearsal for the program on Friday. I'm thinking of dressing as an elf in green Lycra."

"Now, I'd go to see that."

She moved closer to him. "Would you?"

"You bet." The line of his lower lip curved into a smile and she had the urge to kiss it and to never stop. Instead, she moved into his arms.

He placed his cup on the counter and enveloped her in his warm embrace, and she floated away on that feeling.

"You feel so good," she whispered.

He took a step back. "We'd better stop because you have to go to school. Remember?"

"Oh, yeah. Mrs. Fillmore."

He tucked her hair behind her ear and then touched the frown on her face. "What's bothering you?"

She heaved a sigh. "Emma's friend Bailey is having a birthday/slumber party on Friday night and she's invited Emma. That's a problem. Since Dad passed away, Emma hasn't been away from me except to go to school. She's all excited about it, but I'm just not sure. I feel she's too little to stay away at night."

"Then say no."

"But… I can't believe I'm saying *but*."

He cupped her face in his hands and she lost all train of thought. "Don't think it to death. Things might change by Friday, but if she wants to go I would support her and encourage her. She's improved so much."

She rested her face against his chest and stared at a blank wall. Then she pulled back quickly. "The photos are gone."

"I took them down the other day. It was time. I still have the ones in the living room, but I intend to take them down, too."

She threw her arms around his neck and hugged him. "I'm so proud of you."

He held her against him, and their emotions began to swirl into another direction. Lacey pulled away. "I really have to go. I don't want to, but…" She laughed.

He laughed with her. It was an effort to leave him. The grouchy man had disappeared and in his place stood a man who was becoming more and more a part of her life. She didn't freak out. And neither did he. That was the good part. Christmas was going to be wonderful.

Lacey made it through the week. The children's program went off with a few glitches, but they were six-year-olds so everyone laughed and understood. All the kids, including Emma, were eager to be out of school for the holiday. She chatted on and on about Bailey's party. Lacey had decided to let her go. She had talked to Bailey's mother and the woman understood the situation and had said she would call if Emma became distressed.

But Emma appeared fine as she marched to the front door with her little suitcase in hand. Bailey and her mother stood there. Emma waved and Lacey had to force herself to drive away. What if Emma needed her?

Go slow. Don't obsess. She repeated the words several times until she felt better.

She kept her cell phone in her pocket as she fixed dinner for her and Gabe. It was going to be special. She'd gotten the menu of salmon, fresh asparagus and roasted potatoes from the internet.

Gabe was outside framing the shed. It wasn't long before he knocked at her back door and came in. When she saw him, the spoon in her hand clattered to the tiled floor. She hardly recognized him. He'd cut his hair into a neat, short style. She could only stare. He was clean shaven and his hair was damp from a shower. He'd made an effort for tonight, and her pulse soared at the thought. His dark good looks and light blue shirt held her attention. It was the first time she'd seen him in any color other than black.

She smiled at him. "Love the look."

He touched his head. "I braved the barbershop again and it wasn't so bad. I found this shirt in my closet." He slid onto a bar stool. "How did it go with Emma?"

"So far so good." Lacey picked up the spoon from the floor and put it in the sink. "I'm the only one feeling a little stressed. I just don't want her to panic when she realizes I'm not there."

"If that happens, someone will call you."

She placed some cheese and grapes in front of him. "I've figured that out. So I'm trying to relax." She reached for the bottle of wine on the counter and handed it to him. "And looking forward to relaxing a little more."

"I see."

They drank wine, talked, ate and enjoyed just being together. They cleaned the kitchen and then took their wine to the living room. A college-bowl game was on television and Gabe wanted to watch.

"You like football?" she asked.

"Doesn't every guy?"

She curled into his side, trying to show interest in the game, but with his body so close that was impossible. She picked up his hand and linked her fingers with his bigger ones.

"Can I ask you a question?"

"Sure." He looked at her then.

"How do you see this night ending?"

"I'm hoping the Tigers will win," he said, deadpan.

"Um… I'm not talking about the game. I…" He pushed her down on the sofa and her voice trailed off.

"Your lips need a little red."

She giggled like a silly schoolgirl.

His lips met hers and she wrapped her arms around his neck, reveling in his touch and the feel of him. His hand slid beneath her sweater to her breast, creating a vibrating need within her.

"Too many clothes," he breathed. With one swift movement he stood and swept her into his arms.

As he headed for the hallway, she said, "First door on the left."

They didn't bother with the light. She slid from his arms, their bodies never losing contact. Clothes became an encumbrance and soon they were scattered on the floor as they frantically helped each other. His boots took more time to shed than either of them wanted. A bubble of laughter erupted as they fell onto the bed, arms and legs entwined. This was the way it should be. Warm skin. Male skin. So rough. So enticing. So what she needed.

"Lacey…" His ragged voice seemed to come from far away, but she heard the question in it.

"Don't think," she whispered. "Please."

His lips left the well of her mouth and trailed to her breast, and she wanted to scream from the sheer bliss of his breath on her sensitive nipple. His hands touched every part of her while hers were equally at work on him. Her fingers found the taut muscles of his arms, shoulders, rib cage and then moved lower. She'd never touched anything as heavenly as his aroused body.

It could have been seconds, minutes or an hour before his body finally joined with hers. All she knew was it was the most exquisite pleasure she'd ever experienced. She welcomed him with a fever that brought them both to the brink of total ecstasy.

Somewhere between need and the ecstasy, she moaned, "I love you."

He stilled for a moment, but didn't say the words back. She hadn't expected them, but she had to admit it hurt a little. The sting vanished as he gathered her into his arms and rocked her gently. They lay entwined, their bodies bathed in sweat, their breathing less labored. Lacey didn't want to ever move again. She wanted this moment to last forever, with their skin touching and the world unable to intrude and ruin the moment.

A nagging chime roused her. Her cell phone! She jumped from bed and reached for it in the pocket of her jeans on the floor. It was Bailey's mother.

She quickly clicked on and glanced at the clock. It was barely 8:00 p.m. "Hello."

"Lacey, it's Denise. I hate to bother you, but I think Emma wants to come home. She's said about four times that it's dark and Lacey is probably scared."

"Can I talk to her, please?"

Emma came on the line quickly. "Hi, Lacey."

"You want to come home, sweetie?"

"Yes." No hesitation. No doubt.

"I'll be right there."

"It's dark, Lacey."

"I know. Get your suitcase. I'm on my way."

Lacey hurriedly slipped into jeans and pulled her top over her head.

Gabe sat up in bed. "Is Emma okay?"

"She just wants to come home. I'll be right back." She started for the door and then turned. "Please don't overthink what I said. We'll talk about it later."

Within seconds, she was in the car and backing out of the driveway. She so badly wanted to go back inside and be with Gabe, but Emma pulled her in another direction. Emma was more important this time.

Gabe scooted to the edge of the bed and ran his hands over his face. What had he done? He'd gone with his feelings, but now it felt wrong. Lacey loved him, and that wasn't supposed to happen. He wasn't ready. He needed her, but need wasn't love. Oh, man. He'd screwed up and now he had to hurt her. That would kill him.

He found his clothes and slipped into them. In the kitchen, he poured the little bit of wine that was left down the drain, washed the wineglasses and put them away. He went out the back door and to his house. As he entered, loneliness engulfed him and a smothering feeling came over him. He took a couple of deep breaths. His chest ached and his emotions were raw.

He should've thought the situation over a little more, but he'd wanted her. At the time that had been all that had mattered. But now her emotions were involved and his were still steeped in the past. He'd come a long way, but he wasn't ready for a serious relationship. Lacey should have a man who could love her for who she really was, not a man who was still struggling to get through each day. Now he would have to step back and disappear from her life. But he didn't know how to do that. Breaking her heart would also break his. He needed her, but he didn't love her the way she deserved.

How did he tell her that?

It started to drizzle as Lacey parked in front of Bailey's house. The umbrella was somewhere, but she didn't take time to look for it. Emma was standing at the front door in her pj's, her suitcase in hand. Denise stood behind her.

Lacey jumped out, ran up the walk, spoke to Denise and lifted Emma into her arms. Without another word she ran to the car as the rain started in earnest. She put Emma in her booster seat and dashed to the driver's side.

Emma didn't say anything as Lacey drove the three blocks to their house. As she parked in the garage, she noticed that Emma was sound asleep. She lifted her out of the car and carried her into the house. Emma awoke as Lacey tucked her into bed.

"It's raining," Emma murmured.

"Yes, it is, but you're safe at home."

"I wasn't scared," Emma stated.

Lacey kissed her sister's forehead. "I know, sweetie. Go to sleep."

Thunder rumbled outside and Emma jumped. "Sleep with me for a while, Lacey."

She was torn between going to her room to see if Gabe was still there or assuaging her sister's fears. The sensible part of her brain told her Gabe would have left long ago. "I have to get out of these wet clothes. I'll be right back."

"Lacey?"

Pulling a big T-shirt over her head, Lacey called back, "I'm coming."

She climbed in with Emma and cuddled with her. In seconds, Emma was asleep again.

When Emma became restless, Lacey slipped from the bed and made her way to her room. She grabbed the pillow Gabe's head had been on and curled up. Thunder continued to echo and lightning occasionally streaked across the sky. The tip-tap of the rain against the window lulled her to sleep.

Before she succumbed completely, she relived their night together. It had been more than she'd ever expected. She hadn't meant to say "I love you." The words had just slipped out in the heat of the moment. She had to make sure Gabe realized she didn't expect anything from him. But in her heart she knew she was lying. Her expectations might surprise him, though. Having him around was enough for her. Her responsibility to Emma would prevent her from having a life of her own for a while. Gabe made her life a little brighter, and she hoped he understood that. The way she felt about him could cause some problems, because she knew he wasn't ready for any type of love.

Why not? The question echoed through her mind as darkness claimed her.

The next morning, Lacey overslept. It was after nine when she woke up with Gabe's pillow in her arms. Baby sis was sound asleep, too. Lacey had cereal and a banana ready when Emma climbed onto the stool, brushing hair from her face. She'd slept rough and her hair was everywhere.

"I don't like it when it's dark," Emma said.

"I know, sweetie. Eat your cereal."

Lacey's phone buzzed and she picked it up from the counter. It was Denise.

"I'm so sorry about last night."

Lacey walked into the living room so her sister couldn't hear. "It's okay. I had my doubts that she would stay."

"When the thunder started, all the little girls wanted to go home and Bailey was disappointed. So today we're having a big party with pedicures and manicures and princess gowns with an old-fashioned tea party. It's going to be fun, and we'd like for Emma to come back. The other girls are coming back, too."

"I'll talk to her and let you know." She hung up the phone. "Sweetie, that was Bailey's mother. They're having the party today with all kinds of fun stuff. They want to know if you want to join them."

"Do I have to stay the night?" Emma asked around a mouthful of cereal.

"No. It's just for the day."

"'Kay, but you'll come get me when it gets dark?"

"You bet. Now, we'd better hurry to get there in time for the tea party."

Emma jumped off the stool. "Oh, boy!"

Thirty minutes later Lacey once again delivered Emma to Bailey's birthday party. She waited in the car for at least ten minutes to make sure Emma was okay.

Hurrying home, she planned to take the cupcakes she had made for last night to Gabe. They had been too busy with each other to eat dessert. And they really needed to talk.

Gabe sat nursing a cup of coffee and a foul mood. He had to talk to Lacey, but Emma was home and he wasn't sure when he'd have the opportunity for a private conversation. It was important, though, that he do it as soon as possible.

His doorbell rang and he got to his feet. Was it Lacey? She never came to his front door. At least, she hadn't recently. He opened the door in stunned disbelief. Dana, his ex-wife, stood there.

"Did you think I'd never find you?" She walked past him into the living room without an invitation. She stared at the photos on the wall. "Oh, my God, Gabe. Take the photos down. It's time to let our son rest in peace."

"What are you doing here, Dana?"

She had on a dark suit with a cream silk blouse— the kind she usually wore to work. Glancing around the room, she said, "Could we talk somewhere besides this depressing room?"

He walked into the kitchen with her a step behind him. "Would you like a cup of coffee?"

"No. This won't take long."

"How did you find me?"

"Your sister, Kate. I've called her at least three times in the past year, and she said she didn't know where you were. Then I called again last week and she finally told me."

"She didn't know for a long time where I was. I didn't want to see anyone."

"You can't keep hiding, Gabe. It's time to start living again. That's what I'm doing. I've met a man. A lawyer, actually, and we want to get married on Valentine's Day. But you left without signing the divorce papers. I really need you to do that."

"I thought I signed them."

"You didn't."

He couldn't speak. His old life had found him and he could feel the walls closing in. He fought to breathe. Fought to maintain his composure. He managed a couple of deep breaths.

"I'm glad you've found someone." He meant every word, but part of him felt a loss he couldn't describe. But then, he knew what it was. Dana was his last link to Zack. He'd thought it had been Pepper, but it was Zack's mother.

"What's wrong with you? You're very pale."

He ran a hand through his hair. "It's just seeing you and realizing once again that we've lost our son."

Her perfectly made-up face crumpled like a tissue. "Please, Gabe. Don't do this. I'm trying to live with it and move on."

He collected himself. "Okay. I'll sign the papers. Can you send them to me?"

"You have to return to Austin. We have to sell the house and go through Zack's things. We've never done that and I'm not doing it alone. I just can't."

The walls pushed in a little closer. He wanted to fight back and not let the pain return, not let that dark hole suck him back in. The only way to do that was to face that terrible time. He knew that as well as he knew his own name. Lacey had helped him take so many steps forward. Now he had to take the final one himself.

"I'll be there in a couple days."

"Good. I've been making the payments on the house from your check, which I have deposited every month."

"The firm is still sending me checks?"

"They're expecting you to come back. Don't you understand that?"

No, he didn't. When he'd left, he'd told the senior partner that he was done and wouldn't be returning.

When he didn't respond, Dana added, "Everyone wants to help you. You just have to let them."

He drew air into a chest that was slowly collapsing. "I'm sorry I left you with all that responsibility, but I knew we had money in the account to cover it. I had no idea the firm would keep me on the payroll."

"Just come home, Gabe. We have to end our marriage. We have to end so many things."

"I'm not sure where our marriage went wrong, but it was over a long time before Zack's accident."

"It started to deteriorate when I pressured you to work for a big law firm. You resented that, even though you wouldn't admit it. Your idea was working alone in a tiny office as a private attorney. I wanted better things for our life. I wanted money to do those things, so I pushed and you withdrew. Your idea of a fun weekend was spending it on Rebel Ranch with Zack. That was a nightmare for me." She tossed her long dark hair back. "In college I thought we were compatible, but once we started living our dream we both realized we weren't. By then we had Zack and we centered our lives on him. That's why his passing hit us so hard." She studied the tip of her high-heeled shoe. "I'm sorry I blamed you for Zack's death. I was just grief stricken."

"I'm sorry I blamed you for the same reason."

She raised her eyes to his. "Then let's end this relationship amicably."

Before Gabe could respond, a knock sounded on his back door and Lacey came in with a cupcake in each hand. She looked from Gabe to Dana.

"I'm sorry. I didn't realize you had company."

Dana stepped forward. "I'm Dana, Gabe's wife."

An expression shifted across her face, as if she'd been blindsided by an eighteen-wheeler. Gabe wanted to go to her and reassure her, but his pain kept him grounded.

"Oh…um…" She moved backward out the door. "I'll just…go."

"No need," Dana said. "I was just leaving."

But Lacey wasn't listening. She disappeared down the steps, and he knew she was running to her house with tears in her eyes. His body trembled at the thought that he'd hurt the one person he cared most about in this world.

"My cell number is the same," Dana was saying. "I'll expect you in Austin before Christmas."

Gabe was aware of Dana leaving, but he had only one thought on his mind. He had to get to Lacey.

Chapter 16

Lacey marched into her house, set the cupcakes on the table and then grabbed a carton of milk out of the refrigerator. She didn't bother with a glass. Sitting down, she said a curse word, peeled the paper away on one of the cupcakes and started to eat.

He was married. He was still married ran through her mind like a crazed rat on a little Ferris wheel. She'd had sex with a married man. She took a gulp from the carton and set it back on the table. The more cupcake she stuffed into her mouth, the angrier she got. How could Gabe do this to her? So much for her fantasies and dreams. Crap! She was pitiful thinking there might be a life for her and Gabe. The reality check was a downer.

Her back door opened and Gabe walked in. She kept eating. He sat on the chair next to her and she wanted to move away—far, far away from all the heartache he was about to dump on her.

"Isn't one of those for me?"

"Not anymore."

"Where's Emma?"

"She went back to her friend's house." Lacey hadn't meant to answer him, but the words slipped out.

"We need to talk."

She took a gulp of milk. "I think *wife* pretty much says it all."

"Lacey—"

"Please leave. I'm busy."

"I'll get you a glass."

"You will *not* get anything in my house. Please leave." She stuffed more cupcake into her mouth.

He picked up a napkin from the table. "You have chocolate all over your face."

"So? That's none of your concern."

"Lacey, listen to me. Can you do that without wanting to smear chocolate in my face?"

She couldn't answer because she was about to choke on the cupcake. She coughed, sputtered and grabbed the carton of milk. It took a moment, but she finally swallowed the mass of cake in her throat. She felt like a total fool.

He pushed the napkin toward her and she wiped her mouth.

"Yes, I'm still married—technically. When I left Austin a year ago, I just forgot to sign the divorce papers. Now Dana has met someone and is planning to get married, so she wants me to wrap things up and make it legal."

Lacey reached for the milk and realized she was

drinking out of a plastic container. God, she was a mess. But she focused on what he was saying.

"So you're going back to Austin?" The words sounded just as bad as they'd felt inside her heart.

He took the napkin and wiped chocolate from her face. So gently. So Gabe. She wanted to cry, but refused to be that weak.

"I tried for a solid year to deal with Zack's death in every way I could, but it just got worse. I couldn't stand being around people. I couldn't stand the looks, the stares and the sympathy. One day some lawyers were laughing in the conference room and I lost it. How dare they laugh when my son was dead? The thought set me off and I said things I don't even remember, but afterward I walked out. I got in my truck, drove to the house and picked up Pepper. I started driving and ended up here. You know the rest."

She studied the poinsettia she had on a table in the corner. The red leaves heralded the beauty of the holiday season. But there was nothing beautiful about the pain in his voice.

"I just went through the motions of living, if you can call it that. I ate just enough to keep me alive. Pepper's health was what kept me going. As long as she was with me, that was all I needed. But I knew I would have to let her go and I didn't know how to do that. Until you. You were like sunshine and smiles all rolled into one. New and exciting. No matter how much I yelled at you or threatened you, you still came back, just like the blasted sun, every day. And you made me angrier than I've ever been. How dare you invade my darkness?"

"Gabe..." Her throat ached and she couldn't say another word.

"Then a miracle happened. The sunshine in you slowly sparked a light in me, and the darkness started to fade. I've loved seeing you, talking to you, being with you. I've used you as a crutch to bring myself back to life. You've saved me in more ways than one, and for that I will never forget you."

He was leaving.

A choked sob left her throat without her even knowing it. She prayed she could keep the tears inside, but she feared she was failing.

"Last night should never have happened."

She finally found her voice. "No, don't say that."

Please, don't say it meant nothing to you.

"I'll remember it always, but now it makes it that much harder to leave."

She swallowed something that tasted like fear, panic gripping her system like water filling a drowning person's lungs.

"I've been hiding from my responsibilities in Austin. I have to go back and apologize to the partners of the firm. Dana and I still haven't sold our house, and we need to do that. And we have to go through Zack's things and give them away. I'm not sure I can, but because of you I know that I'm stronger and I will try my best." He crushed the napkin in his hand. "Living next door to you has been an epiphany. I never knew people like you existed—kind, loving and selfless. In a perfect world I would stay and life would go on. We'd ignore the outside world and all the problems that could tear us apart. But that would be unfair to you."

"Wh-why?"

"Last night, when you told me you loved me, I knew I would have to disappear from your life."

"Wh-why?"

"Because I don't know what love is anymore. I need you, but I'm unable to love you the way you deserve to be loved—by a whole man who won't drag you down with sadness. Please understand that I have to go."

Her heart exploded in her chest. It shattered into a million little pieces and bled until she couldn't breathe. She didn't want to breathe. Life suddenly wasn't worth living. But there was Emma… And for her, Lacey found the strength to choke out a breath.

"When will you leave?" Her voice was low and weepy. She couldn't help it.

"I want to finish the shed first. I promised Dana I'd be there by Christmas."

She lifted her eyes to his. "You won't be here for Christmas?"

"No. Christmas doesn't mean much to me anymore. You'll be fine. Don't worry too much about Emma. She'll adjust because she has you."

But you won't be here.

Silence intruded in a way it never had before. Awkward. Painful. Then she did something to alleviate the pain of parting. It might have been wrong, but she couldn't help herself.

"Are my lips red?"

His face, etched in pain, relaxed. "No."

"They need to be. Badly."

He reached for her then and pulled her onto his lap. Her arms went around his neck and their lips met in a sweet, touching kiss that turned passionate instantly. They kissed with everything in them. They kissed as if it was their last time. Because it was. Finally, she rested her forehead against his, and this time the silence was soothing. Comforting. But only for that moment.

"I'll talk to Emma," he whispered against Lacey's face. His warm breath fanned her heated cheeks.

"You'll let me know when you're leaving?"

"I wouldn't leave without saying goodbye." He stood and gently held her elbows as she stood, too. He gazed into her eyes for a moment and then walked out, much the same way he'd done the first weeks she had known him.

She wrapped her arms around herself to still the ache in her chest, to still all the fears that gripped her and to still the tears clinging to her eyelashes. Finally, she gave up and went to her room and cried like she'd never cried before. She'd found someone special and now she'd have to learn to live without him.

Lacey wasn't sure how long she stayed in her room for the biggest pity party in the world. Afterward, she was prepared to face whatever she had to. She knew she had to let Gabe go. He had to find the peace he needed. The peace he deserved. And she had to have the strength to let him go without guilt. That would be the hardest part of all.

Besides her father's illness and death, the next couple of days were the hardest Lacey had ever lived through. Gabe worked tirelessly on the shed. Even in the late hours of the night she could hear hammering, drilling and the buzz of a saw. She had invited him to eat several times, but he always refused, so she knew he was eating little and working himself until he couldn't think. She couldn't stop his pain, so she left him alone.

Emma wasn't as understanding. She was over there

every day to help Gabe, as she put it. He hadn't told her yet that he was leaving. Lacey dreaded that moment. Too many people had left Emma. Lacey wasn't sure how her sister was going to take it. But she would be there to comfort her and hopefully they both would get through it.

On Tuesday afternoon, Gabe came over. Lacey was making Christmas cookies using a recipe she'd gotten from a cooking show. Emma was thoroughly enjoying decorating them with icing, sprinkles and candy pieces.

Emma was on her knees on a stool. Gabe slid onto the one next to her. He was dressed in jeans, the blue shirt and boots. He was clean shaven and his hair was combed. *He was ready to go.* Tiny pinpricks of pain shot through Lacey, but she resolved to be strong.

"Want a cookie?" Emma held out one to him.

"No, thanks, kiddo. I want to talk to you."

Emma sank back on her heels. "'Kay."

Gabe's throat worked, but no words came out, and Lacey wanted to reach across the counter and hug him so it would be easier. But she resisted with everything in her.

"I have to go back to Austin."

"Why?"

"I was very sad and down when I left, and now I have to go back and face my responsibilities. You might not understand that, but I have a house there and I need to sell it. And I have to go through Zack's things. I never did that."

Lacey held her breath for what seemed like an eternity. The emotions on Emma's face shifted and Lacey couldn't gauge what her sister was thinking. Then she did something remarkable. She held out her arms to Gabe and he lifted her onto his lap.

"Don't be sad, Gabe."

He kissed her forehead and held her. "Would you do something for me?"

Emma nodded.

"Would you take care of Pepper's grave and make sure those pesky birds don't dig around too much?"

"'Kay. I'll take care of it real good. When will you come back?"

The question that Lacey couldn't bring herself to voice Emma asked without hesitation.

"I don't know, kiddo. I have a lot of things to take care of and figure out about myself. Just know that I have to go."

Emma hugged him. "Don't be sad. Wait!" Emma jumped from his lap and ran to her room. She came back with one of the wide, stretchy woven bands. It was yellow. "Lacey and I made it for you."

Gabe slipped it onto his left wrist. "Thank you." He glanced at Lacey. His eyes, which lately had been happy and sparkly, were now dark and foreboding. All the old pain had slipped back to grip him. He walked around the counter and took her in his arms. She rested against his chest, loving this last moment with him. And hating it at the same time. The frantic pounding of his heart told her how hard this was for him, too.

"Take care of yourself. I'll remember you always." Saying that, he released her and fished a key out of his pocket. "You might need this."

She took the key and they stared at each other for endless moments. He was the first to break eye contact. "Lacey..."

"It's okay." The words came out soaked with tears

but she couldn't help it. "Please find the peace you so deserve."

He inclined his head. "You'll always be my crazy lady," he whispered for her ears only. "Goodbye."

She didn't say the words back to him because she couldn't. She would never say goodbye. Ever.

He walked to her front door and she and Emma followed. Without glancing back, he strolled to his truck, which was parked at the curb, and got in. Slowly, the truck pulled away. They watched as he stopped at the street sign and then disappeared out of sight.

And out of their lives.

Christmas Eve arrived cold and windy. Lacey spent the day getting ready for the holiday. She put on a brave face for Emma, but every moment she wondered what Gabe was doing and if he was okay.

Tonight when Emma went to bed, she would go over to Gabe's house, get the gifts and lock his house up for the last time. He'd never said what he planned to do with the house, and she feared one day she would come home to see a for-sale sign in the front yard. Then she'd know for sure that he would never return. But until then she'd allow herself a tiny grain of hope.

Emma was busy wrapping something in her room. Lacey had no idea what it was. She had her Christmas dinner organized. She was going to make a roast with all the trimmings for her and Emma. Once again it would just be the two of them, but she would do her best to make the day as fun as possible.

Lacey called her mom several times, but Joyce never answered. Finally, she left a Merry Christmas message.

That afternoon she and Emma got dressed to go to

the big celebration on the square. The Wiznowski Bakery closed at four. Coffee, hot chocolate and free kolaches would be offered to everyone until they ran out. Then the store would be closed until after Christmas.

Everyone was in the square, eating kolaches, drinking coffee and chatting. Everyone was happy, especially when it grew dark and the huge Christmas tree in front of the courthouse was lit. Some of the kids began to sing songs, and Lacey enjoyed a moment of happiness with Peyton and Angie, but it was fleeting.

Later, Lacey and Emma put flowers on their dad's and Mona's graves, then attended the eight-o'clock mass. The church was packed. The Wiznowski family sat in the second and third rows on the left. Lacey and Emma slid into the last pew. Even though she was surrounded by people, Lacey had never felt as lonely as she did at that moment.

Erin got up and walked back to them. "Mama wants you to sit with us."

Lacey almost burst into tears, which was silly, but she was feeling a little emotional. She and Emma squeezed in with the big Wiznowski family. The service was moving and Emma sat very still beside her. Candles were passed out and lit and then the church's lights were turned off. The congregation sang "Silent Night." It was moving and touching, especially since Emma sang right along with everyone.

As they walked out into the cold night air, Angie said, "Please come for dinner tomorrow. We'll have tons of food and we'd love to have you."

"Thank you," Lacey replied. "That's very nice, but I have dinner already planned for us." She'd told Angie about Gabe leaving, so Angie knew she was feeling lonely.

"If you change your mind, just come," Angie told her.

Lacey walked away feeling good about the friends she'd made in Horseshoe. She and Emma weren't really alone, so she couldn't explain why she felt otherwise.

Back at the house they changed into their Christmas pajamas: red-and-black-plaid ones with feet and Santa Claus hats. Emma looked adorable. Lacey looked ridiculous. But it was fun.

"We have to watch Ralphie," Emma said. "Daddy and me always watched it on Christmas Eve."

"I know, sweetie, but let's have a snack first."

Emma climbed onto a bar stool. "What kind of snack?"

"A sandwich."

"Peanut butter and jelly."

"Grilled cheese," Lacey shot back.

"No, Lacey. PB&J."

"Okay, since it's Christmas."

Neither of them ate very much, and soon Emma was running into the living room to turn on the TV. Lacey sat in her dad's chair and Emma squeezed in beside her as *A Christmas Story* began.

Emma giggled every time Ralphie or Randy did something silly. Her laughter was what Lacey wanted to hear. Her sister was happy. Maybe this Christmas wouldn't be too bad after all.

Lacey was almost asleep when Emma sat up. "Lacey, our tree is not decorated. Why haven't you decorated our tree?"

Lacey blinked like a deer caught in a hunter's crosshairs. "Really? Seriously?"

"Daddy always decorated it after Thanksgiving. What's taking you so long?"

Lacey sat up. "Are you kidding me? Aren't you the kid who said you didn't believe in Santa anymore and you didn't want to decorate the tree?"

Emma shrugged. "I'm a kid. What do I know?"

Lacey grabbed her and tickled her rib cage. "I'm gonna tickle you senseless."

Emma wiggled and screamed, "No, Lacey, no!"

After a few minutes of roughhousing, Lacey got to her feet. "Let's decorate this tree. It's long overdue."

Emma had relented. That in itself was a miracle. Lacey got the decorations out of the attic. It was past midnight when they finished putting the last ornament on the tree. Lacey turned it on and the bright lights glowed, welcoming Christmas into the Carroll house. Finally.

"It's beautiful, Lacey."

She picked up her sister as if she was two years old. "Now let's go to bed and wait for Santa." Lacey didn't have to say it twice. Emma was already half-asleep on her shoulder. Lacey tucked her in and sat for a moment with her.

She gazed out the window at the cold night and wondered where Gabe was. Was he in a hotel room all alone? Was he thinking of them? Was he hurting?

Getting up, she sighed and tucked the blanket tighter around Emma. *S-l-o-w.* How she wished she could tell Gabe that Emma had decorated the tree. His advice had worked.

Lacey slipped into bed and clutched her pillow a little tighter. "Merry Christmas, Gabe. Wherever you are."

Chapter 17

Lacey woke to a light touch on her cheek. She didn't freak out or scream. She knew it was Emma. Her sister had done this a lot since their father passed away. She'd wake up and sneak into Lacey's bed.

"What's up, snuggle bunny?"

"There's no Santa, Lacey."

Lacey opened one eye and stared at the clock on her nightstand. It wasn't even 5:00 a.m. "Did you look in the living room?" She'd spent over an hour putting out toys and gifts.

"I did and I saw my bicycle and lots of other stuff. I like my bicycle. I sat on it and everything."

Lacey scooted up in bed. "How long have you been up?"

"I don't know."

Lacey was trying to figure this out, but her brain

was still in sleep mode. "Why are you saying there's no Santa Claus? We decorated the tree and you were happy. What has you so down this morning?"

"There's no Santa Claus, Lacey." Her sister's voice rose as if Lacey was hard of hearing.

"Okay, I hear you, but you'll have to explain because I'm still half-asleep."

"I didn't get what I asked Santa for at the mall."

Oh, good heavens. She'd forgotten about that with everything that had happened with Gabe. "What did you ask Santa for?"

"I asked for a puppy and there's not one in the living room."

Lacey wanted to smack herself on the forehead. A puppy! That was so easy. How could that have escaped her?

"I asked for two other things and I didn't get them, either. There's no Santa Claus. He's not real." Emma curled up beside her, a sad, forlorn little figure.

Lacey gathered her sister close. "What else did you ask for?"

"I... I asked for Daddy to come back one more time so I could tell him I loved him."

"Oh, sweetie." Lacey hugged Emma tight. "Santa can't grant those kinds of requests. He deals with toys. You asked him for something very personal and difficult."

"I don't care. If he was real, he could make it happen. You told me if I believed strong enough, it would happen. And I believed right here—" she jabbed a finger into her chest "—real hard and I didn't get what I asked for."

Lacey was wildly flipping the pages of the book in

her head for an answer to soothe her sister's wounded heart. But she feared there was no answer for this. No answer for the dreams or wishes of a six-year-old girl.

Lacey glanced at the window. It was still dark outside, but moonlight streamed in with bright promises. Lacey was trying to figure out how to find a puppy on Christmas Day. If she called around, perhaps someone would know and maybe she could get a puppy before the day was over. And Emma would still believe. That might be wrong, but Lacey was determined to make this day as special as possible.

"I didn't get the other thing I asked for, either."

Lacey looked down at her sister. "How many things did you ask for?"

Emma held up three fingers. "I asked that Gabe would be with us forever."

Lacey was lost for a response. It was all tangled up with her own emotions of having to let Gabe go. How could this day be happy when they were so miserable?

In that moment Lacey decided she wasn't going to do this. She wasn't going to sink into a well of despair. It was Christmas and they would have Christmas.

With her thumb and forefinger she touched the corners of Emma's mouth. "Smile, snuggle bunny. We're going to have Christmas, and we're going to laugh and be happy and open our gifts and be grateful for what we have. Daddy would want us to do that."

"Yeah." Emma rose to her knees. "Let's open gifts. We don't need no Santa Claus."

"You got it." Lacey crawled from the bed. "I'll make coffee and hot chocolate and we can eat some of our delicious cookies."

"Just don't make any toast, Lacey. We don't want to

burn the house down today." Emma laughed and ran into the living room.

Lacey kept forgetting to buy a new toaster. Oh, well, maybe one day she would remember. She made the coffee and hot chocolate and carried it to the coffee table in the living room.

She sat cross-legged on the sofa, sipping coffee, hoping it would wake her up. She'd only had a few hours of sleep.

"I have to get our hats." Emma dashed off again and came back with their red-and-white Santa hats. Lacey slipped hers on, as did Emma.

Emma clapped her hands. "Now we have to open presents."

"Drink some of your hot chocolate. The marshmallows are melting."

Emma lifted the mug to her lips and drank, leaving a marshmallow ring over her upper lip, which she licked off with her tongue.

"What gift do you want to open first?" Lacey asked.

"You have to open yours first. I'll go get it." Once again, Emma charged off and came back with a wad of wrapping paper around something. Every inch of the red and green paper had tape on it. "I wrapped it myself."

"I see."

"You're gonna love it. Open it! Open it!" Emma's eyes flashed like a Fourth of July sparkler.

"You're excited."

"Yeah."

"Remember, I told you that sometimes giving is better than receiving. You're excited and can't wait for me to see your gift." She reached over and touched Emma's chest. "That feeling in there is what Christmas is all about."

"It feels like jumping beans are in there."

Lacey smiled, placing her cup on the coffee table. "Well, then, I better open this before you explode."

She could hardly tear the paper away for Emma's little face being in the way and the tape that constantly stuck to her fingers. Emma had probably used a whole roll of tape. As she peeled the last piece of paper away, she saw a piece of Emma's artwork in a frame.

Emma pointed to the picture. "That's me and you in front of our house."

"Yes, it is."

"Mrs. Fillmore said it was really good."

"It is, sweetie. I love it."

The colors were really bright and pretty. A big yellow star hung in the blue sky and they stood on green grass. To the left was a shadowy figure that Lacey couldn't make out.

"Who's that?" she asked Emma.

"That's Gabe at his house."

"Oh." Of course. Why hadn't Lacey figured that out? Gabe had been a big part of their lives. But not anymore. She wondered how long it would be before they stopped missing him.

Emma pointed to the star. "And that's Daddy, because he watches over us."

"It's beautiful and you did a wonderful job. I'm so proud of you." Lacey ran her fingers over the dark wood frame. "Where did you get the frame?"

"Gabe gave it to me. He took down all the pictures of his son. I told him I needed a frame for your gift and he gave me one."

Lacey wasn't going to scold her for asking for things because now wasn't the time.

"I'll hang it in my room so I can see it all the time."

Emma clapped her hands again. "Oh, boy!"

"You have a lot of gifts to open—you better get started."

Emma grabbed a package and ripped off the bow that Lacey had carefully made. A noise sounded on the roof and Emma jumped onto the sofa and curled into her.

"What's that, Lacey?"

"It must be the wind. Go ahead and finish opening your gift."

A loud stomping sounded from the roof, and Emma stayed glued to her.

That wasn't the wind. Lacey wasn't sure what to think. Weird things were happening. She waited for the sound to stop, but it only got louder. Someone was walking on the roof.

"I'll go see what's going on." She got up, and Emma held on to the back of Lacey's Christmas pajamas, not willing to let her get too far away. Lacey opened the front door and the wind blew it back, almost knocking her down. The pinecone wreath clattered against the door.

"What is it, Lacey?" Emma whispered into Lacey's back.

"I don't…" Her words trailed off as she spotted a kennel at her feet. Someone had left it at their front door. A small dog was inside. The porch light and Christmas lights were on, but Lacey couldn't see anyone.

Emma spotted the dog. "Look, Lacey. It's a puppy. A puppy!" Emma knelt down by the kennel. "There's a note on it. What does it say? I see my name."

Lacey bent down to investigate. What was going on?

"Read it, Lacey."

She tried to focus on the paper while keeping an eye on their front yard. "It says, 'To Emma from Santa… Claus.'" She read slowly because she wasn't believing what she was reading. "At the bottom it says the dog's name is Merry Christmas."

"That's what I would've named her, too. Can we get her out? She's so pretty."

"Let's see what's on the roof first."

Lacey stepped over the kennel and almost kicked an unwrapped box with a bow on it. Looking down, she saw it was a toaster. *A toaster!*

Emma saw it then. "Lacey, Santa left you a toaster. He knew what you needed. Santa knows everything."

Did he? She walked out into the yard to look around. Emma was right behind her. It was still pretty dark out and Lacey couldn't see much but a dark sky with the sun lazily rising to the east.

"Lacey, Lacey, look!" Emma pointed to the sky. "It's Santa. He was here. Daddy sent him." Emma waved with both arms. "Daddy, I love you. Bye, Santa."

Lacey looked down at her sister. "Sweetie…" She was going to say something, but for the life of her she couldn't find words to disappoint her sister. Maybe there were miracles in a child's imagination.

"It was Daddy, Lacey. He knew I was sad and he sent Santa so I would believe and be happy. I saw him."

"You saw Daddy?"

"Yeah, weren't you looking? He was right there on the roof and he went back to heaven."

Lacey knew she should say something, but she'd encouraged Emma to believe, and she had to go with what she had told her. She didn't have much time to analyze the situation as the Wilson family came running up her walk.

"What's going on, Lacey?" Sharon asked, huddled in her housecoat. "The boys say they saw Santa outside your house and on your roof."

"We did," Brad said. "He left something at your door and then he was on the roof and just disappeared."

"You saw Santa?" Lacey asked, thinking she had to be dreaming.

"Yes. Jimmy and I were looking out the window, waiting, and suddenly there he was."

Emma got in Brad's face. "Santa is real. You lied. You don't know nothin'."

Lacey placed her hands on Emma shoulders just in case she was planning to throw a punch.

Instead of answering Emma, Brad said, "Come on, Jimmy. We have to go home and wait for Santa to come to our house."

Sharon hurried after her boys, but her husband hung behind. "Did you pay for a Santa?"

"No. I have no idea what's going on."

"Weird." He took one long look at her in her Christmas pajamas and then he walked off, shaking his head.

"Come on, Lacey." Emma took her hand. "We have to tell Gabe."

"Emma, no." But Emma ran across the yard to Gabe's front door and pounded on it with her fist.

"Gabe, it's Emma. Open the door."

"Sweetie, Gabe went back to Austin. Remember?"

"No, he's here," Emma insisted, pounding harder on the door. "Gabe, open the door. It's me. Open the door! Open the door!"

Lacey took a deep breath and wrapped her arms around her waist. It was cold and they needed to go back to their house, but how was she going to make Emma understand?

"Sweetie, stop beating on the door. We have to go back to our house. You have a new puppy and we have to take care of her."

"No." Emma defied her and Lacey was at a loss for what to do next.

She squatted and turned Emma to face her. "We have to go to our house. It's cold and Gabe's not here."

"He has to be. I got everything I asked Santa for, so Gabe has to be here. I believed, Lacey, just like you told me. Right here." She poked at her chest. "Gabe has to be here."

"Sweetie—"

"No!" Emma turned back to the door and resumed pounding. She beat on the blasted door until Lacey thought she would scream. Finally, Emma sank to her knees, heartfelt sobs racking her little body, "Gabe, it's me."

Lacey couldn't stand it any longer. She gathered Emma into her arms and stood. Emma sobbed onto her shoulder. "No, Lacey."

"Sometimes we don't get everything we ask for. You got two amazing gifts. Let's go home and be grateful and take care of Merry Christmas."

Emma sobbed into Lacey's neck. Lacey turned and carefully made her way from the door. Since it was dark, she was careful where she stepped. A clicking sound stopped her. She swung around and saw Gabe standing in the doorway; a light behind him showcased him clearly in jeans and a black T-shirt. His hair was tousled and he wore his cowboy boots. She blinked. She was dreaming. She had to wake up.

Emma had heard the sound, too, and lifted her head. She jumped out of Lacey's arms and flew to Gabe. "You're here. I knew you were. Why didn't you open the door?"

Gabe squatted. "What's up, kiddo?"

Lacey could see and hear Gabe. This wasn't a dream. He was here…in his house. How long had he been here? And why had he been hiding from them?

Emma took Gabe's hand. "Come on, you have to see what Santa brought. He was here. I saw him on our roof. Can you believe that?"

"No."

"Come see." Emma tugged him farther into the yard, giving him no choice but to follow. Lacey trailed after them, her mind a jumbled mess of confusion.

Gabe picked up the kennel and the toaster, and they went inside to the warm house. He helped Emma get the small dog out. It was a brown-and-white Jack Russell terrier mix. The dog ran around the living room, into the kitchen and down the hall to the bedrooms. Emma was right behind it, giggling.

Lacey encouraged Emma to come open her presents. Total pandemonium ensued as the little girl tore into the gifts. Now that Gabe was there she was all sparkly and happy. Lacey felt a little sparkle herself.

Gabe sat on the sofa and Lacey curled up beside him. There was a scratch on his face and several on his hands. A suspicion formed in her mind. It didn't take a Mensa member to figure out that Gabe had created a little magic of his own this Christmas.

After Emma had oohed and aahed over everything, she went over to Gabe. "Why did you come back?"

Lacey scooted a little closer. She definitely wanted to hear his answer.

"Because I wanted to spend Christmas with you and Lacey."

He was smooth; she'd give him that. He had a lot of questions to answer, but they could wait.

"'Cause you love us," Emma said.

Gabe's skin paled and Lacey came to his rescue. "Let's hurry and get dressed so you can ride your bicycle," she said to Emma. Her sister was off like a shot.

"I rather like what you have on," Gabe remarked.

She made a face at him as she walked out. She quickly changed into black slacks, a white pullover sweater and boots.

Gabe was sitting on the sofa when they came out.

Emma pointed to the box with the toaster in it. "Gabe, look what Santa brought Lacey. Now she won't burn toast anymore."

"That'll give the smoke alarm a rest," Gabe teased.

"Thank you," she mouthed, her eyes holding his for a moment. It wasn't a romantic gift. That would get too mushy, and they hadn't reached that level in their relationship. They never would now. So she would take the toaster and be happy.

Gabe took Emma outside to help her ride the bicycle, and Lacey stayed behind to put a roast on for dinner. He didn't plan to stay, but he found himself lingering even though he knew he should go.

Emma mastered the bicycle in a few minutes and

he sat on the curb and watched her ride back and forth. Soon Lacey joined him.

"Look, Lacey. Look at me," Emma shouted, Merry Christmas running behind her.

"I see you. You're doing good."

"Do I look cool?"

"Frosty."

There was silence for a moment, and then she looked at Gabe. "Why did you really come back?"

He wanted to say what she wanted to hear, but he couldn't. He went with the truth instead.

"I made it to Austin and rented a room in a hotel, called Dana and got something to eat. Later, I drove to a gas station and there was a little boy outside who was trying to find a home for the dog. I looked at it and thought Emma would love her and, before I knew it, I was driving back to Horseshoe. I bought the toaster on the way."

He rested his forearms on his knees. "I kept thinking how hard it was going to be for you with Emma not believing in Christmas. I just wanted to create a little magic."

"You did that. The Wilson boys saw you on the roof and are sure you were Santa. They now believe, too. And Emma even says she saw Daddy on the roof. You created a lot of magic."

"It was dark. How could they see me and mistake me for Santa Claus?"

"It's Christmas morning. Kids are looking for Santa, and when they see a shadowy figure on a roof they automatically think…ah, Santa."

"Mmm."

"From the scratches on your face and hands I take it climbing onto the roof wasn't so easy."

"I wanted to get your attention to come to the door, and the only way I could think to do that was to climb to the roof and stomp around. Cowboy boots did me in. I slid off into your bushes."

She suppressed a laugh. "How did you know she wanted a dog? She never told me."

"I just went by how much she loved Pepper."

"It's what she asked Santa for at the mall. So, as Santa, you're right on target, especially since you were here this morning. She also asked that you would always be in our lives, and she wanted to see Daddy one more time. Everything she asked for has come true, and now she believes more than ever. All because of you."

"Maybe there is something magical about Christmas, because I had no idea she wanted a puppy and I have no idea how she saw her dad on the roof. It was me."

"It was enough." Lacey laid her head on his shoulder. "You're wonderful. You made one little six-year-old very happy. I'm not too unhappy myself."

"I planned to quietly leave, but I heard Emma crying and I couldn't do it." He leaned his head against hers. "I still have to go, Lacey. I can't stay."

"You're staying for dinner," she said, as if he hadn't spoken. "No arguments."

He didn't argue. Lacey cooked a fabulous meal and they were finally able to drag Emma into the house. Merry Christmas rested at her feet. Emma chatted nonstop, which helped alleviate the tension between the adults. She was happy and that was what Gabe had wanted, but the sadness in Lacey's eyes tore at his heart.

After dinner, Emma fell asleep on the couch with the dog. He helped Lacey with the dishes. She was very quiet.

He leaned against the counter. "I guess I shouldn't have come back. It's too hard for both of us."

She wiped the counter and then turned to him. "Have you thought about what made you come back?"

"Lacey, I can't analyze it any further than I have. I have to go to find me. I don't know if I'm supposed to live in my other world or if I belong here. I have to make the right decision for all of us. Please, don't make this difficult."

She carefully laid the Frosty the Snowman dish towel on the counter. "I'll always be grateful for what you did today. But I can't go through another goodbye." She walked past him into the dining room. "Please say goodbye to Emma. She'll be disappointed if you don't."

"Lacey…" The pain in her voice ignited so many responses, but he had to ignore them. He couldn't stay and regret that decision later. He had to be sure of what he wanted, even though it seemed as though he was looking at everything he'd ever dreamed about.

She lifted her head and met his eyes. "Take care of yourself, and don't let grief overtake you again." Her voice cracked on the last word and she walked out to the patio, quietly closing the door.

There was no need to go after her. They'd said everything they had to say. Now they just needed time.

Emma came in from the living room rubbing her eyes, her blond hair everywhere. Merry Christmas barked at her feet. He picked Emma up and sat her on the stool.

"It's time for me to go, kiddo. Take care of Lacey and Merry Christmas."

"I will. When are you coming back?"

His gut clenched. "I don't know." He hugged her and kissed her cheek. "Never stop believing."

"I won't. Bye, Gabe."

He walked out of the house, got in his truck and drove away. This time he knew it was for good. But he couldn't explain the feeling that everything he loved was in Horseshoe, Texas.

Lacey sat on the patio, tears rolling down her cheeks. She didn't want to cry, but she couldn't help herself. The wind stirred the fall leaves and blew them against the fence. They clung to a bare rose bush like ugly Christmas ornaments. Children's laughter sounded down the street. It was Christmas. Everyone was happy. Except her.

Emma crawled into her lap, facing her. "Don't cry, Lacey."

She drew in a deep breath. "I'm not crying."

With her forefinger, Emma touched Lacey's wet cheek. "You're weird, Lacey."

"Okay. Maybe a little," she admitted.

"Gabe'll come back."

"You think so, huh?"

"Yeah, because I believe in here." She jabbed at her chest. "And you have to believe in there." She jabbed at Lacey's chest. "That's what you told me and it's true. All you have to do is believe."

Lacey smiled through her tears. "Do you know how much I love you?"

"Bunches."

"Oh, yeah. Bunches and bunches." She held her sister. She would believe until Gabe returned. That was all she could do. With belief, she had hope, and she would never let go of that. Not ever.

Chapter 18

As Lacey went back into the house, the doorbell rang. She paused, wondering who that could be on Christmas Day.

"I'll get it," Emma said and ran to the door.

Lacey slowly followed.

"Who are you?" Emma asked.

Lacey pulled the door wider and froze. It was her mother, dressed to the nines in a stunning navy-and-white dress and to-die-for heels. Mervin stood behind her, holding a big package.

"Mom!"

Her mother was here.

"Hello, dear. I hope we're not intruding."

"No. No, please come in. I called you several times and you didn't answer."

"I had to do a lot of thinking," her mother replied.

Lacey pulled Emma to the side so they could enter.

"It smells good in here," Mervin said.

"I made a roast for lunch today. Would you like a piece of pie and coffee?"

"That's too much trouble." Her mother dismissed the offer with a wave of her hand. "We're on the way to spend Christmas with Mervin's daughter in Dallas."

"Is the pie homemade?" Mervin asked.

"Yes."

"Then that settles it," he decided. "We'd be happy to have coffee and pie. My daughter buys everything from the bakery."

"Mervin—"

"Joyce, relax and visit with your daughter."

Emma looked up at Joyce, evidently tired of being ignored, and asked, "Who are you?"

Her mother tried to look everywhere but at Emma. Eventually, she brought her gaze to the child. "I'm Lacey's mother."

"You're pretty."

Her mother blushed and the tired expression on her face vanished. "Thank you, dear." She took the package from Mervin and handed it to Emma. "We brought you something."

"Oh, boy! Thank you." Emma took the package and ran to the sofa to open it.

Lacey had never thought this day would come. Maybe her dad had been here that morning, because this certainly was a miracle.

Emma tore the paper away and Merry Christmas sniffed around her mother's feet.

"Oh, dear. A dog." Her mother was not that fond of dogs.

"That's Merry Christmas," Emma told her. "She won't hurt you. Look, Lacey." Emma opened a big wooden box full of pencils, crayons, markers and art paper. Emma jumped up and hugged Joyce around the waist. Joyce stiffened; even Lacey could see that. "Thank you. I love to draw. I draw real good." Emma went back to the box and Lacey's mother stood as if frozen in place.

Then, as if in slow motion, another miracle happened. Her mother removed her cashmere coat and laid it on the arm of the sofa. She sat on the sofa with the box between her and Emma.

"You look just like Lacey did when she was your age."

"I know," Emma replied. "Everybody tells us that."

Lacey hated to leave them alone, but everything was going so nicely that she didn't think her mother would do or say anything to hurt Emma. "I'll make coffee and serve pie."

"Okay, dear."

All Lacey could think was that her mother had come. She'd made the effort, and it was the best Christmas gift ever, except for seeing Gabe that morning.

"This pie is delicious," Mervin said.

"Thank you."

"Everything looks so nice, dear," her mother said as Lacey handed her a cup of coffee.

Lacey wanted to cry. She could feel the tears welling up at the back of her eyes. Her mother had praised her instead of criticizing.

The rest of the afternoon went the same way. Her mother talked more and more to Emma instead of over her head. When her mother mentioned that Lacey loved Barbies, Emma ran to her room to get hers, which totally shocked Lacey. Emma never played with the Barbies. But that afternoon Joyce and Emma sat on the sofa and dressed and redressed Barbies. It was a moment out of time.

All too soon, Mervin said it was time to go. Lacey felt a tug at her heart because she didn't want them to. She wanted to hang on to this moment when maybe… just maybe they had started to become a family.

Then Emma shocked her. "Can you be my grandma?" she asked Joyce.

Joyce clutched her chest. "Oh, dear. I'm too young to be a grandmother."

Mervin choked on his coffee. "Good one, Joyce."

He sat down by Emma. "You know, Emma, I have three grandchildren and they call me Pappy. If you need a grandpa, I'm your man."

"Oh, boy. I don't have a grandpa, either. You can be my…pappy." Emma giggled as she said the last word.

Her mother was now on the spot, and Lacey did nothing to help her. It would be a defining moment. Joyce played with the pearls around her neck and time stretched. Still, Lacey said nothing.

"Well, I guess, you can call me Jo… Nana."

Lacey hadn't even known she'd been holding her breath until air swooshed out of her lungs at her mother's reply.

"My friend Bailey calls her grandma nana."

"Then I'll be your nana."

Emma hugged Joyce, and Lacey saw tears in her mother's eyes. What a revelation. What a moment.

As they were leaving, Lacey hugged her mother and held on. She needed to. "Thank you," she said. "You've made me very happy. I love you."

It was a time in her life Lacey would never forget: The day her mother had finally accepted Emma as part of their family.

When Gabe made it back to Austin, he went to sleep and didn't wake up until the next morning. He thought of Lacey. He wanted to feel all the emotions Lacey was feeling, but his were twisted and shredded and he didn't know if he could ever make sense of them. Or if he could love her the way she wanted. That was the reason he was in Austin alone, and had never felt more lonely than he was today.

He met Dana at the attorney's office and signed the divorce papers. The attorney and Dana would go before a judge, who would sign off on the divorce decree, and that would be that. From there, they drove to the house they'd shared with their son. Gabe braced himself for the emotional impact, but was surprised when he didn't have the urge to run.

Going into Zack's room, though, was another matter. He found himself touching the yellow band on his wrist as if he could draw strength from Lacey. Even so, he didn't have that overwhelming, crippling feeling. He had tucked it away in a vault in his heart, just like Lacey had told him to.

The room was full of Zack's belongings, from his TV, video games and movies to the basketball hoop over the bathroom door to his baseball, his glove and his soccer ball. Everything that was Zack was in here. And there wasn't one thing Gabe wanted to keep. All his memories were stored in his heart, and that was all he needed, again just like Lacey had told him.

He and Dana agreed to donate all of Zack's belongings to a shelter so kids could enjoy them. Zack would like that. He told Dana she could have everything in the house. He wanted nothing except his clothes.

Before he left, he forced himself to walk to the spot where Zack had died. The bits and pieces of the four-wheeler were still there, scattered on the ground. He took a deep breath and said goodbye to all the pain and suffering. All he wanted now were peace and good memories of the child he'd loved. He was able to do that because of Lacey and her loving nature. As he made his way to his truck, the tangled mass of confusion inside him still raged on.

Over the weekend, he and Dana cleared out the house. They put the house on the market and, on Monday, Gabe went to the law firm to meet with the senior partner, Ted Silversteen. He was welcomed back with open arms. His old office was waiting for him and everything in it was just as he'd left it.

The next day he went to work and time slipped away as he got back into the routine of being an attorney. It was as if he'd never left. But a big part of him knew that he had. He also knew he was well on the way to full recovery.

The next week he rented a furnished one-bedroom apartment and moved in. He settled into his life in Austin. He was invited to dinners and parties by partners in the law firm. Inevitably, there was a single woman he just had to meet. He took all of this in stride because he knew they were trying to help him adjust. They just didn't know it was always the wrong woman.

The days passed quickly for Lacey. She stopped listening for the sound of Gabe's truck. The news of Santa visiting Emma had spread through Horseshoe quickly, and Emma told her story over and over to anyone who would listen. She now believed there was a Santa, and no one dared to tell her otherwise.

Lacey's mother had done a complete about-face concerning Emma. She called several times and came to visit before Emma's break ended. Lacey didn't question it. She just accepted the amazing gift.

With Emma back in school, the house was very quiet, and Lacey grew restless. She had to find something to do with her life. Emma was growing more and more independent. She had friends now and her aggressive behavior had stopped. She didn't even care if Lacey was late picking her up. All the anger she'd had inside was gone, and she didn't need Lacey as much.

Lacey wasn't sure what she could do in the small town, but then something fell into her lap. She was visiting with Angie at the bakery and discussing her plight when Angie mentioned that the woman who owned the flower shop two doors down was looking for someone to take it over. Lacey met with Mrs. Hinson, and after thinking about it for a couple of days, she bought the shop.

Her first order of business was to do a lot of redecorating. She painted and replaced the worn linoleum with big pink-and-white tile squares. The blinds were dingy, so she took them down and installed pink-and-white-striped shades. She bought two white wicker chairs and had the cushions covered in a pink-and-white stripe. The look was fresh and feminine.

She had looked at the previous owner's books, but she had no idea how busy she would be. It turned out she had two weddings the first week and there always seemed to be a special occasion that required flowers. The shop kept her running during the day. She loved working with flowers and decorating. She opened at nine and closed at two because she had to pick up Emma. If she had deliveries to make, she made them then. After that, it was Emma time.

Weeks turned into a month and then another. Still, she had no word from Gabe. As more time passed, she knew the likelihood of him returning was small. She kept believing, though.

At the end of February, Lacey helped Peyton give a baby shower for Angie. Lacey made the decorations extraspecial with pink, blue and white flowers. It was a fun day for everyone.

By mid-March Lacey had to face the fact that Gabe wasn't coming back. Even Emma had stopped asking. She still checked on Pepper's grave, but Lacey noticed she was doing it less frequently. Time had passed and his feelings had changed. Lacey had to accept that.

She just hoped he'd found peace.

Gabe had worked late. The firm had represented a hospital in a lawsuit and they'd won. Two of the single lawyers in the firm invited him out to celebrate. Of course, such celebrations were always in a bar. Tonight the bar was on Sixth Street. The other two guys were dancing with women they'd met. Gabe sat at the bar with a woman named Sonya, who presumably was his date. She was blue-eyed and gorgeous.

"What would you like to drink?"

"Strawberry margarita" was her reply. It was hard to hear with all the chatter, laughter and the band playing in the corner.

Gabe signaled the bartender and made the order. He'd already ordered Scotch on the rocks for himself.

"What's that yellow band on your wrist?" she asked as the bartender placed the drink on a napkin in front of her.

He raised his wrist. "It keeps me sane."

She took a sip of the margarita, her eyes on him. "Are you known for going insane?"

"Regularly."

"I like a man who's not afraid to have fun."

He swirled the ice in his glass. This was where he was supposed to make his move and they would spend the night at her place or his. In that moment, he realized he wasn't in his twenties anymore and the parties and the late nights were just a way to get through the day in another way.

She pointed toward the entrance. "Your friends are leaving. I guess we should go, too."

Following her gaze, Gabe ran his finger over the yellow band and all the emotions that were tangled inside him suddenly began to unravel. He knew what he wanted. He wasn't confused. He wasn't blinded by grief. He wasn't going through the motions anymore.

Setting his glass on the bar, he replied, "Yes, it's time to go."

Lacey was having a bad day. The flower delivery had been late and she'd had several arrangements to go to the funeral home. She got them there by twelve.

Emma's bows had gotten the attention of the mothers at school, and they'd asked if Lacey would make bows for their daughters. Now she had several to make by tomorrow. Right after she made an arrangement for the

D.A.'s secretary. It was her birthday, and Hardy wanted the flowers delivered after lunch.

Who knew she would be so busy in this little town? But she'd found a home here with wonderful people in a place where she could raise Emma without the worries of the big city.

After finishing the arrangement, she ran across the street to the courthouse to deliver it and then hurried back. Merry whined, wanting to go to the bathroom. Lacey opened the shop's back door. There was a graveled parking area and a grassy verge. "Hurry, I have work to do."

Merry darted out at the same time the shop's front door bell jingled.

"I'll be right there," she called. "Come on, Merry," she said to the dog. Once Merry was back inside, Lacey hurried to the front. Nobody was there. She turned and saw a man sitting in one of the wicker chairs. She almost didn't recognize him. He wore jeans, a white shirt and boots. A Stetson lay in his lap.

Gabe!

What was he doing there?

He stood up with his hat in his hand. "You look good." He pointed with his hat. "Your hair's longer."

She touched it self-consciously. "Uh…yes, I'm letting it grow. I only cut it when my dad was so sick and I didn't have time to take care of it. The short style was easy." She was rambling because she didn't know what else to say. Her palms were sweaty and her nerves were tied up like a pretzel. It was just such a shock to see him.

"Can I get you a cup of coffee?" She moved toward the front counter.

"No, I've had more than enough for the day." He

glanced around the shop. "Very nice. You found something to do that suits you."

"Yes." Lacey was so nervous she didn't know what to do with her hands, so she shoved them into the pockets of her smock. There had never been this kind of awkwardness between them. Now it was a viable thing she could feel. It was more about nerves and disappointment than anything else.

She raised her eyes to his and stared into his dark ones. For the first time she noticed that all the pain and disillusionment were gone. His eyes were clear and bright. The lines pain had etched on his face had also disappeared. He had finally put the tragedy behind him.

To calm her nerves, she rushed into a speech. "How are you? You look good, too. The city agrees with you."

"Could you please come out from behind the counter?"

"Uh…" She didn't want to. She wanted to postpone the heartache as long as possible. But she graciously walked around the counter to his side.

Merry sniffed at his feet.

"Hey, Merry Christmas." Gabe bent to rub the dog's head. Then he straightened and set his hat on the counter. "Aren't you curious why I'm here?"

She bit her lip. "Yes."

"I've finally found that peace I've been searching for."

"Oh… I'm happy for you." She wanted to reach out and touch him, but she kept her hands firmly in her pockets.

"When I left here, I was a man adrift and I didn't know if I could love again the way a man should. You deserve to be loved, Lacey."

She curled her hands into fists, bracing herself for what would come next.

"I've had a lot of time to think in the past few weeks, and I know now that I can have those feelings. I've had them all along, but the pain blocked them. The block was caused by guilt—guilt over my son's death. If he didn't have a life, then I didn't merit one, either."

Gabe raised his left wrist. "This yellow band has gotten me through the past weeks. As long as I could touch it, I could walk into my old home, even go through Zack's things without falling apart. I even went to the spot where he died. I did all these things with my hand on the yellow band. I dived into my work never realizing what this band meant to me, but now I do. I know exactly where I belong. I know exactly who I am and what I want in life." He cupped her face with the palm of his hand. "I can love you now the way a man should. Completely." He ran his thumb over her bottom lip. "Your lips aren't red."

A smile blossomed in her chest and rose up through her throat to her mouth. "They need to be. So badly."

He took her in his arms and his lips met hers with passion and power. The anguish of the past few weeks faded away as she tasted happiness once again.

"I love you," he whispered into her mouth. "I belong here with you and Emma. This is where I want to be for the rest of my life."

She rested her face against the warmth of his neck. "Are you sure?"

"Look into my eyes. What do you see?"

The smile rose up once again. "I see a man who has finally recovered from tragedy. I see us. I see a future."

He swung her around and sat in the chair with her on

his lap. "I'm going to open a law practice here in Horse-shoe. I always wanted to be a small-town lawyer." He tucked her hair behind her ear and she kissed his palm. "Will you share that life with me?"

"Yes, if I can bring a six-year-old along."

"I wouldn't have it any other way."

They sat there for a long time—her head on his shoulder, his arms around her waist as he told her about everything that had happened in Austin.

"When I was with that woman in the bar, I knew I didn't want to sleep with anyone but you. The crazy, lovely lady is the only one I want."

"I love you," she murmured. She touched his face, his throat, his hair. "I can't believe you're here. I've missed you so much, and Emma—" She jumped from his lap. "Oh, good heavens! I have to pick up Emma. She'll be so excited."

"Let's go, then."

"In a minute." She slid back onto his lap and wrapped her arms around his waist, resting her head on his chest. "I just need to feel you a little while longer."

He kissed the side of her face. "I'm going to love you and Emma forever."

Forever would be just enough time.

Epilogue

Two weeks later...

Christmas was supposed to be the happiest time of the year, but for Lacey it would always be this April day when she stood at the back of the church in the designer gown her mother had insisted on and stared at Gabe in a tux at the altar, his dark eyes as warm as the love in her heart.

A ripple of excitement ran through her. Her fantasy had come true. She was marrying the man of her dreams.

Her mother and Mervin sat in the front row on the left, and the Wiznowski family and the rest of the town were gathered behind them. Angie and Hardy were at the end of the pew with their new baby son between them. The Rebel family took up the pews on the right and gave new meaning to the roguish-outlaw look. Lacey was getting used to Gabe's nephews and their charming appeal.

After the reception, she and Gabe were flying to Hawaii for a week. Her mother was staying with Emma. Lacey didn't worry because she knew Emma had formed a special connection with her new nana.

"The Power of Love" by Celine Dion filled the church. Emma looked up at Lacey. "Is it time to get married, Lacey?"

Emma looked like a doll in her white dress with a band of white miniature roses Lacey had made in her hair. "Yes, sweetie. It's time."

Emma stepped out with her basket in her hand and dropped rose pedals all the way to the altar.

How Lacey wished her dad could have been there to walk her down the aisle. She closed her eyes briefly and he was there, just as he'd been for the past several months.

The music stopped and "Here Comes the Bride" began. Lacey took one step, then another, her eyes on Gabe. Her breath caught as he came down the steps to meet her. After he lifted her veil, their eyes met and Lacey saw everything she'd ever wanted.

He took her arm and walked her the rest of the way to the priest. They would never be alone again. No more books in her head to consult or angst. Through all the heartache, pain and tragedy, they'd made it. The sun had burst forth through the darkness in a dazzling array of bright colors, and the future was theirs to reap. A future full of love, happiness and sharing.

All because they'd believed.

* * * * *

Cathy Gillen Thacker is married and a mother of three. She and her husband reside in North Carolina. Her mysteries, romantic comedies and heartwarming family stories have made numerous appearances on bestseller lists. A popular Harlequin author for many years, she loves telling passionate stories with happy endings and thinks nothing beats a good romance and a hot cup of tea! You can visit Cathy's website, cathygillenthacker.com, for information on her books, recipes and a list of her favorite things.

Books by Cathy Gillen Thacker

Harlequin Special Edition

Texas Legends: The McCabes

The Texas Cowboy's Quadruplets
His Baby Bargain
Their Inherited Triplets

Harlequin Western Romance

Texas Legends: The McCabes

The Texas Cowboy's Triplets
The Texas Cowboy's Baby Rescue

Texas Legacies: The Lockharts

A Texas Soldier's Family
A Texas Cowboy's Christmas
The Texas Valentine Twins
Wanted: Texas Daddy
A Texas Soldier's Christmas

Visit the Author Profile page at Harlequin.com for more titles.

THE TEXAS
CHRISTMAS GIFT

Cathy Gillen Thacker

This book is dedicated to
Grant James Thacker, the best
little brother two sisters could ever have.

Chapter 1

"Derek McCabe is *still* on the phone?" the office manager asked.

In *her* private office, no less. Doing her best to curtail her irritation, Eve Loughlin smiled. "Yep."

Sasha handed her a beautiful red poinsettia from a grateful client. "Well, at least he's easy on the eyes."

Worse, Eve thought, hazarding a glance through the glass door, the amazingly successful venture capitalist had to know it. With his dark brown hair, ruggedly chiseled face and mesmerizing blue eyes, he was handsome enough to stop traffic. His broad-shouldered, six-foot-three-inch frame, currently garbed in an elegant, dark gray suit, made him even more of a catch. *If* she'd been looking. She wasn't.

Luckily, at that moment his call ended.

Taking a deep, calming breath, Eve squared her shoulders and walked back into her office.

"Sorry about that," Derek said. "I'm investing in a technology company. There were some last-minute details to work out."

"I understand," Eve replied. Even though she didn't. Why did Loughlin Realty's well-heeled clients think *their* time was somehow more valuable than the agents they employed to buy and sell their houses?

She set the plant on her credenza, next to several other gift baskets and a ribbon-wrapped bottle of champagne, then returned to her desk. "So back to where we were," she continued crisply. Which hadn't been far, given the fact that Derek had taken the call on his cell thirty seconds after he had walked in. "Have you had time to answer the questionnaire I emailed you?"

He shook his head and lowered himself into a chair in front of her desk. "We don't need to bother with that."

Of course they didn't, Eve thought with mounting frustration. She settled into her ergonomically designed swivel chair.

"I know exactly what I'm looking for," he stated amiably.

Eve picked up her notepad and pen. "Then suppose you tell me."

"I want a home in Highland Park, preferably on or near Crescent Avenue. I'd like to pay between seven and eight million for it. It must have at least three bedrooms and two baths. There'll be no need for bank financing, as I plan to pay cash." He paused, allowing her to catch up. "I'd also like to close next week and take possession immediately."

Eve finished writing and looked into the most gorgeous eyes she had ever seen. "I gather this is just an investment?"

"Much more, actually." His sensual lips lifted into an easy grin. "I plan to live there with my daughter." Affection laced his low voice. "So if you could just find something and let me know..." He glanced at his phone again, which was chiming quietly, then rose as if to leave.

Eve stood and moved around her desk. Because of the eight-inch difference in their heights, which was modified only slightly by her three-inch heels, she had to tilt her head to look up at him. "When will you be available to look at properties?" she asked, knowing from experience that he was going to be one of those demanding clients who didn't want to waste an instant.

Derek grimaced. He shoved back the edges of his suit jacket, the impatient action briefly diverting her gaze to his flat abs and lean hips. "I only want to look at one."

Lifting her chin, Eve studied him for a long beat. She couldn't help wondering if the sexy venture capitalist was this way with everyone he hired. Or just the nonessential personnel? "You expect me to choose your home?" she asked drily.

He glanced at his watch as his phone chimed again, his deep blue eyes narrowing. "Yes."

Wanting to make this work—but only to a point— Eve held up a palm. "Then I'm going to need a lot more information."

Derek frowned. He might be only thirty-four, if the information she had found on Google prior to meeting him was correct, but he was all autocratic executive. "I'm too busy for that right now."

Which left her no choice. She walked him to the door and opened it wide. "Then," she said, just as imperiously, not about to make herself miserable—especially at this time of year—by working with a man who was far too big for his britches, "you'll have to find yourself another Realtor."

Derek stared in amazement. "You're firing me as a client?"

Eve nodded and ushered him out. Then she smiled one last time. "Consider it my Christmas present to myself."

Two hours later, as she entered the conference room for the Friday afternoon staff meeting, Eve was still trying to figure out how to tell her mother what she'd done.

The two other sales agents, Vanessa and Astrid, were already there. Eve's mom—the owner of the company—was seated at the head of the table. As always, Marjorie Loughlin was beautifully dressed, today in a red wool suit and heels, her short silvery-blond hair perfectly coiffed. Despite the artful application of makeup, Eve couldn't help but notice her mother looked tired. But maybe that was to be expected. Like the rest of the staff of the all-female realty firm she had founded, Marjorie put in long hours.

"I have great news," she said. "We are still ahead of Sibley & Smith Realty in annual sales by several million dollars." She paused and massaged her left shoulder. "And you all know what that means."

"More exclusive, top-dollar listings and sales," Astrid declared, already pulling out her calculator.

Vanessa winked. "Not to mention that new Mercedes convertible I've been coveting."

Marjorie dabbed a bead of sweat from her hairline. "Luckily, we all have clients wanting to close on homes before the end of the year." Briefly, she went over the list of Astrid's and Vanessa's clients, as well as her own. Then she turned to Eve, addressing the properties and clients of primary concern. "There's Flash Lefleur's condo—which we really need to get sold before the listing expires—and Derek McCabe."

"Right." Eve steeled herself for her mother's disapproval as she prepared to talk about the latter. "About that…"

Marjorie's hand went to the left side of her neck. "Don't tell me there's a problem there."

Except for the fact I fired him? Not a one.

Eve noted her mother was pressing her hand against the bottom of her jaw. "Mom, are you all right…?"

Marjorie winced, as if in pain.

Something was wrong! Eve rushed toward her in alarm. "Mom!"

Her skin a peculiar ashen gray, Marjorie swayed slightly. "I feel a little dizzy," she said, then slumped in her chair in a dead faint.

One harrowing ambulance ride, admission to the hospital and balloon angioplasty later, Marjorie was finally declared stable and moved to a room in the cardiac care unit. Once she was settled, the doctor came in to go over the results of all the tests, as well as the emergency surgical procedure. "You were lucky. It was only a mild heart attack," the cardiologist announced.

"Impossible," Marjorie declared, still looking awfully pale and anxious, despite the medicines they had given her to help her relax. "I'm in perfect health. It was indigestion. A lunch gone wrong. That was all."

The doctor turned to Eve. "Is your mother always this difficult?"

"Yes," she said.

"No," Marjorie stated at the same moment.

Dr. Jackson smiled and shook his head in silent remonstration, obviously having dealt with similar situations before. He turned back to his patient. "We're going to keep you in the hospital, as a precaution, for forty-eight hours, Mrs. Loughlin. After that, I'd like you to go to the cardiac rehab unit, in the annex across the street, for another month, for further evaluation and treatment."

"That's impossible!" Marjorie folded her arms belligerently. "I have *work* to do."

Clearly unintimidated, the physician countered, "It's absolutely necessary, Mrs. Loughlin. You need to rest and rebuild your strength, and above all else, rethink how you've been living your life."

Marjorie sent Eve a look, begging her to intervene.

"I agree with the doctor," Eve said as the physician slipped from the room, wisely leaving the persuasion to a family member.

"But the annual sales award…"

"I'll see we still get it," Eve promised gently.

Still, Marjorie fretted. "I have a new client, that Houston oilman, Red Bloom, coming in soon to see the Santiago Florres–designed home."

Eve smiled. "Not to worry, Mom. I'll take care of that, too."

"You have Derek McCabe.…"

Eve had had plenty of time to regret her foolhardiness. "I'll handle his sale, too," she reassured her mother. *At least I hope I will.*

"You're sure?" Marjorie started to relax, as the meds finally kicked in.

She nodded. Her mother had done so much for her over the years. It was now her turn to be the caretaker. "Just rest now." She bent and kissed Marjorie's temple. And then, hoping like hell it wasn't too late to undo the damage, Eve went to make good on her vow.

"What do you mean, it didn't work out?" Derek's ex-wife said over the phone late the next afternoon. "Marjorie Loughlin is the best Realtor in Dallas!"

"I didn't get her. I was assigned her daughter."

Carleen paused. The sounds of their infant daughter and Carleen's lively household could be heard in the background. "I haven't met Eve Loughlin, but she's supposed to be good, too."

She was beautiful, Derek mused, that was for sure. Temperamental, too. A knock sounded at his door. Aware that his assistant had already left for the day, he said, "Can you hang on a minute?" He walked across his private office and opened the door.

On the other side was the show-stopping beauty who had sent him packing. In a long cashmere coat, vibrant blue business suit and suede heels, Eve Loughlin was the epitome of Texas elegance and style. Around five feet seven inches tall, she was slender and lithe, with great legs and even more spectacular curves. From her full breasts to her narrow waist and hips, there wasn't an inch of her left wanting. And despite his irritation with her, his attraction didn't end there. Her skin was fair and utterly flawless, her nose pert, her cheekbones high and sculpted. Her shoulder-length golden-brown hair was so lush and thick he wanted to sink his hands into it. Most mesmerizing of all, though, were her intelligent, wide-set amber eyes, which seemed to hide as much as they revealed.

Derek swallowed around the sudden dryness of his throat, and tore his eyes from her plump, kissable lips. No good could come of this. "Listen, Carleen, I've got to go."

As always, his ex understood. "I'll see you at five-thirty. Craig and I will have Tiffany ready to go."

"Thanks. See you then." Derek ended the call.

Meanwhile, Eve Loughlin waited with a patient, angelic smile.

Not about to make it easy on her, after the way she had summarily dismissed him the afternoon before, Derek lifted a brow. Waited.

Her smile only became more cordial and determined. "I'm sorry to interrupt."

If that was the case, Derek thought, she already would have left. "What brings you here?"

"I wanted to apologize for what happened yesterday."

She looked as if she actually might be regretting her actions, if the shadows beneath her eyes—shadows that hadn't been there the day before—were any indication. Derek's attitude softened just a little, even as the rest of him remained wary as all get-out. "I'm listening."

She held her red crocodile briefcase in front of her like a shield. "If you can find it in your heart to forgive me, I'd like to retain your business for Loughlin Realty."

Maybe it was the way his marriage had turned out, or the experiences he'd suffered through with women he had dated since, but he'd had enough fickle women to last him a lifetime. Regarding her skeptically, Derek lounged against his desk, his arms folded. "If that's the case, then why did you fire me as a client in the first place?"

* * *

Time to grovel, Eve thought, setting her briefcase on the seat of the armchair beside her. Not her favorite thing, but in this case, extremely necessary if she was to make good on her promise to her mother. Eve noted the spacious office matched him well. Done in varying shades of gray, with large masculine furniture befitting a man of his physical stature, the executive suite had a beautiful view of downtown Dallas.

Gathering her courage, she looked into Derek Mc-Cabe's vivid blue eyes. "Let's just say it was an all-around bad day." Bad time of year, actually. Christmas always made her feel out of sync and vaguely depressed. "I took my frustrations out on you," she admitted, "and that was definitely not the right thing to do." She lifted her palms apologetically. "I wasn't brought up that way, and as a real estate agent, I certainly wasn't trained to behave like that."

Derek looked her up and down, then paused, his broad shoulders relaxing slightly. "I wasn't brought up that way, either." An awkward silence ensued, and then he slid her a long, thoughtful look. "I probably shouldn't have kept you waiting outside your office for a good half hour while I handled other calls."

Understanding flowed between them, as tangible as their previous frustration. Eve easily met him halfway. "Thanks for acknowledging that."

His eyes twinkled. "So maybe we were both at fault yesterday?"

"Maybe." And there it was, she thought as his rueful smile broadened, the legendary McCabe charm.

"Well, good." He came forward and briefly shook

her hand to seal the truce. "Then we have something in common."

Eve's skin tingled as they broke contact and politely stepped away from each other. He inclined his head. "So what's next?" he murmured.

She drew a deep, bolstering breath, then took a seat in the armchair and opened her briefcase. "I'm ready to meet your demands."

His phone chimed. He peered down at it, then set it aside. His full attention on Eve once again, he asked, "What stopped you yesterday?"

Watching him take a seat behind his desk, Eve sensed sugarcoating the situation would get her nowhere with the accomplished businessman. "I didn't want to proceed because I felt selecting a property for you, without knowing anything about you or your specific needs, would be a disservice to us both."

He pressed his fingertips together. "In what way?"

"If you end up purchasing a home you're unhappy with, that dissatisfaction will eventually be heaped on Loughlin Realty. And more specifically, me." Hesitating for a moment, Eve crossed her legs and discreetly tugged her skirt a little lower over her knees. "My reputation depends on being able to find the exact right home for my clients. If I can't do that, I may as well not continue as an agent."

His dark brows furrowed. "That's why you wanted me to fill out the forms?"

Finally, they were getting somewhere! "I don't even know how old your daughter is. Or if she lives with you full-time or part-time, or simply visits."

"Tiffany lives with me fifty percent of the time. My ex and I share custody."

"Do you want her to go to public or private school?"

"Probably public, if we're in the Highland Park district, but we're not there yet. She's just turned one."

What was it about this man that had Eve losing her equilibrium? Usually, she was much better at maintaining a casual, inscrutable demeanor. Blowing out a breath, she attempted to rein in her reaction. "You must be very recently divorced."

"It was final last summer. We were separated for a year and a half before that," he related mildly.

And his child was one now, Eve thought, doing some quick calculations.

"Aren't you going to say it?" Derek asked, something akin to disappointment on his handsome face. He studied her bluntly. "What a terrible person I must have been to have left a pregnant wife?"

This felt like some kind of a test. Deliberately, she held his gaze. "I'm sure you had your reasons." Her manner matter-of-fact, she continued, "In any case, it's none of my business."

He appeared to be mulling that over. "So when did you want to get started?" he finally said, after a long, awkward pause.

Glad he had decided to use their firm for his home search, after all, Eve smiled. "I'm available anytime."

"Right now?"

Another test. Eve inhaled and smiled again. "Absolutely."

Derek stood and reached for his coat, all McCabe determination once again. "Then let's go."

Chapter 2

"Mind if I drive?" Derek said as they walked out the door of his swanky office complex.

Whatever the client wanted. Within reason. That was the rule. "Not at all," Eve fibbed. "Where are we going?"

"I have to pick up my daughter by five-thirty. I'll have her until tomorrow evening." He paused to help Eve with her coat, and then escorted her out to a late-model Jaguar SUV. He opened the passenger door, waited for her to slide in, then circled around to the driver's side.

Impressed with his good manners—it had been a long time since she had met anyone so naturally chivalrous—Eve pulled out her notebook again. Determined to keep things strictly business, she asked, "You want to take her with us when we look?"

"Tomorrow, when we go see the house we select, yes. As for this evening, I plan to take her back to my hotel, feed and bathe her, and then put her to bed."

Eve wasn't sure where that left her and the business she needed to conduct.

Derek continued, "And while I do all that, we'll have a little chat about what property would be best suited for my daughter and me."

Eve wasn't surprised. Most single parents were adept multitaskers. Still, she would have preferred they talk under less intimate circumstances. She wanted to know only enough about him and his life to do her job well. Anything else would be just too personal.

He turned onto Crescent Avenue. "I assume you have most of the property specs on the computer?"

Eve nodded. "Including visual tours."

"Then we should be able to pick one."

Derek parked in the driveway of one of the largest, most elegant properties in Highland Park. "Mind giving me a hand? There's a lot of stuff when we switch back and forth."

So now she was a bellboy, too. What next? A nanny? Tamping down her irritation, Eve flashed a smile. "No problem."

This time, she managed to exit the sedan before Derek could gallantly lend a hand. If he noticed her effort to keep things on an impersonal level, he didn't show it. Instead, he seemed distracted, almost eager, as they walked to the front door. The doorbell was answered by an attractive brunette in a silk shirt, heels and jeans. She had a pair of reading glasses perched on the end of her nose and a pen tucked into the short, sophisticated curls above her ear. Her expression was intellectual—and kind.

"Hey, stranger!" She greeted Derek with a friendly pat on the arm and a peck on his cheek. "How's the house-hunting going?"

Derek inclined his head at Eve. "We haven't really started yet. Carleen, this is Eve Loughlin. Eve, Carleen Walton, my ex-wife."

The woman grinned and extended her hand. "It's nice to meet you," she said.

They certainly were friendly, Eve noted. Maybe the most amiable exes she had ever seen. "Nice to meet you, too," she replied.

A tall forty-something man ambled up with a baby in his arms.

"And this is Craig, my husband," Carleen continued. "With our baby, Tiffany."

And what a beautiful baby she was, Eve could not help but note.

The one-year-old had a cloud of dark curly hair, like her mom's, and Derek's vivid sea-blue eyes. She was dressed in a white turtleneck, ruffled red velvet overalls and shiny, high-topped shoes. Spying Eve, she beamed, her smile revealing four teeth, two on the bottom and two on top.

Eve had never been much of a baby person. She saw no reason to lust after something she likely would never have. But something about this little girl captivated her attention.

Still grinning, Tiffany lifted her chubby little hands to her face and spread her fingertips over her eyes. "Peek—boo!" she chirped to Eve.

Eve couldn't help it; she chuckled. She lifted her

hands to her own eyes and covered them playfully. "Peekaboo to you, too!"

Tiffany threw back her head and chortled. Without warning, she lurched out of Craig's arms and reached for Eve.

Eve caught the infant, cuddling her close. It wasn't the first time she had ever held a baby. However, it *was* the first time she'd held one and felt something catch in her heart.

"She's a real people person," Carleen noted proudly.

Craig agreed. "Never met a stranger..." he teased.

Tiffany settled in Eve's arms. She had that wonderful baby-fresh scent. A smear of what looked like strawberry yogurt at the corner of her mouth. More of it on her hands.

Tiffany tilted her head to one side. She looked at Eve. "Mommy?" she asked.

"No, I'm not a momma," Eve said.

Although for the first time in her life, she found herself wanting to be.

Behind Craig came half a dozen more kids, from toddlers to teens. One of them was holding a wet baby wipe.

"And the rest of our brood," Craig continued. Catching Eve's confused look, he said, "From my marriage to my late wife."

They all certainly looked happy, Eve thought, like the ideal blended family.

Craig took the wipe and handed it to Eve as more introductions were made.

Too late. The little girl's sticky fingers had found their way to Eve's hair and were wrapped in the long, silky strands, transferring strawberry yogurt even as they tugged.

Tiffany giggled.

Derek jumped in. "Honey, you can't do that," he chided, working to free the tiny fingers.

"It's okay," Eve said.

And despite the stickiness, she really didn't mind.

The close contact had given her a glimpse into the little girl's personality. And what was there was all sweetness and innocence.

She could see why Derek was so bent on being as close to his daughter as he could. And she admired the friendship and cooperation his ex and her new family demonstrated, as Carleen put a hat and jacket on their little girl before Derek took charge of putting Tiffany into her car seat. Craig and the kids carried several large bags of clothes and toys, and a stroller, out to the car.

"I hope you can find something for Derek without too much delay," Carleen told Eve pleasantly.

Craig nodded. "Life will be a lot easier for them when they're in a house instead of a hotel."

Where was the acrimony that usually existed in recently divorced couples? Eve wondered. Not that there was a residual attraction between them, either. The only love Carleen and Derek seemed to harbor for each other was the old-and-trusted-friends variety. Although why that would be a relief to Eve, she didn't know. She was just helping Derek buy a house, not becoming part of this unorthodox situation.

Eve returned Carleen's and Craig's smiles. She dipped her head in acquiescence, promising, "I'll do my very best."

* * *

"Anyone ever tell you that you have the patience of a saint?" Derek asked several hours later, as he paced the length of his two-bedroom hotel suite, his drowsy daughter in his arms.

He had shed the suit and tie shortly after they'd walked in, emerging from the bedroom in a pair of worn jeans and the same pale blue dress shirt he'd had on earlier. With the first two buttons undone, sleeves rolled to just below the elbow and the hem untucked, he looked casual and at ease. Having gotten a glimpse of the man he was in his off hours, Eve liked what she saw. It also gave her hope that she would eventually be able to connect with him on a more congenial level, and talk some sense into him when it came to looking for a place to call home.

In the meanwhile, Tiffany had resisted being tucked in, so Derek was now "walking" her to sleep. It seemed to be working, Eve noted, as she watched the little girl lay her head on his broad shoulder and slowly close her eyes.

Eve smiled as Tiffany yawned again and cuddled even closer against her daddy's big strong frame. Eve sighed despite herself. Was there anything more compelling than watching a man tenderly care for a child?

Abruptly aware that Derek was watching her as intently as she was watching him, Eve brushed aside the fantasies he'd been engendering all evening and reassured him with a smile. "Not to worry. Adjusting my schedule to my client's is a necessary component of my vocation."

She hadn't planned to be there through Tiffany's dinner and bath, but it had given her time to get better acquainted with Derek and his daughter and intermittently ask him questions about what he wanted in a home. Which in turn gave her a better idea what properties to show him.

Noting his daughter was now sound asleep, Derek carried her into the adjacent bedroom and set her ever so gently down in her crib. He paused to cover her with a blanket, and then returned to the living room. With his dark hair attractively mussed, the hint of evening beard rimming his handsome face and his long legs emphasized by close-fitting jeans, he was the epitome of masculinity. And *way* too sexy for her own good, Eve reminded herself.

He plucked the bottle of sparkling water from the room service tray, filled two glasses and added ice, then handed her one. "Ready to get down to business?"

She accepted the beverage with a smile. "Let's do it."

She brought up the map of Highland Park on her computer. The town was three miles north of the center of Dallas, and only 2.26 square miles in size. Yet it had approximately 8,900 residents, most living in very luxurious and expensive homes. "Exactly how close do you want to be to your ex-wife's place?"

Shrugging in response, he pulled up a chair beside her at the desk. He turned it around and sank onto it, his long limbs on either side of the seat, his arms folded over the back. After a moment of deliberation, he slanted Eve a glance. "Next door wouldn't be bad."

She turned toward him so abruptly her stocking-clad knee brushed his denim-clad thigh. A flicker of sensation swept through her. "Seriously?"

He lifted his shoulders in another shrug. "Just because Carleen and I are divorced doesn't mean we can't give Tiffany the same level of familial happiness she would have enjoyed had we stayed together." He studied Eve over the rim of his glass. "You don't believe that can happen?"

She paused, not sure how to answer that. "You two seem to get along great."

Her caution made him smile and search her eyes. "And you think that's weird."

Eve wanted to deny it. But she sensed if she was less than honest, she would lose him as a client. She shifted so they were no longer in danger of touching, and leaned back in her seat. "I think it's commendable."

He waited, still studying her.

Eve gulped some water, aware she was going to have to open up even more. "And...unusual," she said finally.

She lowered her eyes to the strong column of his throat and the tufts of springy, dark brown hair beneath his collarbone, then quickly looked back up. Clearing her throat, Eve tried for diplomacy. "I'm not married. Never have been. But from what I've seen, sharing custody can be really challenging."

He lifted a brow. "You mean ugly."

"Or just plain difficult." She shrugged, still feeling as if she were walking through a minefield, courtesy of Derek McCabe. "Given that there are so many emotions involved in these kinds of situations..."

His gaze drifted over her face slowly, before returning to her eyes. "You're wondering why I'm okay with my wife remarrying."

Was she that easy to read? And why did she, a consummate professional who made a point these days to keep her personal feelings out of every business situation, really want to know? Telling herself it would help her find the right home for him if she knew more about the overall situation, she shifted a little closer. "Are you?"

He nodded, then rose and walked back to the room service table where several desserts sat untouched. He picked up a plate and gestured for her to have at it, too. "Maybe if Carleen and I had been head over heels in love, I'd feel differently."

He'd chosen the slice of coconut cake garnished with berries. Eve picked up the crème brûlée.

He settled himself on the sofa. She selected an adjacent wingback chair and spread a napkin over her lap. "But you weren't in love?" This was getting more interesting by the moment.

Derek exhaled, regret sharpening his handsome features. "We were really great friends from the moment we met at Harvard Business School. We both worked in the financial sector, and wanted the same things, including high-powered careers—and kids. And we figured if you were going to have a family, you should be married."

"So you tied the knot."

Savoring another bite of cake, he nodded. "For the first couple of years it was great. We moved back to Texas, where our families were from. We had work and each other. And then Carleen and I met Craig. One of Carleen's coworkers, he had recently lost his wife to cancer. Needless to say, our hearts went out to him. We started helping him with his brood of kids whenever we could. But I was traveling a lot with my job then, so Carleen spent more time over there." There was a long silence. "The experience made her really want children, so we started working on a family of our own. She had just found out she was pregnant when I walked in one day and saw the way they looked at each other."

Eve's heart stilled. She paused, her spoon halfway through the sugary crust on her crème brûlée. "They were having an affair?" She couldn't fathom that, remembering the two people she'd met earlier.

Putting his empty plate aside, Derek exhaled roughly and clamped a hand to the back of his neck. "No, they were both too principled for that. But it was clear to me that Carleen was in love with Craig, the way she never had been with me." He paused, rubbing the tense muscles.

Eve watched Derek rummage around for a coffee cup. Finding one, he filled it from the decanter on the room service tray. "You must have been devastated," she said.

The look on his face said he had been. "I thought about ignoring it," he confided quietly, coming back to sit on the sofa. "Just hoping and praying whatever it was they were obviously feeling would fade."

Eve remembered that they had separated early in Carleen's pregnancy. "But you didn't do that."

He shrugged and turned his eyes back to hers, a mixture of remorse and acceptance visible there. "I realized I couldn't live a lie for the rest of my life. So I asked Carleen about it, and she finally admitted what I had already observed. That, in an ideal world, she probably *would* have ended up with Craig...but she was married to me, and she intended to *stay* married to me."

"You disagreed?"

He gestured with a weariness that seemed to come from deep in his soul. "Pretending feelings don't exist doesn't mean they aren't there. I wanted Carleen to be happy. And I knew she belonged with Craig."

That was gallant. But… "You weren't the least bit jealous?"

He rubbed his jaw in a rueful manner, then drawled, "Let's just say I wanted what they were having for myself."

That made sense, Eve thought. Everyone was entitled to the love of a lifetime. Whether or not a person ever actually achieved that was a different matter entirely.

"So, the two of us split up," Derek continued. "I stayed involved with the pregnancy and was there for the birth. For propriety's sake, we waited to finalize our divorce until Tiffany was six months old. A short engagement followed. And then Craig and Carleen got married in late October and relocated from Houston to Dallas—so that Carleen could have a job with greater flexibility. I made arrangements to follow suit."

Eve studied the attractive man sitting opposite her. He really was one of the most honorable men she had ever met. But she couldn't help but wonder if all that selflessness came with a price.

Derek wasn't sure why he was talking about any of this. He certainly didn't need to tell Eve about his broken marriage in order for her to find him a suitable home. And yet there was something about the way she looked at him, as if she wanted to understand—not just the situation, but get to know him in a way few did— that had started him talking, and kept him talking when he should have stopped.

"This is the point where you tell me I should have made the most of my ex's foibles and fought for full custody of my kid," he said cavalierly, wanting to see her gut reaction to his situation. To find out if she was as skeptical and disapproving as his family and friends had been. Emotional affairs, many had pointed out to him, were a lot more destructive than sex with someone outside the marriage. For that alone he was owed full custody.

Eve looked puzzled. "How would that have benefited Tiffany? She needs a mommy *and* a daddy, doesn't she?"

Glad to see she wasn't the vengeful type, Derek nodded gratefully.

"And you work full-time. And probably still travel," Eve continued.

"Although less than I did before," he said.

She compressed her lips, then took her last bite of crème brûlée and set the dish aside. "Having parents who rue each other's very existence is no help to anyone, believe me."

As interested in Eve as she apparently was in him, Derek sat back in his chair and sipped his coffee. "And you know that because…?"

She got up and poured herself a cup of coffee, too. "My father wanted nothing to do with me, not when I was a kid or after I grew up."

Derek winced. "Wow. That's harsh."

Eve added cream, then sprinkled in a packet of sugar. She stirred the coffee, tasted it, then went back and sat down at the other end of the couch. "You get used to it. For a lot of years, I wished my mother and my biological father had gotten along. Then I began to accept that if they had no use for each other, it was really better that we never saw him. You, on the other hand, have managed to stay friends with your ex and her new husband. The fact you do get along can only benefit all seven of the kids involved."

Her ready understanding boosted Derek's morale. "So you don't think I was a fool?"

Eve shook her head. "I think you were noble." She flashed him an encouraging smile and continued to hold his gaze as she sipped her coffee. "No, I think you were realistic, that you did the right thing for everyone."

Not sure when he had enjoyed a woman's company this much, he smiled back at her. "Thanks."

"So." Her expression determined, Eve rose gracefully and headed to the desk where she'd set up her laptop computer. "Back to the house-hunting."

When Derek joined her, she glanced up at him from the computer. "I don't want to waste your time, but I really want you to look at more than one home." Before he could object, she continued firmly, "There are three immediately available properties in your stated price range in Highland Park, within a two-mile radius of Tiffany's other home. I've emailed you the specs on all three, to peruse at your leisure. Two are having unadvertised open houses tomorrow afternoon, for qualified buyers only. The other is available only by appointment. Would you like to hit all three at once tomorrow?"

Derek did—for reasons that didn't have as much to do with house-hunting as they should. "We'll have to take Tiffany with us," he warned.

Eve's expression softened in a way that let him know what a good mother she would be one day. "Shouldn't be a problem," she assured him confidently.

Derek watched her put her laptop back in the case.

"Can we do it after her afternoon nap, say, at two-thirty?"

"Absolutely." Eve gathered up her belongings and headed for the door.

Derek walked with her. She hesitated in the entry, and for a brief moment he was tempted to kiss her. As if sensing it, Eve drew away. "I'll see you then," she said briskly, before moving off down the hall.

"You're looking a lot better," Eve told her mother happily the next morning after arriving at the hospital to visit her.

Marjorie accepted with a smile the stack of magazines Eve had brought her. "How are things going with Derek McCabe?"

A little too well on the personal side, Eve thought uncomfortably. She moved a chair closer to the bed and sank into it. "We're looking at three properties this afternoon." Marjorie, who had every luxury listing in the area memorized, considered the plan thoughtfully as her daughter specified which ones they were seeing. "Is he going to be easy or difficult to please?"

In what way? Eve pushed the unexpectedly amorous thought aside. "It's too soon to tell." All she knew for certain was that Derek had an enormous capacity for giving—to the point he probably had Christmas in his heart all year long. And Eve envied him that. She had trouble getting into the holiday spirit at all.

Marjorie paused. "I know I've said this before, but… be careful. I don't want to see you hurt."

Eve clasped her mom's hand, happy that she didn't seem as weak and fragile as she had the day before. "Believe me, I don't want to be hurt, either." One devastating love affair had been enough to last her a lifetime.

"You don't need a man in your life to be happy," her mother continued.

Oh, how well Eve knew that. She squeezed her mother's fingers. "You don't have to worry about it, Mom. Derek is just a client. I'm his real estate agent." She paused to let her words sink in. "And nothing more."

It didn't matter how physically and emotionally attracted she was to him, she thought. At the end of the transaction, she and Derek would go their separate ways. And that would be that.

Chapter 3

"Not exactly what you had in mind, hmm?" Eve asked Derek as they left house number two and headed down the long curving stone walk to his car. It was a beautiful December day with clear blue skies, and warm enough that only light jackets were required.

Derek turned to her. He had showered and shaved before meeting her, and he smelled of sandalwood and pine. "I've been in nice homes before, lots of them."

"But no open houses where free Botox injections were offered?"

He mimed a shudder and moved closer, the sunlight picking up the mahogany in his short dark hair. "I know plastic surgery and other enhancements are popular in Dallas," he said in a low voice. "But to do it as part of an open house…"

"A bit tacky?" she asked wryly.

"You got that right." He shifted Tiffany to his other arm while he fished for his keys.

Seeing he needed assistance, Eve held out her arms. She expected the tyke to slide into them as easily as she had the day before. Instead, Tiffany turned away and buried her face in her daddy's shoulder.

"Sorry," Derek murmured.

"No problem," Eve returned easily. She was about to offer to help him reach his keys, but slipping her fingers into the jeans pocket adjacent to his fly did not seem like the best idea. She turned away to survey the beautifully landscaped lawn.

With Tiffany cuddled on his shoulder, Derek fished some more. He finally got what he needed and unlocked the doors. While he put Tiffany in her car seat, Eve slid into the passenger side of the Jaguar.

Yet another anomaly in this situation.

Normally, she drove clients around.

But since Tiffany's car seat was already in his SUV, and they were apparently a hassle to put in correctly, Derek preferred to do the driving.

He settled himself behind the wheel, grabbed his designer shades and adjusted them over his eyes. Which was a shame, Eve thought, because now she wouldn't be able to use his gaze to intuit what he was thinking; she'd have to rely on his body language and tone of voice to try to figure him out.

Stifling a sigh, she put on her own sunglasses to guard against the glare.

Derek stretched his right arm along the back of the front seats, turned to make sure all was clear and reversed out of the drive. "As if that Botox party wasn't weird enough...what was with the free massages at that first place?" He put the car in gear, then sat idling while Eve punched the address of their next possibility into the GPS built into the dashboard.

"It was part of the promotion for the property," Eve explained. "A way to get qualified buyers, ones who can afford a seven-or eight-million-dollar home, out to see it."

Derek drove off when the suggested route popped up on the screen. Shortly thereafter, he made the first turn. "The thinking being, if you actually tried out the home gym and the pool and the sport court, and then had a free massage..." He waited for a traffic jam on Mockingbird Lane to clear.

"And a catered lunch in the gourmet kitchen." Noticing her skirt had ridden up slightly on her thigh, Eve discreetly tugged it down. "You'd be hooked."

He shrugged. "It might work. If that was what you wanted." The home had a billiard room and a home theater, swimming pool and crowd-sized hot tub.

"I'm guessing it was too much of a bachelor pad for your taste." Even though it had been just down the street from his ex.

"It didn't exactly spell *family*," he agreed drily.

Eve brought out the specs she had previously sent him. She refreshed his memory with a few photos from the sales brochure while they sat at a stoplight. "You may like the next one."

"Daddy!"

Derek glanced at his daughter via the rearview mirror. She looked ready to start fussing at any moment. "Hi, honey," he said, turning around to smile at her briefly, before picking up the conversation where they'd left off. "I hope so," he stated quietly. "Tiffany's been a trouper, but she's really tired."

Unfortunately, the next property elicited as many frowns and scowls from both Derek and his little girl as the first two had. Luckily, there was no open house going on, so they were free to talk frankly. "What is it you don't like about it?" Eve asked, trying to get a handle on what it was Derek truly wanted in a home.

He walked around the huge rooms.

Part of the estate of a late oil tycoon, it had been built in the early eighties, and recently staged and updated in sophisticated neutral palettes.

"Let me count the ways," he said, placating the little girl he held in his arms with the baby bottle of apple juice he'd brought in with them. "The marble floors are way too cold and hard. The floor plan is awful, and I think the spiral staircase could be dangerous for a kid."

Okay, Eve noted, that was a start.

She edged closer. "It's five streets over from your ex's home. The staircase could be replaced. And it has a nice big backyard with a fence, and room for a really nice play set."

Finished with her juice, Tiffany pushed the empty baby bottle at Eve, then reached out and touched Eve's hair. The little girl smiled as she got a fistful, and held on tight.

Afraid to move, Eve smiled back at her and stayed very still.

Derek came to the rescue, his touch tender as he extricated her from his daughter. Which in turn made Eve wonder what kind of lover he would be. Probably excellent, if her feminine intuition was any indication. Not that she should be thinking this way...

"It also has a pool," he continued, while Eve put the empty bottle back in the diaper bag slung over his broad shoulder. "I don't think I want a swimming pool with a toddler around, fenced or not. Maybe when she's older. Not now."

Aware that Tiffany was looking restless again, Eve rummaged in the diaper bag and found a set of plastic baby keys she could play with. "Pools can be taken out. The entire decor can be changed."

Tiffany grinned and shook the keys in both her tiny fists until they rattled.

Derek continued glancing around. "It would still be way too big."

As would all the properties in the seven-to eight-million-dollar range, Eve thought, since the asking price was directly related to the amount of square footage.

Trying to be helpful, she asked, "Do you want to look at something smaller?"

His jaw set in that stubborn way she was beginning to know so well. Tiffany grabbed the sunglasses tucked into the neckline of his cashmere sweater, shook them once and threw them to the floor. They landed with a clatter but, to Eve's relief, didn't break.

"I wanted there to be parity in our homes." Derek set Tiffany down on the floor. Happy to be able to flex her legs, she grabbed the keys and sunglasses and toddled happily around the foyer, babbling all the while.

"Okay," Eve said.

Derek blocked the way to the staircase, keeping an eye on his daughter while studying Eve shrewdly. "You don't agree with that objective, though."

There he went, putting her on the spot again. Although it wasn't always what a client wanted, Eve decided yet again to be honest. She shrugged and knelt down to engage Tiffany with another toy the little girl had previously discarded. "Your homes are going to be different, no matter the square footage and price tag."

Tiffany took the stuffed bunny and sat down on the floor to examine it.

Confident that the toddler was entertained, at least for the moment, Eve rose. She looked her handsome client in the eye and continued, "Carleen has a husband and seven kids, if you count Craig's. At your place, it's just going to be the two of you." Eve paused to let that fact sink in, and then forged on. "Tiffany is going to feel the difference. It doesn't mean she'll like one place any more or any less, especially at this age. Your home should reflect who you are, what *you* want, Derek. Not what Carleen and Craig need and want for their brood."

Tiffany stood and grabbed her daddy's jean-clad legs. "So something cozier." Derek smiled and picked her up.

His daughter nestled against his chest, as if in heaven, a reaction Eve could understand, given who Tiffany was nestling against. It had to feel great, being that close to Derek. She knew she would be happy with his big, strong arms wrapped around her.

"There are smaller homes in this area," she told him. "Some have been redone, some not. In any case, the price tag will be quite different." Which, Eve knew, could be a deal-breaker for a venture capitalist who also wanted a house as a monetary investment.

Derek squinted. "How different?"

"It depends on how small you want to go. Not to mention the overall condition of the property."

Derek sighed as Tiffany grabbed his sweater with both hands and let out an impatient shout. "Bye-bye!"

He headed out the door. "Meaning we have to keep looking."

Eve paused to lock up. "If you want to be happy with your choice, you do."

He glanced at his watch. "I have to take Tiffany back to Carleen."

It was almost five-thirty. "You want to call it a day, then?" Eve asked, unable to help but feel a little disappointed that their time together would soon be ending.

"Actually," he said, as if reading her mind and feeling the same way, "I'd like to keep looking tonight."

"Okay, then," Eve smiled. "Let's do it."

"I think we should stop. At least for today," Eve said, an exhausting three hours later.

Darkness had fallen a long time ago. They had physically gone through two more homes, and driven by eight more, only to have Derek dismiss them out of hand for one reason or another.

"After a while, everything begins to blur together. We can start again tomorrow if you like." Plus, without Tiffany as a tiny chaperone and constant distraction, Eve found herself way too physically aware of her hunky client.

The only good thing was that once they had dropped his daughter off, they'd been able to swing by the office so she could pick up *her* car and do the driving. While Derek concentrated on perusing the neighborhoods from the passenger seat, she tried hard not to think about how intimate it felt to have him sitting so close beside her.

"What about that one?" His mind evidently where it should be, Derek pointed to a cozy English Tudor–style cottage with a for-sale sign in front.

Grateful for the latest diversion, Eve steered her car to the curb. Up and down the street, homes were lit up with Christmas lights. However, the one in front of them was dark and neglected. Familiar with the original 1960s interior, she warned, "It's a fixer-upper. Nowhere near move-in ready. And way below your target price."

Derek continued to stare at the ivy-covered brick. "I'd like to see it, anyway."

They wouldn't need an appointment; this property was on lockbox. She could let them in.

"Okay," Eve said, thinking that if anything were to end his desire to keep looking, this particular property would be it. She cut the ignition and led the way up to the front porch. Inside, it was worse than she remembered from the initial agents tour: chill and dank. Bad carpeting, outdated everything.

"What's the story on the property?" Derek asked.

She continued switching on overhead lights. "The owner has gone into a nursing home. The family isn't interested in doing anything to the house." Hence, it had been cleared of all belongings, but not staged or in any way adequately prepared for sale. "They're hoping it will go as a teardown."

He shot her a questioning look.

"Which means that someone will buy it for the lot—which is a premium—demolish this property and start from scratch," she explained.

Derek ran a hand over a wall in the study. He shook his head admiringly at the built-in bookshelves and ornate trim. "Look at this wood."

"Paneling's not really popular these days."

"I like it."

The client was always right. And it could be stripped and refinished to give it a more updated look. "It's very masculine."

He pivoted and regarded her speculatively, as if wondering if she was playing him.

She wasn't.

After a moment, he seemed to accept that.

Eve sobered. "I want you to see the kitchen, though."

They walked down the hall to the rear of the house. Eve hit another switch. Derek blinked at the orange-yellow-and-brown-plaid vinyl wallpaper. "Talk about a blast from the past," he murmured.

The laminate counters were also bright orange, the floor a speckled linoleum. "I know," Eve sympathized, looking past the grime-smeared windows and severely outdated appliances. "Really awful, hmm?"

He peered at a cobweb overhead. "It could use a good cleaning, that's for certain."

Eve moved her foot away from something sticky on the floor. "No joke."

Derek came closer. He stood next to her, thoughtfully looking around, his steady presence and the warmth of his tall, strong body a nice counterpoint to the lingering chill inside the home. "But with all new appliances..."

Ignoring the tingling deep inside her, along with the wish the two of them had met some other time, some other way, Eve drew a deep breath and pointed out the rest of the flaws. "It's going to need brand-new cabinets, counters, flooring and updated lighting, too." She turned abruptly, her shoulder bumping against his bicep. "The kitchen alone would cost you at least fifty thousand. Then there's the furnace and air conditioning, and it will also most likely need all new electrical and plumbing."

"How much are they asking?"

Doing her best to tamp down her continuing awareness, Eve showed him the listing information left on the kitchen counter. "One point five million, but that's too high for the condition of this house." She led the way up to the second floor. There were four nice-sized bedrooms and two full baths, one off the hall and one off the master bedroom.

Derek continued to look around with real interest. "What do you think it should be going for?"

Eve studied the worn carpeting and cramped, outdated bathrooms, the dingy walls and lack of adequate closet space. "One point two million, max. And that's mostly due to the location." She turned back to Derek, in full business mode, but found herself temporarily blinded by his brilliant blue eyes. "I'd, uh, be tempted to go in at one point one million, and then let them talk you back to one point two, as the most you would pay. Although, with your time frame, wanting to be in before Christmas, I can't recommend you take this on."

Derek stood, legs braced apart, hands on his waist, still looking around. "Surely you know contractors who would be willing to do whatever it took, particularly if bonus pay was involved."

He really was serious. "I do." Despite herself, Eve began to get excited, too.

Derek walked around some more, as if dreaming about what a good infusion of cash and a little tender loving care could do for this home. He swung back toward her. "Could you get it done in a week?"

Good heavens, the man was demanding! But all of a sudden willing to be ambitious, too, Eve straightened her spine and replied, "Maybe two, if we come to terms with the sellers right away, and you're willing to pay time and a half for the entire job."

He shrugged off the problem. "I'm okay with that."

They finished looking around the bedrooms and went back downstairs. "Why this house?" she asked curiously, turning off another bank of lights.

Derek shook his head. He prowled the first floor, his expression thoughtful. "I don't know. Something about the way it looks. Feels." He turned to her with a grin, certain now. "I want to put an offer in tonight."

Eve studied him. She hated snap decisions when it came to something this important. "You're sure this is what you want?" she asked finally.

Derek nodded.

The light in his eyes, his sheer enthusiasm, were irresistible. *Okay, then.* They went back to her office again.

Eve called the other Realtor to let her know an offer was coming in, and then wrote up the contract. She had barely faxed it over when her cell phone rang. Derek's offer, to take the house as is, without inspection, had been accepted.

He grinned. "Looks like I just bought myself a house!" he said, wrapping Eve in a warm, Texas-style hug. It was the kind of embrace people gave each other after the winning goal in a football game. Yet the brief expression of exaltation left her tingling and on edge long after they broke apart.

Eve congratulated Derek again, more formally this time, and then bid him good-night. It was a good thing her business with Derek McCabe was almost over. She was going to have a hard enough time forgetting the powerful attraction she felt for him as it was.

Eve was still thinking about the congratulatory hug from Derek—and her unprecedented reaction to it—when she went to the hospital the next morning to help with her mother's transfer.

As expected, even though the facility was bright and cheerful, Marjorie was less than enthusiastic about her upcoming stay in the cardiac rehab unit.

"I'd rather just go home," she grumbled, accepting the bag of comfortable clothing Eve had brought her.

Aware of the irony in taking on the parental role in their relationship, Eve handed over her mother's computer tablet and the weekend newspapers. "This is a necessary part of your recovery, Mom." Although she doubted her mother would change anything about her life without putting up a heck of a fight.

Marjorie made a face and removed the real estate inserts from both papers. "Have you found Derek McCabe a house yet?"

Grateful for the change of subject, Eve gave her the details.

Her mom blinked. "I thought he was in the market for an eight-million-dollar home!"

Eve knew a transaction of that magnitude would have likely given them a solid lead in the annual sales race. Refusing to feel guilty for doing what was right for her client, however, she explained, "He decided he wanted something much smaller in scope and more baby-friendly. The good news is he's very happy."

Or at least he had been the night before. Eve still

had the feeling it was all happening a little too fast for comfort.

Her sense of foreboding increased the next day.

She had been given permission to get contractors in to look at the property in advance of the closing, and she went to the house to let them in. By the time they'd finished, Derek had arrived. The kitchen and bath designer, plumber, electrician, flooring rep and painters all conferred with him, and promised to have formal estimates for him the following morning.

Bad news relayed, they filed out, one by one.

Leaving Derek and Eve alone.

"So what do you think?" she asked, looking around at the empty house. The heating and ventilation system was out of commission, so the interior was chilly and dank. A light rain was falling, and on this gloomy December day the house seemed even more in need of tender loving care. "Feel overwhelmed yet?"

Derek shook his head. "Excited."

Glad to see he hadn't changed his mind about his spur-of-the-moment decision, because deep down she sensed that this was indeed the perfect home for him, she allowed herself to tease, "And here you thought you weren't the fixer-upper type."

He gave her a leisurely once-over. "Sometimes it's necessary to get business out of the way. So you can move on to more important things."

Puzzled, Eve tilted her head. "Like what?"

The look he gave her was direct, uncompromising, confident. "Asking you out."

For a second, she was certain she hadn't heard right. The sparkle in his eyes told her that she had. Her pulse pounding, Eve worked to get air into her lungs. "On a date?" she asked hoarsely.

His sexy smile widening, he inched closer. "That was the general idea," he said.

Eve pressed her palm to her chest, trying to tamp down the immediate spark of excitement she felt. "I'm flattered."

Derek sobered. "I don't want you to be flattered," he told her huskily. He took her in his arms and pulled her flush against him. "I want you to say yes."

Chapter 4

Yes was what Eve wanted, too. Even if she would have preferred not to admit it. Before she could stop herself, before she could think of all the reasons why not, she let Derek pull her closer still. His head dipped. Her breath caught, and her eyes closed. And then all was lost in the first luscious feeling of his lips lightly pressed against hers.

It was a cautious kiss. A gentle kiss that didn't stay gallant for long. At her first quiver of sensation, he flattened his hands over her spine and deepened the kiss, seducing her with the heat of his mouth and the sheer masculinity of his tall, strong body. Yearning swept through her in great enervating waves. Unable to help herself, Eve went up on tiptoe, leaning into his embrace. Throwing caution to the wind, she wreathed her arms about his neck and kissed him back. Not tentatively, not sweetly, but with all the hunger and need she felt. And to her wonder and delight, he kissed her back in kind, again and again and again.

Derek had only meant to show Eve they had chemistry. Amazing chemistry that would convince her to go out with him, at least once. He hadn't expected to feel tenderness well inside him, even as his body went hard with desire. He hadn't expected to want to make love to her here and now, in this empty house. But sensing that total surrender would be a mistake, he tamped down his own desire and let the kiss come to a slow, gradual end.

Eve stepped backward, too, a mixture of surprise and pleasure on her face. Her breasts were rising and falling quickly, and her lips were moist. Amazement at the potency of their attraction, and something else a lot more cautious, appeared in her eyes. Eve drew a breath, and then anger flashed. "That was a mistake."

Derek understood her need to play down what had just happened, even as he saw no reason to pretend they hadn't enjoyed themselves immensely. "Not in my book," he murmured, still feeling a little off balance himself. In fact, he was ready for a whole lot more.

She held up a finger and shook it. Composed again, she stalked away from him, her high heels echoing on the wood floor. When she swung around to face him, he could tell her every defense was in place. "What you're feeling right now is all related to the roller-coaster emotions of buying a new home. One minute you're up, the next you're down. The euphoria you just felt is going to be very short-lived."

Like hell it was! He was adult enough to know the difference between being excited about purchasing a home, and wanting to make a woman his. And so was she. He rocked back on his heels, braced his hands on his waist and sent her an impudent grin. "You're telling me you've been kissed by clients at the end of a deal before?"

"Yes," Eve said. She looked him in the eye, long and hard. "I have."

Her matter-of-fact confession had served its purpose. First, Derek looked shell-shocked, then skeptical, and finally, as she had hoped, blatantly unhappy. He stepped closer, as if that would change anything. "You're kidding," he exclaimed in a low, raspy voice that practically oozed testosterone.

Eve struggled not to get swept up in the moment or the man, as embarrassment warmed her cheeks. "I wish."

He shifted forward, invading her space. "How many times?"

With effort, she kept her gaze locked with his. Determined to handle a situation that was fast escalating out of control, she replied, "Including you?"

He nodded.

"Twice."

Derek looked at her as if he already knew what it would be like to make love to her. "There must be more to the story," he said.

Since the last thing she needed to be doing was thinking about kissing him again, or worse, imagining what it would be like to make love with him, Eve lifted her chin and drew a deep, calming breath. Refusing to fixate on the fact that everywhere he was hard, she would be soft, or that everywhere he was male, she'd be female, she challenged, "Really. What makes you think that?"

Regarding her with a devil-may-care glint in his eyes, he pointed out, "You're not the kind of woman who lets her guard down easily."

That was certainly true. Although she wished he had not intuited the fact.

"So what happened, the other time?" Derek continued, a tad impatiently.

Eve shrugged and kept her voice matter-of-fact. "I was fresh out of real estate school. Ryan was a classmate of mine, from Southern Methodist University. He had just come into his trust fund and wanted to buy a bachelor pad in Deep Elum. It wasn't my area of expertise, but the commission was going to be great if I could find what he wanted. Ryan, of course, had no idea what that was, so we had to do quite a lot of looking together." Eve paused, recalling how naive and hopelessly romantic she had been at the time.

Working to keep the disillusionment out of her tone, she admitted, "One thing led to another, and by the time Ryan closed on his new loft, it was clear there was something between us. Or so we thought."

The chivalrous, protective look was back in Derek's eyes. "What happened?" he prodded.

"Exactly what you would think," Eve stated, with a cavalier attitude she couldn't begin to really feel. *My heart was broken and my spirits were crushed.* "Ryan and I came to the mutual conclusion that it had all happened too fast. We didn't have nearly as much in common as we'd thought, so we ended it. And," Eve continued, without the slightest bit of irony, "I learned a valuable lesson."

Derek regarded her gently. "Which was?"

She appreciated his understanding, even as she forced herself to take another step away from him. "I'll never again make the mistake of thinking the intimacy that develops during a home search will continue once a residence is found." She splayed a hand across her chest again. "I'm a Realtor. You're my client." She paused to let her words sink in. "And that is all."

She tensed as the first notes of the country ballad "Need You Now" emanated from her cell phone: Loughlin Realty's emergency ring. "Excuse me." Eve plucked her phone out of her bag and stalked off. "I've got to get this."

Sasha, the office manager, was on the other end.

Eve listened, hardly able to believe what was being said about her mother. "She *what?*" Her heart sank. "No! My God, no!" Then she commanded quickly, "Don't do that. Tell her I'll be right there! Yes, I'm five minutes away, max. Just hold her off, Sasha. Please."

Almost as distraught as she'd been the day of her mother's heart attack, Eve ended the call and grabbed her carryall.

"Everything okay?" Derek followed her, obviously concerned.

Aware she'd already been way too intimate with him, she kept him at arm's length. "I've got an emergency back at the office," she told him calmly. "You can stay as long as you like. Just lock up before you go, and return the key to the office."

"You're sure everything is okay?"

It wasn't, but what could she say besides the obvious? "I'm sorry, Derek, I've got to go."

Giving him no further chance to question her, Eve rushed out the door.

The house was oddly silent and gloomy after Eve's abrupt departure. Not certain what had happened, but accepting her implication that it was none of his business, Derek walked around, switching off lights and making sure all the doors were locked. He had almost finished the task when he saw Eve's red-leather-bound iPad sitting on the counter next to the various contractor estimates. She'd left it behind in her haste to get out the door.

He glanced at his watch and saw it was five-thirty. More than likely someone would still be at the office. And he had to return the key in any case.

He finished locking up, got in his car and drove over there. There were two cars in the lot, one of them Eve's white Mercedes sedan. A taxi was just pulling away. Inside the building, Sasha, the office manager, was in the reception area. The mid-thirtyish woman was as eclectically dressed as always, in a vivid handkerchief hem dress and lace-up high-heeled boots. Face pale, tight platinum curls standing on end, she was pacing and wringing her hands.

In Marjorie Loughlin's private office, voices rose.

"Mom, you can't do this!" Eve was insisting emotionally. "You *know* what the doctor said."

The well-coiffed woman beside her retorted, "I have a client I've been wooing for months coming in later this week."

"I know that, Mom," Eve replied in a soul-weary voice Derek had never heard her use before.

Eve's mother bulldozed on, pacing the office in much the same way Derek had seen Eve do. "And someone has to talk some sense into Flash Lefleur and get his condo adequately staged. Otherwise, who knows if and when his place will ever sell? And with only two weeks left on the listing contract!" Marjorie threw up her bejeweled hands. "I really don't want to let that one go, Eve."

"I told you I would take care of that, too," her daughter said plaintively.

"I want to believe you, honey. But…with all we have at stake here. Especially after what happened with the other sale…" The older woman's voice trailed off when she saw Derek standing in the doorway.

It was hard to figure out who looked worse, Derek thought. Marjorie Loughlin was pale to the point of being gray, and a little physically shaky to boot. Eve looked anxious and distressed.

"May I help you?" the older woman asked, suddenly all genteel Southern charm.

Eve jumped in to make introductions. "Mom, this is Derek McCabe. Derek, my mother, Marjorie Loughlin. I don't think the two of you met when you came in the other day."

They hadn't, Derek realized.

Marjorie came forward to shake his hand. "Mr. McCabe, what a pleasure to meet you! Eve tells me you went to contract on a house."

Not really surprised by the zero-to-sixty change in attitude and demeanor—salespeople were legendary for their ability to morph into what was required—he nodded and returned her energetic smile. "I did. Your daughter was amazing, by the way."

"That's always good to hear," Marjorie replied, a bead of perspiration appearing on her elegant brow.

After a tense look at her mother, Eve stepped forward in turn. "What can we help you with?" she asked in a pleasant but businesslike tone.

He lifted the iPad in its red leather case, glad his presence had stopped the familial quarreling, at least momentarily. "You left this at the house."

Eve slanted a glance at her mother, who seemed to be swaying slightly. "Thank you for bringing it."

Before her daughter could get to her, Marjorie eased into the chair behind her impressive glass-and-chrome desk.

Noticing the way she was trembling, Eve turned paler, too. And it was easy to see why she was worried, Derek thought. Marjorie seemed near physical collapse, though she was trying her best to hide it. "Mrs. Loughlin, are you feeling all right?" he asked with concern.

"I don't see how Marjorie could be, since she just got out of the hospital," Sasha cried, obviously near tears.

"And she's supposed to be in the cardiac rehabilitation unit as we speak," Eve added pointedly.

Although she was ghostly white, and shaking visibly, Marjorie glared at her daughter and the stressed-out office manager. "I don't need it."

Eve glowered back, seeming to forget for a moment they had an audience. "That's not what I heard, Mom. I just spoke to your cardiologist, and Dr. Jackson said you checked yourself out against medical advice!"

Another dot of perspiration appeared on Marjorie's forehead, but she wiped it away. "I told the cardiac rehab staff I'd go when my schedule clears up. Right now—" she squared her shoulders and turned to the stack of messages on her desk "—there is work to be done here."

Eve paced, looking ready to explode. "Work the four other employees of the agency can handle."

Once again, Derek stepped in as peacemaker. "How long were you supposed to be at the rehab center?" he asked.

Marjorie shrugged and didn't answer.

"Four weeks," Eve said. "Then she's to continue her physical therapy on an outpatient basis and recuperate at home, until Dr. Jackson gives her the all-clear to return to work, which will probably be not until well after the Christmas holidays."

Derek had been through something similar with his own mother, when pneumonia precluded Josie's return to work. He poured Marjorie a glass of sparkling water and took it to her. Knowing it was sometimes easier to listen to a neutral third party than a family member, he said gently, "That's not too much to ask, is it? To follow medical advice, if for no other reason than to prevent any more issues with your heart?"

The older woman hesitated, but still did not give in.

Eve came and knelt down beside Marjorie, clasping her hands. "Come on, Mom. It *is* the season of giving, after all. And the only gift I want from you…is for you to be well." Still gazing up at her mother, she released a deep, quivering breath. And then burst into tears.

"Thank you so much for all you did this evening," Eve told Derek two hours later, when they finally got back to the office. She glanced across the car at him as he pulled into the parking lot, then paused, her shoulder bag on her lap. "If you hadn't been here, using all your McCabe charm, I don't know if I would have been able to get my mother back to the cardiac rehabilitation center at all."

With the motor still idling, Derek reached across the leather console and took her hand in his. "The important thing is she went, and agreed to stay the duration, providing you take care of everything else. But my question is…" Derek paused, his warm palm still engulfing hers "…who's taking care of *you?*"

Eve caught her breath. Once again, her time with him was not going according to script. "What do you mean?"

"Did you even eat dinner last night?"

Eve didn't know how he could look so cool, calm and collected, when she felt so frazzled. "I…" She paused in turn, unable to remember when she'd eaten last. Warming to his slow, sexy smile, she had to admit reluctantly, "Maybe not."

As if they had all the time in the world to spend together, he continued his tender inquiry. "Breakfast this morning?"

Aware it had been forever since someone had taken care of her, she flushed, and pushed aside the memory of his kiss. "Toast."

He gave her a long, steady look. "Lunch?"

Eve fought back a second wave of heat. "A salad."

"Then you definitely need a solid meal this evening."

Trying not to think about how good it would feel to have a man like Derek looking after her, Eve folded her arms and retorted, "Since when did you become my personal nutritionist?"

He lifted his wide shoulders and she caught a whiff of his sandalwood-and-pine cologne. "Think of it as me returning all the favors you've done me the past few days."

Eve swallowed around the sudden tightness of her throat. "That was my job."

Triumph radiated in his smile. "And at the moment, being a gentleman is mine. Come on." He leaned toward her. "You know a good meal will not just fuel your body, but enable you to care for your mother and work a whole lot more efficiently to boot."

Unable to dispute all that he was saying, Eve lifted her hands in surrender. "Okay, I'll go." She held his gaze resolutely. "So long as we're both clear this is absolutely not a date."

Derek appeared affronted. "Of course not." His eyes twinkled. "It's just me saying thank-you to my most excellent Realtor."

Considering the size of the commission she was going to reap from the sale, Eve was the one expressing gratitude. "No. *I* am taking *you* out, as a thank-you."

His lips quirking with amusement, Derek put the Jaguar in reverse. "We'll fight over the check at dinner."

"No, we won't," Eve said calmly. "Because I'm buying."

It was, she knew, the best way to set an all-business tone for the evening. And prevent another kiss, or any emotional closeness from materializing again.

Unfortunately, the restaurant Derek chose felt anything but businesslike. It was dark and romantic, with deep leather booths that afforded maximum privacy. Adding to the winter wonderland atmosphere were abundant Christmas decorations and soothing holiday music playing in the background. Not to mention the sense that, despite her insistence to the contrary, this was in fact their first real date.

"So I take it you have no siblings," Derek said once the butternut bisque had been served.

Telling herself there could be no harm in getting acquainted in a friendly way—doing so might even eventually lead to more clients, upon his recommendation—Eve drew her spoon through the Granny Smith apple garnish. "No, it's always been just me and my mom."

He regarded her with interest. "Your mom never married?"

Trying not to feel a thrill at being with him in such an intimate setting, Eve shook her head and continued holding his gaze. "She never really even dated. The situation with my father turned her away from that. Although she insists it was really the best thing for her."

Derek poured them both a little more wine, an inscrutable expression on his face. "Do you agree with that assumption?"

Eve shrugged, not sure. "The please-go-away-and-never-darken-my-doorstep-again check my blue-blooded father gave her enabled her to get a foothold here and launch what has been a very satisfying career for her."

From the look of admiration he sent her way, Derek seemed to understand what a feat that had been for Marjorie, who'd come from nothing herself. "Does she want the same kind of life for you?"

"You mean single, high-powered career woman?" *Workaholic?* Eve added silently.

He nodded.

Good question. She finished her soup and moved

the dish aside, giving his inquiry the serious consideration it deserved. "Well, she wants me to be able to support myself. She'd like it if I took over the business when she's gone."

Derek's gaze roved Eve's face, hair and lips, before returning ever so slowly to her eyes. "You don't see your mom stepping down?"

Tingling everywhere his gaze had landed, as well as everywhere it hadn't, Eve shook her head facetiously. "Not as long as there's breath in her body."

He chuckled. "Having met your mom, I totally understand. Mine is the same way."

They leaned back as their soup dishes were cleared and plates of vinaigrette-dressed field greens peppered with pecans and cranberries were set in front of them.

Derek regarded Eve curiously. "What about you? Do you want to have more of a personal life?" He waggled his brows comically. "Are you dating anyone?"

His exaggerated interest had her rolling her eyes. "Checking to see if there's any competition?"

"Something like that," he said smoothly.

Trying not to think about the way he looked at her—as if she was the most fascinating woman on the planet—Eve sipped her wine. "There is no one in the picture."

"No one you find interesting?" he pressed.

Except you? "Not even marginally."

He smiled in satisfaction, clearly not about to give up on his pursuit of her.

Ignoring her inner burst of excitement, and figuring it was her turn to ask questions, Eve said casually, "What about you? Have you dated since your divorce?"

"Some."

She didn't know why she found that disappointing. Keeping her gaze matter-of-fact, she prodded, "And?"

His lips compressed. "I have to say, up to now my heart really hasn't been in it."

Up to now. "You've been going through the motions." Eve understood. She'd done her fair share of that, too.

"But I've been going along with it, for my family's sake," Derek continued.

Now they were getting somewhere. "They want to see you married again."

He grimaced. "Very much so. To the point they'd like to see me sign up for services with my sister-in-law, Alexis. She's a professional matchmaker for Foreverlove.com."

Another alarm bell sounded in Eve's head. She welcomed the arrival of their entrees, which served as a distraction. "You're resisting, I take it?" she asked when the waiter was gone again.

Derek nodded and cut into his steak. "I prefer a less orchestrated approach."

Her gaze swept over his handsome face. "Meaning…?"

"On paper, my marriage to Carleen should have worked."

Eve had to fight the urge to reach over and take his hand. "But it didn't."

His eyes drifted to the pulse throbbing in her throat. "Maybe the key is finding someone not so much like yourself. Maybe that's the way to a happy ending."

Eve wasn't so sure about that. The only thing she did know for certain was that she and Derek were very different. In their backgrounds, in their wants and needs and most definitely in their outlooks on life.

* * *

"You're looking better this morning," Marjorie murmured when Eve went to the cardiac rehab to have breakfast with her.

Eve felt better after her leisurely dinner with Derek the night before.

She'd slept well, too, and to her consternation, awoke dreaming of kissing him again.

Not that Derek had made a move on her the night before. He'd been a perfect gentleman when he had taken her back to her car after dinner. Which was, after all, what she had wanted.

Wasn't it?

"I'm glad," Marjorie continued. "I was worried about you last night."

"Same here," Eve murmured, looking her over with the same close regard.

Clearly, there were improvements here, too.

Marjorie was dressed in workout clothes for the physical therapy she'd be doing later. Although she wore no makeup, her color was actually a lot better this morning than it had been at the office the previous afternoon. "I gather you had a good night's sleep?"

"Probably because Loughlin Realty is still in the lead in sales. Although—" Marjorie frowned "—maybe not for long. Sibley & Smith is set to go to contract on two more properties this morning, which, unfortunately, would put them only one point seven million dollars behind us." *In other words,* Eve thought, *one luxury property.*

"How do you know this?" she demanded, narrowing her eyes suspiciously.

Marjorie pushed the cottage cheese and fruit around on her plate. "I still have my ear to the ground."

Everything fell into place when Eve spotted the BlackBerry that was peeking out of her mom's pocket. Her appetite suddenly almost nonexistent, too, Eve nibbled on a whole wheat pancake provided by the cafeteria. "You're supposed to avoid stress, Mom."

Marjorie scoffed. "Keeping an eye on my business is a lot easier on me than being kept in the dark."

Unfortunately, Eve knew that was true. "I'll make the sale to Red Bloom happen, Mom." The Houston oilman not only loved collecting unique homes, he had tons of money to spend.

An imperious brow arched. "That's what you promised when it came to Derek McCabe."

"And I did find a property for him. One he's very excited about." Although Eve still felt Derek had rushed into the deal, and might end up regretting it if everything didn't go the way he hoped.

Marjorie sneaked a peek at her BlackBerry. "I would have preferred he be excited about an eight-million-dollar listing."

Eve stifled a groan. She liked to put property under contract as much as the next agent, but didn't want the sales race to dominate her life. "Mom. Please. It's Christmastime. Let's stop worrying about competition. And work on finding the joy in our lives."

Marjorie slid her phone back into her pocket. She peered closely at Eve. "Since when did you become so romantic?"

Eve flushed.

"Or maybe," Marjorie continued, even more sagely,

"I should ask who is responsible for making you see the world this way?"

There was only one answer to that, Eve knew. And she sensed her mother knew it, too.

Derek McCabe.

Chapter 5

Derek's rancorous business meeting the following day was in direct contrast to his incredibly enjoyable dinner with Eve. The young entrepreneurs sat on the other side of Derek's desk, looking crestfallen when he finished his in-depth analysis of their pitch. "So in other words, you're not going to fund us," the lead programmer said with obvious resentment.

This was the part of the job Derek loathed. He regarded the trio of budding geniuses. "As I said, your ideas are great. The business plan is not."

"How do we fix that?" the more amenable software designer asked.

"Find an executive with experience running a small software company, and a chief financial officer, to help set things up."

The marketing guru shook her head vehemently. "We

don't need someone already set in his or her ways telling us what to do! The whole point of starting our own company is so we can run things ourselves!"

Knowing he'd done what he could to set them on the right path, Derek stood and shook their hands in turn. "Then I wish you luck," he said.

But they wouldn't be getting any venture capital from his company.

Alma May, his fifty-something administrative assistant, popped her head in the door after the surly trio departed. "Your parents called while you were in the meeting. They said they'd catch up with you later."

Aware his folks would probably be full of questions about the house he was buying when they did end up talking, Derek nodded.

His family would also be full of questions about Eve, if they had any inkling how interested he was in the pretty real estate agent. Luckily, they hadn't a clue. Derek wanted to keep it that way. Pursuing her was going to be a delicate business. She was cautious to a fault, overburdened with work and worried sick about her mom.

Hence, it wasn't an ideal time to jump-start a romance, Derek rationalized. And yet, to wait would risk losing what momentum they had gained.

Oblivious to the direction of his thoughts, Alma tossed her springy silver curls as she continued going down her list. "I rescheduled your appointments, as requested, so your afternoon is free."

Derek wondered if Eve would have any spare time, too. He wouldn't mind taking her out to lunch. Since she'd paid for dinner the night before, this would be his treat. And since the transaction would be closed by then, there would be nothing stopping them from interacting in a purely social way. Except, of course, Eve's theory about it being only the house-hunting that had brought them together.

"The bank called. They have the cashier's check ready for the closing. Which is…" his assistant consulted her watch "…in forty-five minutes."

Derek shut down his computer, glad to be done in the office for the day. He smiled. "I'm headed there now."

Eve was waiting for him, gorgeous as ever. She was wearing an elegant business suit with a black watch plaid skirt, dark green silk blouse and fitted black blazer. Black tights and matching suede heels set off her sexy, spectacular legs.

One thing that was different about her today, Derek noted appreciatively, was her hair. The silky golden-brown strands had been brushed off her face and twisted into a chignon at the nape of her neck. On another woman, the sophisticated style would have highlighted imperfections. However, on Eve, it pointed out the lack of them. From the oval shape of her face, to her wide-set amber eyes, straight nose, chiseled cheekbones and full, bow-shaped lips, she was absolute perfection.

Derek knew it. And it was evident that the sellers, the attorneys and even the other Realtor involved knew it as well. Only Eve seemed oblivious to just how lovely she was.

Derek promised to remedy that as soon as humanly possible. But first things first; they had to close on the property.

Two hours later, it was a done deal. The lawyers and sellers departed. Hal Brody, the listing agent for the other party, stayed behind to tie up loose ends. After taking the lockbox off the door, he glanced over at Eve. "Congratulations. Looks like Loughlin Realty is going to win. Talk is, despite their recent sales, Sibley & Smith is still going to fall short."

With a pleasant smile fixed on her face, Eve cautioned her colleague, "Let's not be too hasty, Hal. As you and I both know, anything can happen, especially this time of year."

He went to get the real estate stand out of the front yard. "Well, just so you know, since it can't be us," the distinguished-looking Realtor said as he returned, "I'm rooting for your team."

"Thanks, Hal," Eve replied. But her expression indicated they would just have to see what developed.

"Pleasure doing business with you, as always." Hal slid the sold sign into his trunk.

Behind them, a familiar canary-yellow truck pulled up to the curb. Derek's heart sank. As much as he loved the occupants, he did not need this now.

Eve caught his expression and frowned. "Expecting company?" she asked quietly as Hal waved and took off.

"No," Derek said, but after his email announcing his plans the day before, he should have guessed his parents would show up in person, rather than just call him at the office.

Smiling and waving, his parents got out of the pickup. As always, they made a handsome couple. The kind you could look at and just know they belonged together, and always had. It was that kind of comfort and compatibility that Derek wanted, too.

Beside him, he felt Eve's attention turn to his folks. She seemed curious—obviously, she hadn't put two and two together yet, and wondered what he had in common with this couple—yet she appeared as welcoming as always.

Derek understood. He was standing here in a suit and tie, having just come from his downtown Dallas office. His mom was dressed in her usual jeans, boots and wool jacket. His dad, also in jeans and boots, had a shearling-lined suede jacket on, a black Stetson slanted across his brow. Both looked very West Texas and proud of it.

"Eve, I'd like you to meet my parents, Josie and Wade McCabe. Mom, Dad, this is Eve Loughlin, the Realtor who negotiated the purchase of my new home."

Josie greeted Eve warmly, and then turned back to Derek. Wade did the same. "I gather the closing went without a hitch, then?" she asked.

Derek tried not to notice the hint of disappointment in his mother's eyes. "Usually does when you pay cash for a property," he quipped.

Another glint of disappointment appeared.

Ever the peacemaker between Derek and his mom, his dad stepped in like clockwork. Wade's years successfully investing in troubled companies of all kinds had given him an ability to talk affably with everyone, no matter what the circumstances. "Want to show us around?" he asked Eve.

Derek knew the agenda here. His mother wanted to talk to him alone, as she always handled the "emotional" issues in the family. His dad would get to know Eve, and figure out what, if anything, she had to do with his hasty actions.

Apparently unwilling to get swept up into his family drama, however, Eve lifted a hand and took a step backward. "Actually, I should be going—"

"Actually," Derek cut in, "if you have a minute, Eve,

I'd really like you to stay." He knew his parents were worried about him. They'd been concerned ever since he had given up on his marriage without a fight. He just didn't want to hear about it.

Derek pivoted to Eve, awaiting her decision.

Their eyes met and held. "Certainly," she said at last, with a look that conceded she owed him when it came to running interference with family. "I'd be glad to help out in whatever way I can."

Eve wasn't sure what was going on between Derek and his folks. She did know they were the last people he had wanted to see at that particular moment. And if his tense body language was any indication, that feeling seemed to intensify when his parents stepped into his new home and had their first look around.

Clearly, they were in shock as they scoped it out. Wondering, even if they were too polite to actually come out and say so, what in the world Derek had done.

Finally, Josie drew a deep breath. "It will be a wonderful home when it's redone."

Wade nodded as he strolled through the downstairs. He looked out at the spacious backyard through a bank of grimy single-pane windows that were definitely going to have to be replaced. "I think so, too."

"But what are you going to do in the meantime?" his mother asked. "I thought you wanted to be out of the hotel by the holidays." Her youthful face radiated concern. "For Tiffany's sake."

"And I will be," Derek promised.

Josie's gaze narrowed in a way that let Eve know this woman would not accept any useless excuses from her son. "Surely you know that you can't have a baby around ongoing renovation."

"It's going to be finished by Christmas, Mom, with a week to spare." Derek went on to state in excruciating detail what all was going to be done.

Josie and Wade stared at him as if he had lost his mind. "That will all be finished two weeks from now?" his mother repeated with a mixture of shock and disbelief.

Derek nodded. "They've promised."

More alarmed looks transferred between his folks.

"I know what tradespeople say," Josie declared. "But when it comes to renovations there are *always* unexpected delays. You cannot go by the best-case-scenario estimates, son."

Derek folded his arms across his chest. "Eve has assured me that won't be an issue with these particular contractors."

Josie turned back to her, and Eve had an idea what it would be like to be at the top of Josie's Not Happy With list. Sighing inwardly, she couldn't help but sympathize with Derek. It was the same with her mother. As long as they felt you were on the right path, all was golden. The minute you weren't... Mama Bear personality returned.

Once again, Derek's dad stepped in to calmly defuse the situation. "How about you show me the upstairs?" he suggested. The upshot being so Derek and his mom could talk.

Knowing he was no more likely to get out of that than she was to avoid her own mother's scrutiny, Eve smiled despite herself.

Feeling as if she had unwittingly stumbled into a hornet's nest, she said, "I'd be glad to."

The rumbling of voices continued while she and Wade looked around the second floor. Eve took her time explaining what Derek had planned for each room.

"Naturally, he also has an interior designer helping him pick out the soothing, neutral color scheme he wants. She will get it move-in ready for Derek and Tiffany, right down to the dishes and the towels. All Derek will have to do is turn the key and walk in."

"That's good. Interior design isn't exactly the forte of any of our sons."

Eve hesitated, reluctant to insert herself into a situation where she didn't belong, yet wanting to assist Derek in alleviating his parents' worry. "I know how disconcerting it looks now, but knowing what kind of relaxed and easy home life he wants, I think Derek's made a very good choice, as well as a sound financial investment."

"With the exception that it is well under my son's initial financial goal."

"I don't think it's an issue as far as his portfolio goes, since Derek still plans to invest more money in real estate by the end of the year. Besides, it's close to Carleen, close to Derek's work." Even close to Eve's office and her condo. Not that she should be thinking that way...

Wade smiled. "I think Derek's chosen wisely, too," he said quietly, in that instant looking very much like his son. "Maybe more than he knows or realizes."

Eve wasn't sure what Derek's father meant by that.

Wade frowned, continuing, "I think the real issue is that he had told us a while back that his next home was going to be a ranch, so that Tiffany would be able to enjoy the outdoors as much as he did when he was a kid."

Caught off guard, yet trying her best to hide it, Eve shrugged. "He didn't say anything about that to me...."

"That's what worries us," Wade returned. "Not that it matters what the plan was. Apparently, there's a different one now." Lips compressed, the older man turned and headed for the stairs.

The air was thick with tension when they rejoined the others in the living room.

"You're sure you won't have lunch with us?" Josie asked Derek, clearly trying to make amends.

He shook his head, his shoulders as set as the expression on his face. "I already have plans. Maybe another time, Mom."

Josie searched his face. "We will see you for the family Christmas party, though."

Derek nodded. His current aggravation with them notwithstanding, he clearly loved and respected both his parents. "I made arrangements with Carleen to take Tiffany to Laramie for the weekend before Christmas," he reassured them.

Josie smiled. "Good." Her expression gentled. "My favorite time of year is when I have all you boys with us." She gave her big, strapping son a fiercely maternal hug, then stepped back and gave him another long, beseeching look. "Don't be too angry with me."

Derek exhaled, his irritation back full force. "Got to let us go, Mom," was all he said in return. He shook his head in silent remonstration. *"You've got to let us go."*

Eve waited until the elder McCabes had departed, then turned back to Derek. From her shoulder bag she withdrew an envelope with his name scrawled across the front.

"Well, thank you again for choosing Loughlin Realty," she said formally.

Derek accepted the envelope she pushed into his hands. He opened it, saw the thank-you and the gift card for a five-star restaurant, and smiled in satisfaction. "This means our business is done?"

Suddenly wishing her reasons for being around Derek weren't over, Eve forced herself to stay professional. "As far as the closing goes. Naturally, if you encounter any post-sale problems, I'd like to know. We want you to be happy with the final result." How many times had she said these same words? And felt relieved, not sad?

Derek paused, as if choosing his words carefully. Finally, he said, "I am happy."

Their gazes met. Eve could see that was true—about the sale. As for other aspects of his life, he was not as pleased. She walked back upstairs with him, checking the rooms, making sure the lights were turned off, the shades pulled.

Wanting him to put his thoughts and feelings into words, she continued, "I'm sorry your parents weren't thrilled with your choice of a home."

In no hurry to leave, he sat down on a seat built into the wide shed window in the master bedroom. "You weren't either, so long ago."

Eve moved closer, so they wouldn't have to talk as loud, and leaned against the wall.

Outside, the sun was peeking through the winter gloom, sending splintered rays into the master suite. The light caught the dark strands of Derek's short, rumpled hair, bringing out glints of brown and maple. She could see how closely he had shaved that morning, as well as how deep blue his eyes were, how masculine his features. She could never tire of looking at him, being with him. Which was, again, a mistake.

One she had sworn not to repeat.

Eve swallowed and kept her place with effort. She flashed another brisk, efficient, I-have-everything-completely-under-control smile. "I didn't know you as well then."

He folded his arms, studying her. "So you don't think I made a mistake?"

"No, of course I don't think you made a mistake with this house." Eve was now seeing what he had all along, how it would look once it was redone and Derek and his daughter were in residence. "Why?" She paused, alarm bells sounding. "Are you having a case of buyer's remorse?"

He chuckled and shook his head. "When I make a decision, that's it, as far as I'm concerned. The problem is, my mother thinks I make them too quickly."

Aware that her knees were suddenly feeling a little shaky, Eve took the only available seat—on the window bench next to him. She dropped her gaze to the fine fabric of his suit trousers and swallowed again. "And you don't think that is the case."

Derek shifted slightly, his knee almost touching her thigh. "Probably because I wasn't always like this." He settled back in the deep window well and loosened the knot of his tie, tugged it down an inch. Undid the first button of his shirt. "I didn't always go with my gut instincts."

Trying not to think what he would look like with

that shirt off, Eve pushed the thought away and asked, "What were you like?"

His lips twisting ruefully, he admitted, "Analytical to a fault. It's what got me into my first marriage, which was, in hindsight, the biggest mistake of my life." Abruptly, the distant brooding look was back on his face. Sorrow and regret crept into his low tone. "The only good thing about it was Tiffany. Had I not married Carleen, I wouldn't have my daughter."

Able to see he needed comforting the same way she had the night her mother had checked herself out of the hospital, Eve reached over and squeezed Derek's hand. "You're very lucky to have her. She is such a beautiful child. Always a good way to look at it."

He brought his other hand around to cover hers, and squeezed slightly, inundating her with his warmth and strength. Then, restive again, he stood and began to pace. Finally, he pivoted to face her and admitted gruffly, "When it came to choosing a mate the first time around, I ignored my instincts, which told me that although I liked Carleen very much, and we were great friends, we never had the physical passion we should have had." He let out a long, slow breath. "And I know now you should never marry someone you aren't completely wild about."

"So it's not a mistake you intend to make again."

Derek slid Eve a pointed look and shook his head. "If and when I marry again, it will be because I know for certain that the two of us have what it takes to grow old together."

She stood, too, realizing they had lingered for far too long. She felt Derek's eyes on her as she straightened her skirt and walked toward the door on legs that felt shaky again. "You agree with my position, I take it?" he drawled.

Eve nodded and moved past him toward the stairs. Hand on the rail, she made her way down to the first floor. "I think marriage is serious business. To be successful, you have to be one-hundred-percent sure it's the right thing."

Derek was close behind her. "We're on the same page, then."

She paused at the newel post in the foyer. "Apparently."

Another silence fell, more companionable this time. They walked through the downstairs, switching off lights here and there, closing more blinds. "But back to business," he said, when at last they had finished and were about to head for the front door. "Now that we've concluded ours, there really is nothing stopping us from moving on."

There was something new in his voice. Something that had an exciting ring to it. Eve's throat grew dry and tight. "Moving on how?" she rasped.

He smiled, sexy and self-assured. "By having that first date."

"A date," she repeated, achingly aware of how good it felt to be flirting with Derek, without the specter of business between them. Too good, if she was honest....

He gently cupped her shoulders with his big palms, keeping her in front of him when she would have run. "You know," he explained in a deadpan tone. "A social occasion between two people that usually is romantic in nature."

Pretending she wasn't totally thrilled with the very idea, Eve nodded with mock gravity. Damned if he didn't have the most mesmerizing eyes. And smile. Darn it if she didn't like—and lust after— nearly everything about him. "Ah," she quipped. "That kind of date."

"Yes." He stepped nearer, standing so close she could feel the heat of his body, inhale his cologne and see the sudden intensity in his eyes. "Would you like to go on one with me?"

More than he knew. But wary of rushing headlong into anything only for them to both regret it a few weeks from now, Eve held up her index finger and extricated herself from his grip. Then she walked a short distance away, pulled her phone from her purse and quickly accessed her calendar.

Aware of his eyes lingering on her, she said, "Sure. Just let me check my schedule." Flushing slightly, she scrolled through a host of open Friday and Saturday nights, finally settling on a date several weeks away. That would pretty much guarantee whatever fire they had flickering between them now would be completely cooled off. "How about Thursday, January 15?" she asked finally.

Derek tilted his head slightly to one side. "Don't you mean December?"

Eve shook her head, doing her best to hold her own with this sexy, determined man. "January."

The glimmer of hot pursuit lit his dark blue eyes. "That's all you've got open?" he probed.

Being careful to keep her screen where he couldn't see it, she scrolled some more, past many an empty evening. "Well, January 30 is available, too." She looked up, poker-faced. "At lunch."

"I'll take the fifteenth."

She should have known he wouldn't back down.

Well, she wouldn't, either. All brisk efficiency once again, Eve asked, "What time?"

"Seven-thirty."

She typed his name into the slot. "Seven-thirty it is."

Derek strolled closer. "In the meantime, should an opening arise…"

Eve slid her phone back into her pocket. "I'll be sure to let you know. But given that I'm especially busy right now, covering for my mom—" she wrinkled her nose playfully "—I doubt it will happen." *Unless, of course, I give in to the extraordinary chemistry between us. Which I won't!*

Derek gazed at her in concern. "When will Marjorie be back in the office?"

Eve recalled the kindness he had shown her mother, a fact that only deepened her attraction. "Early January."

He smiled in relief, apparently as glad to hear the news as she had been. "When you see her, give her my best."

"I will," Eve promised.

"In the meantime, we both have to get back to work." Reluctantly, Derek let Eve go. They said a cordial goodbye. He went off to listen to more proposals from hopeful entrepreneurs in the tech industry.

Eve devoted the rest of the afternoon to preparing another list of architecturally interesting homes to scope out in case the Santiago Florres house that Red Bloom was flying in from Houston to see didn't work out.

After that task was finally done, she spent the evening with her mother. Yet busy as she was, Derek was never far from her thoughts. She couldn't help but wonder if he was thinking of her, too.

On Thursday, she went to see two potential clients

who were planning to list their homes in the first quarter of the next year. Eve toured the properties and spoke with the owners about their expectations, then promised to get back to them with a suggested listing price by the end of the week.

She was just heading back to the office when her phone rang again. It was a text message from Derek. Ignoring the little thrill that went through her—it had only been twenty-four hours, and she had missed him more than she liked to admit—she took a deep breath and scanned the text. It said simply: Meet me at my house? Problem with the HVAC. I could use your advice.

Chapter 6

"Why did you text the Realtor?" Harvey Jefferson, the HVAC installer, asked Derek.

Why indeed, Derek thought. Except that he was jumping at just the thought of seeing Eve again…and his ego told him she was probably feeling the same way, even if she was too cautious and too stubborn to admit it.

"Are you sure Eve even wants to be involved in this?" Harvey continued with a beleaguered frown. "I mean, technically—"

Derek knew where the installer was going. "The sale is complete. Her job as a Realtor is done."

Harvey nodded.

"I'd like Eve's opinion." *And I'd really like to see her again, even if it is only about business.* An answering text came through. "We're in luck." Derek grinned at Harvey, happy his hunch had paid off. "She's on her way." Even though—technically—she did not have to be.

Ten minutes later, Eve showed up, looking every bit the polished professional in a tweed jacket, red silk blouse, trim black skirt and heels. With her golden-brown hair glinting in the winter sunshine as she emerged from her Mercedes, Derek decided she was gorgeous enough to stop traffic.

Feeling a pang of guilt for objectifying her that way, he tore his eyes from her spectacular legs as she moved up the sidewalk.

With a concerned look on her face, she crossed the weed-choked lawn to where he and his contractor were standing next to the dual units on the rear wall. Like everything else, the big metal HVACs were rusty and out-of-date. Both were on and making hideous grinding noises.

Eve glanced cautiously at the whirling fans inside the units. Then at the two big boxes beyond, containing brand-new state-of-the-art machines waiting to be installed. "Hey, fellas, what's up?"

Harvey Jefferson, the HVAC installer, winced. "I'd rather just show you both." He motioned them inside, then led them through the mass of workers tearing up carpeting and damaged flooring, to the kitchen. The burly man stopped beneath a vent in the ceiling and lifted a hand. "Feel anything?"

Eve and Derek both raised their hands. Their glances met. "Nothing," they murmured in unison.

Still grimacing, Harvey led them to the guest bath. "Feel anything here?"

Eve and Derek stood under the vent. It was faint, Derek thought, but he could feel a flow of air. So could Eve.

"Let's try the family room," the contractor suggested.

There, small, staticky bursts of air were coming out of the vents, although the slats in the grates were wide open.

"Do you think something might be blocking it?" Derek asked.

"Like a squirrel nest?" Eve interjected.

Derek looked at her.

She gestured matter-of-factly. "It happens in houses that have been untended for a long time. Our furry friends decide to move right in."

Derek chuckled at her wry tone. He liked a woman who could not only take the most challenging situations in stride, but joke about them.

The HVAC guy was not laughing, however. "I only wish it was that simple," Harvey muttered. He led them over to a ladder, beneath where an air duct grill had been removed. He took a mirror and a flashlight out of his shirt pocket. "It's going to be kind of hard to see, but if you climb up the ladder and look that way…" He pointed in the direction of the HVAC units outside the house.

Derek gestured for Eve to go first.

She started to do so, then stopped, removed her black suede pumps and handed them to Derek. In stocking feet, she climbed the ladder. Squinting, she looked where the contractor had pointed. "I don't… Ohhh." Her voice turned as grim as her expression as she glanced down at the contractor. After inching back down the ladder, she wordlessly exchanged the flashlight and mirror for her shoes.

Derek offered his forearm in support as she slipped her heels back on. Despite the decidedly unromantic circumstances, he couldn't help liking the way it felt to have her leaning on him, even for a second or two. Then, aware that neither Harvey nor Eve wanted to be the bearer of bad news, he went up the ladder and looked around. It took him a moment to figure out what was what, but as his eyes adjusted to the dim lighting, he eventually saw the problem, too. "The ductwork inside the walls is collapsing." And where it wasn't collapsing, it seemed to be almost crumbling to bits.

Big sighs and more grave looks were exchanged between Eve and the contractor.

Derek came back down the ladder. "What does this mean?" Obviously, something bad. Harvey winced as if bracing himself for an angry reaction. "There's no other way to say it. All the ductwork is going to have to be replaced. Otherwise, there's no point to putting in new units. And the only way to get at it is to cut through the drywall and the ceilings. That will take time."

Derek could only imagine. His dream of having Tiffany in their new home in time to celebrate the Christmas holiday began to fade. "How much time?" he asked grimly.

Again, Harvey seemed to brace himself. "Two, three more days than what we figured."

Eve added, "The interior painting can't be started until they're done and the drywall is repaired or replaced."

And every day counted. Derek turned to Eve, knowing she would have a good overview. "How many more issues like this can we expect?"

She kept her gaze locked with his and replied with a frankness he admired, "I don't know. If you'd opted to have an inspection, we'd have some idea."

But he hadn't opted for one. Hadn't wanted to take

the time to get one done, or let the results in any way infringe on his purchase of the property.

Derek silently racked his brain for a solution that would keep them on schedule. "Can your crews work around the clock if I pay double time?"

Eve tensed and stepped in. "There is a city ordinance preventing that. And even if there weren't, Derek, it'd be a bad idea to disturb your neighbors or their kids with construction when they're trying to sleep. Never mind disrupt the horse-drawn carriage tours of the holiday light displays."

Derek hadn't thought of that. He had simply been focused on his goal.

Harvey added, "The best we can do is work seven days a week with as many guys as I can round up. And have the other contractors do the same."

"We'll find a way to have you and Tiffany in your new home by Christmas," Eve promised.

Derek hoped so. Failing in his marriage was one thing; failing his child was something else entirely. This was Tiffany's first Christmas with him, as a divorced single dad. He did not want her spending it in a hotel.

"How upset was Derek McCabe?" Marjorie asked later that afternoon, after Eve had filled her in.

Eve took a seat next to her in the solarium on the roof of the hospital annex. Glad Marjorie was well enough now to handle small amounts of stress, she paused.

"It was hard to tell." Sometimes she was able to read Derek like a book. At others, she hadn't a clue. And when he had departed he had seemed unusually quiet and more brooding than she had ever seen him, even during that frustrating house-hunting search that had repeatedly left him empty-handed.

Marjorie put down the novel she had been reading when Eve arrived for her daily visit. Another first. Before her heart attack her mom had never taken time for leisure reading. Or any other hobby or relaxing activity. It had been nothing but work, work, work for Marjorie.

"But you suspect he was unhappy," the older woman said.

Sighing wearily, Eve sipped some of the decaf peppermint tea she had brought them from the hospital cafeteria. "Wouldn't you be if you had news like that?" She searched her mother's face, heartened to see she was looking a little less pale and drawn every day now. "Especially because we don't know what else could go wrong with the house. I mean, for all we know, it could be a real money pit."

Marjorie reached for her teacup. "Fortunately, Derek is a man of means and steely determination."

Aware what a good judge of character her mother was, Eve nodded. "He is that."

"And it was his decision not to have an inspection. I don't think he'll blame you for that."

"You're right. He isn't the kind of man to push responsibility for his actions off on someone else."

Both women smiled.

"But you're wise to be concerned," Eve's mom continued. "When a buyer is unhappy with the home they've purchased, the Realtor involved invariably ends up taking the blame."

"I've done everything I can do to help when it comes to Harvey Jefferson and the other contractors," Eve said. And though she knew she was becoming too personally involved, she couldn't help it. She had promised a client he would be able to spend the holiday with his baby girl in their new home. It was a promise neither she nor Derek had taken lightly. A promise that, if broken, would have lasting repercussions.

"Then there's only one thing left to do," Marjorie advised with a maternal pat on the forearm.

Eve grinned, recalling the business training her mother had given her. "The triage approach. Identify the problem, come up with a solution and apply it."

Marjorie beamed with pride. "Exactly! Glad to see you were paying attention, after all."

Suddenly eager to put her plan into action, Eve stood and kissed her on her cheek. "Thanks, Mom. I knew you'd have the answer."

And the answer, Eve thought, was finding Derek, and making sure that their relationship, business and otherwise, was still okay.

An hour later, Eve arrived at Derek's hotel, determined to not only bring tidings of good cheer, but find out if anything else was wrong that he had yet to tell her about. If there was, she was resolved to do what she could to help him rectify the situation.

I have something for you and Tiffany, she texted him. *Shall I leave it at the front desk?*

He texted back, *It would be better if you brought it up.*

Well, that was a good sign, wasn't it? Eve took the elevator to his floor, determined to help him start celebrating the holiday season more fully.

Derek was waiting for her when she stepped off with overflowing shopping bags in both hands. She smiled at him, then at the baby girl cuddled in his arms. Tiffany's cute little face was red, her lower lip trembling, her cheeks wet with tears.

Derek shot Eve a grateful glance. He looked so harried and distraught that her heart went out to him.

"You couldn't have come at a better time." Tiffany still in his arms, Derek opened the door and ushered Eve into his suite.

She set her bags down, gifts momentarily forgotten. "What's going on?" she asked.

Derek pursed his lips in concern. "She wants her *m-o-m-m-y.*"

Oh, dear.

Tiffany's lower lip thrust even farther out. Abruptly, she started to cry again. "Mommy. Mommy. Mommy…"

Derek murmured, "It's all right, honey," and patted her back consolingly. To no avail. Tiffany wailed on, clearly miserable, and Eve's heart went out to the child, as well. This was the part of divorce and split custody that no one wanted to talk about.

"What can I do?" Eve whispered.

Before Derek could reply, Tiffany looked at her, said "Mommy!" again and stretched out her arms. After shifting her weight, she lurched unexpectedly toward Eve. Derek made sure she had caught his little girl before letting her go. Then he stepped back, clearly exhausted and grateful for the emotional backup, while Eve cuddled the infant close.

"Mommy!" Tiffany squealed, happier now. With a giggle, she wound her hands in Eve's hair and tugged.

Derek made a face, as if knowing how uncomfortable that must be, and stepped in to try and extricate the tiny fists. While he worked at it gently, the warmth of his body so close by flooded Eve's.

"It's a new thing, apparently." Derek untangled one fist, only to have Tiffany reach again for Eve's mane when he went to work on the other.

Still untangling carefully, Derek continued, "It's been going on the past two days. Whenever Carleen and Craig are both there, Tiffany is fine. But if Craig leaves, Tiffany cries for *d-a-d-d-y*. And now she's started doing it with me. If Carleen isn't here, or it would seem, you, she wants an *m-o-m-m-y*."

"Or, in other words, an adult female, and a male presence."

"Right." Derek gave up on extricating Tiffany's hands and went to get two toys. He held them out in front of his daughter. Tiffany thought about it for a moment, then let go of Eve's hair so she could reach for them.

With Eve more comfortable, Derek continued with what he'd been saying. "Carlene talked to Tiffany's pediatrician—Dr. Maydew—and she said it's no wonder Tiffany's confused, with the recent moves, in addition to growing up in a split-custody arrangement. Dr. Maydew said Tiffany is old enough to be aware of her surroundings, and is just reacting to being in a hotel one moment, Carleen and Craig's huge new house the next...."

Eve gazed down at the sweet little girl in her arms, wishing there was something she could say or do to help.

"Eventually, the pediatrician said, Tiffany will be fine wherever she is, as long as she's with people who love her. But right now, she just wants what every child wants."

"A mommy and a daddy and a secure place to call home," Eve guessed, privately sharing Derek's worry and anxiety. This had to be tough.

Well, she'd been right about one thing at least, Eve thought. It hadn't been just the failing HVAC ductwork that had been bothering Derek today.

Glad she had come, she bounced the baby girl in her arms, noting that the brooding look was back in Derek's eyes. "Well, then it's a good thing I brought a distraction," she said cheerfully, smiling when Tiffany started wiggling, signaling she wanted down.

Eve set the toddler gently on the floor, and she scampered off in the direction of the shopping bags.

Derek inclined his head. "What's all that?"

Eve grinned and sashayed forward. "You'll see," she promised with a wink.

With Derek and his little girl watching intently, she opened the first oversize bag and pulled out a box. Inside was a two-foot-tall artificial Christmas tree with battery-run lights. Made to sit atop a table or desk, it added instant holiday cheer to the otherwise bland hotel room.

With Derek's help, she drew it out of the box. "Where do you want it?"

He looked around the living area of his two-bedroom suite. "On the bar, I think. Out of reach, but where she can see it."

Eve set it there, then went back to her bags and reached for one containing tissue-wrapped presents. "This is for Tiffany. It's meant for a baby's first Christmas tree."

Derek sat down on the sofa with his daughter snuggled beside him. He let Tiffany unwrap the tissue paper and pull out several cloth ornaments. The little girl chortled when she saw the Santa and Mrs. Claus. She giggled at the reindeer with its bright red nose, and smiled at the gingham candy canes and miniature teddy bears.

"Now she's happy," Derek murmured in a deep voice.

Eve draped the bottom of the little evergreen with a quilted skirt embroidered with the words *Merry Christmas, Everyone!*

Finished, she turned back to him, a little embarrassed that she had let herself get so into this. "I know it's not the same as being in your house right now," she told him soberly, ordering herself to keep at least some emotional distance. She pulled two stockings out of the bag. One embroidered with Derek's name, the other with Tiffany's. Eve hung them side by side on the doorknobs of the tall armoire housing the television set. Again, both were safely out of reach of the toddler. "But hopefully, this will add a little touch of Christmas to your world in the meantime."

"Thank you," Derek said in a voice that was husky and soft, and so tender it brought forth an answering well of warmth in Eve.

Grinning, Tiffany scooted toward the edge of the sofa. Once she'd climbed down onto the floor, she toddled around, a stuffed ornament in each little hand. Jabbering nonstop, she placed the ornaments here and there and everywhere, beaming all the while.

Derek sat watching, relaxed and content. He exhaled again, then turned and locked eyes with Eve. "This was just what we needed. Thank you, Eve."

Glad she'd acted on instinct instead of letting her usual reserve rule her, she smiled back. "You're welcome." Then, knowing it was time she left before she was tempted to do anything else "instinctive," she looked around for her purse.

Once again, Derek was beside her, his hand on her arm. "Don't go," he said in a gently compelling voice. "Stay and have dinner here tonight."

As it turned out, Tiffany had already eaten. She just needed her pajamas, bedtime bottle and story. And she wanted them from Eve, not Derek.

Everything in Eve that wanted to be a mother was eager to participate. But wary of jumping in even deeper into a situation that could easily leave her with a broken heart, she hesitated. "Should we? Because I'm not usually going to be here with the two of you."

Derek sat down beside Eve with Tiffany on his lap.

The little girl grabbed a fistful of each of their clothes, trying to bring them closer together. Derek obliged by scooting over until the side of his body touched Eve's. "Who knows what tomorrow will bring? All I know is she's happy to have both of us with her, so I think we should just go with that."

Because if they didn't, Eve knew, Tiffany was likely to start crying again for a mommy. It had been hard enough earlier, seeing her so upset.

"You're the expert." Eve smiled down at Tiffany, who crawled off Derek's lap and onto hers. Looking utterly content, the little girl leaned her head against Eve's chest and propped her pajama-clad feet on Derek's lap. Grinning and babbling, she held her bottle with one hand, looking happily from one adult to the other as she drank.

By the time she'd drained the bottle, her eyes were closing. And by the time Derek finished reading the story about the bear who accidentally slept through Christmas, she was sound asleep.

"Now for the really tricky part," Derek whispered, easing the empty baby bottle out of his daughter's hand. "Getting her into bed without waking her."

Eve held her breath as he stood, leaned over and slipped his hands between Tiffany's relaxed form and Eve's chest. Oblivious to the immediate tingling in her body that resulted, he started to lift his daughter.

The pout on the little one's face was back.

Derek waited, not moving, and Eve barely breathed, for another minute, then two.

Tiffany relaxed back into sleep.

Slowly, carefully, Derek lifted her, shifted her gently, then carried her into the adjacent bedroom where her crib was set up.

Aching with a similar need to be held and cared for, Eve stood and tried to calm her racing heart. Her taut nipples, her body's awareness, meant nothing, she told herself. But when Derek came back to her, she could see that it did.

He was grateful. Gratitude in that man-who-has-just-been-rescued-by-an-intuitive-woman kind of way. Which was, Eve realized with no small amount of irony, not what she wanted from him at all.

"So how about that dinner?" Derek said, watching the conflicting mix of wistfulness and hesitation cross Eve's face. He sensed she was as attracted to him as he was to her, yet determined not to act on the chemistry again, too. Feeling a little frustrated about it, as well as the fact that he hadn't been able to comfort his child on his own, yet deeply grateful for Eve's intervention, he walked toward her with a casual smile and handed her a leather-bound menu. "It seems I owe you whatever room service can provide."

Eve glanced at her watch, noting that it was after eight. "Thanks," she said politely, "but I really should go."

"Sure?" Derek asked, oddly disappointed that she didn't seem to think they should be enjoying these interactions as much as they actually were. He searched her face, looking for a way to persuade her. "It doesn't have to be a date."

A furrow formed along the bridge of her nose. "But you'd like it to be."

He took a deep breath and stuffed his hands in the pockets of his slacks, aware it wasn't like him to get attached to a woman so quickly, never mind one as gorgeous as Eve. And she *was* gorgeous tonight, with her hair down, her lips soft and bare, the light of awareness shimmering in her pretty amber eyes.

Derek shrugged and continued frankly, "I'm not going to pretend I don't want to spend time with you." *Man-and-woman time. The kind we're not likely to forget.*

She hitched in an uneven breath, even as she quirked her lips in a sassy smile. "At least we cleared that up," she joked.

He let his gaze drift over her, noting the imprint of her nipples beneath her blouse. "You don't want me to be honest?"

A turbulent light came into her eyes and she stepped away. "I don't want you to move so fast."

Derek edged closer anyway. He knew she was wary at heart. He also knew that wariness was keeping her from getting really close to anyone. "Why did you come over here tonight, then—if not to further our...whatever you'd like to call this?"

She angled her head to one side, as if studying him that way would give her greater insight into what was going on inside him. Silky hair fell across her shoulders, onto her breast. "I didn't want you to be an unhappy former client," she said softly.

Wishing he didn't want to take her to bed quite so much, he drawled, "Bad for business?"

She smiled as the flirtatious mood between them intensified. "Very, as it happens."

Derek cupped her shoulders between his palms. "You know what I think?"

Her tongue came out to briefly wet her lips. "I'm not sure I want to know," she told him hoarsely, but, to his satisfaction, didn't move away.

Feeling the pressure building at the front of his jeans, he noted with a wink, "I think the Christmas tree and the trimmings were just an excuse to be with me again."

She blushed. "You've got no shortage of ego."

"No shortage of desire," Derek corrected, glad the interest wasn't one-sided. He wrapped his arms around her and brought her closer still. Eve caught her breath but didn't move away. Her nipples were taut, her knees trembling slightly.

Derek lowered his head, aware he wasn't the only one who was so turned on he could barely breathe. "Kiss me," he whispered, even more softly, "and tell me you don't feel the same."

Chapter 7

Eve wanted to tell Derek she didn't desire him. She wanted to tell him she didn't want him to pull her against him. But the moment his lips found hers, all rational thought dissipated. Need entered the picture, and it was a yearning that refused to subside. When Derek finally lifted his head, the question she knew was coming glimmered in his beautiful blue eyes: Was this what she wanted? Because if not, they both knew they needed to stop. *Now.*

Eve forced herself to be practical. And practicality told her she would not be able to stop thinking about him like this unless she answered some very fundamental questions. Such as, was making love to Derek going to be as heavenly as merely kissing him?

Aware that if he had any doubts, he sure wasn't showing them, she hitched in a tremulous breath. "Normally I am not into one-night stands, but we need to get each other out of our systems."

A corner of his mouth lifted in a sexy smile. He tucked a strand of hair behind her ear. "We need something, all right."

And Eve knew exactly what that was.

She'd been wondering what gift to get herself. At first, way back in the beginning, she'd decided it would be not working with him. Now, she wanted something different. Still holding his devastating gaze, she flashed a smile. "It *is* Christmas…."

His eyes crinkled at the corners, the idea of making love to each other evidently as enthralling to him as it was to her. She lifted her face to his and teased, "What's Christmas without at least one gift to ourselves?"

"Ah." He nuzzled her neck, then danced her backward toward the bedroom he'd been using as an office. "A woman after my own heart."

He let her go just long enough to gather all the folders and the computer, and stack them on the chair. Eve shrugged out of her red cashmere cardigan and toed off her black suede heels. "Just so you know, this one time is all it will be."

He unbuttoned his shirt. "I hear you."

Eve helped him remove it and then his T-shirt. His chest was sleek with satiny muscles, and a dusting of hair that arrowed down to his navel and disappeared into the waistband of his trousers. Damn, but he was beautiful. Inside and out. Forcing herself to concentrate only on the physical, she ran her hands over the warmth of his skin, appreciating the masculine strength. "But you don't believe me."

Derek let her explore to her heart's content. "I think

you mean it now." He eased down the zipper at the back of her black-and-red sheath dress.

"What you'll want after I do this…" The fine wool fabric fell over her hips and puddled on the floor at her feet. He bent to kiss the exposed arch of her throat, and then paused to admire the nipples protruding through the semi-sheer fabric of her red bra. "And this…" His lips dropped to her breast.

"And this…"

She trembled as her bra came off.

"…may be something else entirely." His lips found the aching crowns, the valley between, the sensitive uppermost curves.

Eve closed her eyes, luxuriating in the feel of his tongue making lazy designs on her skin. She had never felt more beautiful than she did at that moment.

The next thing she knew, her black tights were being peeled off. Then her sheer red panties.

Moments later, Derek joined her, naked, between the sheets.

Eve had thought if she accepted her desire, and celebrated it freely, she would be able to control her reaction to him. She hadn't banked on how it would feel having his bare form pressed up against hers. She hadn't counted on the abundance of his masculinity or the skill with which he took her in his arms and made a leisurely tour of her entire body. Starting with her lips, then her throat and breasts, before moving lower still, across the quivery plane of her abdomen to the inside of her thighs. She arched as he found the most sensitive part of her, and caught his head in her hands.

And then all was lost in the glorious possession of his lips and caresses, and the tenderness he bestowed.

Satisfaction roared through Derek as Eve shuddered and fell apart in his hands. He waited until her trembling subsided, then moved up over her and slid between her thighs, his need to make her his stronger than ever. Clasping her against him, he kissed her hard and long, soft and deep, and every way in between. He kissed her until she moaned, her hands moving over him, finding him every bit as ready for more as she was. Their eyes locked again, and the sound of their ragged breathing filled the room.

"Now?" he whispered, touching her yet again.

"Now." Eve arched, and he slid all the way home. She was as hot, silky and wet as he had imagined. Her lips found his and her body closed around him, demanding, pleading, urging him on. They moved in perfect union, again and again, until Derek was lost in the sweet essence that was Eve. And suddenly, for him, life was better than it had been in a long, long time.

"Stay."

With a sheet draped loosely around her, Eve bent to retrieve her clothes.

Her body might be sated, but her emotions were in tatters. "I can't."

Derek lay on his side, all six feet three inches of him sprawled out across the queen-size bed. Unlike her, he found no need to cover up, now that their first—and only—lovemaking session had ended.

Flushing, Eve turned her glance from the part of him that indicated he was as ready for more as she secretly was.

She steeled herself against the desire still roaring through her. "I've got two important meetings tomorrow." Pretending an ease she couldn't begin to feel, she slipped into the bathroom and put on her bra and panties. "The first is with a client from Houston, who collects interesting houses the way others amass fine art."

Realizing she had yet to locate her tights, Eve came back into the bedroom. Feeling suddenly self-conscious in her red satin-and-lace undergarments, she circled the bed where Derek lay watching her, a mixture of delight and satisfaction in his gaze. "He's interested in one designed by Santiago Florres."

"The Texas architect who builds homes like ultramodern mazes."

"Right." Spying her tights at last, Eve snatched them off the floor and started putting them on. "My mother has been courting this investor forever. He's coming to town to look at a property tomorrow. I have to pick him up at Love Field in the afternoon." Nearly dressed, she stepped into her sheath. "In the morning, I have to meet with Flash Lefleur—"

Lazily, Derek stood and tugged on his boxer-briefs, still listening to her intently. "The hockey player who was traded to Montreal last summer."

The snug-fitting cotton highlighted the sensual contours of his generous physique in a way that made Eve want to undress him all over again. Forcing herself to remain as strong and disciplined as she needed to be, she smiled. "Yes. I listed his condo almost five months ago. But Flash has refused to do the things required to actually sell it. Luckily, he's going to be in town for tomorrow night's game, and agreed to meet with me while he's in Dallas…."

Trying to keep her mind from veering into forbidden territory, she cleared her throat, then continued. "Because there has been so little interest in the property despite its stellar location, I'm hoping to talk sense into Flash at long last. But I only have a few minutes, after his morning practice wraps up, to do it." She located her pumps and slipped into them.

Derek put on his pants and then his shirt, unabashed admiration in his eyes. "If Lefleur's smart, he'll listen to you. You know your stuff."

Aware that Derek could easily make her forget everything but making love to him again, Eve drew in a jerky breath. She held him off with a roll of her eyes and a look that would have sent a lesser man running for the exit. "Flattery will get you absolutely—"

"Where I want to go?" With a teasing smile, he pulled her against him. His eyes mirrored everything she felt, and the knowledge was staggering. So tender, so yearning… It would be so easy to fall in love with him.

Too easy. Eve gulped and did her best to keep her vulnerable heart in check. "The sex was great, Derek." Pretending to be a lot more casual about all this than she was, she splayed her hands across his hard chest.

His heart thudded heavily beneath her palms. Ignoring her efforts to keep him at bay, he playfully nuzzled the side of her neck, finding the nerve endings just beneath her ear. He kissed her again, in a way no one else ever had. Or likely ever would.

Finally, he drew back, his eyes meeting hers. "No argument there," he said softly. "It was spectacular for me, too."

Eve wet her lips. "But I meant what I said about this being a make-love-once-and-we're-done affair."

His grin widened. "I know."

She willed her knees to vanquish their trembling. "Then...?"

His blue eyes twinkled. "Even so, a Texas gentleman never ends an evening without a proper good-night."

Eve should have seen the last kiss coming. Should have seen a lot of things coming. Like the fact that, since Derek was the kind of man who went after what he wanted with no holds barred, he wasn't likely to end their one-and-only encounter without a kiss.

And not just any kiss, but one that made another chink in the wall around her heart, and nearly drove her to her knees. When he finally lifted his lips, she was a puddle of desire once again.

Derek walked Eve to the door, said a casual goodbye and watched her slip away. He knew she had told him that this was a one-time event. But he didn't believe that would be the case.

For starters, she wasn't the kind of woman who could make love without feelings being involved, even though she had clearly tried her best to do so. Second, even though she didn't want to get emotionally involved, they already were. The fact that they couldn't seem to stay away from each other, and the hot, reckless way they'd just made love, proved just how interlinked their lives were becoming.

Getting Eve to admit that, however, was not going to be easy.

Not only was she one of the most independent and elusive women he had ever met, she was cautious to a fault. Part of it likely had to do with the way she and her mom had been abandoned by her wealthy, well-connected father. The rest was because she had gotten involved with the wrong guy for the wrong reasons before, and consequently was scared of laying her heart on the line.

Derek understood that, but he wasn't willing to throw away the best thing he'd ever had, either.

The kind of connection he and Eve had found in each other was a rare occurrence.

So he would do whatever it took to make sure they continued to build on that connection. And have faith that patience and understanding would ultimately bring them the happiness they both deserved.

Her tense but ultimately productive meeting with Flash Lefleur behind her, Eve was at the airport the next afternoon, awaiting the arrival of Red Bloom's private jet, when a text from Derek came in. Need advice re house. Free to meet tonight?

Eve contemplated the message, her heart racing. This was the point where she should be gently but determinedly extricating herself from her former client, to concentrate more fully on her current ones. Yet she couldn't bring herself to do so, any more than she had been able to tear herself from his arms before they'd made love and satisfied their mutual curiosity once and for all, the night before.

She bit her lip, still thinking. After further deliberation, she typed, May still be tied up with client tonight. Particularly if things went as well as she hoped with the Houston oilman and home collector. Can someone else in the office help you? She hit Send.

Thirty seconds later, Derek replied, Prefer you. Will check with you later.

Which, Eve thought as she studied the screen, left

a lot of options open. They could end up spending another evening together. Or be involved in something that was strictly business. Or not see each other at all. She knew what she was privately hoping for. And it wasn't the sensible route to take.

But then nothing about her involvement with Derek was sensible, she thought, sighing wistfully. And that worried her almost as much as her upcoming appointment with Red Bloom.

For her mother's sake, she really needed to make the sale.

Unfortunately, as much as Red Bloom liked the uniquely designed contemporary home, he was not going to be reasonable.

"I can't present the owners with an offer like that," Eve protested, upon hearing what the businessman was prepared to bid. "It's only half what the property is listed for!" The owners weren't about to take a two-million-dollar loss.

Unimpressed, Bloom looked around the elegantly appointed home. Like many self-made men, the sixty-something bachelor was dressed to suit himself, in designer jeans, alligator boots and a tailored suede jacket with patches on the elbows. Freckles dotted his weathered face, and a dark brown Resistol was tipped up over his fading auburn hair. "How many bids have the current owners had?" He stroked his mustache thoughtfully.

"None," Eve conceded reluctantly. The mazelike floor plan and starkly contemporary exterior, in an area of mostly traditional homes, had seen to that. "But I believe it will sell eventually, at close to what it's priced."

Bloom clearly did not agree. He persisted curtly, "Make the offer."

Somehow managing not to sigh in frustration, Eve reached for her phone and did as her client bid.

"Well?" he said, when the round of calls had finally been completed.

"The answer is no." Unequivocally, angrily, no.

His handsome brow furrowed. "They understood that I was the one placing the bid?"

A fact that had made it all the more insulting, since Red Bloom was well known as an astute collector of unique architectural designs. Eve affirmed this with a nod. "They did."

"And they didn't even counter?"

Deliberately, she kept her manner matter-of-fact. She might not want to waste any more of her own time with Red Bloom, but in this situation she had little choice. Her mother had been courting the oilman for months, trying to get him to come to Dallas to see the Santiago Florres home that Marjorie was certain was perfect for Red's collection of eccentric properties. "Their view is that it's the asking price or above. Or nothing."

Bloom scoffed in disbelief. He took off his hat and slapped it against his thigh. "That's too bad. It would have been nice to add a Santiago Florres to my real estate portfolio."

It would have been nice, Eve thought, to get the sale on her mother's behalf. And keep Loughlin Realty firmly in the lead of the Highland Park real estate sales race. But she hadn't. And now she would have to tell her mother that disappointing news, too.

Unable to interest Bloom in looking at anything else that day or any other, Eve drove the oilman back to the airport. The two of them said a cordial goodbye, despite the fact they knew they would likely never see each other again.

Dispirited and exhausted, Eve called Sasha and her mother to let them know what had happened, then headed back to the office. And found an even bigger surprise waiting.

Derek had expected Eve to be pleasantly stunned to see him waiting for her with a yuletide horse and buggy. However, he hadn't expected her to look so incredibly gorgeous after such a long day. In a cranberry wool coat, suit and heels, her hair drawn up in back, she was the epitome of sophistication.

The look she gave him, when she realized what he was doing there, was cool, however. He moved out of earshot of the driver, as did she.

Aware they were being observed by everyone in the vicinity, especially those coming out of her office building, she repeated his invitation as if she couldn't possibly have understood him correctly. "You want to look at Christmas lights? Right now?"

He shrugged affably and kept his gaze locked with hers. He'd known even before they'd hit the sheets that Eve would regret making love prior to them really getting to know each other. He'd seduced her anyway, and now was paying the price for their mutual recklessness. Her coolness toward him would likely continue unless they took several steps back and established even more of a close personal relationship.

Knowing it was going to take a lot of persuading to get her to go out with him, he ambled close enough to take in her hyacinth perfume. "I hear yuletide carriage rides are a tradition in this neck of the woods."

She studied him, offering no clue as to what was in her heart. "It's quite a gamble, showing up with a horse and buggy." She looked him up and down and narrowed her gaze. "What if I hadn't been here?"

A fresh wave of guilt wafted through him. Figuring if Eve was going to hear it, she may as well hear it from him, Derek admitted, "Sasha told me when I called the office that you were expected shortly."

Determination stiffened Eve's slender frame. "Then she should have also told you that I had a very long day, and will probably have an even longer one tomorrow."

If ever a woman needed tender loving care, Eve was it. "Then it's a good thing I'm here with just the holiday distraction you need." He paused. "Unless...you've already taken a leisurely tour of this year's best holiday light displays?"

Briefly, a wistful look crossed her face.

Clearly, Derek thought, she hadn't.

He'd known his instinct was a good one. "It's also a nice way to wind down, make the transition from time on the job to time off," he said, adding for good measure, "Not to mention get in the spirit of the holidays."

His expression hopeful, the driver tipped his hat at them. The horse snorted and pawed the ground restlessly. Derek grinned again and all three waited for Eve to decide.

She looked them over for a long moment, then propped her hands on her hips and drawled, "Well, I guess it's either this or spend the evening saying 'Bah, humbug!'"

Everyone laughed as she finally relented.

Delighted with her response, Derek helped her up into the cozy confines of the carriage and settled beside her. The evening was chilly and damp, and a luxuriously thick velvet lap robe had been provided for extra warmth. Together, they tucked it across their laps and around their legs.

There was comfort and joy to be found, Derek realized, in just sitting cuddled together on a cold and starry December night.

The carriage swayed as the horse trotted down the avenue and turned onto a suburban street. Santa's sleigh was on one lawn. A manger, complete with animals and a baby, on another. Across the street, there was a Star of David on a roof. Cartoon characters decorated another lawn, and everywhere there were festive wreaths and Christmas trees, colored and white lights. Sometimes music accompanied the displays. All were beautiful. Some moving, some funny.

Eve studied their surroundings, quiet now, at peace. Finally, she turned to Derek, her shoulder gently nudging his. "Thanks for this," she said sincerely. "I think I needed some R & R more than I knew."

He resisted the urge to reach over and squeeze her hand. Contenting himself with a long look into her eyes, he replied softly, "You're welcome."

Another companionable silence fell. Eve took a deep breath and turned back to him, her hip and thigh briefly touching his. "When you texted today, you said you needed my advice regarding your new home."

Derek nodded, serious now, too. "Even though Tiffany and I can't move in yet, I want to go ahead and decorate the outside of the home for the holidays. But I'm not sure which direction to go."

Eve squinted as if doing some mental calculations. "And you thought you'd ask me?" she asked eventually.

He admired the soft, luscious curves of her lips, and the cute way she wrinkled her nose when she was perplexed. "You do have impeccable taste."

She lifted an eyebrow. "So do you," she acknowledged. Then she waited, as if wanting to know what was really behind his unexpected request.

Derek knew he could make something up—and eventually give her further reason to want to keep him at arm's length. Or he could be honest. "Okay," he admitted with a smile. "It's just an excuse to spend time with you."

She studied him, her eyes taking on a turbulent sheen. "You thought it wouldn't happen any other way?"

Derek sobered. "Not as fast as I'd like it to happen, anyway."

She peered at him through a fringe of thick golden-brown lashes, smiling briefly as she asked, "Does anyone ever say no to you?"

She seemed to think, erroneously, that this went back to him being part of one of the most powerful clans of Texas. "That's not really the issue." It had nothing to do with him being a McCabe. "The issue is, do I ever say yes."

Eve shifted on the carriage seat again. "What do you mean?"

Ignoring the heat her brief, accidental touch generated, Derek forced himself to focus on his reply, not on how good she felt whenever she pressed up against him.

"At work, as a venture capitalist, I'm constantly sifting through proposals and hearing pitches from start-up businesses," he explained. "I turn down ninety-nine for every one that I fund, because they're just not ready for prime time, so to speak, or the idea is terminally flawed in some way."

A mixture of understanding and compassion lit her smile. She seemed to realize what so few others did— how much he hated being the bad guy in a situation. "So you're always saying no," she guessed, with no small trace of irony.

"In my business life," Derek specified. "Which is why, in my private life, I want to say yes as often as possible."

She gave an encouraging nod, as if that made sense to her, so he reached over and took her hand. "I'd think you would want to say yes a little more often, too."

"When it comes to you," Eve returned softly, looking down at their entwined fingers, "I do." After a moment, she withdrew her hand. "But that doesn't mean we *should,* Derek."

Clearly, he thought with a frustrated sigh, he had a lot more convincing to do. But he'd get there. When he wanted something as much as he wanted to be with Eve, he always did.

Chapter 8

"So what do you think?" Derek asked, a half mile of beautifully decked out houses later. "What kind of decorations should I go for?" There was another manger on one lawn, a menorah several houses later and a Charlie Brown Christmas display at the end of the block.

The truth was, Eve didn't know him well enough yet to say. Wishing he didn't look so handsome in his cashmere coat and scarf, or that she still didn't want him quite so much, she demurred, "You could always call your designer."

He watched her adjust the velvet lap robe. "That would take all the fun out of it."

She fought the urge to cuddle against him. "True."

He sat back and draped his arm across the top of the seat, seemingly content to just be there with her. In a low, gravelly voice that sent prickles across her skin, he said, "The only thing I know for sure is that it should be something that would delight Tiffany."

Unable to help herself, Eve shifted to better see his face. "Well, there you go," she teased in a soft, sultry voice.

"But," Derek said, "in that realm, as we have seen, there are a lot of choices." Everything from Sesame Street characters to teddy bears and reindeer.

Curious, she asked, "Do you want her to believe in Santa?"

He nodded. "Carleen and I both do."

It was nice, the way he and his ex worked together to co-parent their child. Eve wished there was more of that in divorced couples. Certainly her own experience, with her mother and father detesting each other, had been less than ideal.

Aware that Derek was waiting for her reaction, Eve said, "Then there you go. Something to do with Santa and his workshop would be perfect."

Derek radiated enthusiasm. "Next question. Where do I get the stuff?"

Glad for something else to focus on aside from the dashing man beside her, Eve opened up her bag and whipped out her phone. She scrolled through several options, paused to type another more specific query, then finally came up with a list of choices. "I would recommend this place." She pointed to a popular home improvement store.

Derek glanced at his watch. "How late are they open?"

She checked the posted hours. "Until ten o'clock."

"Which means we could go now," he suggested.

For a second, Eve was tempted, but then she shook her head. "I have a big day tomorrow."

"I understand."

Moments later the carriage arrived back at Eve's office. Derek climbed down and helped her to the ground. A little sad that their time together was over, she looked up at him. "But good luck." She reached out and squeezed his hand. "I'll be thinking of you."

"And I," Eve thought she heard Derek murmur as she walked away, "will be dreaming of you."

Derek went to the hardware superstore that night, then recruited two of his brothers and his sister-in-law to help put up the decorations on Saturday morning.

"You're certainly in a cheerful mood, considering what you're dealing with in there." Derek's older brother, Grady, pointed to the crowd of contractors working on the interior of his newly purchased home.

Grady's wife, Alexis, was unraveling several outdoor extension cords. Above the sounds of hammers and saws, and vehicle doors being slammed, she called, "It's because there's a woman in his life."

Grady turned to his wife, the love he felt for her shining in his eyes. He ignored the whine of a power saw coming from the open garage. "How do you know?"

"Easy." Alexis pulled out a set of thin metal stakes and unboxed those, too. With all the authority of a professional matchmaker, she stated, "I haven't seen Derek smile the way he has today, ever. And no house, no matter how much potential it has, will ever light up any Mc-Cabe male's face like that. That kind of smile, my dear husband, comes from falling head over heels in love."

Squirming, Derek averted his gaze. He wasn't in

love. *Yet.* It was way too soon for that. He was head over heels in lust. And so was Eve, if the way she had kissed him and made love to him was any indication.

Grady grinned at him. "I would have to agree," their brother Rand teased, lifting his voice above the ongoing racket. An environmentalist, he generally disliked anything that used too much energy, but for sentimental reasons made an exception when it came to Christmas lights. He lifted the boxed yard ornament from the back of his pickup truck. "I think I know who it is, too."

Although Derek was happy to see his baby brother—who was passing through Dallas on his way to a job in East Texas—he didn't want his family nosing around in his private life. They'd already done enough of that already, questioning first his marriage and then his divorce from Carleen.

"You can't know," Derek retorted.

That was the beauty of living several hundred miles away from everyone but Grady and Alexis, who resided in nearby Fort Worth. His family couldn't usually just drop by and check in on him. It had taken big news—like the fact he was buying a home on the spur of the moment—to get his parents to drive to Dallas to see him.

Grady exchanged knowing glances with his wife and then grinned slyly. "So you admit there *is* a woman."

"No one special," Derek fibbed, growing increasingly impatient. The last thing he needed was more familial interference.

"I heard you were sweet on the Realtor who sold you this place," Rand stated. "At least that's the impression Mom and Dad got when they stopped by to congratulate you the other day."

"Mom and Dad are wrong," Derek said, noting that Alexis suddenly had a very peculiar look on her face. "Eve and I are friends. That's it." *As far as I'm going to admit at this point, anyway.*

"Good to know," a cool feminine voice said from behind him.

Swearing silently, Derek turned to confront the interloper.

Eve looked as appealing as ever, in professional garb even on a Saturday. A large embroidered carryall was slung over her shoulder, and she had a pamphlet in her hands. "This is from the neighborhood association," she said briskly. "It details their requirements for any light displays. Tells you about the parameters for taste, when they'd like the lights on and off, etcetera. I thought you would appreciate having a look at the guidelines before you got everything up."

"Thanks," Derek replied, doing his best to telegraph with his eyes that he hadn't meant what he'd just said, that he'd just been trying to keep his nosy family from interfering in their budding relationship.

If you could even call it that.

But Eve either didn't get, or didn't want to get, his message.

That impersonal look still on her face, she smiled again, gave a desultory wave and took off down the walk.

Derek called Eve several times throughout the day. She didn't pick up. Nor did she respond to any of the messages he left, asking her to phone when she had a minute.

Unwilling to let things stand with a misunderstanding of that magnitude between them, he found out where she lived and drove to her condo, a rectangular three-story building made of white stone. Luck was with him. Since it was 7:00 p.m., her car was in the lot and the lights were on in her unit.

Hoping she didn't have company over—it was Saturday night, after all—he walked up to her front door and rang the bell. Eve opened on the second ring. In a V-necked T-shirt, snug, worn jeans and shearling-lined lounging boots that came to midcalf, she looked ready for a comfortable evening at home. Her hair was tucked into a messy knot on the back of her head, and on close examination he discovered that her face was scrubbed of all makeup. Which made her skin look all the fairer. Seeing him, she sighed. "I heard you were trying to find me."

"News travels fast."

Another sigh. Her amber eyes glittering, she clamped her arms beneath her breasts. "What did you need?"

Derek noted that her delectably soft lower lip hadn't relaxed in the slightest. He dragged his gaze back to hers, swallowed around the telltale constriction in his throat. "I owe you an apology."

"No," she said sharply, "you don't."

"You misunderstood what was being said today."

She took a moment to consider that. "I think you were pretty clear, McCabe."

It was the first time she had called him by his last name. He kind of liked the reverse-intimacy of it. "I was trying to maintain my privacy."

She made a shooing motion. "So go! Maintain it!"

It was the last thing he wanted right now. Derek settled in, his shoulder braced against the door frame. "My family can be a little nosy."

She glared at him as if to say, *Beat it, buster!* Out loud, she snapped, "Not. My. Problem."

"Well, Loughlin, the fact that you're clearly mad at me is mine. And I would say it's a pretty big problem. One that needs to be dealt with right away before any more damage is done."

Scoffing, Eve folded her arms in front of her like a shield. "I would have to be interested in you to be ticked off at you."

Derek peered at her mischievously. "And you're not interested in me," he drawled, not believing it for one red-hot minute.

"Now you're getting the picture, McCabe."

There she went again with his last name. Derek grinned. Resisting the urge to take her in his arms and kiss her until she forgot why she was so mad at him, he said instead, "Let me make it up to you."

She shrugged, demonstrating her disinterest. "There's nothing to make up."

She was wrong about that. "Have you had dinner?" Derek persisted.

Temper gleamed in her eyes and her lips clamped shut. "Again. Not your concern."

Once more Derek dug in his heels. "So you haven't," he remarked genially, as if they had just made a date, after all. "What would you like?"

A smug look on her face, she replied sweetly, "Pizza and wine. Here."

There was no "we" in that equation. *Yet.* Derek vowed to keep working on her. "Okay. Tell me exactly what you want, from which pizza place, and I'll have it delivered for you. Same with the wine."

Clearly, she was as tired of sparring with him as he was of arguing with her. Her slender shoulders began to slump. "Again, McCabe, it's really not necessary."

Derek said, even more tenderly, "Why don't you let me be the judge of that?'

She sized him up for a long, long time. Then sighed, and said finally, "You know, McCabe, just because you like to say yes a lot in your private life doesn't mean everyone else does."

This time he laughed. "Why not?" He edged closer. "It can be fun."

She didn't step back. When she finally spoke again, resignation laced her voice. "We had our fun, remember? We made love once, to satisfy our curiosity, and now we're done." She paused. "Surely some of this must sound familiar."

It did, unfortunately.

Determined to change the narrative, Derek spoke again, even more cajolingly. "Please." He held her eyes, doing what he never did—laying bare his soul. "Give me a second chance. Let me make this up to you."

Eve could have refused a lot of things. Cool reason, a mea culpa. Teasing, or outright seduction. But to see a man like Derek practically get down on his knees and beg her to forgive him unthawed her heart. Not all the way. Just enough to allow her to open her front door and wave him in.

"You won't regret it."

She rolled her eyes, wondering what it was about this man that got to her so. "I already am."

"Has anyone ever told you that you're beautiful when you're angry?"

Eve chuckled despite herself at the dated cliché. Knowing he wasn't the kind of guy to ever deliver a line to a woman, unless it was a joke, she swatted his biceps playfully. "Watch it. Or I might put you in the deep freeze again."

He flexed his shoulders and rose to his full height. "I do not want to go there."

Eve could see that. Just as she could see how desperate he was to set things right between them. And that told her something, whether she wanted to admit it to herself or not. "What kind of pizza do you want?" she asked. If he was going to be here, they may as well eat. She was starving.

He spread his hands, obviously eager to please in whatever way necessary to get back in her good graces. "Whatever you want."

Eve groaned facetiously. "I've had a heck of a day, McCabe. Just make a decision." Telling herself that no matter what he thought, this wasn't a date, or anything close, she handed him a take-out menu.

He glanced at it. "The Everything."

A man after her own heart. "Works for me." She let him place the order. Opened up a bottle of zinfandel and poured two glasses. "I gather Tiffany is with her mom today."

Derek clinked glasses with her. "Carleen and Craig took her to see family. They won't be back until late tomorrow evening, so I won't see her until Monday after work."

Eve settled on the sofa opposite him as they waited

for their dinner. It did seem quiet without his daughter. "You must miss her."

"I do," Derek confided in a low, husky voice. "Although I'm kind of used to the schedule. And the split custody arrangement allows me time to pursue other things that are important to me."

I can't say I mind that, Eve thought. Then, realizing how premature it was for her to be thinking that way, she pushed that notion away and continued chatting casually. "I saw the yard decorations on my way home tonight." He and his family had done a great job decking out his new place. "Santa and Mrs. Claus at the North Pole. Very nice."

Derek grinned. "It was just about all the store had left, but thanks."

Their eyes met. "So how was your day?" he asked.

There was, Eve knew, only one way to describe it. "Tiring."

He listened intently, as much friend now as potential lover. "Yeah?"

Eve ran a finger down the seam of her jeans. "I finally got Flash's condo cleaned out and properly staged. We're having an open house tomorrow afternoon."

"Think it will sell now?"

"I hope so. We have only two more weeks on the listing, and he's threatening to sign with another firm if I don't get it done."

Derek's jaw flexed. Gallantly, he jumped to her rescue. "Lefleur can't blame you if he wouldn't do what was needed all this time."

"Actually, he does, and he will," Eve answered. "But enough about business." She wanted to escape from real-estate drama tonight, not wallow in it.

She stood and went to the window that looked out over the parking lot. But despite her grumbling stomach, there wasn't a delivery vehicle in sight.

Derek rose, too. "Where's your Christmas tree?" He looked past her galley kitchen, which was on the other side of the half-walled breakfast bar, and down the hall, where open doors revealed an ultrafeminine master suite, and an eight-by-ten space that seemed to be half den, half clothes closet.

Eve shrugged, suddenly feeling a little embarrassed to be living in such a small space. "I don't have one."

He turned back to her, his brow furrowed. "This year?"

She shook her head, embarrassed again. "Ever, really."

When he stepped nearer, she could see how closely he had shaved. Could smell his familiar, appealing scent. "Why not?" he asked. Eve pressed her lips together and, all too physically aware of him, paced back to the window. "Putting up holiday decorations is nothing my mother and I ever really had time to do."

Derek blinked and followed after her. "You're kidding, right?" Darkness had fallen. Although her immediate neighborhood was all brick condo units erected side by side, in the distance, colored lights twinkled and lavish homes beckoned.

She smiled. "When I was little, we had a tabletop tree—like the one I brought you and Tiffany at the hotel. But after I realized there was no Santa Claus, we stopped even that. Marjorie saw no reason for the charade."

"Christmas is a charade?"

"Expecting that miracles might happen, or that everything changes for the better this time of year, is, in my mother's view, nothing more than a fantasy, and a harmful one at that. As she's fond of saying, only hard work and clear eyes will get you where you want to go in life."

"And your perspective...?"

Of course he would ask her that. Eve sighed. "I don't know what I believe." She looked him in the eye.

"Don't know, or don't want to say?"

How about a little bit of both? Eve thought. "Not everything in life has to be definitive, Derek."

"That's true." He bent closer to study her, then murmured, "But everyone knows deep down what they believe."

Eve stiffened, unsure just how emotionally vulnerable she was ready to leave herself. "Okay," she said, with a lift of her chin. "Then tell me about you."

His blue eyes warming affectionately, he rose to the challenge. "I think Christmas is a magical time of year."

"Because...?" Eve prompted.

After pondering it for a moment, he gave her a long, telling look. "Because Christmas opens up people's hearts and makes all things seem possible."

It was certainly making *this* seem possible, she thought. She barely knew Derek, and already they felt incredibly connected. "You really are romantic, deep down," she whispered.

To her satisfaction, he didn't even try to deny it. "What does Christmas mean to you?" he asked instead.

He'd been remarkably honest. Eve knew she should be, too. Struggling to put her feelings into words, she raked her teeth across her lip. "I think it's great, if you have a big happy family, like you apparently do."

Once again, he seemed to sense all she wasn't saying. "But otherwise?" Derek tucked a strand of hair behind her ear. It was becoming a familiar gesture.

Eve savored the tender touch of his fingers against her skin. "It can be—it has been—the loneliest time of the year for me."

He smiled and dropped his hand. "Then it's time that changed."

His confidence made her laugh and groan simultaneously. "Really? And how are you going to achieve that miracle?"

"I don't know yet." He squinted, then rubbed his jaw. "But I'll come up with a plan."

Suddenly, Eve sensed they were in dangerous territory. "You're not responsible for me and my happiness."

Derek sobered, all protective male. "I know that," he told her in a low, husky voice that seemed to come straight from his heart. "But here's the thing, Eve. I want to be."

Chapter 9

The words hung in the air between them. Derek knew it had been a cornball thing to say. It was true, nevertheless. He did want to be responsible for Eve and her happiness, in a way he'd never been with anyone before.

Problem was, she wasn't buying it. Not yet, anyway.

"Which brings me to my next question," he said. "Exactly how tired are you?"

The sparkle was back in her eyes. "Why?" she countered softly, as the doorbell rang.

Derek went to get it. He paid the pizza guy, then brought their meal back to where she was sitting, and put it on the coffee table. When he opened the box, the fragrance of fresh hot pizza filled the air.

She'd already set out stoneware plates and plenty of paper napkins. "Because," he said, returning to her side, "the evening is still young."

She glanced at the clock on the wall, noting it was half past eight. "Maybe for you. For all you know, my bedtime could be nine o'clock."

Realizing too late how that could possibly be interpreted, she flushed.

Gallantly, he let the faux pas pass, and asked instead, "What would you usually do on a Saturday night?"

A serious question deserved a serious answer. "After a week like this past one?" Eve heaved an enormous sigh and stretched. "I'd probably bake something sweet and decadent and watch a movie."

His dark brows furrowed. "Alone?"

"Usually." Eve nodded. "I like my quiet time."

"Me, too."

For several minutes, they enjoyed their pizza in silence. Eventually, she dabbed the corners of her mouth and said, "Although, for some reason—" she winked flirtatiously "—quiet time doesn't happen a lot when you're around."

He laughed, deep and low, then waggled his eyebrows. "You never know." He left the implication hanging.

Eve looked down her nose at him like a prim schoolmarm chastising a rowdy teenage male. "I think I do."

Derek returned her slow smile with a sexy one of his own. "We could go out this evening."

She considered the possibility. "And do what?"

He smiled and took another bite of the delicious pizza.

Eve took a bite of hers, and when she'd swallowed it, said, "Obviously you have something in mind."

Derek gave a slight nod. "Something," he said, both serious and hopeful now, "that should help you get in the Christmas spirit."

* * *

"I'm not exactly Ebenezer Scrooge," Eve drawled a few minutes later, as they cleaned up and put the leftovers in the fridge.

Derek tossed the napkins in the trash. "No one said you were."

She pushed the cork back in the wine bottle and put it away. "But you think I could use some improvement."

He folded up the pizza box. "I think your spirits could use some boosting." He reached out and rubbed the back of his hand across her cheek. "There's a difference."

Tingling from his touch, Eve went to get her jacket. Chivalrously, he assisted her as she shrugged it on. "You guarantee it's going to be worth my while."

Derek put his leather bomber jacket on. "Promise."

She grabbed her bag and together they walked out her condo door. "I don't know why I keep letting you talk me into things."

They stepped into the empty elevator and pushed the button for Lobby. "I think it's my irresistible McCabe charm," he bragged.

Eve laughed, unable to help but think how handsome he looked, no matter what time of day or night. Like the Prince Charming of her dreams. "It's something, all right," she quipped back, aware that she felt more a woman when she was with him than she had in a very long time. A woman with needs...

Oblivious to the disturbing nature of her thoughts, Derek took her hand in his. "Seriously, I promise this will make you happy."

The funny thing was, Eve realized, Derek did make her happy. Just hanging out with him on a Saturday evening made her feel giddy with excitement. And that wasn't something she'd ever experienced before.

Was this infatuation? she wondered. Or something much more?

She had no answer as Derek drove the short distance to the nearest Christmas tree lot. Set up by a local Rotary Club, it was filled with a nice selection of Fraser firs. They were about to close for the evening, but some fast talking and the promise of an extra donation from Derek kept them open a little longer.

Up and down the aisles he and Eve went. Derek looked at one after another. "What do you think?" He tucked his hand in hers and drew her close. "Seven feet tall or eight?"

Eve clasped his gloved hand and tilted her head to see his face. "Where are you going to put it?"

He looked at her as if that was an odd question. "Probably in the living room."

O-kay. Her brows came together quizzically. "You do know they're still doing construction in your home, right?"

He erupted into laughter and leaned down to touch his nose to hers. "Then it probably should go in yours."

His "Eskimo kiss" left her all aflutter. Eve drew back slightly, her eyes locked pleasurably with his. "For now," she said.

Another perplexed frown creased his handsome face. "At least until New Year's, I would think."

Eve blinked. "What are you talking about?"

Derek cupped her shoulders. "I'm buying you a Christmas tree."

She was dumbfounded.

He continued looking at her as if she wasn't the only one feeling infatuated. Persuasively, he added, "You bought me and Tiffany one, after all."

"A two-foot artificial tree." It was hardly the same thing.

"Which is perfect for us, since we're in a hotel." He went back to examining the fresh, fragrant fir he had been looking at. "This one is perfect for you."

Eve moved so he had no choice but to look at her. She curved her hand around his biceps. "What if I don't want a tree?"

Derek curved his free hand behind his ear. "What was that you just said?" he shouted, pretending he was half-deaf. "Bah! Humbug!"

Eve laughed despite herself. She could easily see a man like this taking over her life. She could easily see *Derek* taking over her life.

He leaned down to whisper in her ear. "Come on. You know you want one."

The warmth of his breath sent a shiver down her neck. And caused new heat elsewhere.

"It's for a good cause," the Rotary volunteer interjected helpfully.

The guys had her there.

"Okay," Eve said, deciding it was less treacherous to agree than to prompt Derek to continue persuading her. "But no bigger than six feet."

"Six feet it is," Derek and the Rotarian volunteer agreed in unison.

Minutes later, they had it tied to the top of Derek's Jaguar SUV, along with a nicely decorated, fresh evergreen wreath for her door, for good measure. "Now where are we going?" she asked when they took off once again.

"Exactly where you would think." Derek parked in front of the nearest megastore with a big red-and-white circle on the front. "To buy some decorations."

They went inside together. Despite the fact it was nearly ten-thirty, the place was still packed with harried shoppers taking advantage of the extra-late holiday hours.

Derek grabbed a red plastic shopping cart, then paused to study the layout of the store. Eventually, he went left. Amazed by how at-home he was doing ordinary things, Eve trailed along after him. It seemed there were many intriguing facets to this man.

Not that he was right about everything. She tapped him on the shoulder. "If you're looking for ornaments, we should go right."

He stopped, chagrined, and smiled down at her. "I knew I brought you along for a reason."

Eve knew she had invited him in that evening for a reason. She just didn't want to think what that might be.

"So what do you think?" Derek said, as they reached the holiday decor section of the store and studied the array of possibilities.

Eve pointed out her favorites. "I like the velvet and satin bows."

He tossed several packets of each in the basket. "For the tree topper?"

It was a hard decision. "An angel," she said finally.

Derek handed her the prettiest one. "What about lights?"

Eve picked out strands of miniature colored bulbs.

He put a tree stand in the cart, then moved to the next aisle. "Got to have some ornaments."

Eve bypassed everything that was breakable and went for the kid-friendly ornaments. "In case any children come over," she said with a self-conscious flush, one very special little toddler in mind.

"Safety first," Derek agreed soberly.

Eve studied their finds. "I think we've got everything."

She brought out her wallet at the checkout line. He stopped her with a shake of his head. "This is on me."

"I—"

"Consider it my thank-you to you for helping make my holidays wishes come true."

Again, they locked glances, and again something passed between them. Something tender and sweet, and undeniably uplifting.

As it turned out, getting the Christmas tree into her condo was easy. Getting the trunk centered in the stand? Not so much.

First it listed to the right, then to the left. Finally, Derek got down on all fours and, lying on his side beneath the branches, adjusted it in the metal pan. While Eve held the tree in place, he tightened the bolts around the base of the trunk.

When they were both finally satisfied the tree was straight, Eve went to get water to keep it fresh. Still sprawled on the floor in a way that engendered way too many secret sexual fantasies for Eve, Derek poured in the liquid, then rose up on one elbow to hand the pitcher back.

Her pulse racing, but determined to appear unaffected, Eve set the pitcher aside and offered him a hand up. He locked palms with her, and a second later towered above her once again, all big brawny male. And Eve realized all over again this was no simple friendship. This was no simple anything.

"You okay?" he asked, peering down at her curiously.

Yes and no, Eve thought.

Somewhere in all the activity, she'd gotten her second wind. And then there was her ongoing, escalating reaction to him.

Pretending it was the holiday activity that had her so distracted, she murmured, "Are you any good at stringing lights?"

"As it happens—" he winked at her "—I'm an ace."

He certainly seemed to know what he was doing. Curious, Eve asked, "What were your traditions like at home, when you were growing up?"

He plugged in one light strand to make sure it worked. "The usual, I guess. Stockings above the fireplace, a tree, lights inside and out, a wreath on the door."

"And socially?"

He smiled reminiscently. "It seemed like we were always busy. There were lots of extended family gatherings and community functions to attend."

It sounded…nice. Like a Hallmark movie of the way things should be. "And on the holiday itself?" she asked.

The fabric of his jeans snugly cupped his muscular thigh when he knelt to drape lights on the lower branches. "We usually had a catered dinner brought in." He threaded the strand through the fragrant evergreen and stretched it out. Their fingertips brushing, she caught it from the other side and pulled it through.

"What did you and your mom do?" he continued, equally curious.

Eve went to get another strand to plug into the first. "We went to a restaurant for dinner on Christmas Eve, opened presents on Christmas morning and usually baked cookies and watched holiday movies together later on Christmas Day." It had been really nice, and yet she'd always had the sense the holidays made her mother a little sad, so she'd been sad, too.

Derek looked at her thoughtfully. "What's your favorite movie?"

With a slightly embarrassed shrug, Eve admitted, "It's a cartoon, actually. *A Charlie Brown Christmas.*"

Derek paused. "I like that one, too. Although I never really understood Charlie Brown's melancholy until a couple years ago."

"After the whole Carleen and Craig thing…?" Eve guessed.

Derek nodded, grim. "Up until then, in a lot of ways, I'd led a charmed life."

Eve smiled up at him. "And would like to do so again."

He hunkered down to finish the lights, his sweater riding up slightly as he moved. "It'd be nice to provide Tiffany with a mommy and a daddy at both of her homes."

Dangerous territory, that. Eve tore her glance away from his flat, muscled abs. No need recalling how nice he looked naked.

Her mouth dry, she went to open up the ornaments,

deliberately cutting off her view of him. "What was *your* favorite Christmas movie?"

"A Christmas Story."

Her emotions under control, Eve pivoted back to the tree and started hanging ornaments and placing velvet bows. "I don't think I've ever seen that one."

"It's set back in the late 1940s, so a lot's different than life today, but the chaos in it between siblings, and parents and children, is reminiscent of my childhood." His lip curved with amusement. "My mom used to say that her life would have been so much quieter if she'd had five girls instead of five boys."

Eve chuckled. "I wouldn't bet on that. Girls can get pretty rowdy, too. Just in different ways."

They both smiled. Then she tossed him a cookbook. He caught it one-handed. "What's this for?"

Eve stood back to admire the twinkling lights and ornaments, and finally handed him the angel to set atop the highest branch. "You helped me with the tree. I'll bake you some cookies before I send you on your way."

He adjusted the angel, and then plugged in its cord. The angel lit up, too, adding an even more magical quality to the scene. Finished, he dusted off his hands and turned back to her, his gaze intent. "You're kicking me out?"

He didn't look as if he wanted to go any more than she wanted him to. "Eventually." She nodded at the cookbook, which he'd set aside. "What kind would you like?"

He picked it up again, an inscrutable look on his rugged face. "I can have anything I want?"

More dangerous territory—if he wanted the same

thing she wanted, that was. Eve smiled and approached him lazily. "If I've got the ingredients, sure."

He flipped through the pages. "Spritz cookies."

"Chocolate or vanilla?"

"Both."

"Taskmaster," she complained.

"Hey." He angled his thumb at her chest. "You asked."

She had.

While she worked, he perused her shelves and eventually found a Chris Botti Christmas CD a client had given her. Derek slid it into the stereo and turned it on. The soothing trumpet music added a sultry aura to the apartment. Looking a bit restless and distracted himself, he returned to the kitchen and took a stool on the other side of the breakfast bar. Elbows on the counter, he watched her stuff dough into the cookie press and fit a star mold over the tip. "Is that hard to use?"

So he needed something to do with his hands, too.

With a shake of her head, Eve held it out. "Want to try?"

He rose with the same economy of motion he did everything else and strode around the counter. "I won't screw it up?"

Eve mugged comically. "If you do, we'll just reload the press with more dough and do it again."

"Well, hey, when you put it like that…"

She motioned him closer, then stepped behind him and fitted the cookie press in his big hands. "You position the end right over the baking sheet and press the trigger. That's good." She moved a bit nearer. "Keep pressing until a quarter inch or so of dough is on the sheet, then let go of the trigger and lift the press. And voilà!"

To his amazement and her delight, they ended up with a cookie shaped like a star.

"Hey, what do you know, it worked!"

Eve stepped away from him and lounged against the counter, watching. "Just keep going."

Derek pressed several more cookies in a neat row. "I am good at this."

She wrinkled her nose. "And modest, too."

He finished filling up the empty spaces on the sheet. "Helps to have a good teacher."

Eve smiled. There was no denying it—she and Derek were a good team. Wondering if there was a way for them to be friends in the future, despite the fact they'd given in to passion once already, she said, "Let's get these in the oven."

"Okay." Derek washed and dried his hands while she shut the stove door and set the timer.

He turned back to her. "Now what?"

"We do another sheet, of the chocolate ones this time."

For the next half hour, they worked side by side. Eventually, they had two more trays in and out of the oven. Delighted by their success, Eve took a warm cookie and popped it into Derek's mouth. She waited for his reaction. "Well?"

He savored the taste with the same intensity he made love. "Delicious."

She relaxed in relief. "I'm glad you like it."

"Almost," Derek added, wrapping his arms around her and tugging her close, "as delicious as you."

Eve caught her breath. "Derek…" she warned.

Eyes shuttering, he lowered his head. His lips hovered just above hers. "One kiss, Eve, before I go. That's all I'm asking."

Chapter 10

But one kiss, Eve found, was impossible to give, never mind receive. The moment her lips fused with Derek's all common sense vanished. She arched against him, until there was only the press of hard flesh and the fierce erotic pleasure of his mouth over hers, and a kiss that seemed to go on and on and on. A kiss that was everything she had ever dreamed of…

It was the perfect Christmas gift.

But to her disappointment, it came abruptly to an end. Tensing, Derek lifted his head. He stroked his thumb across her lower lip, his eyes dark with desire. Their gazes locked, both of them breathing hard. "If you want me to leave," he warned softly, "now's the time."

She loved the brusque humor in his low tone, as much as she loved the way he looked at that moment. A little rough around the edges, and a lot aroused. "There's only one problem with that," she whispered back, lifting her hands in helpless surrender. "I don't."

One corner of his mouth crooked up. He reached for her again, dragging her against him. "Exactly what I was hoping you'd say..."

The next thing Eve knew, he had backed her against the wall. Which was good, because she was feeling a little wobbly, and the solid surface behind her helped keep her upright. Not that the hard cradle of his muscular physique wasn't doing the same. He was trapping her nicely with his big, gorgeous body and stubborn Texas resolve. He tasted innately male, like chocolate and sugar, and an essence that was unique to him. Loving every inch of him, of this, Eve pressed against him a little more. He was just as aroused, his skin burning with fiery intensity through his sweater and jeans, as he continued to kiss her, long and wet and deep.

Eventually, he lifted his head. "Here or the bed?"

Another easy decision. "Here."

He grinned and reached for her again, his blue eyes gleaming with desire and something else as well. He pushed her hair out of the way and then his lips were on the nape of her neck. "Can do."

He made her feel hot, so hot.

She held on to his shoulders with both hands as he nuzzled the sensitive place beneath her ear. His hands were moving lower, undoing the fastening of her jeans, then the zipper. The feel of his fingertips brushing against her skin made her quiver. Knees weakening all the more, she managed to gasp, "Or the bed."

He stopped what he was doing long enough to take in the sight of her. "You keep talking about Christmas presents. I think you're mine." He eased a hand past the elastic of her panties, going lower, lightly brushing back and forth. This time her knees nearly buckled, and he hadn't even found her yet.

She gasped again, still looking into his eyes. "Then that makes you mine."

His smile slow and hot, he slid a muscled thigh between her legs. "Just so you know...we're not rushing through this time."

His soft chuckle brought forth another quiver. "I'm getting that." She leaned forward and nipped his shoulder. "It doesn't mean I'll let you have all the fun."

Throbbing all over, she eased a hand between them. Determined to give as well as receive, she worked free the buckle of his belt. He watched her with pure male satisfaction, and then he was busy, too, kissing her again, while moving his hands beneath the hem of her T-shirt, up across her ribs, to cup her breasts through the thin lace of her bra. The feel of his palms on her taut nipples sent another rush of desire through her.

"Now...inside me."

Still keeping her pinned against the wall, he lifted her so she was straddling his waist, and had no choice but to put her arms around him and hold on tight. "In time..."

His hands found her breasts; his lips found her mouth. There was nothing to do but let him have his way, and claim her he did. Without even undressing her all the way, he found a way to touch her like no one else ever had, a way that made her feel safe and wanted, pleasured and desired. Although she had promised herself she would wait for him, there was no delaying. Eve could no more control her response than she could her feelings. The next thing she knew, she was being carried down the hall to her bed. Ever so gently, he set her down. Undressed her, let her undress him.

His eyes alight with mischief and something else—something deeper than pure pleasure or want or need—he joined her.

Eve reached for him and he sprawled over her. "Are we hurrying?"

Grinning lazily, he pushed her knees apart and slid between them, settling between her spread thighs. "What do you think?"

Her hips rose to pull his body even tighter to hers. She wreathed her arms about his neck. "I think you intend to take your time."

His eyes darkening, he lowered his mouth once again. She shivered as the hardness of his chest teased the sensitive skin of her breasts into taut awareness. "Derek…" She was already so wet and so ready.

He lifted his head to look into her eyes. "Some things are worth waiting for, especially this time of year."

And wait they did, as he took her mouth again in a long, hot, tempestuous kiss. She wrapped her legs around his waist and arched up against him, enjoying the pressure of his sex nestled against hers, the intensity of his kiss, the warm cage of his arms. He kissed her until she throbbed in response, and then he kissed her some more until she clung to him and whimpered low in her throat. And only then, when they were both filled with a longing that went way beyond the physical, did he grasp her hips and slide into her, filling her completely, taking her and making her his, until she was awash in a pleasure unlike any she had ever known.

Eve woke hours later to find sunlight streaming in through the edges of the blinds. The sight of the naked man next to her was enough to make her groan.

Derek smiled and rolled onto his side. "It's a good thing we're not dating. Otherwise, who knows what would happen next, or how we would end up?"

Eve groaned again and tried, without success, to sit up. They'd made love two more times during the night and she felt as physically wrung-out as if she had run a 5k race. Wrung-out and sated. Forearm across her eyes, she stayed on her side of the bed and avoided his gaze. "It's the holidays."

Baffled, he kissed the crook of her elbow. "Meaning...?"

Grumpily, she explained, "They always leave me feeling off-kilter."

His chuckle was low and infectious. "So that's what that was."

Determined not to encourage him, Eve tamped down her own amusement. "You know what I mean." She continued to keep her face hidden, her eyes closed.

Derek rose on his elbow and gently removed her arm. "I know you keep pretending that we don't have something special, when we actually do."

Eve averted her eyes and sat up. Abruptly remembering she was naked, she clamped the top of the ice-blue satin sheet to her breasts, and then said, "Physically, yes." She couldn't exactly deny that after he'd given her innumerable orgasms through the night. And she'd given him more in return. Still smiling with masculine satisfaction, Derek lounged among the pillows. "Physically and in all the other ways that count," he corrected.

Deciding to get some clothes on before they both got turned on again, Eve disappeared into the bathroom. She came back wearing a knee-length white spa robe. "Which are?"

Looking like a Greek god who had magically landed in her bed, Derek folded his arms behind his head. "You understand me."

She didn't even understand herself! "I wish."

He stood and pulled on his shorts and then his jeans. Unfortunately for her, he looked just as mouthwatering half-clad as he had naked. He came toward her, still zipping and snapping.

"Seriously, Eve, you always know instinctively what I need. And I seem to have the same innate ability when it comes to you." He paused in front of her and continued making his case with matter-of-fact ease. "Plus, you and Tiffany get each other the same way you and I get each other. And that isn't all that common."

That was the problem—none of this was usual. She'd thought by being intensely physical when they made love, that they would be able to keep their feelings out of it. It hadn't worked; her emotions were more tangled than ever. And now Derek was doing what he did best— leaping ahead, toward his stated goal—which currently seemed to be establishing them as friends *and* lovers.

Eve released a shaky breath, more sure than ever that, at the end of all this, she was going to get hurt. "I get all that, Derek, but this is still happening way too fast."

He looked at her, his eyes warm and assessing, even as she struggled to get a handle on herself. "Or not fast enough," he drawled.

She was saved from having to reply by the ringing of her phone.

She went to get it. "Obviously, you haven't been checking your messages," Marjorie said.

Eve knew that tone. She sat down on the edge of the

bed, filled with dread, while Derek lingered nearby, watching her with concern. "What happened?"

"Sibley & Smith brokered another sale last night, which puts them ahead of us in the sales race."

Eve signaled to Derek that he didn't have to worry about the call. He nodded and slipped out of the room to give her privacy.

With him gone, Eve was able to concentrate on the problem at hand. "By how much?" she asked her mother.

"Close to one and a half million."

Eve rubbed her suddenly aching forehead. "You're sure?"

Marjorie scoffed. "I wouldn't be calling you if I wasn't."

"There's still time for us to move ahead again, Mom. Flash's condo was finally staged the way it should have been all along. We're having an open house there this afternoon."

Her mother sighed, her pessimism apparent. "Even if it sells today it won't be enough."

"Astrid and Vanessa are pushing their own properties hard, too," Eve added, comforting her mother the best she could.

Marjorie's voice was suddenly tearful. "I thought we finally had it this year." So had Eve. This was exactly the kind of tension and stress none of them needed, particularly now.

Worried about more important matters than just the sales race, she asked, "How's your heart?"

"Broken!" her mother cried. "What do you think?"

Well, at least she wasn't being overly dramatic. "I meant medically, Mom. You're not having any chest pains again, are you?"

There was another pause. "No. I'm not. My heart is fine, honey." Her mother spoke again, contrite this time. "I'm sorry if I upset you."

This was new. Marjorie never apologized for venting or anything else. Eve walked out into the living room. Derek was fully dressed and making coffee, giving her a glimpse of what it would be like to have him around all the time. Very nice.

With effort, she focused on the situation at hand. "Are you sure you are okay, Mom?"

"I'm fine."

Eve relaxed in relief. "I'll see you this evening, then, for dinner, after the open house."

They said goodbye and hung up.

"Everything okay?" Derek asked.

This would be a good place to draw a line. To tell him thanks but no thanks. Unfortunately, Eve knew she needed to confide in someone. And right now that someone was Derek.

She went into the kitchen and brought out two mugs, as well as some pastries from the bakery. "My mother is fine, although how long she will stay that way if Vanessa, Astrid or I don't make another big sale is anyone's guess." While Derek listened intently, she explained about the annual Highland Park home-sales race.

He poured coffee for both of them. "Sounds like a pretty big deal."

Eve added creamer to hers. "It is. My mother has come close before, but she's never won it, so to have the lead in the competition for most of the latter part of this year, only to lose it right after her heart attack, is devastating for her."

Derek guided Eve to a stool at the breakfast bar and sat down next to her. "Should you go and see her?"

Eve picked at her cranberry-and-almond scone. "Right now? Heavens, no! The only thing my mother wants me doing at the moment is working on making another sale."

Derek broke a blueberry scone in two. "I'm assuming you have other leads."

"I do. I just need to pursue them more aggressively." *And stop putting so much time and attention into my personal life. At least for now...*

"You're looking good," Eve told her mother in surprise, hours later. Sunday evening, the rehab center cafeteria was sparsely populated with patients and families, but her mom had saved a table for the two of them in a far corner.

Her cheeks pink with excitement, Marjorie smiled. "I feel better. The yoga workouts they have me doing are really helping me deal with stress."

Eve set out the glasses of decaf iced tea and grilled chicken entrée plates she had picked up in the line, then moved the plastic tray aside. "That's good to hear." Although she still worried that her mother would be able to pace herself as directed, when she was finally permitted to return to work.

Marjorie took two small bites, then pulled a small leather-bound notepad and a pen out of her pocket. "As long as I have you here, I have a few reminders."

Eve paused, her fork halfway to her mouth. "Are the doctors okay with you doing this?"

"Within reason, yes." Marjorie put on her diamond-studded reading glasses and flipped to the correct page.

"First of all, don't forget the annual black-tie Highland Park Holiday Gala on the seventeenth of December." The proceeds of which went to a host of local charities.

Because it was something she and her mother typically did together, Eve murmured, "I was thinking I might skip it this year."

Marjorie straightened in alarm. "Don't you dare! It's more important than ever, in the wake of my heart attack, that Loughlin Realty be well represented. I've already given my ticket away, but I presume you still have yours?"

Eve swallowed a bite of steamed broccoli. She'd also made a considerable donation on behalf of the firm. "Yes."

"Good. Then I expect you to go. Next, I know you're discouraged about the sales race. Astrid and Vanessa were, too, when I spoke with them. But there's no need to be, because I just got off the phone with Red Bloom."

Doing her best to keep her manner neutral, Eve asked mildly, "Red Bloom called you?"

"Actually, I phoned him. I asked him to reconsider the Santiago Florres house."

Eve tensed. Her mother sometimes had the tendency to push too hard. When she did, the results were often not positive. "And?"

"He remains fascinated by the architecture, and turned off by the asking price."

Eve frowned, frustrated, because her mother could have inadvertently put a kink in the solution Eve was working on behind the scenes. She sat up straight. "I thought you wanted me to handle this, Mom."

Marjorie gave her a look of innocence. "I do."

Eve tried not to be hurt by her lack of faith. "Then

trust me to do so, Mom." She sighed wearily. "And in the meantime, there's something *you* can do for *me*. Concentrate on getting better so I won't have to spend so much time worrying about you."

Her mother looked slightly taken aback by Eve's entreaty. Silence fell and the two women resumed their meals. After a few long, tense minutes, Marjorie finally set her fork down and turned to her daughter. "You can sell the Santiago Florres home to Red Bloom with the right approach, Eve. And if you do…"

"We'll win the sales race." Eve guessed where all this was going.

"But just in case neither of those options work out, there is one other alternative," Marjorie continued stubbornly. "I know you've been spending a lot of time with Derek McCabe."

Probably too much, Eve thought, given how huge a part Derek and his daughter had started to play in her life in such a short amount of time.

"I also know that when he came to us, he originally intended to invest seven to eight million dollars in real estate before the end of the year. I imagine some of that cash is going into the fixer-upper he bought."

"A fair amount, actually," Eve conceded.

"But that still leaves a lot of money to invest somewhere else."

Her mother did not need to tell her there was more money to be made here. Normally, this was an opportunity Eve would be pursuing with all her might. Her growing feelings for Derek, however, made even the idea of taking things back to a strictly business level both unpalatable and upsetting. Although she might not know exactly what they were feeling besides lust and longing, and an increasingly intimate friendship, she was sure she didn't want whatever this was with him to end. And certainly not for business reasons.

Impatiently, Eve asked, "What exactly are you suggesting, Mom?"

"That you leverage your friendship with him, and use your powers of persuasion to help Derek meet his original investment goals. And in the process, help make Loughlin Realty the winner in this year's Highland Park sales race."

Winning top honors appealed to Eve, although clearly not as much as it did to her mother. Using Derek did not.

"Of course, I could call him and broach the topic, if you'd prefer," Marjorie offered. "Perhaps suggest he use Vanessa or Astrid as the agent, if you're not able to help."

Eve ignored the unspoken question: What exactly was stopping her from jumping on this opportunity?

"Thanks," she said, stifling a beleaguered sigh. She knew the last thing Derek probably wanted or needed was a hard sell from her mother, or the other agents in the office. "But—" *if it must be done, and I wish to heck it didn't* "—I'll do it."

Chapter 11

Eve was already waiting when Derek walked into the hotel bar. She had a glass of sparkling water with lime in front of her, a frown pursing her soft lips.

Derek slid into the cozy leather booth opposite her. Like her, he'd spent the day working. Now, at 8:00 p.m., he was ready for a little rest and relaxation.

"I'm glad you called." Although he couldn't say he was totally surprised, given what he had received via messenger that afternoon. "It was my second surprise of the day."

Their eyes locked and he felt the connection between them deepen.

"What was the first?"

The mystified note in her voice made him smile. "The ticket from your mother."

Eve blinked, then stared at him in confusion.

Derek leaned closer, inhaling a whiff of her hyacinth perfume. On impulse, he covered her hand with his. "For the Highland Park Holiday Gala on the seventeenth?"

The breath stalled in her throat, while her cheeks flushed with color. "Mom sent you that?"

"Along with the suggestion that I might attend with you, if I didn't want to go alone."

Eve inhaled sharply. He tightened his grip on her hand, feeling the omnipresent need to protect her. "I take it that it wasn't your idea?"

Eve glanced away, clearly struggling to remain impassive. "No. I didn't know anything about it until just now."

Disappointment moved through him. "You don't have to go with me," he pointed out gruffly, releasing her hand and sitting back.

She lifted her chin, for a second putting decorum and expectation aside. The way she looked at him let him know her pride was on the line. "And vice versa."

He couldn't blame her for being upset; he wouldn't want his family setting up social engagements for him, either. On the other hand, this was a prime opportunity for them to be together in another not-really-a-date-even-if-it-feels-like-a-date way.

He let his gaze drift over her, taking in the snug fit of her clothes and the heart on a chain nestled in the V of her black cashmere sweater. Appreciating the fact she'd done something different with her hair again—tonight it was styled in sophisticated waves that tumbled to her shoulders—he grinned at her as if this was no big deal, after all.

"However, I wouldn't mind going to a black tie event

with you on my arm." Then he winked at her for good measure, in case she needed more encouragement to override her pride. "Especially since the gala benefits all the Highland Park charities, and it would be a great opportunity for you to introduce me around to all the movers and shakers in this town."

Eve paused and wet her lips. Finally, she admitted, "I wouldn't mind attending with you, either."

Derek had an idea what it had cost her to say yes, especially to such a public function that might cause one heck of a lot of gossip and speculation about their relationship.

To lighten the mood, he teased, "So is it a... I was going to say date, but—" he pulled out his phone and pretended to look at his calendar "—we're not scheduled to have that until January 15 of next year, so..."

This time Eve grinned, and soon after, a soft laugh escaped her.

Derek chuckled, too, finally feeling as if they were on the right track again. He signaled the bartender and asked for a draft beer and an order of Southwestern egg rolls.

She sipped her sparkling water. He shifted a little, trying to get comfortable in the cozy space. In the process, his knees briefly brushed hers beneath the table. Like him, she was wearing slacks and soft leather boots. Unlike him, she seemed to have a lot on her mind that was still troubling her.

"So what's happening?" he asked. Why had she requested to meet him in the bar instead of his hotel suite? Why did she still seem so reserved?

Abruptly, her manner turned professional. "I wanted to talk business with you."

That was a little bit of a letdown, Derek acknowledged privately. But then again, any reason to spend time with her was appreciated. Telling himself he should accept the time with her for the gift it was, he accepted his beer and sipped the mellow brew. "Fire away."

The waiter returned with a platter of piping-hot appetizers, garnished with pico de gallo, guacamole and sour cream. Derek took one of the serving plates and handed it to her. He kept the other for himself.

Eve helped herself to an egg roll. "You said you were still interested in investing in property before the end of the calendar year."

That, Derek thought, was even more of a disappointment. He cut through the crispy golden-brown skin, revealing a mixture of gooey melted cheese, spicy peppers, black beans and diced white chicken. "That's right. I am."

Eve carefully spread her napkin across her lap. "I'd like to help you with that."

He added condiments to his plate. "You don't think it will make things too complicated?"

Eve sliced into her egg roll, too. "We could put whatever this is on hold until after any transaction is complete."

Derek didn't want to spend the holidays pretending he wasn't interested in her. Aware this was where he drew the line, he speared her with a brutally honest glance, and then murmured, "What if I don't want to put whatever this is between us on hold? What if I want to do both simultaneously?"

Eve swallowed with difficulty. She continued holding his gaze and said, "Here's the thing. I don't want to be seen as unfairly influencing you."

Derek waved off the possibility. "No one who knows me would ever think that could happen."

Eve went back to eating. "So you'd be okay with this?" she asked casually.

"Absolutely." He paused to study her evasive expression. "Although, I have the feeling that this wasn't your choice in the matter." That she wouldn't even be suggesting it, if not for the pressure at the firm to meet year-end sales goals in wake of her mother's unexpected absence.

Eve straightened. She flashed another businesslike smile. "I admit I prefer to work in a more leisurely fashion." She took another dainty bite. "I also know, for a variety of reasons, that it isn't always possible. So I'm prepared to adapt."

"So am I," Derek said, glad she was finally meeting him halfway.

Eve visibly relaxed. "When would you like to get started?"

Damned if she wasn't the most beautiful woman he had ever known, no matter what kind of light she was in, Derek mused to himself. And damned if he didn't want her in the worst way. Sensing that would never change, he forced himself to get back on track.

"Tiffany and I are headed to my hometown of Laramie, Texas, the weekend before Christmas."

Eve quickly brought up the calendar on her phone. "The nineteenth?"

"Yes. So if you'd like to accompany me, and see the ranch I've got my eye on, then that would be great."

Eve finished typing and set her phone down. "You want to buy property in Laramie County?"

Derek nodded. "There's a ranch there that's not on the market yet, but it will be after the New Year. I'd like you to see it. Maybe help me negotiate a deal on the property before it's even listed." Derek could tell by the look on her face that she wasn't surprised by his aggressive tactics. She knew that was how he operated when it came to business, that only the first-on-the-scene got results.

"So long as you know that area is not my premier stomping ground," Eve cautioned.

Derek took another sip of beer. "I'm confident you have the tools to assess proper market value."

"Okay, then, that's great. I'm looking forward to it."

She made a note on the calendar on her phone, then glanced up, with the same stressed-out expression in her eyes he had seen when he'd first walked in.

Derek caught her wrist before she could attempt to leave. "So now that that's set," he said huskily, wanting to help her the way she always helped him, "do you want to tell me what's really bothering you?"

Once again, Eve thought, Derek had read her like a book.

"Did the open house at Flash's condo not go well?"

Eve shrugged. "It went fine."

"Then...?"

His eyes fell on her, full of warmth and tenderness. "You don't want to hear this," she said irritably.

"Yes. I do."

Knowing she had to unburden herself to someone, and that, irrationally, she wanted that someone to be Derek, she briefly explained the way her mother had undermined her with a Houston-based client.

"Is she this way with everyone, or just you?"

Eve gestured helplessly, even as she appreciated Derek's support. "Pretty much everyone."

He looked at her with compassion. "But it still hurts." He took her hand again, and this time didn't let go. "You wish she had more faith you."

Eve basked in the protectiveness of his grasp. "I do."

Derek's gaze roved her face. "Have you told your mom that?"

She stifled a groan. "Oh, yes."

He flashed a sympathetic half smile. "And Marjorie's response…?"

Eve grimaced. "To tell me how to do whatever it is I'm trying to do, only better."

Derek let out a low chuckle. "Sounds like a parent."

Eve pouted. "It's not funny."

His glance turned tender once again. "I know, but what are you going to do?" He shrugged in a way that encouraged her to let it go and move on. "Especially when you know you're going to get that Santiago Florres house sold."

Eve didn't protest when he took her other hand, too. "How can you be so sure?"

"You're telling me you don't have a plan to accomplish your goal?" He held her hands gently.

"Well, I do have a little something I've been working on…."

"See?" he said bracingly. "It's all going to work out in the end."

"Thank you for boosting my spirits tonight."

"Now," Derek said, "how about you do a little something to help me?"

Eve had come here tonight hoping to get things back on a purely business track with Derek. Instead, she had ended up pouring her heart out to him and feeling even that much closer.

The unexpected outcome should have worried her. Encouraged her to take yet another step back from the prospect of falling so hard for him that she would never be able to recover, if and when this whatever-it-is they were sharing came to an end.

But sitting with him in the dimly lit hotel bar, with Christmas music playing softly in the background, all she could think was that spending all this time with him was making this the best holiday season she had enjoyed in years. *If ever.*

Before she could stop herself, she leaned toward him and murmured, "What did you need?"

Derek grimaced.

It was, Eve thought, his turn to look uncertain and disgruntled.

"I think I should get Tiffany a baby doll for Christmas. The problem is, I can't figure out which one to get."

Eve smiled, as ready to help him as he had been to assist her. "Did you have any particular type of doll in mind?"

He sighed. "I went over to the doll store in the Galleria Mall this afternoon."

Eve approved. "That is the place to go."

"Yeah, well, I was pretty overwhelmed." He shook his head. "As I soon as I walked in, I realized I was way out of my league."

"Isn't there someone you could ask?"

He made a comical face. "I am."

It had been a long time since Eve was a kid. "I'm not an expert."

Affection lit his eyes. "You know my little girl, though. And unless I miss my guess, you probably had dolls when you were growing up."

Another wrong perception. Reluctantly, Eve admitted, "Actually, my mom favored educational toys. Or in other words, she didn't want me spending all my time playing house when I could be learning about the ins and outs of real estate."

Derek stared at her as if he didn't know what to make of that. "You're kidding."

Eve sighed and rested her chin in her hands. "I wish."

He caught the check before she could get it. "So you really don't know anything about dolls?"

In frustration, Eve watched the waiter walk off with Derek's bank card instead of hers. "I know Tiffany will like anything that you get her. Especially a baby doll."

Derek threw up his hands. "Which leads us back to square one. How do I pick out the right one for her?"

Silly man. "Why don't you let her do that?"

He lifted a brow.

"Take Tiffany to the big doll store at the Galleria and let her *show* you which one she likes," Eve suggested practically.

Derek stroked his jaw, clearly liking the idea. "I hadn't thought of that." Then he turned to her. "I have one more question." Eve waited with bated breath, certain without him even saying it that this involved her somehow.

"Will you go with us?"

She knew if she had one ounce of common sense left, one flicker of hope for keeping her expectations from going way out of bounds—and her heart from being broken—she should say no. "Sure," she heard herself saying instead.

Derek accepted his bank card and receipt. They rose.

"Six o'clock tomorrow night okay with you?" he asked, walking her out to the front of the hotel, where they waited for the valet to bring her car.

"Sounds good," Eve returned, even as she continued to wonder what she was doing, getting in so far, so fast. It had to be the season.

"Great." Derek leaned down and gently touched his lips to hers. "Tiffany and I will see you then."

"Doll shopping, hmm?" Sasha said the following day.

Eve flushed, beginning to regret asking the three moms of daughters in their office for their advice on which of the exclusive dolls would be best to buy for a one-year-old. She wanted to be able to steer Derek to the right area in the store, in case Tiffany had limited patience for looking. "Don't razz me."

Astrid lifted both her hands. "We wouldn't think of it."

Vanessa's brow furrowed. "Are the two of you dating?"

"No," Eve said.

At the same moment Derek walked into the office and said, "Yes." At her scathing glare, he added, "Unofficially."

Sasha, Astrid and Vanessa all smiled. Which was no surprise. All three of them were happily married and, unlike her mother, had been urging Eve for some time to perk up her social life.

Eve shut off her computer and slid her tablet and phone into her bag. Desperate to get the conversation on more neutral ground, she asked cheerfully, "Where's Tiffany?"

Derek lounged in the doorway. "Still waiting for us to pick her up."

Eve sent her coworkers a look that said, *See? We're going to be well chaperoned by a demanding one-year-old. It's not what you think, after all.*

They didn't buy it.

Unable to bear the scrutiny, Eve slipped out the door.

"So how was your day?" Derek asked. His arm slid around her waist as he walked her to his SUV.

Tingling, she eased away and climbed into the passenger seat. "Good. One of the Realtors who was at the open house at Flash's condo called today to find out how far below the asking price he might be willing to go." Modestly, she tucked her skirt around her legs.

Derek slipped behind the wheel. "Think you're going to get a bid?"

"My guess is, if all goes the way we like, by the end of the week."

Pleasure lit his handsome features. "That is good."

Eve nodded in agreement.

"Any luck with the Santiago Florres house?"

"I talked to both parties to see if I could get them to meet in the middle."

"And?"

"No go. So now I'm tracking down Florres himself. I'm hoping he'll be interested in meeting the investor and to talk about the house he designed and built, explain why the property is so unique, and hence, worth the asking price."

"Hmm. Nice approach."

"Thank you." Eve grew pensive. "I just hope it works."

Fortunately, all talk of business soon faded.

Tiffany was happy to see Derek after a weekend away, and just as happy to see Eve. She babbled all the way to the mall, and was still grinning when they entered the Galleria. She was too excited to sit in the stroller, so Eve pushed the empty carriage alongside Derek while he carried his little girl in his arms.

Tiffany was even more delighted when they entered the beautifully appointed doll store. It was filled with little girls of all ages and their parents, all gazing raptly at the amazing array of dolls and accessories. Eve wasn't surprised to see a number of shoppers from the Highland Park area, people she had met or knew casually from her years in the real estate business. More than once, she found herself waving or mouthing hello as she directed Derek to the section that held the My First Baby Doll designs.

"I think I know which one she likes," he said eventually.

A doll with light skin, red hair and blue-gray eyes.

Eve had seen Tiffany go back to that one again and again. "You want to find a clerk?" The models that were out were only for display.

Derek nodded. He handed Tiffany over to Eve. "I'll be right back."

Eve snuggled Tiffany close, the now-familiar weight in her arms feeling as good as her sweet baby smell. Tiffany enjoyed the cuddling, too. "Mommy," she said, patting Eve's cheeks.

Eve was about to correct her, when behind her, she heard a strident feminine voice. "Well, as I live and breathe. Eve Loughlin, I knew you'd succumb to the joys of motherhood, just like the rest of us!"

Eve turned to see a former college classmate. Linda Brashear had been the president of the women's business club until she'd left school to get married. She was one to never let anything—or anyone—go without putting in her two cents.

Eve forced a smile. "Linda, hi." The two women hugged, Texas-style. "It's been forever," she said.

Linda beamed. "Hasn't it?"

"Mommy," Tiffany repeated even more joyously, once again patting Eve's cheeks.

"I didn't know you got married," Linda continued, her eyes widening in surprise.

"I, um, haven't," Eve said uncomfortably, just as Derek rejoined them.

"Daddy!" Tiffany said, arms outstretched for him.

"Well," Linda said, still seeming a little shocked as she looked Derek's big, strapping form up and down, "I can see why you'd be willing to forgo the legalities. Although," she sniffed, "now that you two have a little one, I would think—"

"We probably should get married," Derek interjected. Sensing correctly that she was ripe for rescue, he wrapped his arm around Eve's shoulders and tugged her close to his side.

Linda, who had never been shy about voicing an opinion on anyone's love life, heartily agreed with him. "You-all really should. Although—" she elbowed Derek playfully "—I have to congratulate you for getting her this far. Because Eve always said she was never ever going to have kids."

"Want to talk about it?" Derek asked quietly half an hour later. Clearly, Eve thought, he felt they should.

Their purchase completed, they were sitting in the doll store bistro housed on the upper floor of the enormous space. Specially designed for little girls, the elegant restaurant sported white linen tablecloths and dinnerware that was ultrafeminine and still child-friendly.

Happy to be away from the crowds and chaos below, Eve busied herself cutting up the mini pretzel balls from the appetizer plate for Tiffany to munch on. She slid them over onto the toddler's high-chair tray.

If only they hadn't run into Linda Brashear! Ever since Eve had known the other woman, she'd had a reputation for being a real busybody.

Not that Eve could keep something like this from Derek forever.

Still feeling a little chagrined by her former friend's disclosure, Eve forced herself to lift her chin and meet his eyes. "What do you want to know?"

Seemingly as on edge as she felt, Derek helped himself to a baby carrot. Eventually, he asked, "Is it true? Did you vow never to have kids?"

Eve wanted to lie, even though she knew she couldn't. "Yes. I did." She took a strawberry-and-cheese kabob for herself.

He sent her another guarded look. "Why didn't you want children?"

Tiffany lounged back in her seat and contentedly watched the other diners. Aware how much of a family they felt at times like this, how much she had grown to love it, Eve swallowed. Would Derek think less of her if she told him everything? Finally, she said, "It's complicated."

His blue eyes glimmered with interest. "I've got time."

Of course he did. He always did. Aware they were about to enter an emotional minefield, she chose her words carefully. "I guess I've never really seen myself as being lucky enough to find a guy who would love me forever. It doesn't really run in the family, you know? And I didn't want to go the route my mother went and be a single mom." Eve took a sip of peppermint tea, then shook her head. "It was just too hard."

Derek studied her with the kindness she had come to rely on. "For her or for you?" he asked.

She flashed a rueful smile. "For both of us. My mom was always working. I always wanted more of her time. It seemed like neither of us ever got what we wanted and needed from each other when I was growing up. And—" her voice caught "—I didn't want to put a child through that."

Too late, she realized the implication of what she'd said. Derek himself was a single parent—at least half the time, anyway. Eve stared at him in chagrin. "I'm sorry. I shouldn't be talking like this."

His eyes darkened with a mixture of compassion and sorrow. He leaned toward her and captured her hand. "Why not?"

"Because..." She looked down at their intertwined fingers, taking comfort in both his strength and his refusal to let her drift away, as she was otherwise likely to do. "I don't want you to think that your situation will be as tough as mine was, because our situations aren't the same." Wary of stepping in where she didn't belong, Eve treaded carefully. "You have Carleen, and Craig and their kids, and your extended families. Tiffany is going to have plenty of people in her life who will be there for her. She's never going to feel like a burden."

There was no judgment in his eyes, only curiosity. "Is that the way you felt? Like a burden?"

Eve released the breath she'd been holding. How was it Derek could see what no one else did? Reluctantly, she conceded, "Sometimes, but that's as much my fault as hers. I know my mom did the best she could under what were very tough circumstances. She gave me a good life and I owe her a lot."

Derek's hand tightened on hers. He seemed to understand that she loved her mom very much, and always had. "Do you still not want to have kids?"

Eve was beginning to want it all. And that scared her more than she wanted to admit. "If I was married, then yes, I would definitely want children."

He paused. "But not as a single parent."

She conceded with a nod, withdrew her hand from his and said emphatically, "For me, it would be just too hard."

Again, he understood. His lips crooked ruefully. "Having done it on my own, even half the time, for the past year, I agree." His deep blue eyes met hers. "It is hard raising a child on your own."

Aware, as always, that Derek had options most people did not, Eve suggested, "You could always get a nanny for backup."

He shook his head. "That's not the same as having a mommy and a daddy in residence."

Eve had certainly missed having both. "True," she said with a sigh.

She looked at him, and realized this was striking a chord with him. She thought back to that conversation when he'd confided his desire that Tiffany have equal love and happiness in both households where she lived.

"Which is why," Derek continued, even more firmly, "one day soon I intend to get married again."

Chapter 12

Eve stared at Derek in shock. Once again, he knew he had pushed her too hard, too fast.

"You can't just decide that without having anyone in mind," she declared, aghast.

Who says I don't have anyone in mind? Derek thought to himself. But aware it was far too soon to be hammering Eve with that, he shrugged. "Getting married again in the very near future is still one of my goals." She looked so indignant, he couldn't help but tease, "Like not getting too involved is one of yours."

Her lips curved ruefully as his joke hit home. "You're cute."

"Thank you." Derek preened comically, while Tiffany giggled and waved her baby spoon at both of them. "I'm constantly being told so."

Eve rolled her eyes.

Derek smiled, although he wished she had said that, like him, she was looking forward to tying the knot sooner rather than later.

The waiter appeared with their entrées: macaroni and cheese for Tiffany, quiche Florentine and salad for Eve, a chicken pot pie for Derek.

Derek sobered. He wanted to nail down their next non-date, or two or three. "So what are your plans for tomorrow?" he asked.

Eve mugged at Tiffany, who mugged back. Then, still grinning, she pulled out her phone and checked her calendar. "I've got appointments all day."

"Clients?"

She nodded and continued scrolling through the day. "A quick dinner with my mom at cardiac rehab, then shopping tomorrow evening."

He widened his eyes, intrigued.

She grinned at his continued teasing, and explained, "I have to get a dress for the gala."

"Hmm. I could help with that."

Amusement lit her eyes, along with a hint of desire. "I bet you could, Mr. McCabe. But no. Thanks, anyway."

She just wouldn't let them get close, Derek thought ruefully. "That's okay. I like to be surprised." Letting her know with a glance that he wasn't about to give up on either her or them, he flashed a smile. "So what time am I picking you up on the seventeenth?"

Eve fed Tiffany a little more of her macaroni and cheese so Derek could concentrate on his own entrée. "Seven-thirty okay with you?"

He nodded, ready to be as patient as he needed to be. "Seven-thirty is great." *Any time I'm with you is great.*

As comfortable as if she really was the "mom" in this equation, Eve turned back to him amenably. "How's your house renovation coming, by the way?"

Derek imagined her living in the house with him. Making love every night, waking up in the morning wrapped in each other's arms. "I'm set to move in on December 18."

"Really?"

He nodded in anticipation. "Want to come over and celebrate our first night in the new home with Tiffany and me?"

Excitement sparkled in Eve's amber eyes. Still, it took her a moment to say yes. "What should I bring?"

The only thing he really wanted and needed, Derek thought. He smiled again. "Just yourself."

"How serious are you about Derek McCabe?" Sasha asked Eve several days later.

Eve walked out of the conference room, where she had just signed another post-holiday home listing. "Why?"

"He called this morning and was fishing for information on what kind of gift you might like for Christmas."

"Tell me you're kidding."

"I am not kidding."

"Was it— Was he—?"

Sasha grinned. "Use your words."

Eve tried again. "Are we in the category of a thank-you-for-helping-me-buy-a-house gift?"

"I don't know. Does jewelry fall into that?"

She sucked in a breath. "I don't suppose we're talking costume jewelry."

"Hmm." Sasha struck a thoughtful pose. "The man

makes millions." She considered some more, then straightened. "I kind of don't think so."

Eve flushed in embarrassment. "Well, I can't accept anything extravagant!" It would mean... Well, she wasn't sure what it meant, but nothing casual, of that she was certain. Derek did not do casual, in his work or personal life. He was either all in or all out.

The office manager tilted her head. "Calm down." She patted Eve on the back. "He hasn't given anything to you yet."

Sasha was right. Eve knew she was overreacting. Determined not to be so transparent with her emotions, she drew a deep breath and went back to her desk, where yet another stack of messages awaited her. Knowing how busy he was, she imagined it was the same for Derek. "Did he say anything else?"

The other woman grinned and handed her a few more papers, all relating to another listing about to close. "Besides wanting to know what your birthstone was, you mean?"

Birthstone? That sounded better. Eve breathed a sigh of relief. "You told him garnet?"

"Duh." Sasha smiled as she adjusted the blinds on the window. "He wanted to know what kind of diamond you prefer, too."

Was it hot in here or what? Eve fanned herself with the stack of papers in her hand. "Holy..."

"Moly, I know."

She had heard of women being romanced this way. Many of her well-heeled clients had been. But it had never happened to her. Eve tugged the neckline of her silk blouse away from her collarbone. "Maybe he's just..."

Sasha peered at her, sensing as accurately as Marjorie had that something was up between Derek and Eve. Or had been on several occasions now. "What?"

"I don't know." Eve brushed a hand through her hair and sank down in her chair. Just thinking about Derek in that capacity made her heart race and her knees go weak.

Sasha lingered a moment longer. 'What are you getting him?"

Eve fanned herself again. "Um, some sort of housewarming gift for the get-together, when he moves into his house." A get-together that as far as she knew included only three people: Derek, Eve and Tiffany. How family-oriented was that?

Sasha walked back to the break room and returned with two bottles of water. She handed one to Eve. "You're getting him a plant?"

Eve uncapped the bottle and took a long drink of the ice-cold water. She waved an airy hand, glad she didn't have to meet with a client right this minute and instead could take the time to compose herself. "He doesn't really seem like the watering can kind of guy."

Sasha quirked her lips and perched on the windowsill. "I didn't think so, either."

Feeling even more uncomfortable, Eve rocked back in her desk chair, muttering under her breath, "This is the part of Christmas I hate." Deciding there was something wrong with the ergonomic adjustments, she reached under the seat to alter the forward tilt. To no avail. It still seemed...off-kilter, somehow.

Sasha watched as she stood up and looked under the chair. "So you *are* dating?"

Frustrated, Eve got down on her knees. "I don't know

what we're doing." That was the problem. But now she had to get him a gift. At least for the housewarming. And probably Christmas as well, unless she wanted to look like the kind of person who took and never gave back.

But what? What could she get him? Should she get Tiffany something, too?

Just because she and Derek had made love a few times—and he intended to get married again someday soon—did not make them an item. They weren't even dating yet. It was all too complicated. Way too complicated. Although buying a present for Tiffany would be easy. All Eve would have to do was go to the doll store at the Galleria Mall and pick out an accessory for her new baby doll. Derek was another matter.

Eve attempted another adjustment, then sat down once again. The tilt was worse than before.

She swore, frustrated beyond measure.

Once again, Sasha walked out and sauntered back in. "Cheer up." She tossed a stack of holiday sale catalogues on Eve's desk. "McCabe's probably got everything there is to have, so anything you get will be a duplicate, anyway."

Eve groaned loudly and massaged her temples. "Thank you for pointing that out. And for the record, if he wasn't still a client…"

"You'd already be hooked up with him?"

Guilt roared through her like a tidal wave.

Sasha gasped in shock. "*Have* you hooked up?"

Wishing she had a better poker face—when it came to Derek and her feelings about him, anyway—Eve lifted a hand and waved off any further questions.

Sasha's grin widened. Eve noted that her friend

hadn't looked that happy and optimistic since she had fallen in love with the man of her own dreams and headed off down the aisle.

It was Christmas, that was all, a season that had so much romance in the air.

Belatedly, Eve realized she should have kept to her usual "Bah, Humbug" script.

After another considering look, Sasha quipped, "Did anyone ever tell you that you're cute when you're falling in love?"

This time Eve blushed fire-engine red. It was hot as blazes in here. "I am not." She got up to check the thermostat. Seventy degrees! It could not possibly be seventy. It felt like ninety!

"You are falling in love," Sasha insisted with a knowing wink. "You just can't admit it yet. But have faith. In time, you will." The happily married Sasha sauntered out, calling over her shoulder, "And good luck with your dress shopping tonight!"

The door shut behind her.

Eve groaned loudly and dropped her head down on her desk. The only good thing was that she wasn't seeing Derek for several more days. She needed time apart—make that a lot of time apart—so she could come to her senses and keep from falling into bed with him yet again.

Time apart was not the least bit helpful, Eve decided the evening of December 17, when Derek showed up at seven twenty-five.

Incredibly good-looking under normal circumstances, he was devastatingly handsome in black tie.

He smelled heavenly, too. Like sandalwood and birch and cardamom.

She, on the other hand, was not at all ready. Her hair and makeup were done, but her dress was only half-zipped, and she couldn't find one of her shoes. Or any of the jewelry she wanted to wear. Although why that was, she hadn't a clue.

"Take it easy. We've got time." He gestured for her to turn around. His hands brushed her bare skin as he tugged the zipper up. Finished, he paused to kiss the nape of her neck. "I like the dress." He caught her hand and spun her around, eyeing her sparkly cranberry-red strapless gown appreciatively. Blatant desire tugged at the corners of his mouth. "You look good in red."

Eve knew she might as well be honest. She paused to straighten his bow tie, then stepped back to make sure it was centered. Her glance caught his. "You look good, too." Almost too good. Standing here with him, she was tempted to never even make it to the event.

Derek smiled. "Perhaps we should join a mutual admiration society."

Noting he hadn't brought any jewelry with him, Eve laughed and began to relax. "Why don't you make yourself comfortable?" She disappeared into the bedroom, calling over her shoulder, "I'll just be a few minutes."

When she came back out, Derek was sprawled on her sofa, flipping channels on the TV. He smiled when she glided toward him. Rose to his feet. "I knew you were worth waiting for." Even as he admired the simple silver heart on a chain around her neck, he reached into his pocket and withdrew a slim velvet case. "And make no mistake, I have been waiting." He pressed it into her hand.

Eve's heart skipped a beat. Were they ready for this? She wasn't sure, but apparently he was. She drew a deep, enervating breath. "What is this?"

He let his gaze drift over her slowly, before looking back at her face. "Open it and see."

Fingers trembling slightly, she undid the ribbon. Inside was a beautiful garnet-and-platinum necklace, anchored by interlocking hearts. It wasn't overly expensive by Derek's financial standards, but it was gorgeous. She looked up at him. "What is this for?"

"The start of something wonderful," he said simply.

Derek had known it was a gamble, giving a woman like Eve a gift. But he had wanted her to know she was special to him, and since she wouldn't let him say it, wouldn't believe him if he did, he'd contented himself with this symbol of togetherness.

Looking as if she wanted to say so much but couldn't, she drew in a jerky breath. "It's beautiful."

She removed the necklace she was wearing, and Derek helped her put the new one on. Eve sashayed over to the hall mirror with a rustle of shimmery silk, and checked out the effect.

"It really is perfect." She hesitated, showing the doubt he had expected from her all along. "Although I'm not entirely sure I should accept it," she finished softly.

Determined to win her over, no matter how long it took, Derek teased, "Consider it on loan, then. Until we officially start dating, that is."

Eve chuckled. "Confident, aren't you?"

"Absolutely," he fibbed. Placing his palm at her back, he walked her out the door and escorted her to his Jaguar. He opened her door for her and waited while she got in. Hand braced against the top of the car, he leaned in to drawl, "Now, when we get to the gala, are you going to be all business or just a little bit of business?"

Eve wrinkled her nose apologetically. "A lot business. It's a major opportunity for networking. I hope you don't mind."

He shook his head. "Not at all. As I mentioned the other day, I could do to expand my contacts here, too."

No sooner had they walked into the ball than they each spotted people they knew: Derek's brother Grady, and his wife, Alexis, and the architect that Eve had been playing phone tag with the past few days.

"Would you mind if I went to speak with Santiago Florres first?" she asked.

Derek gave his brother and sister-in-law the "one minute" sign, then leaned down and whispered in Eve's ear, "No problem. I'll go with you."

With his hand at her spine, he escorted her through the crowd of elegantly dressed guests to the line queuing up at the bar. Eve made the approach as graciously as always. "Mr. Florres? Eve Loughlin, Loughlin Realty." The two shook hands.

The architect, an affable-looking man in his late forties, got straight to the point. "I'm sorry I haven't returned your calls, Eve, but frankly, after I heard what Red Bloom offered for the home I designed, I wasn't sure what the two of us might have to say."

She nodded empathetically. "I'm aware it was insulting."

"Very." Santiago looked tense.

"I think," she continued, "that Mr. Bloom did not understand just how unique the home is."

The architect shrugged. "What does that have to do with me?" he snapped.

"A lot, actually." Her skill as a Realtor in full force, Eve smiled. "I think Mr. Bloom might change his mind about the value of the home currently for sale if you were to meet him and go through it with him, pointing out all the architectural features in that particular design that cannot be found anywhere else."

Derek noted that Florres's hostility had faded; the architect was now listening intently.

"Of course, if that should happen," Eve continued, "if a deal were to be made, then that would likely inflate the price of what you could charge for future architectural designs."

Florres considered that. Clearly, he felt his reputation had been harmed by the low offer. He moved nearer. "You're saying Mr. Bloom wants to meet with me?"

Eve lifted a hand. "I'm still trying to reach him, but if I can get something set up, would you be amenable?"

Santiago nodded with a mixture of relief and interest. "Yes, I would. And thanks, Eve, for giving me a chance to defend my work."

She handed him her business card. "I'll be in touch."

After chatting for a few more minutes, Derek and Eve walked off. She sighed. "Now all I have to do is get Red Bloom to come back to the house for another look, and I'll be all set."

Derek paused, not sure he'd heard her right. "Red Bloom, the Houston oilman?" he asked in surprise. That was the guy Marjorie and Eve had been chasing?

Eve nodded, distracted. She went on to refresh Derek's memory. "He is the client who amasses unique houses the way others collect fine art."

Derek slid a hand beneath her elbow and gave her a sidelong glance. "Do you anticipate having a problem getting Bloom to cooperate with your plan?"

She shrugged, then smiled at a colleague who caught her eye from across the room. "No way to say. To be perfectly honest, I haven't had any luck getting him on the phone."

Derek was about to suggest a solution to that when Eve stopped in her tracks. Looking abruptly ill at ease, she elbowed him gently. "There's your brother and his wife."

Hoping this meeting would go better than the first encounter between Eve and his siblings, Derek wrapped his arm around her waist and pulled her close as Grady and Alexis came toward them.

"I'm glad we have a moment to talk," Alexis told Eve sincerely, after the two men had gone off to get champagne. "I want to apologize for what you overheard that weekend at the house. Derek's brothers were razzing him about his crush on you, so he pretended it was nothing, the way guys do. Which is when you showed up."

Embarrassed, Eve felt heat rise to her cheeks. Derek wasn't the only one with a crush. "It's okay."

"I figured Derek would make it up to you." Alexis's gaze drifted to the jewelry around Eve's neck. "If that necklace is as new as I think it is, I see that he has."

Eve's hand flew to her throat. She felt even more embarrassed now, probably because whatever it was that they had was too new and fragile to stand up to scrutiny.

Wondering if the veteran matchmaker thought she and Derek would last much beyond the holidays, which were admittedly a popular time for fleeting hookups, Eve asked, "How did you know this was from him?"

"Because he's my brother-in-law, and I know him." Alexis grinned. "Even when he was trying to convince us that the two of you weren't an item, for privacy's sake, I had the sense it was more than that. And this necklace proves it."

"I don't understand."

Gently, Alexis explained, "It's a McCabe thing. All the men buy the women jewelry when they are getting serious."

Eve wasn't sure whether to be elated or nervous. The only thing she knew for certain was that once again things seemed to be moving way too fast.

Luckily for her, the rest of the evening flew by. She and Derek both did a fair amount of networking, together and apart. And it was only when Derek was walking her to her front door that the conversation became truly intimate again. "Did Alexis say something to you tonight?"

Eve had been afraid this would come up. She fished her key from her bag and unlocked the door. Well after midnight, the condominium was blissfully quiet and still. "Why would you think that?" Derek shrugged and followed her inside. He undid his black bow tie and slipped it into the pocket of his tux. "Just a sense I had when my brother and I got back to the table. You had a funny look on your face." He peered at her. "In fact, it's still there."

"It's nothing."

He helped her remove her wrap, looking confident as ever. "It's something. Otherwise, you wouldn't still be so pensive."

She started to turn away, but found she couldn't. "Alexis thinks the fact you bought me a necklace is significant."

"And that upsets you?" he asked huskily, inching closer.

His voice washed over her, warming her from the inside out. "Is it significant?" Eve pressed.

Derek moved closer still and took her in his arms. "This," he said, lowering his lips to hers for a deep soulful kiss, "is significant. This…" he backed her toward her bedroom, leaving a trail of hot, fevered kisses over her throat, shoulder, breast "…is what we should be concentrating on."

Yearning swept through her, as powerful as the sensations his mouth and hands were generating. Eve curled her fingers in the fabric of his suit jacket. "Sex doesn't solve anything."

Derek bent her backward from the waist. "It doesn't have to." Draping her over his arm, he kissed her again. "It's a wonder in and of itself."

Eve had to admit, as they undressed each other slowly and carefully, that he was right.

There was something incredible about being with him this way. Maybe it was the season. The fact she'd been alone too long, or he missed his daughter on the days and nights that Tiffany was with his ex and her new family. Or just the fact that he liked to say yes in his personal life whenever possible.

All Eve really knew was that when he kissed her and held her so intimately, the world narrowed to just the two of them and she felt treasured in that special man-woman way. And even if love wasn't involved, everything else that mattered was.

He was gentle and kind, and tender beyond measure. More important still, they were becoming very good friends. The kind who would always be there for each other, she thought as they kissed passionately, and she surrendered to him all the more.

Able to feel how much Eve needed him, Derek lay down with her on the satin sheets. His own body throbbing, he kissed the hollow of her stomach and the soft insides of her thighs, then drifted lower still, to deliver the most ardent of kisses. Overcome with pleasure, her heart pounding in rhythm with his, she whispered, "Derek…"

Shifting position, she moved to explore him, too. Seducing him, urging him on, molding her body to his, until they were both on fire. It was all too much. He brought her upward, claiming her mouth, claiming her. She lifted her hips and then they were one, riding the wave, going deeper, more intimately still, and then she was his, really his. Not just for tonight, he thought, not just for the holidays, or until their mutual loneliness passed. But until they found a way to give each other everything, heart and soul.

Chapter 13

Sasha greeted Eve at the office door on Thursday morning. "Red Bloom phoned, asking to speak to you. He'd like you to return his call right away."

Finally, Eve thought. "Thanks." She took the message, went into her office and shut the door.

He answered promptly. "I hear you've got Florres ready to meet with me," Red boomed.

Although she had no idea how the brash Houston oilman could possibly know this, Eve affirmed with customary zeal, "I do."

"I'm going to be in Dallas later this afternoon. Does three o'clock work for you?"

Hoping and praying she could get the architect there, too, Eve said, "Absolutely."

"See you at the house, then."

Luckily, Santiago Florres was free to meet them, too.

Probably because he was eager to defend his reputation as a creative genius.

Eve got to the house first. Red Bloom arrived next, in a white Rolls Royce with a Christmas wreath attached to the front grill. He squared his dove-gray Stetson on his head and strode toward her, the edges of his cashmere coat flapping open as he moved. As soon as cursory greetings were exchanged, he said, "I'm afraid I owe you an apology. I had no idea you were a friend of the McCabes until I spoke with Derek this morning."

Of course. Not sure how she felt about Derek interfering in her business life, Eve smiled brightly and pretended this wasn't news to her. "The two of you spoke?"

Red nodded. "He emailed me late last evening, and we spoke first thing today." The edges of Red's mustache curled upward. "His mother and I go way back. I've known Derek and his brothers since they were kids. His dad, too. Derek told me what a great help you'd been to him and his little girl. Said I couldn't go wrong listening to you, or your mother, for that matter."

Eve fished the key to the lockbox from her handbag. "I'm glad to hear Derek was so happy with the service he received from our company."

Not so glad Derek had gone behind her back to lobby for her, but that was another matter, Eve thought. One that would be dealt with privately when she figured out if having him involved in every aspect of her life was a good or bad thing.

Trying not to feel overwhelmed in the way Derek always made her feel, Eve started up the walk, just as a third car pulled up at the curb. Red turned. "Santiago Florres?" he asked as the driver joined them on the sidewalk.

"One and the same." Santiago reached out and shook his hand.

Eve could see she'd been right. When face-to-face, the two gentlemen had entirely different attitudes toward one another.

Hoping this session would have a better ending than the last, Eve led the way to the front steps of the starkly angular contemporary home, and on inside.

An engrossing two hours later, Eve said goodbye to both men and drove downtown to the McCabe Venture Capital office. Derek was in a meeting when she arrived. She elected to wait.

Eventually, he came out of a conference room. Smiling cordially, he shook hands with the group of techies he'd been talking with, all of whom were bearing Tech Wizard T-shirts. Eve guessed the young businessmen and women were part of the small percentage that Derek said yes to, because they looked as if they had just received serious encouragement.

Looking incredibly happy to see her, as well as incredibly attractive in a dark suit and tie, Derek motioned Eve into his private lair and shut the door behind them.

Derek pulled her into a brief hug. "This is a nice surprise."

Eve withdrew. Part of her knew she shouldn't have been surprised by what Derek had done. After all, the McCabes were known far and wide for their kindness and generosity. Which was maybe the reason she had kept Red Bloom's identity from him for so long. Because she had feared if he did know just who it was that was giving her and her mother so much trouble, Derek might interfere on her behalf, rather than let her solve her problems herself.

Eve draped her coat over a chair and set her shoulder bag down in front of it. "Guess who called me this morning?"

Derek gazed at her, his poker face intact.

Eve stalked closer, her footsteps muffled by the thick carpet. "Red Bloom."

If there was one thing her mother had taught her, from the time she was a little girl, it was the importance of being self-reliant. The key to personal strength, Marjorie had said time and time again, was independence. Relying on others to support or defend you was the surest path to unhappiness.

Eve had seen enough divorces to know it was true.

When a woman gave up everything to marry a man and raise his children, it left her vulnerable in more than just a financial sense.

And it always started with a man rushing to the rescue.

"Ah, yes. Red Bloom." Derek pulled a couple water bottles from the glass-door refrigerator built into the bar. He handed her one and twisted the cap off his own.

Eve sat down in a chair a distance away. She crossed her legs at the knee. "Apparently, you did a hard sell on my behalf?"

He came around to lean against the front of his desk, facing her. "I may have forgotten to mention he's an old family friend."

Eve sensed that was as close to an apology as she was likely to get. Like most gallant men, Derek would not harbor any regret for rushing to help a lady "in need." Especially if that lady was intimately involved with him.

She attempted to untwist the cap on her bottle, only to find it...stuck. Sighing, she set it on her lap, unopened. "I could have gotten through to him on my own."

Derek's expression remained impassive. He took a slow sip of water.

"But you don't believe that." She tried again to open her own bottle, and failed.

Derek set his water aside and ambled closer. "I think eventually you would have found a way to get the two men together." Wordlessly, he took the bottle from her and did what she could not, with a single, easy twist. His eyes locked with hers, he handed her the chilled water, stepped back. "Although perhaps not before the end of the year."

Eve snorted and took a sip. The icy water cooled her dry throat, but didn't do the same for her temper.

Derek leaned against his sleek mahogany desk once again. "How did the meeting with Bloom and Florres go, by the way?"

Eve took another sip. "Wonderfully. When they left, Red was talking to Santiago about designing a summer home for him in Galveston."

"The place in Highland Park that your mother listed? What about that?"

Eve took another sip. Feeling unbearably restless, she got up and wandered to the window. Arms tucked against her waist, she looked out at the city she loved. "At the end of the day, the two men still disagreed about the price. Santiago thinks it is worth every penny. Red still feels because of the unique design in an area of mostly traditional homes, that he'd have a hard time selling it if he did pay top dollar. And Red, as you know, does not like to waste money." Eve pivoted back to Derek. "However, he does understand Santiago's approach to design now, so in that sense the meeting was definitely a plus."

Derek tossed his empty bottle in the trash. "I'm sorry." He walked toward her languidly. "I hoped it would lead to a deal so your firm could take top spot in the sales competition."

Eve leaned one shoulder against the window. The chill of the glass was a marked contrast to the heat of his gaze. "It's not your problem."

He leaned a shoulder against the window pane, too, a small distance apart. "Funny," he said, his response as carefully measured as her own, "sometimes, when I see you looking so down, I feel as though it is my problem."

Eve slid him a wry look. It was a good thing he didn't know how much the vulnerable part of her wanted to throw herself in his arms and let him take all her troubles away. "If we ever retake the lead, I want it to be because Loughlin Realty has earned it, not because my guy friend has pulled some strings on my behalf."

Her declaration hung between them for a long moment. "Is that what I am?" Derek asked finally, masculine challenge in his eyes. "A *guy friend?*"

Eve ignored the implication to his question. "You know what I mean," she said shortly.

Abruptly seeming to realize it wasn't a good idea to push her—about anything—Derek dipped his head in acquiescence. "I do, and I'm sorry if I overstepped my bounds. I hope you'll forgive me?"

What was it about this man that made him so irresistible to her? Eve couldn't say; she only knew it to be true.

Eve released the breath she had been unconsciously holding. "I do."

Derek smiled. "Still coming to help me and Tiffany celebrate our first evening in our new house tonight?"

That, she was looking forward to. "I wouldn't miss it," Eve replied. She paused again, aware all over again how much she would like to kiss him, then and there.

Realizing that they were still in his place of business, and should act accordingly, she stepped away and went to grab her coat and bag. "What time?"

He gave her another heart-stopping smile. "Seven-thirty."

Eve was still at the office, wrapping things up, when Derek called her. "Do you want the bad news first, or the even worse news?" he rasped.

With her cell phone cradled against her ear, Eve walked a stack of letters to be mailed out to Sasha's desk. "Hit me with both."

"There's something wrong with the HVAC. It's not working at all."

"Oh, Derek, no! Did you call the contractor?"

Weariness radiated in his low voice. "He was just here. He thinks there's a flaw in the electronic ignition. Because it's brand-new, he's demanding a whole new unit from the manufacturer, but it won't be here until Monday."

Eve felt for Derek.

"The really big problem is I already checked out of my hotel, and they can't take us back. They're booked solid through the holidays."

As would be the case at many of the area's finer hotels. Eve shut down her computer. "Where's Tiffany?"

"With me at the house. In her coat and hat."

It was such a chilly day already, with the temperature set to dive into the twenties by nightfall. Eve didn't even have to think what to do. "Come to my place. You can stay there."

Sasha turned to Eve in surprise.

Eve waved her off.

With relief in his voice, Derek asked, "You're sure?"

She shut the door to her office. "We were headed to your hometown tomorrow morning, anyway. This will make it easier to get an early start." It didn't have to mean anything.

"We'll be right over. And, Eve?" he rumbled softly. *"Thanks."*

"The two of you are getting close," Sasha remarked as Eve prepared to leave.

More than she felt comfortable with, that was for sure. Still, she couldn't turn away a man and his child when they were in need. "I feel for him and Tiffany. That's all."

"Mmm-hmm." Again that raised eyebrow.

Okay, so she could have helped him find another hotel, on the spot. Or had him call his brother Grady. Or let Carleen and Craig, or even his own assistant, Alma May, help. Trying not to flush, Eve shrugged on her coat. "He did me a favor. I owe him one."

"Of course."

She hunted around for her shoulder bag and keys. She'd just had them! "And Mom's place is still empty, since she's in rehab. I can stay there, while he and Tiffany bunk at my place."

Sasha gave Eve a look that reminded Eve just how well they knew each other. "Be careful," Sasha warned. "I know you like Derek and Tiffany a lot."

"But what?" Eve demanded impatiently, sensing there was more.

Sasha frowned. "Playing house with a man and his baby is not the same as the real thing."

That wasn't what they were doing, Eve reassured herself as she walked out to her car. But somehow she couldn't quite make herself believe it.

To her chagrin, Derek had his own doubts, too. "Maybe this isn't such a good idea, after all," he said half an hour later.

Eve looked at the scowl on Tiffany's face, aware once again how little experience she'd had with young children, or really, children of any kind.

Her mother had always been urging her to grow up, quickly! Not take care of other people's offspring.

Eve reached for a tissue. Gently, she blotted Tiffany's red, tearstained cheeks. The toddler studied her from beneath her fringe of thick wet lashes, as if silently beseeching her to do *something!* Eve just didn't know what. "It'll be fine," she said, smiling despite herself when Tiffany reached out and curled her fingers around one of Eve's.

Without warning, the little girl threw herself into her arms. Eve caught her and held her close.

Tiffany's lower lip rolled out. She looked to be on the verge of another sob. Watching, Derek shoved his hands through his hair. "She's been fussing since we left the house."

Eve walked Tiffany around her apartment, rubbing her back gently. "Has she had dinner?"

He nodded. "Carleen fed her before I picked her up."

The little girl let out another wail. A new wave of

tears rolled down her face, silent ones this time, which made her distress all the more heartbreaking. "Does she want a bottle?" Eve asked.

Derek produced one from the diaper bag. Tiffany pushed it away with both hands, and let out another angry, impatient wail.

Eve began to feel a little edgy, too. "Maybe if Tiffany was able to get down and walk around a little bit. Explore."

Eve had already cleared everything not baby-friendly from her reach.

"It's worth a try," Derek agreed.

Eve set her down gently and knelt beside her.

Tiffany wailed.

"Oh, sweetheart," Eve attempted to comfort the adorable baby girl. To no avail.

Derek hunkered down, murmuring soft words of comfort, too. That did not work, either. He eased off Tiffany's hat and coat. She cried even louder.

Derek exchanged baffled looks with Eve and picked Tiffany back up again.

The tears kept coming.

While Derek walked Tiffany back and forth, Eve went to get her teddy bear and blanket.

Those offered no solace, either. They tried sitting together on the sofa. This had pleased Tiffany in the past. Tonight, Tiffany pushed both Derek and Eve away from her. Determined to find a way to comfort her, even if she did not have a rocking chair to sit in, Eve stood. She gathered Tiffany in her arms and began to sway gently, back and forth. The motion lulled the child, but only temporarily. "You don't think she's getting sick or something, do you?"

Derek pressed the back of his hand to Tiffany's cheek. "She doesn't seem to have any fever." He looked at Eve. "What do you think?"

She gently touched Tiffany's cheek, too. He was right. It was wet from her tears, but not in the least bit hot.

Tiffany again pushed her father away. When he stepped back, she twisted and sobbed. "Daddy!" Eve handed the little girl back to him.

He paced the length of the condo living room, his baby in his arms. Eve went down a mental checklist of things that had pacified the child before. "Do you think she could need a diaper change?"

He shook his head. "I changed her before we came over. And there's no diaper rash or detergent allergy or anything that would be making her uncomfortable. So that's not it." He paused, thinking, walking back and forth. Tiffany sobbed louder. Derek looked over his daughter's halo of dark curls. "Maybe if we offered her a bottle again. Apple juice, this time."

Again, it was rejected after barely one sip.

Tiffany demanded Eve hold her again. Eve cradled her tenderly in her arms and walked the room, the same as Derek. The toddler fussed and squirmed and grabbed Eve's hair in both fists and wailed in what sounded like raw fury. Which Eve could kind of understand, since all of Tiffany's efforts to communicate with them had failed mightily. They had no more idea what was wrong now than they had when she'd arrived.

"This is really unlike her," Derek said, reaching over to try and wrestle strands of Eve's hair from Tiffany's little fists.

And that was when his little girl leaned over and bit his hand as hard as she possibly could.

Derek let out a muffled grunt of pain.

Tiffany stopped crying and looked up at him in satisfaction.

And suddenly, Derek and Eve both knew. "Could she be teething?" she asked.

Derek ran his thumb along Tiffany's gum. He pushed back her lip. There were two white teeth on the bottom, and another one coming in next to the two white teeth on top.

"No wonder," he murmured, looking at the red, swollen gum, with a tooth that was only just beginning to tear through the tissue.

Tiffany bit down again. Derek grunted in pain. His daughter smiled.

Eve chuckled. "Well, at least we know what to do now."

There was only one problem, as it turned out.

"Oh, no. I don't believe it. It's not in here," Derek groaned. "I must have left the first-aid kit with the stuff at the house."

And, Eve knew, it was a thirty-minute drive there and back. "There's a drugstore on the corner," she said as Tiffany began to cry once again, softly this time.

Derek looked torn, but there was no doubt in either adult's mind what would be faster. "Is it okay if I leave her here with you while I go?"

"Sure."

The minute he walked out, Tiffany began to cry again, in great choking sobs. Having seen her swollen gum, Eve couldn't blame the child. "You know what?" she told Tiffany resolutely. "We're not going to wait for someone to rescue us. We're going to look for a solution ourselves."

Eve carried the tyke into the kitchen. She opened the freezer, intending to get ice. Then smiled when she saw an even better solution. "Tiffany, sweetheart, I think I have what we both need...."

Derek hurried as fast as he could. It was still twenty minutes before he got back to Eve's condo. He expected to hear Tiffany wailing up a storm. Instead, all was quiet. In fact, he observed as he opened the front door, there was only...*laughter?*

He rounded the corner and found Eve lounging on her overstuffed white sofa. Her shoes were off, her hair looked sticky and her gold silk blouse was smeared with something white. Tiffany was on her lap. Her hair was sticky, too. As were her hands and her face, and her clothes.

She was also smiling.

"More," Tiffany demanded happily, grinning from ear to ear.

"A gal after my own heart," Eve exclaimed, offering a tiny spoonful of what looked to be the last of a small carton of premium vanilla ice cream.

Derek came closer.

And in that instant, as he took in both the woman and his little girl, he knew. He wasn't just enamored of Eve. He didn't just want her as a friend, or a lover, or both.

He wanted her as his wife.

"Asleep at last." Eve and Derek stood in the corner of the master bedroom, which was illuminated only by a night-light. Tiffany was curled up on her side in the port-a-crib, her teddy in her arms, her favorite blanket spread over top of her. She looked incredibly angelic and sweet.

Eve shook her head, thinking of what the little girl had been through that evening before she and Derek had figured out what the problem was. "Poor little thing," she whispered to Derek.

He wrapped his arm about her shoulders and pulled her in close. Bending down, his sandpapery beard brushing her temple, he pressed a kiss to her forehead before turning back to regard his daughter once again. "The combination of acetaminophen and numbing gel are working great at the moment, anyway."

Eve turned to face Derek. Together, they eased from the room, leaving the door open.

"And when it wears off four hours from now?" She couldn't help but worry about the little girl, the way a mom would. It had been heart-wrenching, seeing Tiffany so distressed.

Derek predicted, with the expertise of a very hands-on daddy, "She'll probably be up again. But don't worry... I'll handle it."

Eve wondered if this was what it would feel like if the three of them ever became a family. She only knew she didn't want to let this kind of happiness go, and that scared her. It was too soon to be thinking this way and wanting so much. Too soon to be risking so much of her heart...

Oblivious to the tumultuous nature of her thoughts, but sensing something was amiss, Derek studied her closely. "What's wrong?"

Eve shrugged and forced her mind back to the practical. "Well, for starters, I wish I had an actual guest bedroom."

Then the three of them could have all comfortably stayed there.

Instead, he was going to have to sleep in her room, in her bed, while she went elsewhere.

Derek ambled toward her. "Still planning to sleep at your mother's?"

Eve pushed the mental image of a half-naked Derek, lounging against her pillows, out of her head. She didn't need to know how he looked in her ultrafeminine satin bedcovers. And she certainly didn't need to be envisioning what it would be like to make love to him there. She swallowed around the sudden parched feeling in her throat and turned away from his probing gaze. "I thought you might like your privacy."

He shot her a bold, possessive look. "What I would like is to have you here."

She flushed and struggled to keep her guard up. "On the sofa?"

"Or in bed, with me. Where, just so you'll know, all we will do is sleep."

Eve knew that with Tiffany in there, everything in her bedroom would be totally G-rated. Oddly enough, the idea of bedding down with Derek—without hooking up—seemed even more fraught with peril. Cuddling all night, just for the sake of cuddling, was the kind of thing that could entice one to fall in love. And given how very close she was to that, as it was...

She turned toward him, drew a breath of the bracing scent of his hair and skin, and tried not to fall any harder for him. "Are you sure my place isn't too small for the three of us?"

Derek didn't seem the least bit discomfited by the physical or emotional intimacy of such an arrangement. He met her eyes and didn't look away. "Actually, it's just right for one night." He favored her with a brief, warm smile. "Although I have to wonder…" He paused, slightly perplexed. "Given your success as a real estate broker, why don't you have a bigger place?"

Good question. And one she had been asked before.

Eve went into the kitchen. She opened the drawer where she kept several take-out menus and pulled out a stack. "It's the reality of my business." She fanned the menus across the counter so he could choose one, then turned to face him again. "Real estate is among the hardest-hit business in any economic downturn. When that happens, commissions can be few and far between. So, as a hedge against that, my mother and I both live way beneath our means."

Derek bypassed the dinner selection process and instead made himself comfortable, lounging against the counter next to her, watching her. "Nothing wrong with being cautious financially," he murmured, "so long as you're emboldened to take risks in other aspects of your life."

Risks, Eve noted, that seemed to include whatever this was with him. Her heart stilled and she wet her lips, aware that with Tiffany sleeping on the other side of the apartment, anything could happen here. "I thought this was going to be a G-rated evening." He moved so that she was between him and the counter, and braced a hand on either side, trapping her against his long, hard length. He bent to nuzzle the sensitive side of her neck. "In the bedroom." He found his way to her ear, her throat, then eventually her mouth. "We're not there now," he whispered, expertly fitting his lips to hers. He stopped and grinned. "We're in the kitchen."

And the kitchen suddenly seemed a very erotic place to be. Eve groaned, even as her arms went up to wreathe his shoulders. Before she knew it, she was kissing him back. "You make a tempting case."

"And you are one tempting woman." He nuzzled his way down to the first button of her blouse. "Even with ice cream in your hair."

Eve touched a hand to the stickiness she had entirely forgotten about. He was right; several strands were matted with vanilla ice cream. "Ohhh."

He threaded his fingers through her hair and then bent and kissed her temple, then her cheek. "You're one hell of a good woman, Eve," he whispered as his mouth drifted slowly toward hers. "Do you know that?"

She pulled him flush against her and opened her lips to the investigating pressure of his. She moaned again, her entire body going soft with pleasure. He kissed her again, a deep, giving kiss that had her senses spinning and her heart soaring. "I know you make me feel that way."

They kissed again, even more passionately, holding nothing back, seeking solace in the harbor of each other's arms. "And I know you're one hell of a good man," Eve told him breathlessly, undoing the buttons of his shirt while he made short work of hers.

Derek grinned as both garments fell to the ground. His undershirt went the same way as her bra. As the heat and strength of his erection pressed against her, he cupped the weight of her breasts in his hands, rubbed his thumbs across her taut nipples. "Always something to be said for being on the same page."

Seemingly in no hurry, he lowered his lips to hers again. Eve kissed him back, sweetly and reverently. She ran her palms across the width of his shoulders, down his spine, luxuriating in the satiny feel of his skin and the flex of masculine muscle, aware that nothing had ever seemed as right as this.

Derek hadn't come there with the idea of making love to Eve. Given the way the evening had started out, he hadn't expected to have any opportunity to show her how much he cared for her. But now that the moment was here, he wasn't going to walk away without giving free rein to the primal possessiveness that emerged every time he was near her.

He kissed his way down her body, easing open the zipper of her skirt. Soon she was wearing nothing but a sparkly golden thong.

And eventually that went, too. Nudging her legs apart, he settled between her open thighs, sliding even lower. Eve gasped as his mouth crossed the flat of her abdomen. And she caught his head between her trembling palms when he went lower still, lifting her against his kisses, circling and retreating, adoring, seducing, until at last she fell apart in his hands. Satisfaction roared through him when he heard her choppy breathing and the sexy sounds being ripped from her throat. He held her until the last of her shudders had passed, then moved upward once again. In a flash, whatever clothes remained were off.

And then it was her turn to fulfill his fantasies. Kissing and touching, wrapping her hands around his thighs before sending him into a frenzy of wanting, of need.

He urged her upward. She shifted. Once again their eyes locked, their lips met, and then he was lifting her onto the counter, pulling her to the edge and stepping in. Luxuriating in the hot, intense quality of their connection, he penetrated her slowly, then caught her by the hips and let her do for him, with the most feminine part of her, what he had already done for her. Eve moaned and melded into him, murmuring his name again and again. Already granite-hard, he rocked against her and took his time, going ever deeper, slower, demanding she surrender to him completely.

And she did. Heaven help him, she did, until there was no more blood left in his head. Until there was no more prolonging the inevitable, no more holding their passion and their feelings in check, and the two of them went spiraling over the edge, still kissing, still clutching each other, still giving one another everything it was possible to give.

And then some, he realized shakily, as they clung together through the aftershocks. Affirming, to him and to her, that however this had started, their coming together was a hell of a lot more than just sex. It was, he thought, what she was to him, and he was to her: the best Christmas gift ever.

Chapter 14

Eve's phone rang at seven o'clock the next morning. She was not surprised to see her mother's caller ID pop up on screen. Marjorie wasted no time on preambles. "Have you seen this morning's newspaper?"

"No." Careful not to wake Derek and Tiffany, who were both still sleeping, Eve slid a robe on over her silk pajamas and popped out to get it.

"Check the business section."

Front page was a banner headline: Sibley & Smith Leading Year End Real Estate Sales Race.

Eve groaned. "I'm sorry, Mom."

"Not that one. Loughlin Realty is not about to let that one stand, at least not for the long haul."

Eve imagined when her mother got back to work, things would be different. Marjorie's enthusiasm for the business was always contagious. When she was around, sales were made and deals were closed almost effortlessly, it seemed.

"Farther down the page," Marjorie instructed with her usual zeal. "Next to a photo of someone familiar."

On the lower half was a picture of Derek beside an impressively long article. Eve read aloud, "'McCabe Venture Capital funds Tech Wizard, the next big thing in entertainment streaming and information. Expected to outperform everything currently available…'" Eve quickly scanned the remainder of the story. "Wow." And she thought he was successful now.

"So," Marjorie continued, business as usual, "you should have no problem selling him another property—or even two—before the end of the year, given the money he had originally budgeted and expected to spend." Behind her, Eve heard a gleeful, high-pitched shriek, and pivoted to see Tiffany toddling toward her. Her fluffy dark curls smashed to her head and going every which way, her cheeks pink with sleep, she ran toward Eve, arms outstretched. "Mommy!" she yelled with familiar affection. "Mommy!"

Eve heard a gasp on the other end of the connection. "What is that?" Marjorie pressed. "Or maybe I should say, *who* is that?"

Tiffany grinned at Eve, showing the new tooth that had broken through her gum overnight. She knelt down to hug the child and mugged back at her wordlessly. "Um, a friend," she told her mom.

"Me!" Tiffany grabbed for the phone. "'Lo!" she squealed into the receiver.

Derek intercepted his daughter, swinging her quickly into his arms with a theatrical effect that made her giggle uproariously. Mouthing *"Sorry!"* to Eve, he handed Tiffany his phone to talk on.

She threw it down. The cell phone bounced as it hit Eve's thick, luxurious carpeting. "Bottle!" Tiffany yelled. "Me! Bottle!"

Waggling her brows at Derek, Eve pointed to the fridge and stepped away from where he was heading, baby daughter in tow.

"Since when do you pal around people with babies at seven in the morning? Unless…" Marjorie paused thoughtfully "…you had an overnight guest?"

Unwilling to respond to that, Eve flushed. Her mother would approve of her using everything she had to leverage a sale with Derek. She would not, however, approve of her sleeping with him.

Eve turned and made her way toward her bedroom. A look at the rumpled covers only brought back more memories. Of how it had felt to sleep, fully clothed, wrapped in his arms. She turned toward the living room, only to be reminded of all they had done before they'd headed off to sleep. With her body tingling erotically, she shoved a hand through her tousled hair. "Mom, I have to go."

"Are you still going to Laramie today to look at property with Derek McCabe?"

"Yes." Eve swallowed, trying to get a hold of herself, to sound at least vaguely normal. "But if you need me here, Mom…"

"I need you to make a big sale, Eve. Enough to put us in the lead of the sales race again."

Eve glanced again at the front page of the business section and the stories on her family's business versus Derek's. There was no doubt whose money-generating venture was going better. No doubt about who juggled work and family more effectively.

"I know you can get emotional about property, and the needs and wants of the people buying it, but there's no time for that. Promise me you'll pull this off for us," Marjorie insisted.

Eve rubbed her temples. If her mother wasn't currently recovering from a heart attack, they'd be having a different conversation. One a lot more frank, about Eve's need to start separating her professional life from her personal one, her need to have her own life. Before Derek and Tiffany had come into her world, Eve realized, she hadn't done anything but work, and worry about work. In retrospect, it was not a satisfying way to live.

As much as she wanted to please her mother, Eve didn't want to lose what precious little balance she had already found. "I'll do my best to see that Derek and his little girl get what they need today, Mom," she promised.

Picking up on Eve's reluctance, Marjorie sighed. "I'm sorry I'm pushing, but to see everything we've all worked so hard for this year end on a whimper instead of a bang… It's disheartening."

What an apt phrase, Eve thought. "I know, Mom. I wish…" What did she wish? That she'd already sold all three properties and put them firmly in the lead for the year? Or that she didn't have to worry so much about whether she was ambitious enough to please her mom, and could instead concentrate on trying to make some sort of satisfying home life for herself that included more than just the two of them? There was a choked sound on the other end of the connection. "Oh, honey.

I'm sorry," her mother said abruptly. "Forget all that." Sounding more like the new and improved, post-heart attack Marjorie than the previous go-getter, she continued emotionally, "It's you I care about, Eve. And your happiness."

"I know, Mom," she said.

She knew her mother was struggling to find balance in her life, too. To do what she needed for her health, and yet not neglect the business she'd spent her life building.

Still, old habits died hard. And Eve felt the weight of her mother's expectations like an anchor around her neck.

When she ended the call, Derek was watching her.

He was clad in low-slung pajama pants, and nothing else. With the shadow of a beard on his face, his hair rumpled, his eyes intent, his daughter still cradled in his arms, he was sexy as all get-out. Their eyes met. Her heart took a little leap, and deep within her, desire built.

"Everything okay?" His tone was a seductive rumble. Caring. Protective.

Eve didn't want to talk about anything that would ruin what they had shared the evening before. "You're famous!" She pointed to the business section of the paper.

Derek ignored his own photo and what for him was old news. He frowned. "Sorry about that." He tapped the Sibley & Smith story. "But as they say, it's not over till it's over. And there are still eleven days left in the year."

Yes, there were. And Eve didn't want to talk about that, either. Fearing the end of Christmas would mean the end of their romance, she walked past him into the kitchen. "What do the two of you want for breakfast?"

He set Tiffany down on the floor. She toddled toward the small carryall of toys they'd brought with them, and sat down happily to play.

Derek followed Eve around the other side of the breakfast bar that divided the two rooms. He moved the curtain of her hair and nuzzled her neck just below her ear. "How about something soft and hot…." he whispered, conjuring up images of what they'd done the night before.

Eve turned, poker-faced. "Cream of Wheat?"

He laughed, seemingly content to wait until the right time to put the moves on her again. Playfully, she tapped a finger to her chin. "Or oatmeal?"

He gave her another look that let her know she wasn't going to be able to resist him if he was around for long, and it appeared he intended to be around for quite a while.

Eve swallowed, beginning to feel overwhelmed again. "Seriously…"

He looked in her fridge, saw the loaf of bread, butter, eggs and jam. Then turned back to her, obviously ready and willing to do whatever it took to make her feel better. "How about," he drawled sexily, "you let me make breakfast?"

And he could cook, too. Really, Eve thought with a wistful sigh, what was *not* to love about this man?

"So what'd you think of the Double H ranch, now that you've had a chance to see it again?" Josie Mc-Cabe asked Derek when they got back from their tour of the property.

Derek grinned at his mom. "Same as I recall."

"Another fixer-upper?" his brother Colt teased, refer-

ring to the broken-down house and barns that, thanks to
the family who owned it and didn't reside there, hadn't
seen much in the way of upkeep in many a year.

Derek grinned at him, too, as recklessly sentimental
as ever when it came to choosing real estate. "I prefer
to think of it as in need of some tender loving care."

"What'd you think, Eve?" Wade asked.

"It's very picturesque," she said sincerely. The five-
thousand-acre ranch seemed to have everything, from
tree-lined streams and rocky bluffs to flat, sagebrush-
dotted plains.

"Not to mention remote," Derek's older brother,
Grady, remarked.

Josie scowled. "Well, anything in Laramie County
fits that description."

Derek agreed with his mom. "Nothing wrong with
remote," he drawled.

"Unless you've lived your whole life in a big city like
Dallas," Grady said, with a brief, telling look at Eve.
"Then it can seem like wilderness."

No kidding, Eve thought. During the three-and-a-
half-hour drive to Laramie County, there had been long
stretches of highway without a gas station or town to
be found. Never mind any cell phone reception, which
had made responding to work emails and client texts
challenging, to say the least.

"Well, I for one will be happy to have you-all close
again, at least part of the time," Josie said, hugging
first Derek, then her granddaughter. She held her arms
wide and embraced Eve warmly. "You, too, hon." They
drew apart. "In the meantime, we better do something
about dinner."

A mixture of laughs and groans immediately followed. Josie took the good-natured ribbing about her culinary talents in stride. Apparently, Eve noted, being in the kitchen was one of Josie McCabe's least favorite things. Hence, she was happy to turn the cooking over to others. "Mom, you're in charge of the three grand-kids," Derek declared.

Josie winked at him. "As long as you and Colt stay to help corral them."

Wade headed for the flagstone patio. "I'll fire up the grill."

"We'll help you." Grady, Justin and Rand followed their dad.

Amanda, Alexis and Shelley—the three women who had married into the family—headed for the kitchen. "Not to worry, Josie. We'll take care of everything in here." Wanting to be of some help, Eve followed suit.

The kitchen, like everything else in the sprawling ranch house, was designed for a big family. There were two Sub-Zero refrigerators, two dishwashers, two sinks, a wide kitchen island that spanned the length of the long room and an abundance of windows to look out, and counters on which to work.

In short order, vegetables were brought out to be cleaned and cooked, fruits peeled and sliced, the meats seasoned and prepared for the grill.

Finally, enough prep work had been done to allow a respite. A round of long-necked bottles of Texas-brewed beer was opened and passed out. Conversation ensued about people and places Eve knew nothing about. Not sure where she fit in, or *if* she fit in, she hung back.

Noticing her unease, the six-foot-tall Amanda came over to give her a comforting hug. "Hey. No need to be panicked here. We're all friends."

Eve could see that.

Alexis stopped what she was doing and came over to give Eve's hand a squeeze.

Shelley comforted her with a smile. "The three of us are all only children. I grew up here and dated Colt when we were teens, so I already knew his family. It didn't matter how nice they were to me. They intimidated me for years—until I let them in."

Amanda nodded in agreement. "I got to know Justin and his dad when I was working on the boys' ranch that Justin founded. They made me feel like family from the outset, but I was still intimidated the first time I came to Josie and Wade's ranch to be with everyone."

"Me, too," Alexis recounted with a shake of her head. "As much as Grady tried to prepare me, I was still overwhelmed my first visit here when I saw everyone together."

So it wasn't just her, Eve thought.

She wondered why it didn't help to know that.

"It will get better with time," Amanda soothed, with the knowledge of a woman who had been there, and not only survived, but thrived. "Just relax and soak it all in."

Amazed, and a little disconcerted by how quickly they had accepted her into the tribe and made her feel like part of the family, Eve hugged each of the three women in turn.

Yet as much as she wanted to, she knew she couldn't get used to this, or in any way take it for granted. It didn't matter how much she longed to step into such a Texas-style perfect life. Or how much Derek and his family seemed to want it all to be a done deal.

It was much too soon for that.

* * *

The rest of the weekend passed quickly. Derek wasn't surprised to see Eve getting along well with his family. They were, perhaps, more alike than she knew. He also realized that something was bothering her, and had been since they'd looked at the rural property the previous day. Wanting to talk to her about it without interruption, however, he waited until he had dropped Tiffany at Carleen's house and taken Eve back to hers.

"You've been awfully quiet," he said, carrying her suitcase into her condo. Except for the phone call she'd made to her mother en route, she hadn't spoken much on the drive back to Dallas, and instead had contented herself watching the scenery and listening to Christmas carols on the car stereo.

Eve gave him a wan smile. There was a sadness in her eyes he didn't like. "I was trying to figure out how to talk to you about the Double H ranch."

Derek took off his coat and sat down on the sofa. "I'm listening."

Instead of taking the seat beside him, Eve settled into an armchair opposite. "You also know I'm not the kind of Realtor who is all about the commissions."

Derek got serious, too. "You like to match the right property with the right person."

Eve affirmed this with a decisive nod. "I know what your financial goals are, in terms of investing in real estate before the end of the year. There is still time for them to be met."

Derek braced himself for the bad news sure to come. "Are you trying to say you didn't like the ranch I showed you?" he asked, searching her eyes. "Because if that's the case, we can go back to Laramie County, keep looking."

Her soft lips took on a grim line. "I don't think you understand, Derek. My likes and my dislikes don't enter into this transaction."

What was she talking about? "Of course they do!"

"Not in the way you seem to be thinking," she countered in a tight, controlled voice.

He forced himself to show no reaction. Although this wasn't what he wanted to hear—not by a long shot—part of him had always figured it would come to this. Eve was simply not a woman who wanted to let anyone in.

"Are you breaking up with me?" he asked quietly.

Still holding his eyes—even more reluctantly now, he noticed—she cleared her throat. "Derek, we're not even dating."

He stood, hands braced on his waist. "Right. We're just sharing confidences and spending time together and making love with each other every chance we get."

Pink color flooding her cheeks, Eve stood, too. "Your family pretty much has us married off!"

Derek strode nearer, positioning himself so she had no choice but to look at him. Hands on her shoulders, he held her in front of him when she would have run. "That's because they know the two of us are made for each other," he said gruffly.

Tears misted Eve's pretty amber eyes. "You can't know that."

Aware of all that was at stake here—their future happiness—he held his ground. "I do know that."

Her tears spilled down her cheeks. She pulled away from him. "Well, I don't."

He watched her pace to the window, then stand there as if she had the weight of the world on her shoulders. "What are you saying?"

She pivoted back around to face him, looking edgy and upset. "I'm saying I know how, once you make up your mind about something—like buying a home or vacation retreat— that you just want to find a way to get it done. Ideally, as fast as possible."

It wasn't the first time Derek's success and determination had been held against him, but it had never hurt this much before.

She gazed into his eyes, a soul-deep weariness in her expression. "With that in mind, I know how determined you are to make sure that your little girl has parity in her two homes, so that she doesn't suffer because she comes from divorced parents." Eve drew in an uneven breath. "And I know that Tiffany wants a mommy and a daddy at both of her houses, that the three of us work well as a team, and that Tiffany adores me as much as I adore her."

She was making their connection sound so cold and calculated. "You think I made love with you because I need a bed buddy, and a friend, and I want you to be a mother to my child?"

"No." Eve's eyes were steady, but her lower lip trembled. "I think you made love to me because it's Christmastime and you want someone to celebrate with…and you find me as wildly attractive as I find you. I think you want me because it's easier to have two people parent a child at any given time than just one."

What about heart? Didn't that come into all this? His? Hers? In her view, Derek realized, it apparently did not. Hurt beyond measure, he stared at her. "But you don't want a future with me, is that it?" How could he have been so wrong about her, about all of this?

A shadow of regret crossed her face. "I'm saying what I've been saying all along—that I don't feel comfortable rushing into anything, Derek." She wrung her hands together. "And the truth of the matter is we have rushed into this, for a lot of reasons, none of them good."

Derek reached out and caught her by the waist when she would have moved away. "Okay, you've told me my reasons. As you see them, anyway," he amended brusquely, stung by the look in her eyes. "What are yours?"

She threw up her hands. "My mother had a heart attack and that made me realize how short life is, and how one-dimensionally I've been living." Raw emotion filled Eve's voice. "The crisis made me want comfort, and it made me want a lot more than I've had."

She deserved a whole hell of a lot more, too. Derek drew her against him and tucked a strand of hair behind her ear. "I want more, too," he confessed. *"I want you."*

She splayed her hands over his chest, still holding him at bay. "There were other reasons, too." Her voice sounded thick with unshed tears. "I told you that I get depressed and lonely around the holidays. That I never ever felt like I could quite get into the Christmas spirit the way others did." She paused, her teeth raking across her delectably soft lower lip. "Reaching out to you and Tiffany and celebrating the season with you made all of that go away."

For him, too.

But for him it had been just the beginning.

For Eve, it seemed it was the end. And that scared Derek more than he wanted to admit. "And that's all our love affair was?" he prodded, desperately wanting her to rise up angrily and tell him otherwise. "A temporary reprieve from a family crisis and some scary, uncomfortable feelings?"

Eve paused. She started to say something, stopped. She pushed away from him entirely and ran a hand through her hair. "I don't know if that's what it was or not," she said brokenly. The tortured words came straight from her heart. "I don't know *what* we are to each other. Or how we'll even feel once the holidays pass, and you and Tiffany settle in at your place. Which is why… I want to take a break."

"Now," he repeated, when she still refused to look him in the eye. "Four days before *Christmas?*"

Another nod. A sigh. And this time she did look at him, as calm, cool and collected as the day they'd first met. "For at least a month, Derek. Maybe two."

And then what? he wondered. Did she honestly think this would hurt them any less if they delayed the inevitable? He folded his arms in front of him, legs braced apart. "No."

Eve blinked, obviously as unprepared for his reaction as he had been for hers. "What?" she asked, as if she couldn't possibly have heard him right.

"I'm not going to go through some arbitrary time-out," he told her flatly. Hurt and disappointed beyond measure, he stepped closer and stared down at the beautiful woman he adored so much, the woman he had foolishly hoped he would spend the rest of his life with.

He had wanted Eve to feel as he did, that they were made for each other.

Clearly, she didn't. And if that was the case, he'd

already been down this particular road. He damn well wasn't traveling it again.

Aware that she was still staring at him in shock, he exhaled wearily, then forced himself to go on in a matter-of-fact tone. "If you don't already know that you and I are the best thing that ever happened to each other, then you're never going to know, Eve. And I can't—won't—be part of another relationship where I'm the only one ready and willing to put my whole heart in, and give it my all."

"You're breaking up with me?" she asked, aghast, looking as if this possibility hadn't ever occurred to her.

Derek grabbed his coat and headed for the door. He didn't want to end it, but he didn't want to prolong the pain, either. He nodded curtly. "You've given me no choice."

Chapter 15

Eve spent most of Sunday night crying her eyes out. Monday morning was just as bad. And it got worse when she received the latest news on the real estate front.

Reluctantly, she went to see her mother and tell her in person.

"The offer on Flash's condo fell through."

Marjorie didn't look surprised.

Eve swept a hand through her hair. "There are no other bids. And probably won't be until after the holidays."

Her mom nodded slowly. She put down the novel she had been reading. "The Santiago Florres–designed house?"

The ache of defeat grew. "Red is passing on it. He is, however, in negotiations with Santiago to build him something just as unique on the beach in Galveston. Unfortunately, there's no chance we'll see a commission there, either. Their lawyers will be brokering that deal."

Marjorie pursed her lips, looking surprisingly calm. "Anything else?"

Eve gulped. And here was the worst part, as far as business was concerned, anyway. She looked her mother straight in the eye. "Sibley & Smith sold another four-million-dollar listing over the weekend."

"So in other words, they've won."

Eve went and perched on the edge of her mother's bed. "Unless someone takes over the negotiations on a property for Derek McCabe."

Her mom rose and went to the mini-fridge next to the sink. "Why can't you do it?"

For so many reasons, Eve thought. Most of which were currently breaking her heart. She clenched her hands on either side of her. "It's complicated."

Marjorie passed Eve a can of low-sodium tomato juice and kept one for herself. "Fortunately, I'm in cardiac rehab, so I have all the time in the world when I'm not down in physical therapy, working on regaining my strength." She smiled wryly at her daughter. "So give it to me straight."

Eve looked down as she popped the top on her drink. "I got too involved."

Marjorie sat down next to her on the hospital bed. "Too involved or not enough?"

Eve gave in to the need to be comforted, and rested her head on her mother's shoulder. "He wanted things from me, Mom, that I'm just not cut out to give."

Marjorie wrapped her arm about her shoulders and

pulled her in close, the way she had when Eve was a little girl. "Things like what?" she asked gently.

Eve swallowed a lump in her throat. "Marriage."

"He proposed?"

She straightened, took a drink. "No."

Marjorie moved so they were facing each other, then studied her with a mother's knowing eye. "Then…?"

Eve flushed and took another sip of the sweet, mellow juice. "We were headed in that direction."

"Since when is that a bad thing?"

Barely able to believe she'd said that, Eve blinked. "You've never wanted to get married, Mom!"

"So?" Marjorie shrugged. "I'm not you." After a short pause, she said, "It has to be more than that."

Eve lurched to her feet. "Everything was just happening way too fast." As usual when upset, she started to pace.

Marjorie shifted back against the pillows. "Sometimes life is that way."

Eve had expected her to take her side in this! Whirling toward her mom, she said stubbornly, "I wanted a break. He wouldn't give it to me."

"Hmm."

Once again, hurt mixed with disbelief. Eve scoffed. "That's it? That's all you have to say?"

Marjorie finished her juice and set the container aside. "What do you want me to say?"

That was just it… Eve didn't know. She shook her head miserably. "Something to make me feel better!"

Marjorie smiled sympathetically. "I don't think I can do that, honey."

"You always have before."

"You were never really and truly this—"

Eve expected her mom to say "wildly infatuated before."

Instead, she said, "—foolish before."

It was Eve's turn to study her mother, long and hard. "I know he's well-off financially, Mom. I know he's phenomenally successful, professionally. But just because everything is easy for him doesn't mean it's going to be easy for me, never mind easy for us."

Her inscrutable demeanor fading, her mother nodded sagely. "Especially if you do everything you can to make it more difficult than it has to be."

Honestly! "Whose side are you on?" Eve demanded angrily.

Her mother replied flatly, "Yours."

It sure didn't seem like that was the case. Eve squared her shoulders and regarded her defiantly, aware they hadn't been this far apart in anything since her teenage years. "Maybe we shouldn't talk about this."

Surprisingly, her mother agreed. "It does seem like you need to do a little more soul-searching." Marjorie rose and guided Eve toward the door. She gave her a long, heartfelt hug. "But I have faith that, given enough time and solitude, you'll figure it out."

Acutely aware this was the last place he had expected to be at noon on December 23, Derek stood in the doorway of Marjorie Loughlin's room. He didn't know Eve's mother all that well yet. He also didn't know where else to go for help in, if not making things right, at least trying to make amends. He drew a breath. "Got a minute?"

Marjorie put down the crossword puzzle she'd been working on. She removed her glasses and looked down her nose at him. "For you? I'm not sure, given that you've broken my daughter's heart."

"Hey." Derek lifted both hands defensively. "She's the one who refused to get serious about me." He was the one who had wanted an enduring relationship. Not in the distant future, but right now. "She is the one who kept saying no."

The older woman quirked her lips. "Maybe for good reason, since she says the two of you were never even dating."

Derek sauntered in. He pulled up a chair and got comfortable. "And if you believe that, I've got some swampland in East Texas to sell you."

Marjorie grinned and began to relax. "Why are you here?"

He sobered. "I want help buying enough property to help Loughlin Realty win the sales competition."

A long, suspenseful moment passed. "Why?"

"Because it's Christmas, a time of giving, and it means something to Eve," Derek informed her. "And because I feel I owe her that much."

"For?"

This was tricky. "Hurting her without meaning to." *Hurting us both by pushing her too hard, too fast.*

"Balderdash." Marjorie stood abruptly.

Derek got to his feet, too. "Excuse me?"

The woman stomped closer, at that moment looking a lot like her beautiful, tempestuous daughter. "What a load of hooey."

Like hell it was.

Derek faced off with Marjorie. "Eve wants to win that sales race."

With a shake of her head, her mom corrected,

"*Wanted* to win. For me. I told her it wasn't necessary. There's always next year."

Derek blinked in disbelief.

Marjorie shrugged. "Three and a half weeks of cardiac rehab will make a person examine what does and does not make him or her happy. For me, it's a successful business, always has been, always will be. For Eve, it's a lot more complicated." Marjorie wandered over to adjust the holiday wreath affixed to her wall before turning back to Derek. "She wants emotional satisfaction—not just fiscal—in her work."

Derek listened to the strains of a Christmas carol being played a little farther down the hall. He wasn't sure why; he just knew the rendition of "Hark the Herald Angels Sing" made him feel melancholy. "What does Eve want in her personal life?" What could he have given her, and hadn't?

Her mother's expression gentled. "You really don't know?"

Desperate for help, he shook his head. "Apparently, I haven't got a clue," he remarked drily. Otherwise he would be with Eve right now, celebrating the best holiday of the year. Instead of flailing around, lost and at loose ends.

The older woman sent him another wry smile. "Then it's about time you found out, don't you think?"

"How?" Derek retorted in droll exasperation. "She won't talk to me!" Wouldn't answer his calls or his emails or his texts.

"Since when has that stopped you from going after what you want?" Marjorie asked, unimpressed. "You and I are a lot alike, you know. That's probably what attracts—and repels—Eve the most."

Reluctantly, Derek conceded that she had a point. He and Marjorie were both driven individuals.

"So, I know that if you really want to make something happen, you'll find a way." Marjorie paused meaningfully. "Same as me."

"What do you mean, you're not coming home?" Eve asked her mother on Christmas Eve morning. They always spent the holiday together, and Marjorie's release had already been scheduled.

"I decided to stay another couple of days."

Eve admired her mother's tenacity, even as she worried about her own lack of it. "Then I'll come to the cardiac rehab unit and spend it with you."

"No. I don't think that's a good idea."

Feeling more despondent than ever, Eve said, "You don't?"

Her mother continued brightly, "We can have dinner together in the dining room here on Christmas Day, and celebrate then."

"What about the rest of the time?" Eve demanded. There were over twenty-four hours between now and then! She had wanted a shoulder to lean on, an ear to listen. Comfort. And joy. And love. In short, all the things she could have had with Derek, if she'd only had the courage to take the leap of faith required, and see their relationship through.

"I'll be resting," her mother replied, as matter-of-fact as ever. "And you need the time to reflect, in any case."

Eve wasn't sure she wanted to do a lot of thinking about everything that had happened. Because thinking would lead to crying, and she had done enough of that. "You're sure?" she asked again, wishing she didn't already miss Derek—and Tiffany—so very much.

"Positive," her mother said, sounding positively cheerful and relaxed.

Feeling abandoned all over again, Eve sighed. "Okay…then, I'll see you tomorrow, Mom. And Merry Christmas."

"Merry Christmas to you, too, honey."

Eve hung up the phone.

A moment later, the doorbell rang.

She went to answer. On the porch in front of her condo was a wicker basket containing a DVD of *A Christmas Story,* a red-and-white-striped tin of popcorn and her favorite sparkling water. Attached to a box of peppermint bark, fastened with a big red bow, was a card that said, "You're right. We don't know as much about each other as I want to know. Maybe we should start by watching each other's favorite holiday movies. Derek."

What did that mean? Had he forgiven her? Was he ready to slow down and give her the space she had asked for?

And what was so great about spending Christmas Eve alone, anyway? Eve wondered grumpily. She knew from previous conversations with Derek that Tiffany was spending her evening with Craig and Carleen. Had Derek arranged to be with family, too? Or was he as alone—and miserable—as she was? About to sit down and watch her favorite holiday movie by himself?

There was only one way to find out!

Derek had just turned on the DVD when his doorbell rang.

The melancholy sounds of *A Charlie Brown Christmas* filling his beautiful empty home, he went to see who was on the doorstep.

Eve stood there, looking like an angel from heaven. She was wearing a pretty red dress and a white wool coat. A silk scarf was looped around her neck, the gift basket he had left for her was by her side and two other presents were in her arms. With a hint of color in her sculpted cheeks, her golden-brown hair flowing over her shoulders, she looked as elegant and gorgeous as ever. "I hope I'm not intruding," she began.

If she only knew how much he'd been hoping she would reach out to him, the way he had been reaching out to her. Yet something in her eyes had him erring on the side of caution. Suppressing the impulse to wrap his arms around her and hold her close, he remained where he was and simply said, "You're not."

She flashed a brief smile. "I was out delivering thank-yous to clients and thought I'd stop by to give you this." She handed him a small gift-wrapped box bearing his name, and another with Tiffany's.

Was that it?

Just a business call?

He looked her in the eye, trying to decide.

"Merry Christmas," she said thickly.

Were those tears glistening in her amber eyes? Or was he just imagining the slight tremble of her lips?

She picked up the basket he'd left for her, and handed it to him, too.

"Merry Christmas to *you*." He set the gifts she'd brought him on top of the unopened ones he had left for her, in the basket.

Across the street, neighbors paused to observe.

Eve glanced over her shoulder, then turned back to him. "May I come in?" she asked quietly.

He narrowed his eyes, still trying to figure out what she was up to. Was this the ultimate kiss-off? Or something else entirely? Well, there was only one way to find out.

He nodded and stepped aside. She swept by him in a drift of hyacinth perfume.

Acknowledging that she had the power to break his heart all over again, he closed the door behind them, shutting the rest of the world out. At least for now.

Her head cocked at the distant sound of the *Peanuts* gang rehearsing a Christmas pageant. Derek led the way into the adjacent living area, where a beautifully decorated tree and more presents waited. The television was on. Snoopy and the gang were dancing uproariously, while Charlie Brown stood alone and looked on, exasperated, depressed and disillusioned.

"For the record, I haven't watched the movie yet," he said awkwardly. Although he had seen it before as a kid, many times.

As he set the basket down on the coffee table, he could see the seal on the DVD he'd given her was also intact. He figured whatever this was, they might as well get it over with. Particularly since she hadn't yet moved to take off her coat or scarf. He inclined his head at the gift basket. "You didn't like my gift?" Was she rejecting that, too?

"It was nice."

"But...?"

She lifted a shoulder. "It wasn't what I wanted, after all."

His heart, not to mention his pride, felt stomped on again.

"The being-apart-from-each-other bit," she amended hastily.

A muscle worked in his cheek. "What did you want?" he rasped.

Eve took a deep breath and came closer. "A do-over."

"A do-over?" he repeated dumbly.

She nodded. Took off her coat and then her scarf, and set both aside. Amber eyes locked with his, she came nearer still. Took both his hands in hers and squeezed lightly. She paused to look down at their entwined fingers. "I know I said I was upset because everything was happening too fast." She took another breath, then looked up again. "But I realize that wasn't it at all."

He followed his instincts and wrapped his arms around her. "Then what was it?"

She shrugged, looking tearful—and remorseful—yet again. "It was that it was happening at all," she choked out. "I knew the first time we met that you had the power to change my world. It's why I found you so completely irritating."

Eve drew a breath and pushed on emotionally, "The first time we kissed, I knew you had the power to change my heart." She splayed her hands over his chest. "And the first time we made love, though I tried hard to deny it, it was pretty much a done deal."

Derek stroked his palm over her hair. "You rocked my world, too."

She nodded, truly accepting that in a way she never had before. Her voice dropped a notch. "The fact is, I've never wanted to be with anyone as much as I wanted to be with you, Derek. In truth, I didn't even know it was possible to love like this...."

With joy soaring through him, he pressed a finger to her lips. "Back up a minute," he demanded gruffly. "Did you say 'love'?"

Eve nodded, trembling all the more. "And not in the casual, maybe-we-should-consider-having-a-relationship kind of way, but the forever-and-ever kind."

She swallowed hard, but her gaze didn't waver as she forged on. "And that scares the heck out of me, Derek, because I'm afraid something could or will happen, and we'll lose this—"

Knowing she wasn't the only one at fault here, Derek interrupted her. "For the record, what we feel for each other scares the heck out of me, too. Which is why I've been pushing so hard," he admitted hoarsely. "I wanted everything nailed down in a way that couldn't be undone. So it wouldn't be easy for us to walk away. When what I should have had all along was faith." He lifted her hand, kissed the back of it. "Faith in you, faith in me, faith in the two of us and the love we share. And in the life we could have, if we take the time to build a relationship that is strong enough to last through whatever fate throws our way."

Eve smiled, as at peace now as she was in love. "I do have faith in you, Derek."

"And I have faith in you." They kissed, sweetly and tenderly.

Finally, they drew apart.

Eve continued affectionately, "Enough confidence to want to not just pick up where we left off, but to take it to the next level."

She reached for the presents she'd brought him and had him open the first box, which contained a toy cradle for Tiffany's baby doll. In the second was an expensive gold watch with some simple words inscribed on the back: *No Time like the Present.*

Looking a little misty-eyed, he put the timepiece on and kissed her. "As long as we're getting gifts for each other…" Grinning mysteriously, he went to his desk, opened a drawer and returned with a jewelry box, which he handed her. It also contained a watch, with the inscription: *Slow and Steady Wins the Race.*

Eve laughed. "Great minds think alike."

Derek kissed her deeply. "They sure do. Now that we know time is on our side," he joked.

"And that we have all the time in the world," she added, laughing again.

They embraced, and kissed some more, even more poignantly. "So it's official? We're a couple?" Eve said.

Derek nodded. "For now and forever."

Epilogue

Christmas Eve, two years later...

"I really get to put the angel on top of the tree this year?" Tiffany asked.

"You sure do," Derek and Eve replied in unison. Eve handed her the angel. Derek lifted the three-year-old high enough to reach.

In a red tartan plaid dress, fitted red velvet vest, shimmery white tights and her favorite red cowgirl boots, her glossy brown curls swept into a bouncy ponytail, the little girl was beside herself with excitement.

As were they, Eve thought happily. She'd thought the same thing every year she had been with Derek, but she was sure this was going to be the best Christmas ever!

With his assistance, Tiffany settled the ornament on the top branch of the Fraser fir. With one arm laced about his broad shoulders, she leaned back against her daddy, wrinkling her nose and studying her handiwork.

Clearly possessing an artist's temperament, she asked finally, "What do you think?"

"It's perfect," Derek and Eve said simultaneously.

Tiffany giggled as Derek kissed the top of her head, then set her back down on the floor. She dashed over to accept a hug and kiss of congratulations from Eve, too. "You two always say the same thing at the same time," the child declared, her blue eyes sparkling in delight.

Winking, Derek gathered both ladies close for a family hug. "That's because great minds think alike."

Eve laughed at the familiar refrain. Tiffany did, too, then wiggled out of the group hug. "I have to get the cookies for Santa!"

"The red dish with Santa's picture on it is on the table!" Eve called after her.

"'Kay!" Tiffany disappeared around the corner into the kitchen.

"So how are you doing?" Derek asked, putting a hand to Eve's tummy, where another little one, yet to be born, resided.

Basking in his solid warmth. Eve sighed in satisfaction. "I could not be happier. Which is," she teased, "a fact you well know."

He kissed her. "And a sentiment I share."

She and Derek had celebrated their one-year wedding anniversary the previous month, and found out shortly after that she was pregnant. Much to the entire family's delight, the baby would be born the following summer. Her mother had not only recovered fully from her heart attack, but gone on to win the top home sales award for Highland Park two years running. Marjorie had also found a new beau, Red Bloom, when the two realized they had more in common than a lust for business. And, Eve reflected with a smile, since buying and upgrading the ranch he had wanted in Laramie County as a weekend and holiday retreat, she and Derek saw a lot more of the McCabe clan, too.

Life, it had turned out, was pretty wonderful these days. And with the first of the children they had planned on the way, it only looked to get better. Smiling to herself, she watched as Tiffany glided back into the room, a half dozen of the cookies she had worked so hard on with Eve balanced precariously on the rimmed dish. "I think Santa's really going to like these," the little girl declared, setting them on a table near the sofas flanking the fireplace.

"I know he will," Derek and Eve said, once again speaking at the exact same time.

Tiffany erupted into a cascade of giggles that brought tears to their eyes. "You-all are so funny!" she exclaimed, then ran back to the kitchen to get the sippy cup of milk they'd already poured for Santa.

Derek took Eve into his arms. "Not to mention very much in love," she said softly, splaying her hands across his chest and kissing him tenderly.

"You've got that right," he murmured, kissing her back just as gently. He looked down at her, all the affection he felt reflected in his eyes. "Merry Christmas, Mrs. McCabe."

Eve wrapped her arms around him and hugged him close. She whispered sweetly, "Merry Christmas to you, too."

* * * * *

IF YOU ENJOYED THIS BOOK
WE THINK YOU WILL ALSO LOVE

LOVE INSPIRED
INSPIRATIONAL ROMANCE

Uplifting stories of faith, forgiveness and hope.

Fall in love with stories where faith helps
guide you through life's challenges, and discover
the promise of a new beginning.

6 NEW BOOKS AVAILABLE EVERY MONTH!

"I am so sorry," Daisy told Joe as they walked down the sidewalk together.

The sun had come out and it was warm. The kind of day that made her long for spring.

"I don't know that I need an apology," Joe told her. "But an explanation would be a good start."

She shook her head. "I saw you sitting with your family, and I knew how I'd feel. Ambushed."

"I could have handled it. Now I'm engaged." He tossed her a dimpled grin. "What am I supposed to tell them when I don't have a wedding?"

"I got tired of your smug attitude and left you at the altar?" she asked, half teasing. "Where are we walking to?"

"I'm not sure. I guess the park."

"The park it is," she told him.

Daisy smiled down at the stroller. Myra and Miriam belonged with their mother, Lindsey. Daisy got to love them for a short time and hoped that she'd made a difference.

"It'll be hard to let them go," Joe said.

"It will be," Daisy admitted. "I think they'll go home after New Year's."

"That's pretty soon."

"It is. We have a court date next week."

"I'm sorry," Joe said, reaching for her hand and giving it a light squeeze.

"None of that has anything to do with what I've done to your life. I've complicated things. I'm sorry. You can tell your parents I lost my mind for a few minutes. Tell them I have a horrible sense of humor and that we aren't even friends. Tell them I wanted to make your life difficult."

"Which one is true?" he asked.

"Maybe a combination," she answered. "I *do* have a horrible sense of humor. I *did* want to mess with you."

"And the part about us not being friends?"

"Honestly, I don't know what we are."

"I'll take friendship," he told her. "Don't worry, Daisy, I'm not holding you to this proposal."

She laughed and so did he.

"Good thing. The last thing I want is a real fiancé."

"I know I'm not the most handsome guy, but I'm a decent catch," he said.

She ignored the comment about his looks. The last thing she wanted to admit was that when he smiled, she forgot herself just a little.

Don't miss
The Rancher's Holiday Arrangement *by Brenda Minton,*
available November 2020 wherever
Love Inspired books and ebooks are sold.

LoveInspired.com

Love Harlequin romance?

DISCOVER.

Be the first to find out about promotions,
news and exclusive content!

f Facebook.com/HarlequinBooks

t Twitter.com/HarlequinBooks

O Instagram.com/HarlequinBooks

P Pinterest.com/HarlequinBooks

ReaderService.com

EXPLORE.

Sign up for the Harlequin e-newsletter and
download a free book from any series at
TryHarlequin.com

CONNECT.

Join our Harlequin community to
share your thoughts and connect
with other romance readers!
Facebook.com/groups/HarlequinConnection

HARLEQUIN

HSOCIAL2020